PERFECT REMAINS

Helen Fields studied law at the University of East Anglia, then went on to the Inns of Court School of Law in London. After completing her pupillage, she joined chambers in Middle Temple where she practised criminal and family law for thirteen years. After her second child was born, Helen left the Bar. Together with her husband David, she runs a film production company, acting as script writer and producer. *Perfect Remains* is set in Scotland, where Helen feels most at one with the world. Helen and her husband now live in Hampshire with their three children and two dogs.

Helen loves Twitter but finds it completely addictive. She can be found at @Helen_Fields.

D1193480

HELEN FIELDS

PERFECT REMAINS

HarperCollins
PUBLISHERS Since 1817

This novel is entirely a work of fiction. The names, characters and incidents portrayed in it are the work of the author's imagination. Any resemblance to actual persons, living or dead, events or localities is entirely coincidental.

Avon
A division of HarperCollins*Publishers*
1 London Bridge Street,
London, SE1 9GF

www.harpercollins.co.uk

A Paperback Original 2017

1

First published in Great Britain by
HarperCollins*Publishers* 2017

A catalogue record for this book is
available from the British Library

Paperback ISBN-13: 978-0-00-818155-0
Trade Paperback ISBN: 978-0-00-820094-7

Set in Bembo by Palimpsest Book Production Limited,
Falkirk, Stirlingshire

Printed and bound in Great Britain by
Clays Ltd, St Ives plc

To Helen Huthwaite and the whole team at Avon, for making this real, and for making the process so mind-blowingly wonderful (I've almost stopped crying now). And to my brilliant agent, Caroline Hardman who soothed a ragged ego, answered endless emails, never gave up on me, read and reread – you have the patience of a saint.

To my first readers (those who had to correct terrible typos and battle with my stupid mistakes), I cannot thank you enough. Jessica Corbett, you listened to me rabbiting on about this book and never once fell asleep. (You also provided cake in times of dire need, which may be the most valuable contribution anyone could make.) Allison Spyer, you read, enthused, believed, raved, cajoled and brought enough loyalty to the table to scare away an army of doubters. Andrea Gibson, you lived every blow and victory of this process with me as if it were your own. I am grateful every day that you know vastly more about chemistry than me. Ever positive, ever sure, you got me through. I must also thank Mark Thomas for talking teeth with me (any mistakes are my own). Ruth Chambers, my holiday buddy, who spent more hours trying to comprehend various plots and characters than I can bear to recall (a thousand apologies).

To my mother Christine for teaching me that you can be a mother, a wife and whatever the hell else you want to be, all at the same time. To the glorious, stunning, evocative and wondrous city of Edinburgh (with a special place in my heart for your drinking establishments and eateries), I am humbled by you more with every visit. To friends too numerous to list who kept me going.

And to David, who gave me the time, the space, the facilities and the courage to put my keyboard where my mouth had been. Thank you.

For David, Gabriel, Solomon and Evangeline,
who let me write in a time machine
where *just five more minutes* in my world
is always an hour or two in yours.

Chapter One

He laid out the body with almost fatherly care, stretching each limb wide, allowing air to circulate freely around her skin. She was ashen but peaceful, her eyelashes bold against the greyness of her face, lips colourless. He preferred it to the way she'd looked when they'd first met. The nakedness was unattractive, splayed as she was, but it was necessary. There should be no part of her left. No aspect of her past, no link to the life she was leaving. This was, in many ways, a cleansing. Very precisely, he aimed his foot above the middle of her left humerus, letting his whole weight bear down on her arm, feeling the crackle and shatter of it vibrate through the bones in his own leg. Only when satisfied that the pyre was perfectly prepared did he take the small silk pouch from his trouser pocket. Tipping the white gems into his hand, he rolled them between deft fingers and palm, enjoying the contrasting smoothness and sharpness, dropping them like pennies down a wishing well into her mouth, saving just one. It seemed a shame to burn such immaculate work but no flesh could be spared. He had soaked the body in accelerant overnight, marinating her, he'd joked, just in case someone stumbled in earlier than expected, not that he was so amateurish that it would happen.

As a last touch before leaving the stone cabin, he allowed a fragment of bloodied silk scarf to drift to the floor. Planting a heavy rock over it, he ground it into the earth. The grate of a struck match, the screech of ancient rusty hinges, the woof of flames consuming oxygen and it was done. He carried a metal baseball bat a reasonable distance away and covered it with rocks. He'd polished it free of fingerprints but, invisible to the naked eye and awaiting the black light that would illuminate it, a single smudge of blood remained on the handle. A few feet further and he relinquished the final tooth, sticky threads of gum tissue left dangling, then kicked a token sheet of dust over it. That would do.

There was a walk, not so very far but perilous in the dark, which made it slow. The air temperature was below freezing even in the foothills. His breath misted the sharp focus of the stars above him. It was a fine resting place for her, he thought. She was lucky. Few people left the world from such a viewpoint. Soon enough, the Cairngorms were disappearing behind him in the mist. When the first light hit them, they would turn purple-grey against the sky, barren and rocky, almost a moonscape. He watched in his mirror as the vast formations dipped into no more than shallow hills. This was his last visit here, he thought. A final farewell. It had proved to be the perfect location.

Edinburgh was still more than an hour away and there was rain forecast, not that it would stop the burning. By the time the first drop fell, the heat would be so intense that only a flood could halt the destruction. His priority was to get home as quickly as was prudent. There was so much left to do.

The woman had given in more easily than he'd imagined. If it had been him, he'd have fought to the last, would have

2

focused every ounce of anger and bile on resisting. She had pleaded, begged and in the end cried feebly and howled. Life was cheap, he thought, because the general populace failed to appreciate its value. He understood. He constantly pushed himself to the limits of his capability, strove to learn, to surpass. He burned with a thirst for knowledge like others craved money, making it hard to find an equal. That was why he'd been forced to kill. Without her sacrifice, he would forever have been surrounded by women unable to satisfy his intellect.

He listened to a language CD as he drove. He liked to learn a new language each year. This time it was Spanish. Easier than many, he admitted to himself guiltily, but then he had an exhausting amount of other matters on his mind. He couldn't be expected to pick up anything more complex whilst doing so much research and travelling.

'It's not as if I've had any free time.' A rabbit dashed out from the verge. He slammed on his brakes, less from a desire to avoid it than with the shock of the movement in his peripheral vision. 'Damn it!' He was distracted and he'd been talking to himself again. He only did that when he was overtired. And stressed. He'd stayed up late arguing. Whoever thought it was an easy task persuading an intelligent woman to do what was best for her, was a fool. It was a challenge, even for a man of his faculties. The brighter the woman, the harder it was. But rewarding in the end.

He pulled over at the outskirts of Edinburgh and drank passably warm coffee from a flask. He couldn't risk going into a cafe. In spite of the lack of interest he was likely to generate – no one wanted to stare at a middle-aged, saggy-bellied man with an unsightly bald patch – it would be stupid to have his likeness caught on CCTV returning to the city along this route.

The Spanish voice droned in the background until he hit the off switch. It was such a big day, why shouldn't he take a break for once? A lady was waiting at home, needing substantial care and attention. She wouldn't be able to talk clearly for a while, in fact she would probably need speech therapy. Luckily for her, he was a gifted tutor in many fields. It would be his pleasure and privilege to assist.

Chapter Two

Detective Inspector Luc Callanach wondered how long it would take for the jibes to stop, and they hadn't even started yet. It was his second day with Police Scotland's Major Investigations Team in Edinburgh and he'd found himself in a depressingly grey, ageing building that couldn't have looked less like a hub of cutting-edge criminal investigation. Yesterday had been an easy introduction, consisting only of briefings and meetings with superiors too aware of political correctness to dare crack any gags about his accent or nationality. Those who ranked below him wouldn't be so obliging. It seemed unlikely that Police Scotland had ever had to integrate a half-French half-Scots detective before.

Callanach was scheduled to give a meet and greet speech, explain how he intended to operate, and what his expectations were of the men and women in his command. It would be bad enough when they saw him – archetypally European with unruly dark hair, brown eyes, olive skin and an aquiline nose. Once he opened his mouth, it would only get worse. He glanced at his watch and knew they'd be sharpening their collective wits. Keeping them waiting wasn't going to improve things, not that he particularly cared what they thought of him but he was all for an easy life where he could get it.

'Quiet. Let's get started,' he said, writing his name on a board and ignoring the incredulous looks. 'I've only recently moved from France and it will take some time for us to adjust to one another's accents, so speak clearly and slowly.'

There was silence until what sounded like, 'You've got to be fuckin' kidding,' came from the far end of the room, where too many bodies were crowded together to identify the speaker. It was followed immediately by a shushing noise that was distinctly female in origin. Callanach rubbed his forehead and reined in the desire to check his watch as he prepared to tolerate the inevitable questions.

'Excuse me, Detective Inspector, but is Callanach not a Scottish name? It's just that we weren't expecting anyone quite so . . . European.'

'I was born in Scotland and raised bilingual. That's as much as any of you needs to know.'

'Bi-what? Is that even legal here?' a blonde woman called out, to the enjoyment of her fellow officers. Callanach watched her watching the others, waiting for their response and saw that she was trying to impress, to fit in with the boys. He waited blank-faced and bored for the laughter to subside.

'I expect regular case updates. Lines of command will be tightly managed. Investigations falter when one person fails to pass on their knowledge to others. Higher rank is no excuse for you to blame those beneath you and inexperience is no defence for ineptitude. Come to me to discuss either progress or problems. If you want to complain, phone your mother. We have three live cases at the moment and you've been allocated tasks on those. Questions?'

'Is it right that you were an Interpol agent, sir?' a detective constable asked. Callanach guessed he was no more than twenty-five, all curiosity and enthusiasm, as he had been at that age. It seemed a lifetime ago.

'That's correct,' he said. 'What's your name?'

'Tripp,' he replied.

'Well, Tripp, do you know the difference between assisting an international murder investigation with Interpol and conducting one in Scotland?'

'No, sir,' Tripp answered, eyes shifting left and right, as if terrified that the question was the start of some unexpected test.

'Absolutely nothing. There's a corpse, grieving relatives, more questions than answers, and pressure from the top to get it sorted in no time and at minimal cost. Even under the constraints of budgeted policing, I won't forgive sloppiness. The stakes are too high to let your dissatisfaction at the current overtime rate affect the effort you're willing to put in.' He took a moment to stare round the room, meeting every pair of eyes full on, making his point. 'Tripp,' he said, when he'd finished, 'grab another constable and come to my office.'

Callanach exited the room without farewells or niceties. No doubt Tripp was already getting it in the neck for being singled out, the team was bemoaning their newly allocated detective inspector and bitching about Police Scotland's failure to promote from within. Policing was the same all over the world. Only the coffee really changed from place to place. Here, he was unsurprised to find, it was bloody awful.

His office could best be described as functional. It would take promotion to a higher rank before he transcended into actual comfort. Still, it was quiet and light with two telephones, as if somehow he could split himself in half and take two calls at once. On the floor were just two boxes of personal possessions awaiting transfer into drawers and onto shelves. Not that there was anything vital in them. He'd come to

Scotland for a clean start. The country of his birth had seemed the logical place to put down new roots, not to mention one of the few places he could apply for a police position as a passport holder.

Tripp knocked on his door, a young woman behind him.

'Ready for us, sir?' Tripp asked.

Callanach beckoned them in. 'And you are?'

'Detective Constable Salter. Nice to meet you, sir,' she said, looking down at her shoes part way through the introduction. Her awkwardness was irritating in its predictability. Callanach suffered from the least likely affliction of being good looking to the point of distraction, with a face that could – and had – stopped traffic. Few people understood that it was more burden than blessing these days.

'Salter, take me through procedures from initial crime report, ordering forensics and into trial preparation. Tripp, I want comprehensive notes on forms, filing, the works. Understood?'

'Yes, sir, not a problem.' Tripp seemed delighted to be of use. All Salter managed was a downcast mumble which Callanach took as agreement.

'Would you give us the room please, constables?' a voice cut in behind them. Standing in the doorway was a female officer in dress uniform. Salter and Tripp scattered as she entered and kicked the door shut behind her.

'I'm DI Turner, Ava as we're the same rank.' She gave a wide grin, suffering none of Salter's inability to look him in the eyes. Callanach's fellow detective inspector was around five foot five and slim. Her chestnut, shoulder-length hair was curly although an attempt had been made to restrain it in a ponytail. She wasn't beautiful, not in modern advertising terms, but handsome would have been an insult. Her features were fine, grey eyes widely spaced.

'Callanach,' he responded. 'By the look on your face, I'd say you've been party to something I haven't. Did you want to share it or am I supposed to guess?'

Ava Turner ignored the dismissive tone and answered unabashed. 'Well, I did hear one of the sergeants asking why they'd been sent an underwear model instead of a proper policeman.'

'I get the picture,' he said.

'I'm guessing you're used to it. If it helps, the fact that you're French will be more acceptable to the majority of them than I am.'

'English?' he asked, as he shifted the position of a filing cabinet.

'Pure Scottish, but my parents sent me to an English boarding school from the age of seven, hence the accent. That makes me about as welcome as the plague. Don't worry about it. If they actually liked you at this stage, you'd be doomed to fail. Presumably you've arrived with a suitably thick skin. Give me a shout if you have any problems, you'll find my numbers on the contact sheet in your desk. I'd better go and change. I'm just back from a community awards ceremony and I can't stand being in uniform. Your team are a good bunch, just don't take too much shit from them.'

'I have no intention of taking any shit from anyone,' he replied, picking up one of the phones and checking for a dial tone. When he looked up again, he was speaking to an empty space and an open doorway. Callanach dropped into the chair behind his desk. He took out his mobile, programmed in a few of the more important numbers from the contact sheet and was just considering emptying the first of his boxes when Tripp bundled in.

'Sorry to disturb, sir, but we've just had a call from an officer at Braemar. They've found a body and are asking to speak with someone about it.'

'And Braemar is in which area of the city?'

'It's not in the city, it's in the Cairngorm Mountains, sir.'

'For God's sake, Tripp, stop saying sir at the end of every sentence and explain to me how that could possibly be an Edinburgh case.'

'They suspect it's the body of a woman reported missing from the city a couple of weeks ago, a lawyer called Elaine Buxton. They've found a scrap of clothing that matches a scarf she was wearing when last seen.'

'That's all? No other link?'

'Everything else has been burned, sir, I mean, sorry. Braemar thought we might want to be involved early on.'

'All right, Constable. Pull together everything there is on Elaine Buxton then get Braemar on the phone. I want detailed information on my desk in fifteen minutes. If that is Edinburgh's missing person then we're already running two weeks behind her killer.'

Chapter Three

Callanach put down the phone feeling weary and decided it was down to the effort of decoding the Scottish accent. He barely remembered his father and, although his mother had insisted he learn to speak English as well as her mother-tongue French, he hadn't been prepared for full immersion. The sergeant from Braemar managed to mix the singsong cadence with a regular dose of colloquialisms. Callanach suspected it might have been largely for his benefit and, a couple of sentences in, had stopped bothering to ask what any of it meant. He made an idle note of the word 'haver'. Tripp would have to double as interpreter. In the meantime, Callanach had agreed to consult on a case that should technically speaking have been out of his jurisdiction. That wouldn't endear him to anyone, additional money and manpower being expended where it could be avoided, but it certainly sounded as if the body in the mountains was Edinburgh's missing woman.

He saw Salter going past his office and stuck his head out of the door.

'Which of the current cases is nearest to resolution?' he shouted after her.

'Brownlow murder, sir. Culprit's been apprehended, we're just prepping the files for the Procurator Fiscal. Preliminary court hearing is next week.'

'Right. I want you, Tripp and two others from the Brownlow team in the briefing room in ten minutes. Organise it. And how far away are the Cairngorms?' The look Salter gave him was all the response he needed. An overnight bag was required.

The briefing was tense. The squad he'd shifted from the Brownlow case obviously wasn't thrilled at the two-hour drive they had coming, nor starting a new batch of paperwork while they were still finishing another. Detective Constables Tripp, Barnes and Salter were led by Detective Sergeant Lively. The detective sergeant was studying him as if he'd just crawled out of a cesspit. Callanach ignored him and gave the fastest explanation he could for what they were doing, then handed over to the officer sent to update them on the missing person investigation.

'Elaine Margaret Buxton, thirty-nine years of age, divorced, no children, worked as a commercial lawyer at one of the biggest law firms in the city. She went missing sixteen days ago. The last confirmed sighting was on a Friday night as she left the gym to return home. Her mother reported her missing the following evening after she'd failed to turn up for lunch and couldn't be raised on either her home phone or mobile. Her car was in her garage, no clothes or cases gone, passport still there. It was out of character for her not to have checked her emails on the Saturday morning. Her keys were found in a communal hallway. She's described as incredibly organised, borderline workaholic, hadn't taken so much as a day sick in the previous two years.'

'Any boyfriend or obvious suspects?' DC Barnes asked.

'The ex-husband Ryan Buxton is working abroad with a full alibi. There's no known boyfriend. Everyone we've spoken to has confirmed that she was completely obsessed with the law. She was either at the office, at home or an exercise class. We had no leads, until this.'

'Why are the Braemar police so convinced this is your missing person?' asked Callanach.

'The last person to see Miss Buxton had a photo of her on their mobile. She'd stopped by the gym bar to have a drink at a friend's birthday celebration. We circulated the photo and listed the clothes in detail. That's how they came up with the match.'

'Has anyone contacted her family yet?' Tripp asked.

Callanach took that one himself. 'No, and mouths had better stay shut until we've seen the body and crime scene for ourselves. DNA evidence is required before we make a positive link.'

'This might be our missing person but it's not our homicide. What're we doing chasing up country when we haven't got so much as a confirmed identification?' asked DS Lively. 'It's not as if we haven't got our own cases to be getting on with and there's some detective inspectors on that patch who could work this case as well as any former Interpol bigshot.'

'If that is Elaine Buxton, she was abducted from Edinburgh, meaning there's a reasonable chance she was murdered here too. I'm not prepared to lose the opportunity of inspecting the crime scene because you can't be bothered to make the drive. As for any outstanding work on the Brownlow case – learn to multitask.' Callanach snatched his notes from the table. 'We have some distance to cover, so get moving.'

Back in his office, Callanach threw a toothbrush, raincoat and boots into a bag. He considered leaving DS Lively behind instead of putting up with his sour face for the next two days, then thought again. Better to deal with the man than let him win. His squad needed to know from the outset that he wouldn't stand laziness or insubordination. It didn't matter what they thought. For the next six months they would criticise whatever decisions he made, right or wrong, until they found a more interesting target.

Chapter Four

They met with local police at the rural satellite station in Braemar and were transported into the mountains in a four-wheel drive. Some off-roading was required to get near the crime scene and the weather was closing in. It took another hour to get there. The temperature had dropped dramatically by the time Callanach saw the lights and tents of the investigative team. The only blessing, courtesy of the location, was that there was no sign of the press.

'Who found it?' he asked the driver.

'A couple of hikers saw the flames from a distant peak but had to walk fifteen minutes before they got mobile reception to phone it in. By the time the fire service had located the bothy it was nearly burned out. Not much left to see, I'm afraid.' Callanach took out a camera. He always took his own photos at crime scenes. Later, the images would cover his office wall.

The bothy, more refuge than accommodation, was a stone hut left unlocked for hikers caught in storms or mid trek, consisting of a single room, its rear wall set into the rock face. Callanach guessed the original building dated back a couple of hundred years. Now the roof was completely gone, fallen in once the fire had taken hold, making the forensic investigation painstaking. Even the huge stones of the wall base had shifted in the intense heat. Callanach surveyed the horizon. This wasn't a place you could stumble across. Whoever had brought the woman here had chosen carefully, made sure it was nowhere near regular trekking routes, and had been inside before.

'Where is the body?' he asked.

'They've collected the bones already, but their positions are marked inside,' the driver told him.

'Just bones? That's all that remains?'

'Afraid so. The soft tissue was completely incinerated. We've no precise idea how long the fire was burning but it was a matter of hours, for sure.'

They walked to the doorway of the hut, now ablaze with portable floodlights, and watched as two forensics officers trod gingerly through the dusty debris. It was a grim place to die. A hand on Callanach's shoulder stopped his imagination from filling in the details.

'DI Callanach? I'm Jonty Spurr, one of Aberdeenshire's pathologists. Not much left here for you, I'm afraid.'

Callanach shook his head. 'I was told you had located an item of clothing. How did that survive when everything else is ashes?'

'It's not a complete item, just a scrap of a scarf, but the pattern was sufficiently remarkable that one of the constables recognised it as the same as your missing person's. It got trapped under a rock and the lack of oxygen protected it. It's already on its way to the lab for DNA testing. Looks as if there's some blood on it.'

Callanach frowned. 'That's all you've got? Surely there must be something more.'

'These are the cards we were dealt, Detective Inspector. Fire is a crime scene's worst enemy. The accelerant can usually be identified fairly quickly. Unfortunately, it's a peat floor in this part of the Cairngorms which quite literally added more fuel to the flames. Without it, I'm sure it wouldn't have burned so long or so hot. The bones are badly damaged.'

'What about tyre marks? There must have been tracks.'

'You'd hope so, but the fire trucks were called in first and tore up the ground. They had no idea what was inside. We'll get the dogs out tomorrow and do a fine-comb check of the area but it'll do no good tonight, not enough light left.'

Callanach took out his camera again and began collecting images of the grey and black charcoal mess of floor.

'Did she die here?'

'I can't say for sure, and with only bones left I may not be able to pinpoint a cause of death, unless the skull gives me something. Many of the bones are broken, the jaw is in pieces. It seems to me though that this was about disposing of the body. Your murderer didn't want anything left, was probably hoping she'd be unidentifiable,' the pathologist remarked, pulling off rubber gloves and stretching his neck.

'You believe she was killed elsewhere and transported here?'

'You're the detective. That part's up to you. If you're staying overnight, you can come to the morgue in the morning, see what we've got.'

'I'll be there,' Callanach replied, looking around for Tripp. He found him stealing a sip of coffee from Sergeant Lively's flask. 'Tripp, interview the hikers, mark their precise position on a map and the time they first saw the fire. I want to hear their call to the emergency services and you'll need to go to the spot where they were standing to photograph the view they had across to here.'

Sergeant Lively interrupted. 'Statements will have been taken already so I don't see what good that'll do.'

The man's too-long-in-the-job attitude was tiresome to deal with, but far from unusual. Callanach fought the desire to reprimand him and concentrated instead on the matters at hand.

'The number of hours this fire was burning will help us determine the time the murderer left the scene. The height, and perhaps even the colour of the flames when the hikers saw them, might help establish that, enabling us to question local people about unusual vehicles within a specific time frame.'

'You're the boss,' Lively mumbled, not bothering to hide his lack of respect.

'Where are we staying tonight, sir?' Tripp asked, stamping his feet and shoving his hands ever deeper in his pockets. For all his usual enthusiasm, Tripp looked distinctly uncomfortable in the great outdoors and the freezing cold.

'Ask the local officers what's around. There must be accommodation reasonably nearby. Tell Salter she's to attend the morgue with me in the morning and I want Barnes at the scene until it's completely documented. Feedback from each one of you, every two hours.'

'What if that's not Elaine Buxton? It'll have been a complete waste of our time.'

Callanach glared at Lively. 'Whoever's corpse that is, Sergeant, they were almost certainly murdered and if we can contribute to the investigation then only an idiot would regard it as a waste. So unless you have something professional to contribute, from now on you can keep your personal opinions to yourself.'

Chapter Five

The landline rang. King studied the number before picking up. It was a local code.

'Dr King,' he snapped.

'Hello, this is Sheila Klein from Human Resources. I've been asked to ring and see when we can expect you back. University policy is that we need a doctor's note for medical leave beyond three consecutive days.'

Reginald King sighed. He hated the petty rules and regulations that tied him into his banal public existence. The woman on the phone couldn't possibly comprehend that there were aspects of his life demanding more attention than his underpaid, under-appreciated and underwhelming job.

'I'm aware of the terms of my employment contract.'

'So, any idea when we might see you or have confirmation from your doctor?' Sheila asked, her voice trailing off towards the end of the sentence.

King took a key from his pocket as she whined. 'A few more days,' he said. 'Maybe a week. The virus has gone to my chest and set off my asthma.'

'Gosh, that sounds awful. You know we have an open-door

policy. Do call if you think you'll need more leave. I'm sure the department head will be sympathetic.'

The Head of School in the Department of Philosophy would not be sympathetic, King thought. She would be as ignorant as ever, and the ignorant always failed to appreciate him. Just because he was an administrator rather than an academic, because his qualifications came from a university she chose not to recognise, because he hadn't climbed the ranks through socialising and networking, she was not interested in him. Well, the Department of Philosophy could pay his wages while he had some time to himself. Professor Natasha Forge, the youngest Head of School of any department at the University of Edinburgh, would no doubt fail to even register his absence.

King unplugged the phone. Twelve steps down into the cellar he went, switching on the basement light and sliding a wooden panel in the wall to reveal a keyhole. Unlocking the hidden door and stepping inside, he rose twelve steps back up, parallel to the first staircase but concealed behind a layer of plaster, brick and sound proofing. At the back of his house was a secret space, windowless, silent, timeless. It was a place of beauty. He congratulated himself on how well he had designed it with pastel colours to soothe, with gently piped classical music, and art prints adorning the walls. Unless you surveyed the house inside and out, you would never know the back section existed. It was his island. He recited John Donne's lines as he took a key to the last door. The great poet was right. He could not be entire, if alone. That was why he had gifted one fortunate person with the chance to accompany him on his journey. As he opened the door, the woman on the bed began to scream.

Elaine Buxton, recently presumed dead, the bones attributed to her corpse already laid out on an autopsy table, strands of DNA in code form swirling through cyber space so that her death could be formally recorded, cried out until her voice was hoarse.

20

'Your gums are healing nicely,' King said. He spoke softly to her. It was a point of pride that he didn't lose his temper, no matter how much she screamed. Not so with the other woman. When he'd taken her, she'd scratched, bitten and kicked him so hard his groin had been agony for a week. She'd required no delicate handling. She had been beneath him.

'Pleath, 'et me go,' Elaine mouthed, the tears starting again. That irritated him, as he knew it would any man, but it was to be expected for a while. Until she learned to appreciate him.

'In a week your mouth will have recovered enough to fit dentures, then we'll commence speech therapy. It won't be instantaneous but you're a bright woman. You need another shot of antibiotics and more steroids. Please don't fight me, I'm only trying to speed the healing process.'

Elaine began to shudder although the motion made no impact on the metal ankle and wrist cuffs with short chains, binding her to the bed. King took out two syringes. He was respectful when he touched her, would never cause unnecessary pain. She didn't understand that yet, obviously believing that at any moment she might receive the same treatment as her decoy. It was a shame he'd had to kill the woman in front of Elaine, but it had all been part of the education process. She needed to know that he was capable of being strict. Every pupil had to be shown stick and offered carrot. Knowing that one's teacher would not tolerate a failure to comply was an excellent motivator.

He stroked Elaine's arm with his pale, silky hand. She shivered as their flesh made contact but did not tell him to stop. Perhaps, he thought, she was learning already. That was why he'd chosen her. Months of watching, waiting, consuming her days and nights from the shadows. Studying her. Real study with commitment, not the poor excuse for it that universities accepted these days, had borne fruit. She was perfect. Adaptable. Fast. No husband or children to distract her. He'd seen her pick up a set of legal papers at six in the evening and work all night, only caffeine for company, springing into court the following morning as if she'd slept ten hours. Then she'd go to the gym and work the tension from her body. There was no excess. She was driven, like him. Constantly improving.

That was why her choice of body double had been so ironic. King couldn't have found a more dynamic opposite. All he'd needed was a woman of roughly the same age, height and build. The fact that she was a prostitute, stick thin (presumably from years of drug abuse) and barely able to string together a coherent sentence, had made it all the easier to dispose of her. He could have been kinder, but she wouldn't listen when he'd tried to explain the service she was performing, giving him a life partner who was his perfect match.

He'd never even learned her name. As it was, she would forever be the missing Elaine Buxton. And Elaine Buxton, erased from the living world, belonged wholly and exclusively to him.

'I could rename you,' he said. 'It might be an important part of the adjustment process. Compile a shortlist in your head of say three or four. You can explain why you selected each of them, then I shall choose the one I find the most pleasing. It'll be a good way for us to move forward together.'

'You're crathy,' she whispered as he withdrew the needle from her arm.

'You shouldn't use such base terms. But you're upset and I'll be lenient for a while.'

'Wha' 'id you do with the girl?'

'You needn't worry about her. At the end, her sacrifice made up for her wasted life.'

Elaine was staring at the area where he'd carefully laid out a vast sheet of plastic for the girl's body. King had used an old car, hired from a sufficiently disreputable dealership that wouldn't want any contact with the police, and kept it in a

22

garage away from his home. One night he'd driven to Glasgow, picked up the girl who was soliciting in her usual spot (he'd been there several times to select the right one) and driven round a few streets to find a quiet place for her to earn her money. He'd found that concept amusing, even as he'd pressed the chloroform-soaked rag over her face. Earning money. That was all young women thought they had to do for a few pounds these days, believing that men existed to pay for them, that they simply had to don a short skirt and paint their mouths red. It was pitiful. And she'd wanted to charge him thirty pounds to put her filthy tongue inside his trousers. He was ridding the world of a scourge. He may well have stopped the spread of a dreadful disease by bundling her unconscious body under a tarpaulin and driving her away from her next customer.

It had taken immense physical effort to cart her into the hidden room. Down one set of stairs and up another had seemed like a genius plan when he'd conceived it. The reality was more cumbersome. Several times he'd banged her head hard on the steps, not that it mattered. He'd kept her body wrapped in plastic, but allowed her to breathe. Asphyxiation wasn't the plan.

Elaine hadn't liked it when he'd brought the girl in. Perhaps the tiniest hint of jealousy behind the melodramatic hyperventilation and wide-eyed head shaking, he'd thought. How could she ever have believed he would bring such a filthy, low creature into their lives?

King had returned the woman to consciousness long enough to obtain details of past fractures. Previous injuries could tell tales. The thickening of bones long after they'd healed could reveal an unhelpful story, even if all the DNA had been destroyed. She'd been remarkably forthcoming. He'd just had to promise he'd let her live if she provided the information he wanted.

In the event, there wasn't much to be concerned about. A finger broken in a car door and a dislocated shoulder that wouldn't show up. By far the more important thing was to ensure that the girl's left upper arm was fragmented where Elaine's had been fractured after she came off a bicycle as a teenager. If that bone was left intact and the pathologist was thorough, then all of King's hard work would have been for nothing.

Once he had all he needed, King had told Elaine to watch and not look away. When he'd put on the protective glasses the prostitute had only looked curious. When he'd snapped on rubber gloves and a face mask she'd begun to plead. Elaine, for once, had grown silent. When he'd picked up the baseball bat, well, that was a different story. He had no memory of Elaine's reaction for those few minutes. He'd experienced what he assumed was tunnel vision, for the first time in his life. It had been a breathtaking episode. Everything but the screaming, whimpering, dribbling, blubbering pile of living flesh before him had faded out. There had been no peripheral vision to distract him. He couldn't hear anything beyond her feral cries. It was the most intensely concentrated sensation he had ever felt.

He'd awoken, and it was an awakening, standing before her, bat clutched in his hands, to find his pulse racing as if he'd run a marathon. It had been quite the adrenaline rush. For a while there was silence, then gradually Elaine's intermittent sob-screams had broken through. The girl's face was a mess, as he'd intended. He'd needed to bash every one of her teeth out of their sockets and damage the jaw beyond x-ray comparison for the identity exchange to work. He hadn't foreseen that he'd get so carried away, he felt rising shame at the guilty pleasure he'd taken, seeing his handiwork in the bruises on her neck and breasts, guessing there were marks on her stomach and legs too, but unwilling to lift her undoubtedly infested clothing to see. He'd lost control − nothing to be proud of − but didn't he deserve to vent? Better to let it out with her than Elaine. He had no desire to diminish his prize.

King shook himself out of the memory and stared at the woman whose identity the prostitute had taken in death.

'How are we doing with those tapes? I'm sure you've been glad to have an activity to occupy you. I know you already speak French so I thought Russian might be a more exciting challenge. When you're talking properly again, I'll test you and we can make some real progress.'

He flicked a switch on the sound system and a voice began speaking words that Elaine had no inclination to listen to, or repeat. With a baby-soft kiss on her forehead, King placed a protein drink at her side and left.

Chapter Six

The autopsy table looked more comfortable than the bed he'd slept in. That was before it was occupied by the remnants of what was presumed to be Elaine Buxton's skeleton. It had been a bad night. Callanach would have self-medicated with a decent bottle of red, but the only wine on offer had a label with all the appeal of a bargain-bucket binge drinker's delight. Braemar was a slightly touristy but pleasant village lacking much choice in accommodation and the better options had been fully booked. In the absence of good wine, he'd settled for a dilapidated TV with crackling reception, soup he'd admired only because he'd previously thought it impossible to cook it so badly, and half decent coffee.

Jonty Spurr, the pathologist, was quiet as he worked. Callanach appreciated that. He'd witnessed too many autopsies to be disturbed by the body. What he found more disquieting was the forced cheer some pathologists had about them. Too talkative, too determined to lift the atmosphere. Spurr was slow, not annoyingly so, but unhurried and probably unflappable under even the worst pressure.

'The victim was an adult female, aged between thirty and forty, I'd say, approximately five foot six.'

Callanach glanced at DC Salter. She was young but not new to the job and showed no sign of being troubled by what she saw.

'Has the accelerant been identified yet?' she asked.

'We'll need to do more tests on the bones for that. The fire department might have picked something up at the scene.' Spurr chose a bone fragment and held it up for Callanach to inspect more closely. 'The heat and length of time the fire was burning destroyed any chance of getting DNA from the bone marrow. The skull, jaw and upper chest sustained damage not caused by the fire. You can see a pattern of fractures indicating repeated use of a heavy, blunt weapon. Must have taken quite some force.'

'Was that the cause of death?' Callanach asked.

'I'd put my money on those injuries occurring before death. The resulting trauma to the brain may well have been what killed her. With no soft tissue left, I'm not going to do much better than that. Given the planning put into disposing of the body, there'd have been no other practical reason to disfigure the face after death.'

'Bastard,' Salter said.

'Indeed,' Spurr replied. 'We're cross-checking the teeth against Elaine Buxton's dental records. Some have fillings or caps, so it should be easy enough.'

'How soon will we have that?' Callanach was keen to leave. Morgues made him claustrophobic in spite of the bright light and fierce air conditioning. It felt like a prison cell and he'd had enough of those.

'Maybe as early as tomorrow. Will you still be here?'

Callanach wasn't even going to consider another night in the same accommodation.

'No, in Edinburgh. We're going back to the crime scene to get a daylight view then we'll set off. You'll call when you have more information?'

27

Spurr nodded, stripped off a glove and offered Callanach a hand. He disliked the dry, powdery feel of it against his own, as if death was contagious.

'Is there any news from the crime scene this morning?' he asked Salter once they were on the road.

'No. I tried to speak to DC Tripp but mobile reception was poor. He and DS Lively were off to speak with the hikers first thing, but they should be back at the crime scene by the time we get there.'

'She wasn't murdered there,' Callanach said.

'Surely it's hard to tell at this stage,' the young constable commented quietly.

'Why bother taking her so far to kill her? It makes no sense. It may be the perfect site to dispose of a body, but it's not a comfortable or convenient place for playing out his fantasy about her death. A great deal of time passed between her disappearance and the corpse turning up, time the murderer spent elsewhere with the victim. Whoever abducted her had this place in mind for weeks, if not months.'

An hour later the bothy was back in sight. Forensic investigators were shouting to one another, the excitement plain on their faces. Callanach was out of the car before Salter could put on the hand brake.

'What's happening?' he asked a passing officer.

'The dogs tracked a weapon some distance away, buried under a pile of stones.' Callanach watched the back slapping among the handlers.

There would be no fingerprints, he thought. A man who found such a perfect place to destroy a body didn't leave prints.

'Good news, right, sir?' came Tripp's voice from behind him.

'Tell me what you've got,' Callanach replied. Tripp wiped the smile off his face and looked down at his notebook.

'The hikers repeated what they'd said in their statements.

Oliver Deacon and Tom Shelley, both in their early twenties, had been hiking for about three hours, reached the midway point in their route and saw the blaze from' – he looked around, identified a peak and pointed into the distance – 'over there. They had binoculars and took photos with their phones, not that they show anything except a distant orange dot. I've drawn a map of their route.'

Callanach nodded. 'We'll head back to Edinburgh tonight,' he said. 'If I authorise any more overtime, I'll have no job to get back to.'

Two hours later, they were fighting the city traffic.

'Something wrong, sir?' Tripp ventured after dropping Salter home.

'I think so,' Callanach replied. 'I just don't know what yet.'

'We'll be taking over the case, will we, if it proves to be Elaine Buxton's body?'

'As soon as I've cleared it with the Detective Chief Inspector. Take me straight to the station.'

The Major Investigations Team offices were all but deserted. Callanach liked being alone. He could concentrate, undisturbed by slamming doors, the hiss and gurgle of drinks machines and the constant undertone of voices. Quiet was uncomplicated. And it delayed returning to his flat. Somehow the act of unlocking that door would make his transition to working and living in Scotland real. He longed for France, for the culture that ran in his blood. Having one Scottish parent and being fluent in the language was no substitute for the country that had been his home for all but the first four years of his life. Even the cloud under which he'd left hadn't tainted his memories of Lyon.

He opened a box and began dumping the contents into drawers.

'So was your trip to the Cairngorms worth the bollocking it's going to get you?' came a voice from the doorway. Startled, he dropped a file, getting a laugh from his fellow detective inspector. 'Sorry, I hadn't meant to scare you. Apparently Interpol agents are easily caught unawares.'

Callanach retrieved the file from the floor, frowning as he reordered the paperwork.

'DI Turner, I'd assumed I was alone.' He checked his watch. 'It's nearly one in the morning.'

'I practise my best paperwork avoidance at night. No one here to chase me for it. That and the fact that I've done so many night shifts, my brain has long since ceased to differentiate between dark and light,' she said. 'What's your excuse?'

'I thought I might as well unpack before I'm dismissed,' he said.

She smiled. 'I've got some single malt in my office. We could toast your welcome and goodbye in one sitting.' Callanach pinched the bridge of his nose with one hand and breathed in slowly, aware that he was gritting his teeth as he tried to find the least offensive form of words he could. 'Don't worry,' Ava said. 'You've had a long couple of days. Some other time.'

'I just don't believe that socialising at work is sensible. Maintaining professional boundaries is important.'

'Not a problem.' She smiled. 'You've hit the ground running. Probably best to leave the unpacking 'til morning.'

He ran a hand through his hair and stretched his neck. 'Look, you're right, I do need a drink.'

'No, I think you were right. One in the morning is no time to be here. I'm going home. You should too, judging by the look of you. Goodnight.' She let his door swing softly shut as he swore under his breath. He could have handled that better. It was time to face his apartment, accept that life had moved on and that he had to move with it.

Chapter Seven

Edinburgh had been the closest Callanach could get to Lyon, in Scotland. It had the feel of a town, in spite of its size and busy economy, and a history its inhabitants celebrated. The city was easy to love with its sympathetic blend of old and new architecture and a population that seemed to have embraced different races and cultures whilst maintaining its own heritage. If they could only control the wind chill factor, he thought, it would be ideal. Callanach had rented a flat in Albany Street. A hundred years ago, it would have been a grand old terraced house, set over four floors, home to one of Edinburgh's elite families. These days, the inhabitants were busy professionals who would come and go through the central hallway, marking the nearness of their lives with only a raise of eyebrows or curt greeting. He found it wasteful, how little communication passed between neighbours. It was why dead bodies were noticed only by their unbearable odour and how domestic violence could be perpetrated on the same victim repeatedly without intervention. Good neighbours enabled good policing.

He poured a large glass of red wine and picked up a book. Reading himself to sleep had been a habit as far back as he could remember. It was the only thing that distracted him from work. But tonight concentration was difficult. With every page, the image of the bleak Cairngorm Mountains reappeared, forbidding and harsh. Winter was approaching. The Braemar bartender had told them the town would be full of skiers and snowboarders at the first flakes. It was a couple of weeks off yet, but December would bring snow to the peaks. The crowds of summer hikers were long gone, high winds and rain deterring all but the hardiest. The killer's timing, then, was either planned to perfection or lucky beyond the very best of odds.

Callanach woke early, realising he had no food, craving the tiny cafe on the street corner near his old apartment where he could eat freshly baked croissants and read a newspaper in French. Instead, he hurried to the only place close by and open, a health food store across Broughton Street, where he was surprised by the friendly reception, and picked up dried fruit, yoghurt and rye bread.

He plugged in his computer as he ate, wondering what his private emails would bring. They'd been stacking up for a week and he was tempted to simply delete the lot before reading.

There were administrative emails from Interpol dealing with his departure, requesting a forwarding address for documentation, nothing important. Then there were updates about local events in Lyon he'd usually have attended – a wine festival, sports rally, the opening of a new restaurant – and he pressed delete with a sense of resignation. Much of it was the usual e-junk but then he spotted it, hidden between a wine-club subscription offer and a newsletter from his last gym. A bounce-back notice had come from his mother's email address. She had apparently moved beyond steadfastly ignoring his communications and taken action by changing her email completely, as she had already done with her mobile phone number. His letters were returned unopened, his landline calls were screened.

Callanach threw the remainder of his breakfast in the bin and slammed his laptop closed, immediately regretting how he'd let it affect him. Getting angry wouldn't change a thing. He was where he was. What mattered now was Elaine Buxton. Nothing else. He had to make the new start work for him. Offending DI Turner the previous evening was a less than impressive start, and an error it would be tactically sensible to rectify sooner rather than later. With the office still to be organised, he changed from his sweats into a shirt and trousers then left for the station.

Tripp was waiting outside his office when he arrived, looking eager and rested. That was the benefit of being in your twenties, immune to too little sleep and careless of stress. For a couple of seconds Callanach was tempted to send him back to Braemar. Uncharitable, he thought. At least DS Lively hadn't been waiting for him.

'DS Lively was wanting to talk to you, sir.' Callanach rolled his eyes. 'And I thought,' Tripp continued, 'given what we learned in Braemar, you might want to visit Elaine Buxton's flat today, so I've organised that for lunchtime, and her ex-husband's phone number is on your desk.' Tripp had been busy. Callanach mentally rebuked himself for wanting to send Tripp back to Braemar. The young detective constable was sweetly unselfconscious of appearing too keen. That was a rarely seen attribute in any police officer.

'Thank you. Where is the detective sergeant?'

'In the briefing room. Shall I fetch him?'

'No, we'll go to him. Coffee en route.'

Approaching the briefing room, Callanach could hear the exact conversation he'd suspected would be taking place. The door had been left open, sensitivity not a concern, and Lively's voice boomed out.

'How the hell did he end up walking straight into a detective inspector post? That's what I'd like to know. It's not as if there weren't plenty of other candidates, people who know the city and understand the people. Rumour has it, some bastard pulled more strings than make a fishing net to get him in here. He wasn't through the door more than ten minutes before dragging us off our patch into someone else's investigation.'

'Leave it out, Sergeant, he was just doing what he thought was right for the victim,' a female voice spoke up. It took Callanach a moment to identify it as DC Salter's. Tripp tried valiantly to get a few steps ahead and stop the discussion but Callanach put an arm out to prevent him.

'Let it run, Tripp.'

'But, sir,' Tripp started before Lively began again.

'Go on then, Salter, tell us what you think of him. Some sort of genius, is he, coming out of Interpol and all? Begs the question why he moved here. Maybe the detective inspector couldn't cut it in the big league and thought this would be a soft option?'

Callanach booted the door fully open and slammed his coffee down on the desk.

'You asked to speak with me, Detective Sergeant. Is there an update?' Callanach stared at Lively, ignoring the rest of the crowd.

'They found blood on the baseball bat and some soft tissue on a tooth nearby. DNA from both is a match for Elaine Buxton. Her case has been officially upgraded from missing person to murder. The pathologist's report will be through later today. And the Chief wants to talk to you.'

'Set up a board, Salter. Maps, photos, forensics, everything we have,' Callanach called as he walked towards the door.

'It's still not our case yet, Inspector,' Lively shouted.

'It's about to be my case. If you don't want it to be yours then there's a large empty desk in my office where you can leave your letter of resignation,' Callanach snapped.

Lively stood up. Callanach knew he should leave it there and let tempers cool, but the conversation he'd overheard in the corridor was still worming its way through his veins.

'You want rid of me, do you, pal? I bet you do, 'cos I heard what you did. Shall I tell you what we do to men like you in Scotland? You fuckin' froggies might think it's all right to . . .' Lively had stepped forward and punctuated his last few words with a finger poke to Callanach's shoulder. He didn't get any further. Callanach shoved him backwards so hard that Lively went flying into the arms of his fellow officers who broke his fall and probably saved him a fractured coccyx. Lively hid his embarrassment with a laugh that made its way through the group as a strained echo.

'You wanna watch that temper of yours, Detective Inspector,' Lively said, his mouth a hard smirk across his face. 'It'll get you in trouble. Of course, you're used to that . . .'

Callanach stepped further towards Lively and his support group, his fists itching to punch the smug grin, biting down so hard he could taste blood in his mouth.

'Sir, DCI Begbie'll be waiting.' Tripp's voice was soft and unsure but it broke the tension in the room. The fight had already gone out of Lively. He'd made his point and would no doubt continue making it to his audience at the pub after their shift ended. Tripp picked up Callanach's coffee and files, holding the door open for him.

The length and speed of Callanach's strides made it necessary for Tripp to all but jog alongside him.

'DS Lively isn't good with new people. And he was really friendly with the old DI. I shouldn't pay too much attention,' Tripp blustered.

'If I need your help or your opinion, I'll ask for it. Now go back to Salter and get those boards up. I want this investigation in order, no more distractions.'

★ ★ ★

35

His appointment with Detective Chief Inspector Begbie was predictably draining. The Chief was approaching retirement age and of an old school type. Dealing with his superiors had never been an issue for Callanach at Interpol. They'd trusted his judgment, and seen him rise through the ranks. Here, as he'd just been reminded, he still had to prove himself. It wasn't that he minded being spoken to like a wayward child, more that he was embarrassed at having to defend his position when it was predominantly gut instinct that Buxton had been killed in Edinburgh. It sounded so trite. Finally the DCI had given in on a limited basis. Callanach was allowed to visit the victim's flat, talk to witnesses and put together a sufficiently compelling picture to show that he should head the investigation. It wasn't much, Callanach thought grudgingly, but it was a start.

Elaine Buxton's apartment was as immaculate as the address was desirable, in the much sought after Albyn Place, overlooking Queen Street Gardens. The decor was tasteful, only the light covering of dust betraying the owner's disappearance. It was the apartment of a life lived elsewhere, of someone so consummately professional that her standards never slipped. The only room showing signs of life was her study, where two books remained off their shelf on the desk, both doorstop sized and on the subject of contract law. He'd have to review whatever cases she'd been working on when she'd disappeared, but it didn't seem plausible that so dry an area of law could give birth to such a violent crime.

He sat in her large leather chair and leaned back. It wasn't comfortable. The headrest wasn't worn. This wasn't a woman who used her study to contemplate life. As Callanach sat forward to open the drawers, the cushion shifted slightly beneath him. Yes, that was it. Her constant position, head bent towards book or brief. Always working, concentrating.

The interiors of the drawers were as orderly as the surface. A Montblanc fountain pen was in its case, highlighters remained in their plastic container and painkillers, open and half used, were tucked back into their packet. A black glass paperweight, smooth and tactile, held down a neat pile of bills and correspondence. Callanach reached out to touch it, imagining Elaine doing the same as she read or made telephone calls, feeling the cold stillness beneath his palm. It was plain and simple, and it did its job perfectly. Much like the woman herself. Elaine Buxton liked order and routine. What was missing, Callanach thought, was a sense of self. There was not one photo on display. Likewise any plants. No living thing that might require care or attention. Healthy homemade meals were labelled and stacked in the freezer, each in a handy single-person-sized portion. The whole place seemed devoid of human touch.

Callanach retraced his steps and went back into her bedroom. The bed was bare, the sheets stripped by the forensics team looking for signs of sexual activity and DNA. None but hers had been found. There was minimal makeup in her drawers, only two bottles of perfume in her en-suite cupboard. He opened her wardrobe and found two rows of shoes, split between work and exercise. It was ironic how someone who valued order and neatness so highly could have ended their life in such chaos and trauma. At what point had she realised something was wrong? As soon as she'd left the gym, perhaps. Had someone been following her or was he waiting for her at home? Buxton was fit and healthy. She'd have put up a fight if she hadn't been taken completely by surprise. There was no sign of a struggle, though.

Finally, among neatly folded sweaters, Callanach saw the one thing that had been missing. A ragged teddy bear peeked down from the top shelf, much loved, by the look of it, too precious to put away with the other childish things. Something to look at every morning and evening as she dressed and undressed. A fragment of warmth in an otherwise formal home. He closed the cupboard door against the bear's forlorn, waiting stare. It wouldn't help him find her killer and it didn't progress matters to dwell upon the human loss. Only science, logic and research solved cases. Elaine's house offered nothing further. Callanach locked up and was glad to leave the silence and stillness behind.

Calls to her ex-husband Ryan proved unrewarding. He'd been out of contact with her for more than a year. Following the autopsy report, police officers notified Elaine's mother of her death that afternoon. Callanach was pleased it wasn't his job on that occasion. No amount of training or experience made delivering death notifications any easier. The press was given the information shortly afterwards, with a renewed request for information. Callanach chased up the friend whose birthday celebration Elaine had attended at the gym and found she'd been more of an acquaintance in reality. They'd shared a Pilates class, worked out together each Wednesday and Friday but didn't socialise anywhere else. Elaine hadn't mentioned a boyfriend, she'd told Callanach, not that they chatted about that sort of thing. It was in keeping with the way she lived. Work colleagues all said the same. So, surely, Callanach mused, she'd have noticed someone taking an interest in her, watching her, following her. She was a lawyer. She'd have known there were court orders available to protect her. Was her murderer so restrained that he'd never once revealed himself?

Elaine's diary and correspondence had been seized as evidence. Callanach took the paperwork home, expecting little more than meetings and reminders in to-do-list form. It had already been inspected by the missing persons team and no useful information had been identified. The diary was A4-sized, with a sheet for each day, the notations proficiently brief.

Three weeks prior to her abduction was this: *Senior partner review. Resolution statistics good. Increase in billable hours required.* Buxton was an achiever but not someone with a hard head for business then, failing to squeeze her clients hard enough for money. The oddity of a likeable lawyer. Callanach flicked through the remaining pages, finding only a well-organised professional who structured her day carefully and filled her time to the maximum.

The pages of the diary gave nothing away that Callanach didn't already know but tucked inside the back cover was a card from what was presumably an old friend, announcing the birth of a baby girl and updating Elaine as to recent news. A house move, a career break while she enjoyed some parenting time, a joke about a mutual acquaintance. Nothing that indicated the friend had seen Elaine for months, if not years. The return address was London. Behind the card was a half-drafted letter in reply. It began with the expected congratulations, comments about the baby photos and questions about the house move. Then the tone changed.

I'm so sorry I missed the baby shower and it doesn't look as if I'll make it to the christening either. Work is a bit pressing at the moment. You always did tell me I take life too seriously – I'm starting to think you were right! I'll do my best to get down to London for a visit soon. Perhaps I'll amaze you and book a holiday like you suggested. I haven't been away since the divorce. Maybe I'll even meet someone new (you're bound to like him more than you did Ryan). Time to get my head out of the books.

Callanach closed his eyes. There was no good murder, no fair or reasonable circumstances under which a life could be stolen, but Elaine Buxton had been cruelly robbed. How had she felt when the thought crystallised in her mind that she was being abducted? Did the irony of that unfinished letter occur to her, with its dreams of holidays and meeting a new man, or was the panic too all encompassing? Had she finally found her voice and fought for her life? Callanach put the papers down. One hand wandered into a pocket as he paced his small sitting room, and there, as if it was a stowaway, he found Elaine Buxton's paperweight. He took it out, brushed a stray strand of cotton from its unblemished surface, tried to recall the precise moment he'd taken it and how he'd justified it to himself at the time, but the memory was a cloud. Slowly, quietly, almost as if he were being watched, he slid the heavy glass under his pillow.

Chapter Eight

King seethed at Elaine's lack of cooperation. It was usually beneath him to be reduced to obscenities but, if he were forced to use a common phrase, he might say she was being a fucking bitch. He'd tried to fit her new dentures but she'd cried when he'd pushed them into her mouth, moaning at the pain from her gums, saying they were still too sore. The disgusting creature had shaken her head to and fro like a rabid dog, trying to avoid the procedure. He'd known he would have to tolerate her saliva and had gloved-up in readiness. Her head throwing, though, had sent streams of mucus from her snivelling nose across his face. He could have vomited with repulsion.

She had to respect her new situation. If she wouldn't learn willingly then she would be taught. Discipline would do her no harm. The protein shakes he made her weren't appreciated either. Half a dozen times he'd had to hold her nose and tip it into her mouth. She'd soon stopped thinking she could starve herself. King took an old, wooden ruler from a drawer in his study, picked up his laptop as an afterthought and retraced his steps down the official and up the unofficial staircases. A tiny nick at the edge of the panel hiding the keyhole would have to be polished out. It wouldn't do to get sloppy. Not when everything else had gone according to plan.

Elaine frowned when he entered. Like a stroppy teenager, he thought. But it wouldn't last long. If he could just help her progress through this stage, she would see sense. He walked to her bedside without speaking. There was no point engaging with her. It would only create another scene. This help he was giving her, this tough love, was best dealt swiftly and silently. King checked that the chains and cuffs binding her hands were tight enough that she couldn't thrash and cause too much additional damage. She closed her eyes tightly and her mouth even more so, assuming, no doubt, that he meant to try again with the dentures. Her behaviour proved she needed more than just coaxing to comply. This was, he decided, an inevitability of neither his choosing nor his making. It was all her fault.

It wasn't until he pulled her ankle chains tighter causing her legs to part wider, that she began screeching. However, he was delighted to note that no amount of hysteria made a millimetre of difference to her bindings. He was clever to have thought so carefully about the restraints he would need for his guest suite. King giggled shrilly. Elaine stopped shrieking and stared at him as if he'd grown a second head.

'Guest suite,' he muttered aloud.

In a second, she was bawling like a toddler again. Don't talk to her, he counselled himself. Silence until the lesson has been given. That was when she began to beg. He'd known she would.

'Pleath, pleath don' rape me. Pu' in the denture. I'll be good.' King rotated his head slowly from shoulder to shoulder, working out the tension her pathetic whining had caused. He looked coolly into her eyes. He could reassure her, he supposed. After all, he had no intention of raping her. He wasn't an animal.

Only foul lowlifes who couldn't get it anywhere else were reduced to rape. Then again, if the prospect scared her sufficiently to induce compliance, why shouldn't he use the threat as part of his portfolio to help subdue her?

'Not subdue,' he whispered. 'Educate. Damn!' he shouted. Why was he talking to himself? She'd thrown him off balance with the rape comment. He had to concentrate. King picked up the ruler and hit the bare sole of her left foot, hard. The smacking sound it made was like clean, white light. In his head he counted and made it to four before the screaming began, the myriad of nerve endings taking their time to communicate with her brain. Now he would allow himself to speak.

'That took longer than I'd anticipated,' King said. 'This is what the Germans call *Sohlenstreich*, quite literally a striking of the soles. An ancient and well-practised form of correction used in cultures across the world. My father taught me about it at quite a young age. He was a gifted educator.' He snapped the ruler across her other foot. This time Elaine knew what was coming and emitted the scream, if anything, slightly before wood contacted skin. 'Effective because it's extremely painful, but leaves few marks or lasting injury. I shall be careful not to break any of the bones in your foot, although sometimes there are accidents.' He slapped her left foot with the ruler again.

'As for raping you, get your mind out of the gutter. I am not so needy as to require such base rewards.' The level of her screaming was becoming intolerable.

'If you do not stifle that noise,' he said, punctuating each word with a strike on one foot then the other, 'I shall not stop!' Eleven blows in quick succession. More than he'd intended to deal her. She was starting to pull herself together though, eyes wide, watching him, weeping rather than yelling. Her whole body was shaking. It was shock, but she'd come round. The human body was more resilient than the mind.

'I'm going to ask you some questions to check that you are progressing. If you answer correctly this will end and we can be friends again. Will you let me fit the dentures without fighting me?' Elaine nodded furiously. 'Good. And will you drink your protein shakes without fuss?' More nodding. 'What was the German word for this form of correction?' Silence. He raised the ruler into the air.

'No, no, I'm trying to remember, I'm trying,' she whispered, her throat coarse. Even without the dentures she was working harder to speak clearly, playing the diligent pupil.

'You weren't paying attention, were you, Elaine?' He slapped the ruler against her right sole, quite lightly he thought, but still she let loose another assault upon his ears. He supposed the pain was increasing with the bruising.

'Come along, think about it . . .'

'I don't know, I can't think. Don't hurt me any more,' she sobbed.

'*Sohlenstreich*,' he shouted, hitting her left foot hard. '*Sohlenstreich*, say it with me.' There were more blows, he'd lost count by then but the miracle had happened. She was chanting the word with him, over and over, with each blow to her feet. There was no more crying. Elaine had learned. He felt a burst of joy, close to exultation. The knowledge that he had triumphed, that he'd been right about this all along, was as powerful as he could ever have imagined. He felt a thrumming inside. The first step was complete. He had changed her, brought her closer to perfection, brought her closer to him.

He threw the ruler down and went to her side. 'Good girl,' he crooned into her ear, stroking back hair from the mess of tears and sweat that covered her forehead. 'You're my sweet girl, aren't you? That wasn't so hard. Obedience will be rewarded but you must behave yourself. Understand that I only want what's best. Let's move on.' He decided on leniency, released the cuffs around her ankles and tenderly laid her legs back together on the bed. She drew them into her chest and bit her bottom lip. 'Look at you, trying so hard to be quiet for me. I'll put some painkillers into your next drink. They'll help you sleep.' He loosened the chains on her arms enough that she could relax.

'There's one more thing I want to show you. I think you'll be pleased.'

Picking up his laptop, he pulled a chair next to her head and sat down so they could see the screen together. He opened a file and brought up a video clip. There was some crackle at the beginning, the picture dark and grainy, but soon the ambient hum died down to reveal a large video screen, a mass of heads marking the bottom of the view.

'What?' she whispered. King smiled. The pain in her feet was forgotten already. This would be priceless.

'Wait a moment,' he said. 'You'll see.'

A church organ struck up the tune of 'Abide With Me' and the screen came to life. King watched Elaine's face as her mother took a seat at the front, dark glasses shielding her, a handkerchief pressed to her mouth. The camera panned slowly round, showing rows of people sombrely dressed, most with their heads bowed, no one talking. Elaine choked a sob back in her throat.

'I don't understand,' she stuttered.

'Let's not play dumb,' King replied, taking her left hand in his and rubbing its back with his thumb. 'This is your memorial service. The police won't release your body yet, of course. Who knows how long they'll hang on to that bag of bones? But this is your grand exit. Your fifteen minutes of fame.'

'I don't want to watch any more,' she said, looking away.

'But I require you to. I really must insist.'

She didn't look away again. Elaine Buxton was a fast learner. That was why he'd chosen her.

45

Her family sat in the front pews. King knew each by name and recited details about them so Elaine could appreciate the depth of his research into her life. It was a tremendous compliment that he'd dedicated so much of his precious time to her. Her cousin, Maureen, did a reading followed by another hymn. After that came a eulogy, delivered beautifully by a man King didn't know. The man spoke about her when she was younger, a person King didn't recognise from the description, a tale of a disastrous skiing trip, a girl who worked hard but played harder, private jokes that the world would otherwise never have been party to. Now, it seemed, her life was public property. It had irritated him as he'd filmed. Too many had gathered and the church was full, necessitating the outside screen. The police had been there in droves.

'A bit flowery, I thought,' King commented at the end.

'Michael,' Elaine said, as if calling from sleep. King pinched her hand roughly.

'Who was he?'

'My friend from law school,' Elaine answered. 'We lost touch. He moved to New York.' He glared as tears filled her eyes. She really was insufferable.

'You should be grateful. How many people get to see and hear the things I brought you? You were respected, loved, admired and you got to hear it all without dying. I liberated you!'

'Let me go,' Elaine begged in a hushed voice. 'I won't tell anyone. I'll pretend I have concussion. I don't think you're a bad person, just, well, confused.'

King was breathing hard. He could feel hot colour rising in his cheeks. The sound of his own grinding teeth echoed within his skull, and then he could smell her. Unwashed, festering on that mattress. She'd been there twenty days already, and hadn't even bothered requesting use of the bathing facilities. He'd provided a shower stall in the corner of the room for exactly that purpose, and would happily have supervised had she been suitably placid. All she had to do was ask. Putrid cunt. She'd tricked him, hadn't learned a thing. He hated being duped. His judgment had been flawed. Badly flawed. Perhaps she wasn't the right one, after all.

King brought a hand up from beneath the laptop brutal and fast, smashing plastic and metal into Elaine's face as she reeled back in horror.

'Confused, you dumb whore? I'm not the one who's confused. You're dead! Don't you get it? Everyone thinks you're gone. They have your blood, your clothes, a body and your teeth. They have consigned you to history. Do you know what that means, miss smarter-than-me fucking lawyer?' He grabbed the neck of her t-shirt and pushed his face into hers. 'It means you're mine. You belong to me and that's the way it's going to be. So you'll do what you're told, when you're told and learn to like it. No one's coming to save you. Their grief will fade and they'll forget. Nobody's searching for you any more.' He shoved her onto the pillow, straightening his own clothes, knowing he had to calm down.

'You're right,' she hissed from the bed. 'They're not looking for me. But they are looking for you. You'll never find a moment's peace, never stop looking over your shoulder. One day they'll be waiting at your door when you get home and that'll be . . .'

He smashed his arm across her mouth, whipping her head round and sending blood flying from her mouth. He felt soothed immediately. It was what she'd wanted. Oblivion. But he wouldn't be forced into killing her. He still had important plans. Only perhaps he'd have to improvise a little. King left her twisted body as it was and exited. She could wake up and consider her fate alone.

Chapter Nine

The lack of progress was driving Callanach crazy. He'd attended Elaine Buxton's memorial service and watched the vast crowd outside weeping for a woman most of them didn't know personally but who'd been stolen from their city. He knew what the collective was thinking. That it could have been them. That it could have been their wife, sister, daughter or mother. Such crimes left scars on the landscape of a community as vivid as the scorched earth that was once a mountain bothy. The crowd had come not only to mourn, but to jointly experience that unspoken truth. Thank God it was not me. And there was nothing wrong with that, Callanach thought, the clinging on to life. That was what policing was about, after all. Protecting, valuing, cushioning a too short, too fragile existence.

In the fortnight since then, the hours had started to drag. His phone rang less and less often. Public appeals for information had proved fruitless. The police had trawled Elaine's computer files, diary, emails, current and past cases. Nothing had raised a red flag. She'd avoided social media, tended to call friends rather than texting, had never gone near an internet dating site. The usual lines of enquiry were dead-ending.

Callanach had even found the time not only to tip the contents of his boxes into drawers, but to organise them into some semblance of order.

'Is it a bad time?' Ava Turner asked, putting her head round his office door.

'I'm not exactly busy, if that's what you're worried about,' he replied. He'd seen her a handful of times in the last couple of weeks, but never in circumstances when he could apologise for his behaviour. Now too much time had passed and he felt ridiculous referring back to her offer of a drink and his negative reaction.

'I need a couple of spare bodies to chase up a development on a case. Can I borrow some help from your team for the week?' She parked herself in a chair opposite him.

'Absolutely,' Callanach replied. 'It would be good for them to get working on something else.'

'No breakthroughs?' she asked. 'That's tough.'

'It's wrong,' Callanach muttered. 'For a murderer to be so meticulous in their planning, to have thought so far ahead. It's completely at odds with the chaos or fanaticism it takes to kill.'

Ava sat forward, transforming from colleague to detective as she considered it. 'That's because you're looking for a well-organised murderer. You've stopped thinking about him or her as a person. Whoever did this couldn't employ those sorts of skills from thin air. You're looking for someone who's meticulous in their whole life, probably obsessively so, who's never missed an appointment or favourite radio show, who reviews their time expenditure each month on different activities, who diaries when they last changed their sheets. Look for the person first. You'll meet the killer later.' Ava got up. 'So I can take two from your team?'

'As long as one of them is DS Lively,' he said.

'Not a bloody chance,' she answered.

'Do you have an hour or so available for a drink this evening?' Callanach asked as she headed out of his office. Ava stepped back inside to answer.

'I don't think so,' she said.

'If it's about last time . . .' He shrugged his shoulders. 'It's been a difficult transition moving here.'

'The station is awash with rumours about your move from Interpol. There's always gossip when an outsider takes rank instead of promoting internally. I understand you want to settle into the job before starting to socialise and that's perfectly sensible,' Ava said.

'Actually that's not . . .'

DC Barnes walked in, which Ava took as either a cue or an excuse to leave, Callanach wasn't sure which. Barnes' face was alight with a mixture of concern and adrenaline. 'We think we've got another one, sir. A woman's been missing since last night. Her assistant called it in.'

'What's the link with Elaine Buxton?' Callanach asked.

'The woman left work as usual but there's no sign of her entering her home. Similar age to Elaine, single, no children. Totally out of character for her to go off the grid. Missing person report's available in the briefing room and we're bringing in the assistant for more information. We've got units at the woman's home and are making the usual enquiries with colleagues.'

The briefing room was buzzing. Callanach took a seat at the back as he prepared to listen to what information had been gathered, notebook ready on his lap. Ava Turner opened the door and looked in quizzically. He beckoned her in.

'I was coming to collect my extra bodies,' she whispered. 'What's going on?'

'Another woman is missing,' he said.

'Mind if I stay and listen?' she asked. He shook his head and she took the seat next to his.

Jayne Magee's face appeared on the screen. There was a slightly suppressed intake of breath from everyone watching. Callanach didn't know why it was so shocking, only that the surprise came from what was around her neck in the photo. The sergeant who'd taken the missing person report began to speak.

'This is the Reverend Jayne Magee, thirty-six years of age, Caucasian, Scottish national. Her administrative assistant, Ann Burt, called in her disappearance when Jayne failed to arrive for a meeting this morning at the Cathedral Church of St Mary in Palmerston Place, part of the Scottish Episcopal Church. What rang alarm bells is that she appears not to have been home last night. Her assistant says Jayne had no plans. The Reverend had told Ann she was looking forward to a quiet night in with a curry. Her only vice, apparently. When she failed to attend the meeting this morning and couldn't be reached by phone, the assistant went to her house. She has a key and let herself in. There was no sign of Jayne. No bag or coat and in the fridge the curry they'd talked about was sitting untouched. Ann had emailed her at seven yesterday evening, passing on a query and got no response. Usually, the last thing the Reverend does every night is to check emails and respond to them. Ann Burt said she was curious about it last night but assumed something had come up, either illness or an unexpected visitor, and didn't pursue it with a phone call.'

'Where's her home?' Lively shouted from the far side of the room.

The sergeant shifted images and the screen flashed up a map of the city. The cathedral was marked with a blue cross and a red dot denoted what Callanach presumed was the home.

'She lives in a detached house in Ravelston Park, across the river from the cathedral and roughly north-west. She always walks to and from work, even in the worst weather, and we're told she was on foot yesterday.'

'So, she left St Mary's at?' Callanach asked.

'Around seven p.m. She'd been there for choral evensong, stayed to chat with a few people then gone home. There's no sign of a break-in or a struggle, nothing missing that the assistant can identify.'

'I see the similarities,' Callanach said, 'but do you not have anything more tangible that connects this to Elaine Buxton?'

'Only this.' A new photo filled the screen. As one, the people in the room leaned forward to make out what they were looking at amidst the green tangle in the picture. 'Here, at the very bottom, is where Jayne Magee's mobile phone was found. Just inside her front garden, at the roots of a bush. Whether she dropped it or someone else discarded it, we don't know. It's been sent off for prints and data.'

'She could have been trying to make a call, perhaps worried that she was being followed, was disturbed and dropped it,' Salter suggested.

'Or whoever took Magee didn't want us tracing the signal and getting a location,' Ava muttered. 'I'll manage without your lot,' she whispered to Callanach. 'Looks like you've got work to do now.' She left.

That wasn't much to go on as far as linking the cases went. If it was the same person who'd taken Elaine, the one thing they knew was that Jayne Magee might not have much time left. Callanach rose to his feet, running a hand through his mop of hair as he walked to the front. It took all of two seconds for the noise level to reach a point where he couldn't be heard.

'*Arrêtez,*' he snapped, reverting to French in his frustration. 'Stop. There is no time.'

Someone tried a derisive oohing at Callanach's loss of temper, only to be met by DS Lively cutting in.

'We've work to do and the inspector's trying to organise things. So if whoever that was can't get a grip, then get out of the goddamn room,' Lively yelled.

Callanach stared at him a moment, then opened his notebook to go through the list he'd compiled during the briefing, wondering if Lively had suffered some sort of character changing concussion. No doubt it wouldn't last long.

'CCTV footage, see if we can catch any part of her journey home. Neighbours, anyone who might have seen her near her home last night. Presumably the forensics team is already there?' There was a nod from the officer who'd given the briefing. 'Find the last person she talked to before she left the church. Ask what sort of mood she was in, what they discussed, what she was wearing. I want diaries, computer, make the mobile a priority. Tripp, you and Salter find anything that might connect her with Elaine Buxton. I want a full background on them both, from childhood to date. Understand?' There were nods all round. The piss-taking was conspicuous in its absence, which showed Callanach that everyone thought what he was thinking. The clock was ticking. 'Good. Now get back to work.' The team filed out swiftly, buzzing with the combination of adrenaline and pressure. The next twenty-four hours would be crucial.

Lively managed to be in Callanach's office before him. 'I'd like to interview the witnesses at the church,' he said. He was red faced and breathing hard, all evidence of his former cocky bloodymindedness evaporated.

'Any particular reason?' Callanach asked.

Lively nodded and stared at the floor. 'It's that, er, it's where I go. To church, I mean. I know the Reverend Magee. Not personally, we've not spoken or anything, but I've seen her at services. She's a good person and if this is the same man who abducted Elaine Buxton then I'd like to be able to handle the people at the church myself. Sir.' He didn't look at Callanach while he waited for a response. The humiliating addition of the respectful form of address was all Callanach needed to comprehend just how strongly Lively felt.

He wanted to say no, to punish his detective sergeant for the earlier thinly veiled threats and nastiness. But at least by having Lively centred on the church, the man would be out of his way. And there was the fact that Callanach had gone too far in shoving him, not that a man with Lively's ego was going to make a complaint, but it was better to have a rival beholden than aggravated. Reason triumphed over anger.

'It makes sense, as long as this isn't too personal. I need you to be focused,' Callanach decided.

'I'll be fine. I'd appreciate it if we could keep this between ourselves,' Lively muttered.

It was beyond irony, Callanach thought, for Lively to have threatened to reveal whatever muck he'd heard about the forced departure from Interpol, only to ask for his own private life to be respected.

'Take a constable with you and get started straight away. We're already too many hours behind this bastard,' was all Callanach said.

Jayne Magee was about as unlikely a target as anyone could imagine. There was no suggestion that Elaine Buxton was a regular at any church at all, so religion wasn't the link. The pathologist hadn't been able to estimate Elaine's time of death, meaning they had no established pattern to follow, only the knowledge that she'd been missing sixteen days before her body was found. This time, the abductor might keep Jayne alive for weeks or she could be dead already. The killer had become a male in Callanach's mind. There was no evidence, nothing solid, only years of past cases and what was screamingly obvious. Maybe it was more than one person, he considered, but Ava was right about looking at personality first. He couldn't see such an obsessive character working well as a team player.

Callanach met with Jayne Magee's assistant, Ann Burt, that afternoon. She dropped a dripping umbrella into Callanach's bin then removed and folded her headscarf before sitting down. Callanach instinctively tidied his desk as she settled in. Stick thin, shrill and at the far end of her sixties, he guessed, Ann Burt told it like it was. She reminded him of his grandmother, distant though those memories were.

'So I'm talking to the detective inspector, am I?' she began. 'You're the third person I've repeated myself to today. Would you like to tell me what's going on?'

'It's just routine, Mrs Burt. We're covering all the angles.'

'I may be old but I've not lost my faculties. I've had a call to say that there are three police officers at St Mary's and a whole team at Jayne's house. You're thinking the worst, no doubt.'

'There's no trace of her at present and no one has contacted us to say they know where she is, so it's all just standard investigative procedure.'

'And the name Elaine Buxton hasn't come up, is that right?' Callanach didn't say a word. The standard procedure line was one thing. Lying was another. 'I thought as much,' she went on. 'You should know that the Reverend Magee has the heart of a lion. She's a match for anyone. Don't you go writing her off just yet.' The words were brave but her eyes were too bright. Callanach made a few unnecessary notes while she regained her composure.

'We don't know who did this but experience tells us that in every case, a quick start is essential. We're hoping the Reverend will turn up, that it was some personal crisis, perhaps simply that she needed time alone. But if that's not the case then we have to consider all the possibilities,' he said.

'She led a prayer vigil for Miss Buxton shortly after she went missing. Hundreds came, we lit candles, prayed, had a minute of silence. Of course, we had no idea then what had happened to the poor girl.' This time when the tears started Callanach didn't pretend he hadn't seen them.

'We're going to do everything we can. You've brought us her diary and computer, which will help. Tell me more about the sort of person she is,' Callanach prompted.

'She's lovely, genuinely lovely. Not showy or loud, just warm. She has a wicked sense of humour, too. I never expected that from a lady in her position. Just goes to show, you shouldn't judge. She's very approachable, always has time for people. But bright, my goodness. Jayne studied at Oxford University, a master's degree. Always has her nose in a book.'

'And Jayne never said that anything was worrying her? Someone paying her too much attention, maybe?'

'Never,' Ann replied. 'If that girl ever had an unkind thought about anyone, she didn't express it in my presence.' She picked up her handbag. 'You'll find her, won't you, Inspector? Before anything . . .' She couldn't finish the sentence.

'I'll do everything in my power to find her,' he said. Ann Burt patted his hand, a contact he tolerated for a second before pulling away and standing up to see her out.

By the end of the afternoon they were no further forward. The lab had confirmed that the only fingerprints on the phone belonged to Jayne Magee. Interviews of the immediate neighbours were tributes to the kind-hearted woman living next door and reports of how shocked they were that she was missing. Callanach gave in. He took Jayne Magee's file and went home, collecting a take-out curry on the way. If that was the missing reverend's only vice, then it was a good choice.

Back in Albany Street he ate dinner watching television. The evening news brought Ava Turner's face before him, appealing for witnesses about a newborn baby who'd been left on a park bench and died tragically from exposure before he could be found. Ava looked like he felt. Callanach hadn't been aware of the case she was investigating, but any incident involving a child was hard to handle.

Without thinking about it, he dialled her number. When the voicemail message clicked in, he considered hanging up then gave himself a mental kick. It was time to find allies.

'Ava, it's Callanach. I appreciate you're tired and busy, but I could do with a second opinion on the case and I'm afraid you're top of the list. Actually, yours is the only name on the list. So let me apologise and start again, tomorrow night perhaps, if we're both free? Let me know.'

Too caffeine-buzzed to sleep, he opened Jayne Magee's daily diary. It was shaping up to be a long night.

Chapter Ten

The head of the Department of Philosophy had called King in to her office not five minutes after he'd returned to work. She might at least have let him clear his backlog. After three weeks away, the accumulation was frustrating. Could no one have covered his duties while he was away? He may not really have been sick, but his colleagues didn't know that, did they? Not one call to offer sympathy or concern. And this morning the other administrative staff hadn't even asked him about it. This was the way it had always been, no reason to expect anything better at this point. Was it intimidation or jealousy, he wondered, as he deliberately delayed by making tea, keeping Natasha, or Professor Forge as she insisted he call her, waiting just a few minutes more.

By the time King opened her door, she was taking a telephone call and raised her forefinger as if he was a wayward student, keeping him still and silent while she finished her business. Natasha was wearing a dark green suit that emphasised her hazel eyes and ash blonde hair. King hated the way she made him feel. Even though he couldn't bear to be in her company these days, there was no escaping her beauty. He admired her long, slender neck, with skin that would have flattered a woman in her early twenties. Forge's thirty-sixth birthday had come and gone yet she was remarkably untouched by the signs of ageing. But King wouldn't let her affect him like she used to – he had a new world waiting at home that she could never conceive. Like some great Vernean adventure, he would travel into his secret inner domain, moulding it until his utopia was complete. He pictured Natasha there – she could insist he call her Professor to her face, but in his head he called her other names, some she wouldn't like at all – and felt a desire so strong wash over him that the mug in his hand began to shake. Finally she hung up.

'Sit down, please, Dr King. It's good that you're back at work. I'd like you to arrange a speaker for the next evening lecture. It's only two weeks away so we're behind with the arrangements. Can you organise it in that time frame?' She raised her eyebrows at him. There had been a time when he'd loved that expression, her pensiveness. He'd been wrong. It was irritating. He hadn't noticed then how it created tiny frown wrinkles across her brow, or her patronising habit of tipping her head to the side as she waited for a response.

'Easily,' was his reply.

She breathed in as if about to say something more, changed her mind and flipped her diary shut.

'All right. The speaker should address one of our listed titles for the term and we'll need an outline of their lecture seven days beforehand, so time's tight.'

'I know the format,' he said, enjoying her tension. She had her arms crossed defensively over her chest. Little did she know how appropriate it was, he thought. If she could only see what he'd done; all that he'd become. The tailored suits and high heels, her immaculate hair kept short and businesslike, wouldn't be so intimidating on his home territory.

'Right, you'll have a lot to catch up on from your leave, so that'll be all.' She turned her face to the computer monitor. He had been dismissed. All she'd ever done was dismiss him. King had once put forward a paper he'd spent months researching and writing, offering it for inclusion in the department's journal, only to have it rejected out of hand. Three times he'd applied for academic posts in the department. Twice he'd been discounted at the first stage. The third time, he'd been selected for interview. He remembered his elation upon receiving the notification letter with something close to shame. He'd worked hour after hour, consuming every volume on philosophy he could find, studying teaching plans, the history of the department, everything and anything that would impress the board. He was finally going to receive the recognition he was owed. He wouldn't let himself down.

On the day of his interview, he'd been calming his nerves in the gents' toilets, splashing cold water on his face. That was when he'd heard those imbeciles giggling together, thinking they couldn't be overheard in the ladies' next door.

'What are they doing interviewing him? He gives me the creeps and he's horrible to the students, won't give them the time of day. Can you imagine him teaching? I'm not staying here if he's on the faculty, doing his typing, organising his diary. He'll probably make us all address him as sir,' the ugly bleached-blonde receptionist had said. He'd always loathed her. She embodied the worst of young women, concerned only with their grooming and social lives, handing themselves out to the lowest bidder, couldn't write a sentence without a spelling mistake.

'He'll probably make us curtsy when we go in his room,' said another. This was an older voice. Deirdre, King thought. That was worse. She'd always been polite to his face, friendly, even. How quickly women betrayed. Throwing a paper towel in the bin he told himself to stop listening, knowing it was stupid, damaging his confidence before the most important thirty minutes of his life and a chance at the academic career he'd always desired. But he'd stayed. It was the human condition: the need to know the worst, the destructive desire to see how it feels when you hit rock bottom. He'd inched closer to the wall to hear better. The voices were hushed and he'd held his breath to catch the words.

'I shouldn't worry about it,' two-faced Deirdre had hissed. 'Natasha didn't even want to interview him but Human Resources told her she should. They didn't want a challenge to the fairness of their long-listing process. His CV is quite impressive.'

'How do you know so much?' Bleached-blonde had sounded amazed. 'Oh my God, I never hear this stuff.'

'I had to type up the notes of her session with HR. Professor Forge called me in especially to tell me I wasn't to say anything to anyone, so don't you go blabbing. I think he makes her skin crawl like he does everyone's. She's not giving him the job, that's for sure.'

'Bloody right,' the yellow-haired whore had replied.

King hadn't moved, not until they'd finished tarting themselves up and he'd heard the ladies' door swing shut behind them, giggling viciously as they'd trotted up the corridor. When their grotesque laughter had finally faded, he'd let rage take him, slamming a fist into the mirror that was reflecting his reddened face and swelling tears. A second time, then a third, he punched the shattered glass, no pain transferring from hand to brain because everything was black and buzzing and he wasn't sure what he was doing there, why he'd come, only that he had to get out, get out, get out!

He'd grabbed a toilet roll and wrapped the paper around his hand until the bleeding was hidden, shoved the fist into his pocket, wiped the sweat and other unthinkable liquids from his face, and marched down the corridor. He'd forced his pace to slow, held his head high, put his dignity back on like a helmet and left the building. He couldn't remember the drive home, nor unlocking his door and throwing all his notes, all that work, into the bin. He didn't remember cleaning and binding the fist that really required hospital treatment but that still, in spite of all the abuse it had taken, he could not feel. Nor could he recall falling asleep on his bedroom floor, flat on his back, arms over his face as if blocking out the world that had insulted him so badly, the same room where his mother had spent hours patiently teaching him and his sister algebra, French, chemistry, anything and everything. A whole history in this house. He'd wanted his parents to be proud of him then. Had been sure that even in death, this new career path would make them proud of him now. But he'd been tricked. Lied to. Made a fool. What he did remember, with startling clarity, was waking up and knowing he was better than all of them. He would show them how superior he was, humble every one of them with his brilliance. He would not run, wouldn't be forced out, would never let them know the humiliation he'd suffered. Reginald King was a man born for recognition, adoration even, and he would not quit until he had conquered.

He smiled at the memory. What a moment that had been, a pivotal instant in his life. Still, there was work to do before he could progress further. Work that paid for him to live. He couldn't afford to slack. There were mouths to feed. He filed a faked doctor's letter with Human Resources, citing chronic gastroenteritis as his illness then fired off a few emails searching for a speaker. He was particularly keen to secure the attendance of a representative from Professionals Against Abortion. That would get right under Natasha's skin, women's rights being her regular ride of a high horse. It seemed unlikely that they'd be overwhelmed with invitations to speak at such a prestigious institution as the University of Edinburgh. He would follow up his email with a phone call to them in a couple of days.

The rest of the afternoon was spent clearing his desk of trivia before a trip to the supermarket on his way home. There were certain women's supplies that needed buying. Not a chore he looked forward to, but a necessity. He went through the self-service checkout to avoid a nosy employee thinking too hard about the contents of his basket, treated himself to a good bottle of white wine – he might even share a glass with the ladies if they were behaving themselves – and set off to prepare dinner for them. It would be an interesting evening, he thought. Time for them all to get to know each other better.

Chapter Eleven

At Ava's suggestion they were meeting at a pub in York Place, just around the corner from Callanach's apartment. She'd refused to give him the name of it, telling him he'd know it when he saw it.

She was right. Callanach spotted the Conan Doyle at the top of the road and knew immediately he was in the right place. Ava had promised to take him somewhere none of the rest of the squad would go, gossip was a price neither wanted to pay for a quick drink. It was warm and welcoming, eschewing the pretentiousness of trendy wine bars in favour of cosy chairs and a relaxed atmosphere. DI Turner was already there, checking emails on her phone and hugging a glass.

'Can I get you anything?' Callanach asked.

She smiled. 'No, sit down and let me get you a drink. I started early, didn't expect to find a parking space so easily.'

'What's that you're drinking?'

Ava held up the glass mug and he caught the scent of apples and spice in its steam. 'Mulled cider,' she said. 'I can never resist it. I'm guessing I can't tempt you to join me?'

'Glass of red, I think,' he said. While she went to the bar, he held her glass in his hands, enjoying the heat of it as he inspected the place. A large painting of Sherlock Holmes' creator hung above the stairs from the doorway. Callanach wondered what the writer's personal demons had been, to have conceived such an eccentric hero.

'You're a fan?' Ava asked as she handed over a large Cabernet Shiraz.

'When I was young, I consumed his work. It all fed subconsciously into my decision to become a police detective, I suppose. You?'

'I should read, I know, but by the end of the day I'm so drained that concentrating on a book feels like more work. I love the cinema. I go all the time, often to the midnight showings, sit on my own, eat popcorn. It helps me switch off.'

Callanach raised his glass and Ava met it with hers. They sat in silence and sipped until a barman appeared, placing menus casually on their table.

'You said you wanted to talk about your case,' Ava said. 'Anything specific?'

'Not really. I keep wondering why we're not making progress, if it's my fault. Maybe the move to Scotland has distracted me. If I'd found Elaine Buxton's killer, Jayne Magee would be safely at home tonight.'

'You don't know for sure that the same person took them both,' she said.

'There are too many similarities for it to be a coincidence. I studied their profiles today. Excelled at school, both graduated with a first-class degree, each highly regarded in their own profession, hard-working, dedicated. And both disappeared from their home without a trace.'

Ava put her drink down. 'You must have overseen cases at Interpol where there was no break for ages then something happened and one piece of the puzzle landed so you could see the whole picture. You aren't responsible for a lack of progress if there's nothing to find yet.'

'Isn't it our job to seek out the answers rather than waiting for solutions to come to us?' Ava seemed content not to answer. Callanach realised the pomposity of his response to what had been a simple attempt at comfort, and opted for changing the subject. 'Why did you become a police officer?'

'My great aunt was poisoned when I was five, my inheritance stolen and I vowed to find the killer,' she said.

'*Je suis désolé*, I'm so sorry, I had no idea . . .' Callanach spluttered.

Ava began to laugh, tried to control it then the giggles got the better of her.

'I can't believe you fell for that,' she choked, the laughter starting again and Callanach sat with raised eyebrows as he waited for her to stop. 'Policing felt like a good match for the person I was in my early twenties. And I probably wanted to make it clear to my parents that I had no desire to get married and have endless dinner parties until I popped out a couple of grandchildren for them. If I had my time again, I'm not sure I'd choose the same path. What about you? It was a dramatic move to leave Interpol and join a city police force. I'm guessing we're not quite as glamorous as your French colleagues.'

'Glamour is overrated,' he said, finishing his drink. 'I'm hungry. How's the food here?'

'The steak is excellent,' Ava said. 'As is the baked brie, which is what I'm having.'

Callanach couldn't help but smile. It was an unfamiliar sensation. But Ava Turner was so open and upfront that it was completely disarming. They ordered and made small talk until the food arrived.

'Come on then, everyone has a reason. Why the police?' Ava asked as she dipped baguette in melted cheese.

Callanach instantly regretted having asked Ava such a personal question. He should have foreseen having to respond in kind. His pause was long enough that Ava had fully gauged his reticence before he met her eyes again.

'You don't have to answer. It's not a trick. And tell me if I'm misreading this or being dense, but this is the way it usually works. You ask me a question, I ask you one. We bump into each other at work, we get to know each other better so there's more trust. When we have a bad day, we smile at one another, remind ourselves that it's all par for the course.'

'I know how it works,' Callanach said. It came out more brusquely than he'd intended and he regretted it immediately. This wasn't how he'd wanted the evening to go. He readied himself to say sorry.

'Don't,' Ava said. 'Don't apologise again. People are who they are. As far as I'm concerned, forcing a square peg into a round hole is a waste of energy. But you'll have to find a better means of communication than this. Your squad doesn't have to like you, but they do have to respect you. So here's the thing. If you don't say please or thank you to your detectives, they'll still do what they're told but they won't feel a sense of pleasure in working their hardest for you. If you snap at everyone all the time, you'll drag your team down. And if you don't let anyone get to know you, whether it's me or anyone else, then you've got no reason to be here because there'll be no loyalty and no community. And that's all you have in the police. It's what grounds you and supports you. It's the only thing that makes the job tolerable at the end of the day. Feel free to stop me when you want to explain that you already know all of this.'

Ava stood up, picked up her bag and strode away. Callanach realised she'd left her jacket, grabbed it and turned to call after her. He searched the small passageway of steps leading down to the exit but she had already disappeared. Letting out a stream of expletives he returned to the table, threw the jacket back onto her chair and put his head in his hands. He never used to be this person. On top of everything he'd lost – his home, his career, even his mother – he'd become someone he no longer liked. Perhaps Scotland was a mistake, perhaps he was wrong thinking he could take up policing in a new country and that it would be the way it was before. If he was going to run, he should have run much further and never looked back. Slipping on his jacket, he stood up to leave as a glass of wine was thrust into his hand. He stared at Ava.

'Going somewhere?' she asked.

'I assumed you'd . . .' he stuttered, trying to stop the words before he looked even more foolish than he already did.

'That I'd what? Oh my God, you thought I'd left?' Ava laughed, a big belly laugh that contained not the slightest hint of malice or mean spiritedness. Callanach glanced at the large glass of red in his hand and wished furiously for a time machine to start the evening again. 'You can go if you like, but I'm off duty and I have no intention of ruining my evening by flouncing off anywhere. I went to the bar, as you can see. Thought I'd give you a moment to decide if you wanted to join in the conversation or just carry on sitting there like a lemon.'

'*Un citron?*' Callanach's translation skills weren't bad but that phrase made no sense at all.

Ava laughed again, more softly this time. Callanach gave up, took a long sip of wine and forced himself to sit back and at least pretend to relax. Perhaps that was what was required to start a new life. Perhaps the best he could do was pretend that he could still act normally around people. Maybe in time he'd get more convincing at it. He took a breath and forced himself to share the sort of confidences he once wouldn't have thought twice about.

'We lived in Scotland until my father died. I was four years

68

old. After that my mother found it hard to cope, so we moved to France near her family. She had to work long hours to support us and I learned to fend for myself. I got tough very quickly, always fast with a smart mouth, getting in trouble, fighting with the local boys. To them I wasn't properly French, didn't fit in. I suppose I turned myself into the sort of arrogant jerk everyone assumed I was when they saw me. By university I was bedding any woman I wanted, partying constantly. My mother called them my dark years. I almost never went home, was egotistic and unlikeable. Then I met someone and it changed everything. For six months I managed to behave like a decent human being, my grades improved, I was content.'

'You split up?' Ava asked.

'We had a petty row. I went out, got drunk and she found me later that night in her best friend's bed. She left and did not return. I never saw her or spoke to her again.'

'And that changed you forever into the much improved human you are today?' Ava teased.

'Unfortunately not. I was making extra cash modelling so I threw myself into that world, avoiding the university crowd. It was exploitative, drug-fuelled and toxic. Everyone was out for themselves. I spent my weekends travelling with a bunch of crazy thrill-seekers. If we weren't drunk or high, we were skiing, scuba diving, sailing or skydiving.'

'Sounds awful.' Ava raised her eyebrows.

'Everything was excessive which meant, after a while, that it all became commonplace. It's one of the many things I regret – not being sober enough to appreciate how lucky I was. Then the bubble burst. I got arrested for drunk driving. The police officer was female. I was horribly rude about her looks when she was booking me in at the police station and she slapped my face, hard.' He rubbed one hand across his cheek at the memory. 'The officer changed her mind about arresting me. Instead, she put me in a car and drove me two hundred miles back to my mother where she made me stand and listen, sober by then, to the words I'd said to her. For the first time in years, I was truly ashamed. My mother cried with embarrassment. I was at a crossroads, and that police officer sent me the right way. Had it been anyone else who'd arrested me, I would not be here now.'

'She's the reason you joined up?' Ava asked.

'She was a part of it,' he said. 'It was simplistic, but at the time it made sense. I served in the French police force until I was thirty, then transferred to Interpol where I've been for the last five years.'

'So what made you leave?' Ava asked. Her phone buzzed and she paused to read a text, frowning fiercely and muttering under her breath.

'What is it?' he asked.

'Another baby has been left in the same park, still alive and on its way to the hospital but the paramedics don't expect it to survive. How can it be happening again? I'm sorry, Luc, I've got to go. I feel bad for leaving mid-conversation.'

'Don't,' he replied, 'at least I found somewhere that cooks steak properly.'

She smiled. 'Nice to know what your priorities are.' Ava put a companionable hand on his shoulder as she walked past him. He jerked away instantaneously, hoped she hadn't felt it but saw the question in her face. 'See you tomorrow, Luc. You take care.'

Ava left him staring at the books, globes and brass lamps adorning the walls. It was as good a place as any to drink wine and not think. He ordered another large glass of red and watched life go by until time was called.

The next day began too early. It was the first night he'd slept properly in weeks and the awakening beep of his phone was unwelcome. It was Tripp.

'Not sure if it's relevant, but I've been going through Jayne Magee's neighbours' statements. One of them saw a man at about the time we think she was taken, going round the corner at the end of the street pulling a large wheelie suitcase. I know it's unlikely but . . .'

'I'll be half an hour,' Callanach said.

He was there in twenty minutes, uncharacteristically dishevelled, shirt unironed, socks not even distantly related. Tripp stared as Callanach walked in clutching a steaming cup of coffee without noticing that a substantial amount of it was dripping down his jacket.

'Morning, sir. Everything all right?'

'Show me the statement and cross-reference it with a map.'

Tripp rummaged through a box of files then laid out documents on Callanach's desk. 'Jayne Magee's house is here.' He pointed at a red mark on a large scale map of the street. 'And here,' he pointed again, 'about two hundred yards away, is where the neighbour saw the male. Mrs Yale who saw him was walking her dog, coming back into Ravelston Park as the male was exiting onto Ravelston Dykes. She didn't see where he went after that. You think it's our man?'

Callanach was silent. He started scrabbling through desk drawers.

'Er . . . need any help, sir?'

'No, I have it.' Callanach held up a tape measure. 'Lie down on the floor, on your side, tuck your legs and head in as tightly as you can.'

Tripp looked towards the doorway, mouth open, jiggling from one foot to the other.

'*Pour l'amour de Dieu*, Tripp, I'm going to measure you, not kill you. Lie down.'

Tripp assumed the position and held still while Callanach stuck tape to the floor in a rough rectangle.

'Move your feet in a bit,' Callanach said. 'And your elbows. Surely you can make yourself more compact than that!'

'I can't, if I move one limb another sticks out.'

'*C'est des conneries!*' Callanach muttered, throwing the measuring tape to the floor. 'How tall is Jayne Magee?'

'Five foot three,' Tripp answered, giving up and rolling onto his back, arms outstretched as Callanach made for the door.

'Salter!' Callanach yelled towards the briefing room.

Footsteps approached at a pace and she burst through the door.

'What, sir?'

'Tripp will explain. We need to measure you.' He threw the tape at them as he logged on to his computer. 'Make yourself small, we must assume she was bound.'

They finished contorting, taping and measuring just as Callanach found what he'd been looking for on the internet. 'The largest wheelie case available is thirty-four inches long. Is it feasible?'

'Depends on the depth,' Tripp said as Salter recovered. 'But I'd say it's possible.'

'Salter, go to the shops,' Callanach handed her a wad of notes, 'and bring back a thirty-four-inch case, the deepest you can find, strong wheels. Tripp, we're going to Ravelston Park.'

They got out of the squad car at the corner where the witness had spotted the male.

'Two street lights, both the opposite side of the pavement from where he was walking,' Callanach commented. 'Many trees and high bushes. There would have been little light from the surrounding houses, they're all situated well back from the road.'

'He must have been turning west though, or he'd have crossed over before the corner,' Tripp said. 'So he either parked his car within walking distance from her house or he lives close by.'

'He wouldn't risk having witnesses to his route home,'

Callanach said. 'There could easily have been more than one dog walker. The key to this is the vehicle. Have uniformed officers carry out door-to-doors within a quarter-mile radius, checking if anyone saw a man with a case getting into a car, van or truck. We should see if the witness walking the dog can tell us any more.'

Mrs Yale could be heard before she was seen, yelling at her husband to let Callanach and Tripp in, as she controlled an Airedale Terrier who appeared more hungry than friendly. She was large, in her late seventies and obviously excited by the attention.

'Don't mind Archie,' she fluttered. 'Sit yourselves down. Michael will fetch us tea, won't you, dear?' Her husband shuffled dutifully away.

'Mrs Yale,' Callanach began.

'Isabel,' she said. 'Would you like biscuits with your tea?'

'No, thank you. You saw a man leaving the road with a case. Can you describe him again?' Callanach asked.

'There wasn't much to see, I'm afraid. It was dark and cold. He was wearing a long coat, grey or black, a woolly hat and a scarf right up over his mouth. He was all shadows, my darlin'.'

'You noticed a case?' he prompted

'Yes, a big thing. I hate the sound those wheels make.'

'Can you describe it in more detail?' Tripp asked, taking a tea cup from the tray.

'It was soft, like a giant rucksack rather than one of those hard ones. Heavy too, by the look of him pulling it. It was black, with lots of zips. Didn't see any labels, I'm afraid.'

'You seem to remember more about the case than the man, if you don't mind my saying,' Tripp commented.

'That's because I was closer to it. I was bending down as the man came past me, bagging Archie's doings. My first thought was what shiny shoes the man had. You don't see many gentlemen

73

that bother these days. Black lace-ups. Not really the best thing in this weather.'

'Anything else, Mrs Yale? Anything at all?' Callanach said.

'I hadn't realised I'd seen anything of note.' She fussed over biscuit crumbs. 'But there was a faint smell about him. I don't suppose many would recognise it nowadays, but I'm sure it was mothballs.'

'Mothballs?' Callanach asked Tripp, not recognising the word.

'You hang them in closets to stop moths from eating your clothes. Not very common any more.'

'*L'antimite.* You're sure?' Callanach double-checked with Mrs Yale as she fed crumbs to the ravenous Archie.

'It was the smell of my childhood, Mother swore by them. We couldn't afford new clothes during the war, dearie, so we jolly well looked after those we had.'

Chapter Twelve

Dr King was nervous. It was ridiculous. He was in his own home. He'd brought these women here through sheer force of will for a higher purpose and he was about to have his first proper conversation with the woman he would mentor into their new life together. She might even bring the still-rebellious Elaine into the fold.

Jayne would be free of the drugs by now. She'd need food, drink and an explanation. With her extraordinary faith, perhaps she would be more circumspect about how she'd been delivered into his hands. If there was a God, then maybe Jayne had been chosen for him. He put the tray down and unlocked the door. Inside, occupying two beds, were the women who would change his life.

He'd only planned to take one, researching both to find the most suitable. Always have a backup, that was the thing. Jayne Magee had been his. He'd not anticipated taking them both, not until Elaine had proved so unruly. The reverend would be more docile and able to adapt. He'd felt it when he'd placed her on the bed, taking care not to hurt her whilst restraining her wrists and ankles. Human nature dictated that a prisoner would always struggle hardest when they first woke up. Jayne would rise above it though, he was sure.

On entering the room, he was assaulted by the most repulsive odour. He gagged, doubling over, tray crashing to the floor, splattering him with melon flavoured protein smoothie. His clothes were ruined.

'I dressed especially smartly to meet you,' he shouted. 'Which one of you has done that? Which one . . . let me see!' He marched over, glutinous pink liquid aglow from the colour raging in his cheeks as it dripped down his face. He ripped Elaine's covers back. He had expected, actually wanted, it to have been Elaine but she was in her usual cretinous state, rocking to and fro with her eyes jammed shut.

It was Jayne then. He pulled her blanket away more gingerly and the stench was unbearable. He ran to a cupboard, grabbed an electric fan and dragged it to her bed. For a moment he questioned his choice to have the room windowless, but it had been the only way. He snapped on gloves from under the sink and began the clean-up operation. She was awake and he knew it, although her head was rolled away from him and she wasn't speaking. Better that they didn't communicate until this was over. He had to forgive her. After all, she didn't yet know who he was, what his plans were. He could be anybody, any lunatic planning to do unspeakable things to her. It would be better when she discovered the truth and could put his actions into context. King finished up, showered, made a fresh tray of food and went back to introduce himself properly.

The Reverend Jayne Magee's face was still turned away so he pulled up a chair.

'Jayne, I'm Dr King, Reginald, but perhaps we should remain on formal terms until we've progressed. I won't hurt you, I want you to know that straight away.'

Jayne was chanting beneath her breath.

'What's that you're saying? I can't hear.' He leaned over her, trying to see her lips but she strained her face further away. It took him some minutes before he recognised the words. Jayne was reciting the Lord's Prayer.

'That's what we're here to debate. The existence and nature of God. It's one of the reasons I chose you. I read the thesis you wrote during your time at Oxford and I think you'll find I have some interesting responses for you.' Still she wouldn't respond, even after he'd displayed his genuine interest in her. It was becoming tiresome. 'Turn your head, please. It's terribly bad manners not to look at someone who's speaking to you.' Nothing.

King had no wish to chastise Jayne so soon after her arrival. It would put her off completely. Having previously thought that Elaine had rendered herself expendable, he realised she might have a new use, one that could speed things along much faster.

'Jayne, you comprehend the fragile quality of human life and how little time we have to spare. I wish to begin a conversation with you' – the muttered prayer continued – 'so I shall make you responsible for your companion's fate. I'm obliged to maintain discipline, Reverend, and I have many ways of doing so.'

He unlocked the cupboard above the sink, took a needle from the medical kit and walked over to Elaine. She'd been listening, pretending to be in her own world, but listening all the same and she knew something was about to happen. She screamed when he picked up her hand.

'It's a sterilised needle, so there's really no need for all this fuss. There won't be any lasting damage.' He stuck it slowly beneath the nail of her middle finger, pushing down firmly as she struggled, wondering how it was possible to scream and gurgle at the same time. It was as if she was drowning in the pain.

'Stop it!' Jayne screeched. 'Just stop, please.'

'You're talking to me now, are you?' he asked, not withdrawing the needle from Elaine's nail, not until he'd really made his point.

'Yes, I'll talk, I will,' she shouted.

'What do you think, Elaine? Have you had enough?' Elaine spluttered a yes, nodding wildly at him, imploring Jayne to help.

King allowed himself one more jab into Elaine's nail bed, gratified by a final shriek to ensure compliance, then withdrew the needle.

'Do you remember what happened?' he asked Jayne. She shook her head.

'My lips are sore,' she said, 'and my neck aches.'

'Chloroform is a bit hard on the skin, I'm afraid, and then I had to sedate you with ketamine while I went to work in case you became distressed and injured yourself. It's a wonderful drug. It altered your conscious state but allowed me to issue you directions which you were able to follow. You may find you have strange dreams for a few days. And you'll be dehydrated.' He collected the tray. 'Here, drink this.' She jerked her head away as he held the cup. 'You need to drink and I'm not so primitive as to want to drug you constantly. The whole point of you being here is for us to engage with one another. I don't want to have to be any more persuasive today. It's hardly fair on Elaine.'

Elaine started to squeal and thrash on the bed. Jayne took the straw between her lips, sipping cautiously.

'That's better,' King congratulated her.

'What are you going to do to me?' Jayne asked. It was said remarkably plainly in the circumstances, he thought admiringly.

'I'm an educated man, Jayne, not an animal. I am forging a better life for myself and for you.' He leaned forward and whispered conspiratorially. 'Though to be honest, I'm not sure how long it'll be before Elaine has outstayed her welcome. She's not working out the way I'd hoped.'

'Why are you doing this?' Jayne asked. King stared into her eyes, wondering what she was thinking. Was she hopeful of release, curious about him, too scared to understand her position yet? She seemed full of exciting possibilities. A paragon of potential. She reminded him vaguely of his sister. Not that Eleanor had lived to see adulthood, but if she had, she might have been a lot like the reverend. Their parents had always said Ellie was destined to be a leader with her extraordinary academic ability, not to mention her flair for music. She had been almost perfect. Sometimes annoyingly so.

'I'm doing it for us. For a future where we can learn together, appreciate one another, stretch our minds in glorious ways.'

'What if I don't want to?' Jayne asked. King thought about it. She wasn't being defiant, he decided, or difficult. It was a genuine question and it deserved a genuine answer.

'You will want to,' he said. 'Eventually. I'm here to guide you.'

'This is wrong,' she said. 'Please, think about what you're doing.'

'Jayne, don't,' he counselled her. 'Elaine tried, God knows she begged for days, and it won't work. There's a plan, you see. Sometimes a human has to aspire to a life greater than the one they're born to. I am more than the sum of my parts, as are you. The physical being is unimportant. Elaine's finger will heal, pain is transient. It's a conduit for progression, enlightenment.'

'I see,' Jayne said simply. He waited for more, but that was it. He'd won. For today he should be content with that much.

He was exhausted, drained by disciplining Elaine and all the cleaning. Locking the door on his way out, he heard a whisper, considered going back in, but decided not to. They would need time to get to know one another. It wasn't until he reached the bottom of the stairs that his tired brain finally unscrambled the words he'd heard.

'We're going to die here,' Jayne had said, in that plain way of hers.

Reginald King thought that smoked salmon and mushroom risotto would make an excellent choice for supper.

Chapter Thirteen

DC Salter fitted neatly into the extra-large wheelie case, once Tripp had secured her arms with gaffer tape. There was no hard evidence that Reverend Magee had been inside the case or that the man pulling it was her abductor, but there it was, in glorious high definition, inside Callanach's head and he just knew that was how it had played out. Isabel Yale's shoe comment fit exactly with what Ava had intuited about the abductor's obsessiveness. What sort of person made sure their shoes were gleaming before a kidnapping?

Lively knocked the door once and walked in. 'We've finished our enquiries at St Mary's. Only thing that came out of it was a group opposed to women vicars. Seems Jayne Magee had received some nasty letters, a bit of abuse, threats. She didn't report it to the police but we found the notes in her desk. They're being examined.'

'It doesn't fit with Elaine Buxton's killing,' Callanach noted. 'Collate all the outstanding missing persons reports for women in this age bracket from the last twelve months. And I want the forensic report on the mobile phone. It should have been on my desk yesterday. Also, call the police at Braemar. Ask them to go back up to the bothy and look for parallel marks leading to the hut that could have been made by a wheelie case. It's a long shot but still worth investigating.'

Callanach left Tripp cutting Salter free of the gaffer tape, and made his way down the corridor to the kitchenette. The coffee machine was broken, not that he was mourning its loss. When he turned around, Ava was behind him brandishing an empty cup.

'I'll wash, you dry,' she ordered, grabbing a second dirty mug off the draining board and running hot water into the sink.

A uniformed officer appeared just as the kettle boiled, puffed out from the short flight of stairs from the ground floor, and thrust a large cardboard box onto the table in the corner before retreating without a word.

'Biddlecombe,' Ava called after her. 'What is that?'

'Delivery for Major Investigations, ma'am. No name on it. From some posh florist. Must be from a satisfied customer.'

'Our customers are either dead or psychopathic, depending on your viewpoint, Biddlecombe. They don't send flowers,' Ava yelled, picking up the box and eyeing it suspiciously. 'Should I open it or throw it out of the window?' she grinned at Callanach.

'Is it ticking?' he asked. Ava held it to her ear dramatically and shook her head. 'Phone down to the front desk and tell Biddlecombe to come back up here and open it for you. She needs the exercise if nothing else.' Ava was already ripping open the parcel. 'Nothing like a well-adhered-to security policy,' he noted, peering over Ava's shoulder into the box.

Inside was a bouquet of stunning long-stemmed white roses. He reached across and pulled a card from a tiny golden envelope. '"*Detective Inspector, The thorn makes the bloom all the more precious. Yours.*"'

'Is that it?' Ava asked.

Callanach checked the back of the card, the envelope and the box again.

'That's it,' he said. 'Have you arrested anyone for crimes involving dreadful poetry or being overwhelmingly sickly recently? Because it seems you've caught someone's eye.'

'How do you know they're not for you?' she asked. 'My admirers usually just ask for a photo of me in uniform to put up in their prison cell, in lieu of a dartboard, I guess.'

'Can't be for me. Don't Celtic women just hit men over the head with a club and haul them back to their cave?' Callanach asked.

'Oh aye,' Ava mocked. 'And then only if the man'll make good eating. Otherwise we dinnae bother.' She grabbed the flowers, thrust them into an empty desk bin that she filled with water, and left them on the table. 'Well, if they're for me, someone doesn't know I get hay fever, so no points for research.'

'Shouldn't you report the delivery, at least?' Callanach asked. 'These things can get out of hand . . .'

'Because I don't have anything better to do with my time, and a bunch of flowers is a priority right now?' She laughed. 'I'm opposed to undertaking any activity that doesn't help clear the mountain of paperwork from my desk, DI Callanach.'

'It's your funeral,' he replied. 'Any joy with your babies?'

Ava flipped straight back into work mode. 'No. They're unrelated except for a blanket each was wrapped in. Just white towelling, but identical. There must be two very distressed or confused women out there. What about you?'

'Some movement, only a little, but it's progress.'

'Forensics on Jayne Magee's mobile.' Tripp thrust the paper through the doorway. 'Lab said sorry they're late, they were working on DI Turner's baby case.'

Callanach flicked through the paperwork. '*Et voilà*,' he muttered, pouring the remaining coffee into the sink and running his finger along a couple of sentences that were heavy on the scientific language. He read the paragraph twice before calling Tripp back. 'The laboratory confirms the presence of chloroform on Jayne Magee's mobile. He'd have been wearing gloves. That means it's definitely a kidnapping and it fits with the theory that she was disabled before being packed in the case.'

'Yes, sir. And one of the uniforms working the door-to-doors in Ravelston Park just radioed in about a statement he's taken from a man who regularly cycles home along that route. Give me five minutes and I'll get you the details.'

Callanach went back to his office and phoned Jonty Spurr. The pathologist sounded gruff and hassled, the phone obviously on speaker as he continued working while they talked.

'Do you have time to talk?' Callanach asked.

'Four dead teenagers in one car. They'd taken ecstasy and were racing. Never ceases to amaze me how people can be so careless with their lives.' Callanach said nothing because there was nothing to say. 'So come on then, what do you need?' Spurr asked.

'I have an abducted woman who, I believe, was taken by Elaine Buxton's killer. She was subdued with chloroform when he took her. Is there any method for tracing chemicals from Elaine Buxton's remains?'

'Not from the bones or the environment, no. Normally it would be easy if we had organs to screen but the only soft tissue cells we have are from the tooth found near the baseball bat. I'm not promising anything but I'll run a tox screen. The results will depend on how recently she'd inhaled the chemical and in what amount.' Callanach could hear the metallic rattle of tools being picked up and put down.

'One more thing. How long before the effects of the chloroform would wear off after she was first abducted?'

'Number of variables with chloroform, such as size and weight of the victim and quantity of the dose. Assuming he didn't overdose her and she survived, it's minutes rather than an hour, maybe fifteen if he was being careful not to harm her. It can cause burns to the skin, as well as liver and kidney damage if too much is used. You can't use it safely for long-term sedation.'

'Where would someone get chloroform?' Callanach was pushing his luck and he knew it.

'That's two things and you have a pathologist of your own in Edinburgh. The answer is the internet but probably sent from abroad. It's a commodity in certain eastern European countries, otherwise it's a common industrial agent. Difficult to pinpoint sources, I'm afraid, but it's easy to get hold of if you're determined.'

'Thanks,' he said. 'I will repay the courtesy.'

'Holding you to it,' Spurr replied before the line cut off abruptly.

Tripp was standing outside his door waiting for the call to end. Callanach shouted at him.

'I'm not your headmaster, Tripp. You don't have to wait in the corridor. What have you got?'

'Uniform says there's no detailed description, but Liam Granger was cycling home from work down Orchard Road South, just off Ravelston Dykes and went past a man who he noticed because he was talking to himself in quite an animated way. Granger took a second look and saw the wheelie case. Didn't notice his face or clothing. It was too dark for anything other than an outline. The cyclist assumed he was either mentally ill or drunk.'

Callanach strode over to the map on his wall clutching a red pen. He traced a line from Jayne Magee's house into Orchard Road South.

'He must have parked around this area here.' Callanach pointed. 'That walk would have taken five minutes pulling a heavy case. If he only had a quarter of an hour until she regained consciousness, he couldn't have risked parking too far away.'

'It's a densely populated area, cars parked along that road all times of the day. We've knocked every door. No joy with anyone noticing unusual vehicles,' Tripp added.

'Send uniformed officers to knock doors in the vicinity of Elaine Buxton's home. See if anyone noticed a man with a large wheelie case at about the time she got home. This is something he practised. He knew how to fold the body so it would fit, had the chloroform ready. And would you retrieve the photos of Elaine Buxton's home?'

The photos were on Callanach's desk five minutes later as Detective Constable Salter found a vehicle to drive them to Albyn Place.

'Any news on DI Turner's baby case?' Callanach asked.

'No, sir,' Salter answered.

'What's on at the cinema at the moment?' he asked. Salter blushed. 'I just need something to take my mind off this case,' he said, praying she hadn't misinterpreted his question as an invitation.

'I don't know. My boyfriend downloads everything these days.' Callanach offered up silent thanks for the mention of her partner. 'You don't seem the cinema type, if you don't mind my saying,' she noted.

'What is it you think I do at weekends, then, Salter?'

'Eat out at nice restaurants, drink wine, read newspapers, go to dinner parties. That sort of thing? I should probably fetch the car, sir.' She fled and Callanach realised he'd put her on the spot. Still, her answers told him a lot about how he was perceived. Part of it was the stereotype attached to his nationality, he supposed, and too close to the truth of his old life for comfort. Not so for the past year. He'd closed every door, with only the ghosts of parties past for company.

Elaine Buxton's apartment came into view with a 'For Sale' notice displayed prominently in front of it. Callanach guessed

Elaine's mother could neither afford to keep it nor wanted any reminder of the place from which her daughter had been taken.

'Drive around the back,' he directed Salter. He identified Elaine's garage and studied the crime scene photos. He'd visited her home to get a sense of who she was, but hadn't been inside the garage. Using keys taken from the evidence room, he clicked the automatic door and went inside. 'The keys were found inside the hallway that leads to her apartment, correct?' Salter checked the log and nodded. 'Suggesting she'd dropped them there, that whoever took her was waiting for her inside but no one let him in or saw him there. No sign of a struggle, no noise, no trace evidence. It's too clean. I think he took her from the garage, opened the door to the hallway and deliberately threw the keys into the corridor.'

'Garage would have been locked though, according to her mother. The victim was very security conscious,' Salter said.

'There are bushes outside. He would have known her routine. Simple is best. He arrives here before her, it's dark, he stands in the shadows behind the shrubbery, waits for her to activate the automatic garage door, bends down low and creeps in behind the car.'

'He'd need to have been sure she was alone,' Salter commented.

'She didn't bring men back here. He'd have known her well enough to be confident about that. By the time she'd stopped the car and the garage door was back down, he was waiting with the chloroform.'

'You're saying she couldn't have avoided it, no matter what precautions she took. That's not very reassuring for the rest of us. Why throw the keys into the corridor?'

'To deflect attention from the side path which is how he got out of the garage, through the back door, presumably pulling a large wheelie case behind him. Come.'

He led Salter to a side door, leading directly from the garage onto a mud and gravel path back to the street. She went to walk out until he held up an arm to stop her.

'Don't,' he said. 'Call it in to forensics. I want a team here looking for parallel impressions, gravel stuck deep into the mud in lines. The weight of her body would have made a substantial imprint through the wheels.'

The cinema question had been more than just small talk. He looked up what was on when he got home that evening and texted Ava.

'Couple of hours paperwork on my desk,' she replied. 'If you're still awake at half eleven, how about the late showing of *Ice Cold in Alex* at the cinema behind the Conan Doyle?'

He had no idea what the film was. It hadn't come up in the reviews for the latest releases. As it turned out, the reason for that was because it was made in 1958. He found Ava with her legs propped up on the empty chair in front of her, dressed in jeans, a plaid shirt, and clutching the biggest box of popcorn Callanach had ever seen, eyes glued to the opening titles.

'They re-run old films,' she whispered to him. 'So much better than watching on TV. And no bloody HD, super colour, surround sound nonsense. This is film the way it was supposed to be. Story first, everything else second.' She offered the popcorn and he shook his head.

'You're really going to eat all of that?' he asked.

'Absolutely. And if you don't have some, you're missing the point.'

'How's your case going?' Callanach took a piece of popcorn and played with it between his fingers.

'Ssssh!' was all the response he got and he forced his attention towards the screen. Detective Inspector Ava Turner was already immersed in a North African desert in World War II.

An hour and a half later, John Mills and Sylvia Syms had

given Oscar-worthy performances, and Callanach didn't move his eyes from the rolling credits until Ava stood up and coughed pointedly.

'Now you can talk,' she said. They went to a late night pub on Leith Street that also served reasonable coffee and sat in a corner, trying to ignore the couple next to them who were arguing loudly about wedding plans. 'Your opinion?' Ava asked, manoeuvring a tray onto the sticky table. On it was the coffee Callanach had requested and a brandy he hadn't.

'I think they should run away and get married in Vegas if it's causing that much stress.'

'Of the movie?' Ava said, holding out the brandy glass. He raised an eyebrow. 'It's Friday night, in case you hadn't noticed,' she said. 'I, for one, need a drink and drinking alone isn't the Scottish way. Come on, admit it. The film was cinematic perfection.'

'It was not what I expected,' he said. 'I mean that in a good way.'

'Here's to that,' she said, taking a gulp. Her grey eyes appeared bluer in the glow of orange neon lighting. She looked every inch alive, as if just waiting for the next moment, the next challenge. For a second, Callanach wished he could climb into her skin and remember what that was like. 'You're going to ruin it by talking shop, aren't you?'

'Am I so very predictable after such a short time?' he asked.

'It's your safety net,' she said.

'What's yours?' he asked, instantly regretting prying into her personal life again. Ava didn't even blink.

'I play act at being confident, sharp and funny,' she said.

'Why would you need to do that?' Callanach asked, appreciating the brandy more than he'd expected.

'Because then no one will see how terrified and out of my depth I feel most of the time,' she smiled. 'Maybe discussing

89

work would be best.' She drained the glass of brandy and replaced it with her coffee cup. 'Why would two unrelated women leave their babies to die in the same park? I can't think of a good reason, aside from there being a baby-stealing psychopath roaming the city, but then the mothers would have appeared.'

'If this isn't a copycat, and that seems almost impossible in the circumstances, then the two mothers have met, agreed to do this together. They are making a point,' Callanach said.

'Which would be?' Ava asked.

'The public disposal of the children,' Callanach said. 'So maybe they never wanted them in the first place?'

'You're thinking rape victims,' she murmured.

'Perhaps,' Callanach said, 'but there are other possibilities to consider. Often women who are trafficked whilst pregnant have their babies taken from them forcibly. That might explain the lack of complaint from the mothers.'

'It might, but there'd be no point the traffickers leaving the bodies to be found. It just puts the DNA on file. It's something to think about. Why is it easier to see other people's cases so much more clearly than your own?'

'Distance and perspective,' Callanach said. 'I, on the other hand, have a faceless kidnapper turned murderer who plans everything to perfection, suggesting an elevated ability to control his emotions and behaviour, but who talks to himself in public, presumably without even realising it.'

'Internal debate and subconscious reassurance,' Ava said. 'He's lonely, has no one to talk to or to validate his behaviour. There's a theory that we need people to challenge us as much as to praise us, so that we can justify and reason. People lacking that create a second voice, an out loud voice.'

'Do you think that's why he took Elaine and Jayne?' Callanach asked.

'It doesn't make any sense,' Ava replied.

'Why not?' Callanach shifted his chair closer to Ava and away from the previously arguing couple who'd progressed to making up, and were engaging in louder than necessary kissing.

'If he wants them for company, why kill them?' Ava asked.

'He's only killed one of them, so far,' Callanach said, 'but if you're right about the motive for the abduction then there's a chance Jayne Magee is still alive, no?'

They were interrupted by a scuffle at the door. A cursing, drunken twenty-something burst through followed by a couple of mates equally worse for wear, all staggering towards the loved-up couple on the next table.

Callanach glanced at the barmaid who was looking around for help.

'What the fuck, Suze? I still love ya. Tell me you're no' gonna marry this wee piece o' shite?'

'Aw, Gary, really?' the girl answered, looking bored rather than perturbed. 'I've told you, and my dad's told you. You need to keep away from me. It's over.'

'I know you still love me. Ye said you'd always love me. And he's an insurance salesman. What sort of pissy job is that?'

Callanach raised his eyebrows at Ava who huffed and finished her drink.

'You should leave now, pal,' the insurance salesman-cum-fiancé declared, although he sounded more self-assured than he looked.

'I'll go when my girlfriend tells me to go. You'll keep your gob shut, if you know what's good for you. Come on, Suze, we need to talk outside.'

The ex grabbed Suze's arm and began pulling her up from her seat. There was a visible shuffling back from the crowd who'd grown silent to listen.

'I don't want to go outside with you. I don't want to do anything with you. We're done. I love Robert.'

'You're comin' outside to talk this through. You've gotta learn to see sense, woman.'

The ex pulled harder, ripping the arm of Suze's dress and leaving an angry red mark when she tore away from him. She rubbed the reddened skin, tears in her eyes, then the hurt turned to fury and she spat in his face.

'You stinking bitch,' the ex shouted.

Callanach stood up.

'No, you don't,' Ava told him.

'He's going to hurt her,' Callanach said.

'If you do it, there'll be a police brutality complaint. If it's me, the humiliation will stop him from even considering reporting it.'

Ava stepped forward between Suze and her ranting former partner.

'You need to go home. This doesn't seem like the right time or place,' Ava said quietly.

'Who the hell are you? Get out of my face. This is none of your business.'

'You're right, it's not. But I was having a quiet drink and it seems to me that no one wants there to be a fight here. So what do you say? How about cooling off with a long walk?'

'How about you step aside before I use your face to mess up little Robert over there?'

'I don't recommend it,' Ava said, her voice not raised a notch above her original volume.

'Come on then, you stuck-up cunt,' the ex said, launching himself towards her.

Ava seemed barely to move, but she avoided the attack by shifting her body slightly to one side and grabbing his outstretched arm, pulling it downwards. At the same time, she lowered her centre of gravity, stepped to the man's side and swept her leg under one of his ankles, tripping him face down onto the floor. Callanach didn't have time to even contemplate intervening. Watching Ava work was riveting. She followed through by landing her own body onto the drunken idiot's, pushing her backside into his side as she immobilised his arms and leaned towards his head. Despite his best efforts to struggle, it was apparent that he wasn't going anywhere until Ava let him. What began with a few appreciative whispers turned into whistling and then outright laughter at the spectacle.

'Do you boys want to take your friend home now?' Ava asked the backup yobs who were staring in a way that suggested they had no desire to experience any of the same.

'Aye, we'll see to it,' one of them muttered.

'And are you going to go calmly or do we need to spend a bit more time on the floor first?' Ava asked.

'I'll go. She's no' bloody worth it anyway.' Ava stared a moment longer, checking for any hidden signs of ongoing struggle but it was over. A couple of minutes later and the kerfuffle was done, the crowd back to ordering drinks and texting.

'Shall we go?' Ava asked Callanach.

'Thank you,' Suze called as they made their way out.

'Stick with Robert and avoid the ex for a while,' Ava replied, letting the door swing shut behind her. 'I've got beer stains on my trousers. Bloody typical. It's a good job I never buy dry-clean-only clothes.'

'Well, that was unexpected,' Callanach said. 'Police training?'

'Jiu jitsu. My mother expected me to do finishing classes in the evenings when I was a teenager. I would rather have stuck fishing hooks in my eyes. The compromise was that for every class I took, she had to pay for me to do an activity of my choice.'

'That must have made for an interesting CV.'

'I can now pour perfect drinks, play the drums, get into a sports car without fear of flashing my underwear, not disgrace myself in a fight, entertain diplomats at dinner, and I have yet to be beaten by a man at darts.' Ava laughed. Callanach was never sure when she was joking and when she wasn't. He liked that about her. 'And thanks for not stepping in. It's nice not to be patronised.'

'I saw the beer on the floor,' Callanach said. 'Unlike you, I quite often buy dry-clean-only clothes.'

'Well, that's an improvement,' Ava laughed. 'Nice to know you are actually capable of joking around.'

'What makes you think I was joking?' Callanach asked, as he opened a taxi door for her.

The next day, Callanach gave his first broadcast press conference in Scotland. The Reverend Magee's father spoke first, urging anyone with information to come forward, explaining his daughter's extraordinary love of life and her overwhelming capacity for forgiveness and understanding. With Jayne's face firmly lodged in every viewer's mind, Callanach did the rest.

'We have reason to believe,' he began, 'that Jayne is very much alive. Links to the Elaine Buxton murder have not been established and I would remind everyone that this remains an abduction. In the coming days, we may be asking to search properties and outbuildings within a specific radius of Ravelston Park and would be grateful for the public's cooperation.'

A police press officer took over and gave the crime line number and email address, not that Callanach was expecting much. The abductor had been too clever. It was time to force his hand. Hopefully he would try to move her, panic and make a mistake, up-sticks and disappear so that someone else – a landlord, a postal worker, a colleague – would report him missing. Callanach had to make him feel the pressure of the hunt. If the press interest died down too soon, the chances were that they wouldn't find her at all.

Chapter Fourteen

Reginald King ripped up the slip of paper and threw it in the bin. There was no representative of Professionals Against Abortion available to speak at the departmental lecture. They couldn't exactly be in hot demand, he thought. It's not as if theirs was a popular ideology. Natasha was expecting a name and details about the lecture. He remembered how blasé he'd been about finding a speaker and cringed. She would sigh, he knew, not voicing her disappointment, letting her face show it instead.

Professor Forge looked up when he entered her office, too busy to even pretend to smile.

'I've been trying to get the name of the speaker from you, Dr King and I haven't received any information. You've had ten days since we last spoke about this. Who have you booked?'

'I had been trying to contact a very interesting group and I'm afraid they kept me waiting. It's proving difficult . . .' he stuttered.

'I'm in a dreadful hurry, so can we just run over the details. Who is it?'

'Professionals Against Abortion,' he said.

'What were you thinking?' She stood up behind her desk. 'You know the University has a stringent policy about women's rights and equality. Are you trying to start a riot?'

'You're always saying that every side of an argument should be explored. I thought you'd be pleased to step out of the box the department shuts itself in. Other schools test the boundaries. Some of the lectures I've attended in the last year have been most eye-opening.'

'Cancel them,' Professor Forge said. 'I'll pay their wasted costs if necessary. Just make sure I don't have to listen to them lecturing my students on legislating against women controlling their own bodies.'

'They can't make it anyway,' he said more sharply than he'd intended and the look she gave him was one of disbelief.

'Then why are we . . . never mind. Just answer yes or no. Do we have a speaker lined up for this week?' she asked quietly.

There were so many things he wanted to say to her: that he wasn't going to be told his options for answering a question. That she'd left a button open on her shirt (he could see a hint of black lace bra beneath and was finding it hard to concentrate). That he was her equal and she shouldn't speak to him like that. That he could be as cruel and hard as her and, oh, how he wanted to take her to his secret place and introduce her to Elaine and Jayne.

'No,' was the only answer that would leave his lips. 'But I'll get on it this afternoon. By the time you come back from lunch . . .'

'I'll sort it out myself. Make sure all the applications for next year are properly reviewed and arrange a meeting of the academic staff to go over changes in student supervision policy. I'm late,' she said, snatching up her handbag and stalking out, leaving King staring at the space she'd left behind her desk.

He engaged the lock on her door as noiselessly as he could

manage. She'd never left him alone in her office before. It was an oddly intimate sensation, surrounded by her books, her papers, the few pictures she'd put on the walls, photos of children you'd think were hers if you didn't know they were nieces and nephews. He walked around her desk, running his fingers over the silken wood, polished to such softness it might have been her hair. Her chair was firm but worn into the shape of her body from hours of reading. King slid to the very back of it, imagining her buttocks pressed into the leather, warming it, slipping across the seat as she shifted and settled herself. He was aroused. It fascinated and shamed him. He never felt like that when he was with Elaine or Jayne. With them it was pure. It was about a meeting of minds, the anticipation of enjoying their intellects. As he tried to quell the pressure in his suit trousers, he wondered why Natasha affected him in such a low, coarse way.

'It's her base nature,' he said to the emptiness of the room. 'A man cannot help but be attracted. I must rise above it.' He pushed down on the straining material. The ringing telephone shocked him into movement and he ran for the door, sure she would reappear to answer it. In the corridor he stumbled, picked himself up and dashed to his office. King heard tittering and locked his door, pulling down the blind for privacy. 'Natasha's making me feel like this,' he said. 'It's what she wants. I'm better than her. I have women who are better than her too, brighter even. They don't treat me like a fool.'

He was raising his voice, talking too loudly. With one hand still desperately trying to control the bulge in his trousers, he reached to a shelf above his head and flicked on the radio. A man's voice with a pronounced accent and over-perfect English flooded the room. At first King couldn't make out what the man was saying, then he heard her name. He'd avoided the media, knowing it would make him paranoid. Now someone – a

Frenchman, he decided, but a policeman in Edinburgh nonetheless — was telling the world that Jayne Magee was still very much alive. They were searching properties in the city, appealing for help. All because no body had been found.

It was infuriating to be pushed so hard. He wasn't ready. He'd have to get another vehicle and the weasel at the garage was starting to ask questions even though the extra cash he'd paid was supposed to ensure there would be none. The cars were either stolen or written off, had passed through multiple hands since leaving their owners, chassis numbers removed and old enough not to attract interest. None of them would make it more than a thousand miles before being scrapped but that suited him. One car per woman was what he'd promised himself. Keep it untraceable. Then the car was returned to the weasel and passed on to the next dubious user.

He hadn't intended to take both Jayne and Elaine, that was the problem. Having used three cars, he needed a fourth. His research wasn't up to an acceptable standard. He hadn't settled on a proper substitute for Jayne yet and slipshod planning meant less than flawless results. It couldn't be helped. The priority was to stop the police in their tracks. If they wanted a body so badly, he'd have to provide one.

King watched the clock until he could leave his office and retreat to the vehicle legally registered as his. From there, he phoned the man he knew only as Louis and arranged a trip to his yard via a cash point. Louis only accepted payment in ten or twenty pound notes, which was irritating but sensible. An hour later, King had organised for a car to be dropped off at a back street in Causewayside within walking distance of his rented garage, so he could leave his own car there and swap vehicles before his trip to Glasgow.

He set off at ten that night, well after dark but before the pubs turned out, so the streets were reasonably quiet. The car was an old pale grey Saab and the fan belt was whining in a way that grated King's nerves. He was wearing a charity shop raincoat with hardware store overalls underneath. On his head, a cap covered a thinning spot he had a tendency to rub when stressed, a habit that had undoubtedly sped up the hair loss process.

The journey to Glasgow took just under an hour. It was a city of opposites, King thought. The glass and steel structures, the neon-lit bridges and blazing new auditoriums couldn't hide the poverty, deprivation and low life expectancy that had defined the phrase 'The Glasgow Effect'. An historic settlement with its turreted university spires, more akin to a children's novel than a gang violence stronghold, Glasgow was all smoke and mirrors. King knew he would be adding to those grim statistics, even if only by one, but here within the clashing conflict of modernism and second world penury, no one would notice. It would be easy to see the beauty of Glasgow, to visit the tourist sites, to feel only the buzz and hum of it. But it wasn't real. Glasgow, King thought, was a city thriving on death.

By the time he reached the Govanhill area it was raining and he cursed the water as it obscured his windscreen between wipes. The weather would have the whores running for shelter. The hardiest few could still be seen as he took a preliminary, tentative drive down the business end of Allison Street. Both sides of the road presented a living history museum. Four-storey-high tenements were set above shops with signage in every language, selling food for every culture. It was a truly global street, King thought, enjoying the mockery, wondering how Scotland had been overtaken by languages he would never have the time or the inclination to learn. There were tattoo parlours, so-called designer outlets – King laughed out loud at that – money lenders, hair salons and charity shops, everything and nothing. Too many properties 'To Let'. Too many buildings propped up by scaffolding. Too much going cheap. That, of course, was exactly what had brought him here.

He tried to assess the ages and heights of the women he passed, who watched with wary interest. Jayne Magee wasn't tall and these women were perched on high heels, making a comparison almost impossible. Age would have to be the determining factor. He did a second pass, spotting a woman plastered in makeup to fool punters she was in her twenties although her lank grey roots and sagging breasts revealed the truth. He pulled over and put down the passenger side window.

'Evenin', lovey, what is it you're after then?'

'How much?' he asked, playing his role.

'Thirty for hand, forty for mouth, fifty for pussy,' she said.

'Hand'll do,' King replied, popping the door open. She was close enough to a match for Jayne that he wouldn't risk driving around any more. She hesitated. 'Is there a problem?' he asked.

'The light's not working in your car. Why's that?' She took a step away from the Saab, more spooked than he'd expected. It was only a precaution but one he'd had to take. He didn't want onlookers seeing his face and had taken the bulb out before setting off.

'The bulb's blown,' he said, 'and the rain's getting in. Would you just hurry up?'

She stared into the darkness of the car as if trying to see him better then slammed the door.

'I think I'll take a pass tonight, pal. You'd best go home.'

King thumped the steering wheel. Stupid fucking whore. He didn't have time to play games. With a deep breath he willed himself calm and called after her.

'I'll pay double, all right? Just for a hand job. Sixty quid. Come back!'

'I don't think so,' she shouted over her shoulder, walking away. 'Something's not right wi' you.'

That was when the man walked out of the shadows, pulling her by the arm of her coat, marching her back to King's car.

'You pay sixty, right? Just fingers and palm, no extras. Money up front.' He held a hand through King's window, who fumbled in his wallet while the pimp issued a series of reprimands to the unwilling prostitute.

King passed him the money, keeping his face well back and deepening his voice.

'Here you go.' He handed over three twenties. It was proving to be an expensive night. The pimp, who King decided from his accent was Romanian, pushed her into the car.

'I want you back in half an hour. Stay out of the pubs,' the pimp told her.

'Yeah, bollocks to you,' she whispered under her breath once King had put the car in gear and she was beyond the pimp's reach. 'Turn right up there, I know somewhere close by we can stop, assuming you want to do it in your car. It's a bit cold for outside tonight.'

'The car will be fine,' he said, following her directions until they reached a suitable place. He waited until she was busy undoing his zip before reaching into his coat pocket, opening the ziplock plastic bag and taking out a rag.

'You came properly prepared,' she joked. 'Judging by how much work I've got to do down here, you won't be needing your hankie for a while.'

As she cackled at her own hilarity, King slammed the cloth over her mouth and nose, pressing relentlessly backwards into the headrest. In the footwell, her legs did a jig worthy of an Irish dancer as her hands flailed uselessly around, intermittently attempting to pull away the cloth and scratch King's hands. At the end, she was reduced to a juddering, twitching wreck, slumping slowly downwards in the seat until her chin came to land on her chest.

'Laugh at that,' King said, punching the side of her face so hard he heard the vertebrae in her neck protest. She was still very much alive though and in need of more long-term sedation than chloroform could offer. He tied and gagged her, pushed her onto the back seat and covered her with a blanket.

By the time he was hauling her body, shoved into an enormous sack, up the hidden staircase behind the cellar wall, he was tired. Really, deeply tired. His muscles ached, his head was thumping and a knot of pain was rolling over like a spit roast in his stomach. He needed food and sleep.

'No rest for the wicked,' he said, as he unlocked the door. 'Quite literally, you'll probably think. This wasn't my doing though. If that policeman hadn't insisted on hunting Jayne down, the chances are it wouldn't have been you. You're too old and heavy to be Jayne. At least I can do something about the fleshy parts. Let's see what else you have to tell me.'

Elaine and Jayne were exactly as he'd left them. 'Aren't you two a sight for sore eyes,' he said breezily as he dragged the sack into the middle of the room and dumped its contents in a slowly stirring, dazed heap. The women were watching anxiously. He knew what they were thinking. Were they to be replaced? Was this someone new, better than them, making them surplus to his requirements? He was tempted to play it out like that for a while, to see how they would try to impress him and keep their places. Jayne, however, had decided it was time to talk. He braced himself for yet more pleading.

'Who's that?' she asked. She was quiet today, almost at ease. He'd been charting her moods, following the pattern of them. Having passed through fear, disbelief and anger in rapid succession, Jayne was proving much tougher than Elaine.

'Your body double,' he said. 'I've brought this woman to save your life.' He grabbed a handful of hair and pulled the woman's head back to reveal her face. It wasn't pretty, not with the bruises, but then it wasn't pretty before that either. 'Don't judge her too harshly,' he told Jayne. 'I'm sure there's some explanation for how she ended up like this. I'm betting she could tell some tales, if only we had the time. But where are my manners? How was your evening?'

Jayne frowned. He didn't like it when she did that. It reminded him of Natasha.

'We've been chained into these chairs all day, with only one hand free and hospital bottles to pass water. It makes it difficult to have a good day,' Jayne replied.

'More freedom in time, when you've shown you can be good. Elaine, how are the dentures?' King clicked a finger in front of Elaine's face. She opened her mouth immediately and obligingly. 'A little sore, but that's to be expected. Medicated mouthwash will help. I hope you two have been keeping yourselves occupied.' He inspected the chess board between them, placed there to help pass the time and stimulate their minds. It had belonged to his parents, as did practically everything in the house, but this was an object they had loved. He would often come home from school to find either his mother or father playing chess with Eleanor. His sister was being home educated, an easy decision as his father was a science writer and his mother a full-time homemaker. No school was adequately equipped to maximise her potential, that's what his mother had said. Reginald attended the local school and had missed out on the regular afternoon family chess tournaments. It was only after Eleanor died that his father found the time to teach him how to play. It had taken a while, but he'd become a player of some quality. His father had not been shy in drumming strategy into him. Chess was allowed only in recreation time, after homework and testing. Recreation time had been the part of the day King looked forward to most.

Elaine was in dire need of some recreation now. She spent

her whole time with her head bowed, barely communicating. The chess pieces were untouched but the food and drink he'd left had been consumed.

'And how was your day?' Jayne asked. That made Elaine look up, open mouthed, comically aghast.

King tried to answer, had to think about it, stuttered and started again.

'It was difficult, thank you for asking. I'm tired, actually.'

Jayne nodded, an expression that looked oddly like sympathy on her face.

'Why don't you go and get some sleep. If you'll let me up from the chair I can look after the girl. Save you some work.'

For a moment he was tempted. It would be so easy. He wanted his bed desperately. It was the stress of having to deal with the pimp, he thought. That wasn't the way it was supposed to have happened. Someone had been close to him, had heard his voice. And all for Jayne Magee. It was only right that she did some work to thank him for his efforts. Sadly, it was a trick. All women deceived through softness, sucking you in with sweet lies. She didn't want to help him at all. And yet he wished, he wished so much that she could be trusted. King hardened his heart and accepted his fate. He could either be teacher or friend, but he couldn't be both.

'I'd have appreciated the offer, had it been meant to help me. But it wasn't, Reverend, and I don't appreciate a woman of your qualifications and moral substance being duplicitous. Undoubtedly you would like to help this girl but let's not pretend your offer is to benefit me.'

'He's going to kill her,' Elaine muttered. 'There's nothing you can do. Just don't watch. I can't watch again.' She was shaking so hard that the cuffs around her ankles were cutting into her skin. Jayne reached across the table and held Elaine's hand until the shaking lessened. It was a fascinating lesson in the strengths and frailties of the human mind that the two women had responded to their situation so differently. King considered writing a paper on it. An insider's view that would, like himself, be entirely unique.

'Is Elaine right?' Jayne asked calmly. 'Were you planning to kill that woman?'

The self-righteous Reverend's use of the past tense irritated him, as if she was so convinced she'd be able to talk him out of it that she didn't need to address the situation in the present.

'She hardly belongs with you and Elaine, does she?' he snapped. 'A street whore, staying with a respected lawyer and an eminent theologian. It would be an insult to you both.'

Jayne let go of Elaine's hand and leaned back in her chair, taking her time. It occurred to King that this was what he'd dreamed of – proper debate, a meeting of minds – but she was altogether too assured in her opinions. She seemed convinced of her own standpoint. Where was her desire to listen to his?

'We none of us know what any other human being is capable of or what they have to offer. You can't judge a person by their looks or what they do for a living. Should we not speak to her first, find out more? We might be surprised.'

'How you live is evidence of who you are. Doesn't the church teach us that our behaviour is what we'll be judged by?' King said.

'And what of yours?' Jayne asked, voice no more than a whisper, face revealing only gravity and curiosity. If there had been so much as a hint of insolence about it he'd have enjoyed what he was about to do an awful lot more.

'I'm not a religious man,' King said. 'I'm a believer in science, facts and education. There's nothing you can say to dissuade me from this course although I appreciate you trying.'

He took an electric razor from the satchel he'd had slung over his back and placed it on the floor next to the woman's body. She was trying to sit upright, clumsily and unsuccessfully, her feet sliding around on the floor, betrayed by legs that still hadn't regained muscular control. As he removed her foul clothing, armed with a plastic apron, rubber gloves and a bin bag, Elaine began an irritatingly pitched keening noise like a dog left alone too long.

'Can we not talk about this?' Jayne asked.

'No, we can't,' King sniped. 'I don't want to talk any more. I have to go to work in the morning and I need some sleep. I suggest you concentrate on shutting her up before I'm forced to do so myself.' He swung his head in Elaine's direction, not wanting to look at her, knowing she'd be drooling and rocking again. Jayne's chair scraped the floor and King knew she was comforting the lost soul beside her. As hideous as Elaine was proving to be, he felt a spike of annoyance at Jayne's own apparent lack of fear. 'Well, that won't last long,' he said.

'Sorry? I didn't catch that,' Jayne said.

King shoved the last of the woman's clothes into the bin bag and tossed it towards the door.

'Nothing,' he said. 'I wasn't talking to you.'

'Then who were you talking to?' she asked innocently. He'd had enough of being patronised. A degree from Oxford University and praise from the popular press didn't make her superior. Yet here she was addressing him as if he was an errant member of her congregation.

'It's important that you watch,' King said, straightening out the woman's body.

He began to shave the hair roughly from the woman's scalp. That was when she finally snapped back into full consciousness.

Hands tied behind her back and ankles bound together, she began struggling like a giant pink earthworm, thrashing back and forwards, getting nowhere, slipping on the floor. The gag in her mouth made her sound drunk, but she got her meaning across.

'Aw, fuck-shite. I fuckin' knew there was somethin' bad about you. Let me go, you bastard. Let go of my fuckin' hair.' She struggled harder. King sat on the floor behind her head, gripping her skull between his knees as he sheared off the remaining strands. Jayne was talking but he couldn't hear the words. If she wanted his attention, she'd have to break free of that supercilious reserve and scream. Once the scalp was completely hairless he noted with some gratification that Jayne wasn't looking quite so calm.

'What's your name?' Jayne asked the writhing body on the floor.

'Grace,' she said. King began to laugh. It was a mean laugh and he knew it. It sounded the way boys used to laugh at him in the playground. It was hard, mirthless, designed to disorient and humiliate. He laughed harder and harder.

'Grace?' he spat through his tears. 'Grace! Oh the misplaced optimism of your parents. If only they could see you, sucking men's parts for pennies, disease ridden and stinking.'

'My parents are dead,' Grace howled through the gag.

'Amen to that,' King said. 'At least they've been spared some humiliation.'

'Stop it,' Jayne said. King stopped. 'You're being cruel.'

Dr King looked at the monster he'd brought into his house. Jayne Magee was just as bad as Natasha, lording it over him, condescending.

'You stop me,' he whispered low into her face. He strode towards a drawer, unlocked it with shaking hands, selected a pair of pliers then turned back to Grace.

'Open wide,' he said, retaking his seat at Grace's head, tugging away the gag and forcing a piece of wood like a miniature plank sideways into her mouth as she screamed. As he closed the pliers on the left central incisor in her lower jaw, he began to sing. 'Amazing Grace, how sweet the sound, that saved a wretch like me.' Grace was gagging, either from the wood in her mouth or from fear and pain, not that the cause really mattered. It was a blessed relief to sing and drown out the noise. He raised his own volume. 'I once was lost but now am found, was blind but now I see.'

As he paused for breath between verses, Jayne raised her voice enough to be heard above Grace's animal groans and mewling.

'What is it you want?' she shouted. 'Just tell me what you want and I'll do it.' The incisor came out with a soundless spurt of blood, sending Grace's eyes rolling upwards as she fainted. King dropped the yellowed pellet into a glass, wiped the blood from her lower jaw – it was a messy business unfortunately – and took a grip of the next tooth in line.

''Twas Grace that taught my heart to fear . . .' On Grace's name he gave a tremendous wrench with the pliers, bringing her back from painless stupefaction into consciousness once more. 'And Grace, my fears relieved.' He pulled again and she thrashed her legs against the floor. Elaine was banging her head against the table in front of her and Jayne was yelling at him as he crooned. They made quite the alternative band, he thought. 'How precious did that Grace appear, the hour I first believed.'

Another tooth in the glass, blood washing the floor boards, King sensing his own loss of control as he adjusted his position and gripped harder with the pliers to get proper purchase on the tricky lower-left cuspid.

'Through many dangers, toils and snares I have already come.' He had to twist the pliers this time and the effort was sending his voice off key. He coughed and was about to start the verse again when Jayne screeched at him.

'Play chess for her. If I win, you leave her alone. If you win, then . . . you wanted me to learn. I'd love to see how you strategise. I'm sure you can teach me some new moves. Please?'

Dr King continued working the tooth but jiggled it more gently as he considered the challenge. 'All right,' he said, setting the pliers down. 'But I'm tired, mind. I may not be at my best.' He wiped his hands. It wouldn't do to get the chess pieces bloody. There were some things in life that one had to respect. Leaving Grace's hands and feet bound, and stuffing his handkerchief into her mouth for the sake of a quiet atmosphere, he pulled the sack back over her upper body. Distractions were unacceptable whilst playing chess. "Tis Grace that brought me safe thus far,' he sang as he released Elaine from the chair opposite Jayne's and carried her to the bed. She rolled face down and lay unmoving. '. . . And Grace will lead me home.'

Chapter Fifteen

Another baby had been left in the same park and the media was obsessed. This infant, though, whether tougher or luckier than the other two, or because the mother had not really wanted it to die after all, had been so well wrapped up that it had survived until a passing dog walker had found him.

DCI Begbie was in conference with Ava when Callanach went to see how the investigation was progressing. It was late. By rights no one should be at work, surviving on petrol station sandwiches and carbonated drinks, at four in the morning. Still, there was no point going home. Sleep had gone missing from his life at the same time Jayne Magee had disappeared from hers. He went back to his own office and texted Ava to join him for coffee once her debrief with the Chief had finished. Half an hour later she appeared.

'You know you can't carry on working twenty-four hours a day, right?' she asked.

'Hypocrite,' he said. 'What's the news?'

'The baby's going to survive. He's dehydrated but hadn't been outside very long. Same blanket again so they're all linked.'

'No one's reported him missing?' Callanach asked.

'No, but there is something. Forensics say there was some blood clotted and dried in a fold of flesh under his arm. The paediatrician doesn't think it's from the baby.'

'From the mother?' he said.

'That's the hypothesis. Results may be a couple of days, even pushing it through the labs urgently. The issue is how these women are meeting one another. There's been no contact from any GP, midwife, health visitor or other professional saying they're concerned about a baby who hasn't attended for follow-up checks.'

'Prostitutes not using public health care?' Callanach suggested.

'Wouldn't they just have terminations if they didn't want the babies?' Ava ran her hands through her hair, grimacing.

'I suppose some men have fantasies about having sex with heavily pregnant women. Maybe their pimps are forcing them to go full term, making money out of it then dumping the babies.'

'I knew I should have gone home without talking to you. That's such an appalling thought.' Ava put her coat on. 'Do you want a lift?'

'You have two dead babies and one alive with no mother and no name. There won't be a happy ending. And yes, a lift home would be appreciated.'

They walked down to the car together in silence, lost in their own cases. A noise behind them as Ava unlocked her vehicle made them both turn at once, staring into the darkness. When nothing else happened, they climbed into their seats. They were nearly at Callanach's apartment before either of them spoke.

'Did you ever contact the florist to find out who sent the roses?' Callanach asked.

'No time,' she replied. 'What made you think about that?'

'Earlier it felt as if we were being watched. Reminded me about your secret admirer.'

'You have an overactive imagination. It'll be the caffeine,' Ava said as they pulled up in Albany Street.

'Just be careful,' Callanach muttered getting out of the car. He considered whether or not good manners dictated that he should invite Ava up for coffee, looked at his watch and thought better of it. If he was lucky he could grab four hours' sleep before returning to the station. She drove away before he could thank her for the lift.

He was climbing into bed before the realisation struck that he'd nearly invited a woman into his home. A month ago it would have been inconceivable that he could ever be so relaxed around a female work colleague, but DI Turner was different. She was comfortable in her own skin, unimpressed by anything, it seemed, except good cinematography. More than that, she was starting to feel almost like a friend. It had been too long since he'd had one of those. As he rolled over to get comfortable, his hand slid under the pillow to find a cold, hard object. At first when he tried to pull it out, it spun in his hand. In the pale moonlight that spilled through the crack in his curtains it flashed silvery, but the bedside lamp showed a multitude of colours and lines printed on its surface. The miniature globe was part of a key ring, no keys attached, and had previously sat on the Reverend Jayne Magee's dressing table. Did she look at it each night, Callanach wondered, and think of all the places she could go, imagine the sights and sounds of a wider world than the one she ministered? Or was it only of sentimental value? A memento brought home by a travelling parent to show they'd been thinking of her whilst away. Glancing across at Elaine's paperweight, now perched on a book on the table beside his bed, Callanach forced himself to bring the faces of both women into sharp focus in his mind. The physical presence of those two simple objects was his version of a shrine. There could be no forgetting, no avoidance, so long as he kept them close. He fell asleep clutching the tiny globe, and wondering where in the world Jayne Magee might be.

The next day brought confirmation of double wheel tracks embedded into the gravel outside Elaine Buxton's garage. It should have felt like a victory, but the image of a woman bound and folded into a wheelie case was too vivid for him to feel pleased at the step forward. Callanach called a team meeting in the incident room that resembled a living jigsaw. One wall was dedicated to Elaine Buxton, her home, office and what forensic evidence they had. Another wall displayed photos of Jayne Magee. There was more to show for her, including press cuttings, papers she'd written, letters from the congregation and photos of the few people DS Lively had discovered were not in favour of having a female member of the clergy in their church.

Callanach had asked DS Lively to open the case update. 'What we know is that both women were abducted on their arrival home. Their attacker, a male, packs his victims into a wheelie case after drugging them with chloroform in order to transfer them to another location. The presence of chloroform in the soft tissue attached to Elaine Buxton's tooth was confirmed this morning. You've got copies of the witness statements. Police are on the alert in the Cairngorm area in case he tries to dispose of Jayne Magee's body in the same manner as Elaine Buxton's.'

'What about profiling? If we can't find Jayne Magee, can we not find out more about the man who's got her?' a constable asked from the back.

Sergeant Lively looked to Callanach to answer the question.

'It's not possible to formulate a suspect profile for a single murder,' Callanach said.

'Why the hell not?' Lively asked.

'There are restrictions on cases where that assistance is accessible and we don't meet the criteria yet.'

'Because we've only got one dead body? Or is it that profiling is just too bloody expensive to bother with? Reverend Magee is locked up with a lunatic. How many more hours is she going to survive?' Lively was raising his voice. Callanach could see he was more affected by the case than he'd been letting on.

'It's not just a matter of finances,' Callanach explained. 'You cannot profile until there's more than one body because there is no pattern. At this stage, making assumptions about the murderer might blinker us, lead us the wrong way. You can't assess one murder and say the killer has features like this or like that. Right now, keeping an open mind is the greater asset.'

'Bullshit,' Lively said. 'Bloody red tape.'

Callanach was saved from another confrontation with the detective sergeant when a uniformed officer stuck his head in and called two others into the corridor. It was a good enough excuse to call a halt to the meeting. From a hushed conversation outside the door Callanach caught the words 'threat' and 'lockdown' before Tripp handed him a bundle of overtime sheets.

'These came back from the processing office, sir. You initialled them instead of writing your full signature. Accounts are refusing to pay the overtime until they've all been put right.'

Callanach cursed as he took the sheaf of paper from his detective constable.

'Is it always like this?'

'Not usually, but someone new's handling it and it seems they're a stickler for procedure.'

'Of course they bloody well are. What's so important that the briefing was interrupted?' Callanach asked.

'DI Turner had a threatening letter posted under her office door. It's being taken seriously. All CCTV in and out of the building is being checked. The detective inspector's with the Chief.'

Callanach arrived outside Ava's door a minute later only to find himself being ushered away by the forensics team who were taking fingerprints and photographing the letter in situ before taking it for analysis. He opted to wait in the corridor outside DCI Begbie's office until she appeared.

'Busy morning?' Callanach asked.

'You could say that,' Ava said. 'What are you up to?'

'Trying to establish why my briefing was interrupted. I thought I should get the information first hand. Police officers are generally unreliable sources.'

She tutted. 'It's a lot of fuss about nothing. Comes with the territory. Someone dropped off a note to make it clear they don't like me. The most annoying side effect is that my office is out of bounds for a while. I wouldn't mind, only I might as well have got a few more hours' sleep.'

'Could be related to the flowers. Maybe whoever left the note decided they needed to do something more extreme to get your attention.'

'It's a bit of a leap from roses to death threats, don't you think? It's not the first time someone's wanted to kill me and it won't be the last. This morning's good news, however, is that the lab came up trumps with the DNA from the clotted blood, rushed it through the system and we've got results. It's definitely not the baby's DNA but they're pretty sure it's the mother's. They're running it through the database for a match.'

'Unlikely,' Callanach said. 'Chances are she's not been through the criminal justice system.'

'Haven't you got a squad of your own to depress?' Ava asked.

'You didn't tell me what the note said,' was his response. Ava rolled her eyes and tried to look bored. Callanach saw a woman glossing over the unpleasant knowledge that she was a target.

'Something about taking an ice pick to my face and making me wish I'd never been born. I've been ordered not to go home until the forensic results are in. Like that's going to happen.'

'Take the advice,' Callanach warned. 'You never know.'

'Thank you, Detective Inspector, I'll bear that in mind.' She gave a mock salute and marched away.

Chapter Sixteen

The chess game had dragged on for forty-five minutes. King was exhausted, getting bored and aware that Magee was taking advantage of his fatigue. He'd enjoyed it at first, the silence in the room as they'd both settled down to concentrate. Grace had remained restrained in her sack on the floor, rolling over occasionally and emitting a muted groaning, presumably phasing in and out of consciousness. Even the hysterical Elaine had remained quiet, face pushed into her pillow, either asleep or unconscious, he didn't care which. Magee had turned out to be far the more fascinating specimen. He hadn't anticipated that she would do anything either so brave or so brazen as to challenge him to a game for the woman's life. It was a gutsy move, taking responsibility for another soul like that. Not that he'd been fazed by it. His father had required him to study expert gameplay and read books on the subject. He was never quite the player his sister had been, that had been made abundantly clear to him, but he was sure he could beat a woman he'd been clever enough to abduct without a trace.

For the first half hour, he was able to pretend that he was allowing her to succeed, giving her a false sense of security.

Jayne was at a disadvantage and bound to be nervous. What was the harm in letting her take an early lead? By the time he'd realised how skilled a player she was, he was trying to catch up and failing, only just managing to retain his outward calm. After three-quarters of an hour he was fading. He should never have agreed to play when he could hardly keep his eyes open. It couldn't possibly have been a fair match and she knew it. She was a cheat, luring him in, making herself sound desperate but knowing all the while that he was in no state to concentrate. When she moved her king to the centre of the board he knew they were in endgame. It was an effort to stop his hands from shaking. That was the lack of food and sleep. And his fury at the cheating bitch taking advantage of him. He wouldn't concede, couldn't. It was inconceivable that she should beat him.

She declared checkmate a few moves later without a hint of celebration or boastfulness and King loathed her for it. Had she been so sure of victory that she didn't need to appear surprised or pleased by it? Had she assumed him to be such an incompetent that it was a foregone conclusion she would beat him?

'Why aren't you happy?' he hissed. 'It was a game and you won. Only because I'm suffering from exhaustion, but still, you beat me. Isn't this what you wanted – to make me feel small? You've got it, I lost, so the least you can do is be gracious and sociable.'

'Untie her,' Jayne said. 'Let me clean her up.'

'That's it?' he shouted, standing so abruptly the table tipped. Chess pieces scattered at his feet. 'That's all it was about for you? To save her? I brought you here for me!' He was screeching, his voice like a child's. He realised it and hated it and still couldn't stop. 'You're supposed to be interested in me! We were playing a game. It was my time with you. My time. Not hers!'

'We made a deal,' Jayne said. 'You agreed. You knew the terms from the start.'

'Don't lecture me about terms!' he shouted. 'It's all about me, do you get it? For once in my life, I'm the important one. You do what I want, when I want, and you do it for me!'

Jayne's composure was breaking, he could see it. Her eyes were shining with a glimmer of gathering tears that made him feel victorious. He wanted her to cry, to carry on crying and never, ever to stop.

'Please,' she said. 'Please just calm down. I'm sorry. We can talk as much as you want. You played really well. If you hadn't been tired I'd never have been able to beat you.'

'There's going to have to be a punishment,' he said, 'and it must fit the crime.' He picked up the black queen from beneath the upturned table and held it in front of Jayne's face.

'What are you going to do?' she asked. There was a tear on her cheek now. He liked it a lot.

He ripped the sack off Grace's upper body and sat behind her, one leg either side of hers, an arm around her waist, pulling her against him. Even in a questionable state of lucidity, and unable to move her hands or legs for their bindings, she was making a good show of protest, whipping her head forward and back, side to side. Scooping chess pieces into a pile beside himself, he yanked her head back against his shoulder. King pulled open Grace's mouth and caught Jayne looking at the pliers.

'No,' he said. 'Not that again. You chose this for her. You chose it when you asked me to play chess, knowing I couldn't win. You did this to her.'

King dropped the queen into Grace's mouth and snatched a castle off the floor. In it went, followed by a pawn and a knight. He thought fleetingly of how furious his parents would have been to see the treatment their precious chess set was receiving, but then they'd never let him win either. This seemed to be a better use of the antique carved ebony and ivory than it had ever been put to before. He'd suffered enough humiliation from this particular toy.

The blocked airway brought Grace back to consciousness, her body doing its best to make her cough and expel the foreign objects being pushed further down into her throat. Her eyes began to bulge, the lack of oxygen making her thrash even as it weakened her resistance. King decided it was time to skip straight to his favourite verse of the hymn.

'Yea, when this flesh and heart shall fail.' He shoved two bishops in together, scraping them hard against her wounded open gums, blood joining the chess pieces, filling her mouth and sending Jayne into a frenzy. 'And mortal life shall cease, I shall possess within the veil . . .' Finally he seized whatever pieces were left around him in one fist and shoved them down her gullet. Limbs flailing, gurgling and retching, he held her mouth shut, closed his eyes and listened. It was, he thought, the sound of death rising to couple with life. Finally, when his joy at Jayne's tears was starting to ebb, Grace became still. King finished his song. '. . . A life of joy and peace.'

'I told you,' a tiny voice said. He'd forgotten Elaine. She was sitting up on her bed, knees drawn to her chin, rocking from left to right and panting. 'I told you.'

King went to her. 'You did, my darling, didn't you? You told her what would happen and she didn't listen. She'll pay better attention from this point on, I think.' He pulled a blanket over Elaine to keep her warm for the night, smoothing her hair as he tucked her in. 'I'll take out the rubbish in the morning,' he said, kicking Grace's corpse as he walked past it. 'Sleep well, ladies.'

The next day he arrived late to work, hoping Natasha hadn't noticed, horrified by his unironed shirt and the smell of his own body. He'd fallen straight to sleep and not had the time to shower on waking. Any further leave days would attract attention and, much as he'd wanted to sleep the day away, it just wasn't an option. The women in the administration office were staring at him. It wasn't in their breeding to greet him or make small talk but today they were being openly rude. He checked himself. What could they see that he couldn't? He had his usual suit on, hadn't forgotten his tie. It wasn't until he reached the mirror in his office that he saw what had attracted their attention. A blackening bruise sat at the temple corner of his right eye, still in the process of reaching its fullness of colour. He couldn't remember the blow but supposed Grace must have caught him in her writhing and fighting. It didn't hurt unless pressed but it wouldn't do to let Natasha see him in such a state. She'd love it, would revel in his discomposure, would no doubt be desperate for the details. He considered retreating home and knew that would be worse – an admission that something was amiss.

His phone rang. He sighed when he heard the voice on the other end.

'Dr King. We had a meeting scheduled. Did you forget?'

'No, Professor Forge, I was delayed, there was an accident.'

'Come through, would you?' Natasha spoke fast. She always spoke fast to him, as if rushing to end the conversation. He heard her talking to other people and her voice seemed softer, her words slower. She was so tense around him. The atmosphere between them had been charged since the day they'd met. She knew it as well as he. The difference was that he had the courage to admit it to himself.

'Can you tell me what you need on the phone?' He didn't want her seeing him in such a state, couldn't bear to be near her. The thought of Natasha smelling the sweat growing stale on his body was too much.

'Just come to my office, please. I have a biography and photo to give you for the lecture handout.' A click on the line ended the conversation. King took one more look at the bruise on his face and prepared his explanation.

He walked straight into her room.

'I have asked you before to knock and let me know you're coming in. Everyone else does. Could you try to remember?' She was marking papers on her desk and spoke without glancing up. When she did, he saw her eyes flick to the bruise and enjoyed the moment more than he'd anticipated. Maybe it wasn't such a bad thing to challenge her perceptions of him. He waited for the inevitable questions.

'Here are the details of the speaker for the lecture this week.' She turned her attention to her desk and held out a folder to him.

'About the eye . . .' he said.

'No explanation necessary.' She pushed the folder further in his direction.

'It's actually quite a funny story.'

'It's your private business and I think we should keep these conversations professional. Make sure the photo is printed in black and white rather than colour and that her proper title is included. The lecture will start at seven thirty. There'll be drinks in the foyer afterwards. I'll introduce her and attendees will have a ten-minute period to ask questions at the end.'

King took the folder from her hands.

'I know the format,' he said. She wasn't going to ask about his eye. Just how traumatic an event had to occur before she expressed any concern?

'Good,' was her response. It was also a dismissal. He made his way to the door. 'And this is a personal friend of mine, a very close friend, so please make sure everything runs smoothly. She's very busy. There can't be any delays or problems. Clear?'

King didn't credit her rudeness with an answer, just let her door slam shut and bit his tongue.

Natasha Forge was made of ice. When he'd first heard her speak on the subject of whether or not philosophy should be taught as an individual discipline or if it was inherent within every subject, he thought he'd never be able to hear anyone else's words again. A woman so different from his own mother, who had rarely left their house as far as he could tell, constantly cooking, pickling, tidying, writing lists and fussing, Natasha Forge was all clean lines, had professionalism stamped on every part of her, from her razor-sharp wit to her piercing eyes. Not for her a life of domesticity, child rearing or homemaking. King doubted she ever ate anywhere but restaurants, that she ever cleaned her own home or did her own laundry. Her life was lived for academia, seeking enlightenment of the mind. She was the reason he'd applied for the job in the department. At first she'd been welcoming, kind. Then, as they'd spent more time together, Natasha had grown colder. He'd heard some women were like that – their interest decreased relative to the amount of enthusiasm you showed for them. And yet Natasha's intellectual gifts were undeniable.

After his failed application for the lecturing post, he'd collated all the philosophy papers he'd written and published them as a book. Self-publishing was acceptable these days, had almost become the norm. Increasing numbers of respected writers were doing it. It meant he'd been able to send the book to a university in America who'd given him his doctorate in recognition. That should have impressed her. But the rest of the staff hadn't bothered to hide their amusement when he'd taken in his certificate and insisted his title be changed to 'Doctor' to reflect his new status. He'd heard them whispering. So what if it was an online university? The fee he'd paid was purely for administration purposes. He'd worked for his qualification, had earned it with hours spent reading, writing and editing. The name of the university who'd formalised his achievement was as irrelevant as the thickness of the paper they'd printed his certificate on. It was real and it was his.

With an impatient sigh he flipped open the folder Natasha had handed him. If he didn't get on, he'd miss the printing deadline. He stared at the photograph of Natasha's precious friend. Her curly hair made her face look childish. No wonder she'd demanded it be printed in black and white, no doubt to add some maturity to the image. Speaking on the subject 'Society's Moral and Legal Right to Punish Wrongdoers' would be Detective Inspector Ava Turner.

Chapter Seventeen

'It's been twenty-four hours, sir, and I've received no further threat. This is just some wacko trying to get a reaction.' Ava and Detective Chief Inspector Begbie were outside Callanach's door. He was trying to pretend he wasn't listening but failing, as were the other detectives who were gawping in the corridor.

'DI Turner, that wacko managed to get into this building unnoticed and find your office. The threat was a very unpleasant one, as I'm sure you recall. Until we identify and arrest whoever is fantasising about killing you, the protective detail officer stays each day until you're safely at home with your alarm on.' The Chief was strident.

'But I'm just meeting a friend for a drink in a pub. Nothing's going to happen except for me feeling like a prize idiot with my not-very-well-disguised bodyguard escorting me.' Ava wasn't going to back down. Callanach glanced at the time. He was done for the day.

He stuck his head out into the corridor.

'I'll go with DI Turner, if that would assist.'

They both stared at him. Ava had a look of confused hopefulness on her face and the Chief simply looked sceptical.

Callanach didn't read too much into that. He suspected it was Begbie's default expression.

'That's settled then,' Ava said, pulling on her coat.

'Just a minute. You don't leave her side, Callanach, that's an order. Until you've checked her home is clear and locked down, you're responsible for my detective inspector's safety. Interpol or not, you'd better not mess up.'

'Got it, Chief,' Callanach said, grabbing his keys from his desk.

'Can I at least go to the ladies' room on my own?' Ava asked pointedly. Callanach took her arm and began walking her up the corridor.

'What's that saying you have? Quit while you're ahead,' he said. For once, Ava did.

Half an hour later they were in The Pear Tree, jostling for position at the bar.

'Why is it so busy?' Callanach moaned.

'We're near the University's main campus,' Ava explained, passing him a glass of red wine and pointing at a table where seats were just becoming free. They sat down, leaving coats on a third chair to secure it. 'I appreciate you offering to come with me. I can't stand being followed around as if I'm not capable of looking after myself.'

'You understand that's what I'm here to do? You may enjoy irritating the Chief but I'm not ready to fall out with him yet, so no running away.' Ava rolled her eyes then grinned over his right shoulder.

'Tasha! I've got you a gin and tonic already. Sit down. This is Luc Callanach, our newest recruit, fresh from Interpol, no less. Luc, this is a very old friend of mine, Natasha Forge, Head of Philosophy at the Uni.'

'Pleased to meet you. How do you know one another?' Callanach aimed the question at both women who began to speak at once.

'Pony club,' was the response from each at the same time, finished by howls of laughter. Callanach looked confused.

'And this is funny because?' he asked.

'Hated it. Both of us. The result of pushy parents wanting to get rid of us at the weekends so they could play golf or shop or whatever. The first time I saw Tasha she was sneaking off round the back of the stables to have a cigarette. I recognised a kindred spirit and followed her,' Ava said

'We spent every weekend like that, putting on jodhpurs, riding hats and disappearing. I don't think I sat on a horse the whole time. Bloody creatures. Whoever imagined they want humans sitting on their backs was seriously deluded. I got kicked once and never went near one again,' Natasha finished.

'Did your parents not notice?' Callanach asked.

'We got called into the riding school mistress's office one day to explain ourselves. Ava promised we'd stay out of trouble if she told our parents we were doing fine. We got to see each other every weekend, our parents got rid of us and the riding school got outrageous amounts of money for nothing. When Ava got shipped off to boarding school and I was left here term time was dull but at least we got to spend holidays together. The summers seemed like they went on forever.'

Callanach watched them smiling at the memories and saw the carefree, rebellious girls they'd once been. A smashing glass made Ava whip round. She was jumpy, more nervous than she was admitting, and covered it up by bursting into conversation.

'So, tomorrow night. I've got my lecture notes ready. How many people are you expecting? Is there a microphone? What should I wear – uniform or civvies?'

'Wow. Have a drink,' Natasha laughed. 'It's not that big a deal, not for you anyway. I've seen you on the news twice in the last fortnight. Wear whatever you like. Your main problem will be getting away at the end. I'll have to sneak you out the back to avoid the endless questions.'

'What's this?' Callanach asked.

'I'm giving a guest lecture.' Ava held her head loftily. 'Very last minute, mind, to tell the truth. Who cancelled and made you so desperate you asked me?'

'No one cancelled,' Natasha said, shaking her head. 'There may have been a slight oversight when our administrator was unwell but that doesn't mean you weren't my first choice!'

'Who were the other choices then?' Ava asked.

'Some idiot tried to book Professionals Against Abortion, because that would have gone down well with our free thinking, well-educated, balanced students. Luckily you saved me and I'm eternally grateful.'

'Professionals Against Abortion?' Callanach asked.

'A religious group pretending their views are professional rather than moral. They also run pregnancy advice centres where they scare teenage girls so badly they're convinced they'll become infertile or infected or die if they have terminations. The advisors don't disclose their real agenda. They're highly secretive and, as far as I'm concerned, completely poisonous,' Natasha said. 'Right, I'm braving it and pushing my way through to the bar. Same again?'

While Natasha fought the growing mass of bodies, Callanach drained his glass and looked at Ava. She was unusually quiet.

'You okay?'

'Mmm,' was the response.

'You know the Chief will want you escorted by a uniform again tomorrow night.'

'Fine,' she said, not really listening.

'You need to tell Natasha about the threat. The University should have security on hand. If there's a large crowd and you're socialising afterwards, one officer may not be able to protect you.'

'Are you after a promotion? Because you're starting to sound an awful lot like Begbie.'

Natasha put drinks on the table.

'What's with the serious faces?' she asked. Callanach decided to deal with it his own way. Ava was making it quite clear she wasn't going to acknowledge the potential danger of the situation.

'Ava received a death threat,' he said. 'Which is why I'm crashing the party tonight.'

'Arising from your current case?' Natasha asked.

'Maybe,' Ava said, 'or maybe it's one of any number of bored criminals with a hate-crush on me from the last ten years. Who knows? Nothing you need to worry about, Tasha.'

'Why don't you come and stay with me for a while?' Natasha suggested.

'Because you can't stand my music taste and get ratty if I wake you up coming and going in the middle of the night. And because I love you and there's no need for you to worry. We shouldn't have said anything.' The 'we' part of the sentence was pointed. He hadn't given Ava a choice about it and she was mad.

'Of course you should have told me,' Natasha answered. 'I'd feel better if you would stay.'

'But I'd feel as if I'd let whoever did this win. You know me better than that. Listen, I'm going to have to cut the evening short,' Ava said abruptly, grabbing her bag and thrusting her arms into her coat. 'Sorry to be dull but I need to get home. Do you mind, Luc? See you tomorrow, Tash. I'll try not to make a complete dog's dinner of it.'

Natasha kissed her on each cheek. 'You'll be amazing. Good to meet you, Luc.'

Ava lived in a mid-terrace house on a quiet street west of the city. Callanach went back into police mode in a way that was hard to lose if you'd done it for enough years. He checked each room, switching on every light as he went, making sure the locks on the back door were fully engaged and that the downstairs windows were secure. Only then did he let Ava into the property and made her show him that the alarm was fully functioning.

'You wanted to leave the pub very suddenly,' he said, as he made sure he could hear a dialling tone on her landline.

'Something Natasha said sent my mind back to the case. I need a good night's sleep, and drinking with her never ends well. She liked you.'

'How do you know?' he asked.

'If she hadn't, you'd have known it. She doesn't suffer fools. She always decides if a man can be trusted within two minutes, and to the best of my knowledge she's usually right. More than I can say for her taste in women.' Ava put the kettle on and threw her shoes towards the doormat.

'Really?' Callanach said.

'Tasha's a lesbian, although she doesn't flaunt it. She's always been obsessive about not letting anyone at the Uni know, doesn't want to get labelled or stereotyped.'

'I can understand that,' he said. 'Right, everything is secure. Call 999 then my mobile if there's a problem.' He listened as she locked the door and slid on the chain. For all her public bravado, she wasn't taking any unnecessary risks.

Chapter Eighteen

Ava was in the briefing room when Callanach walked past, surrounded by her team and looking like a woman on a mission. Curious, he entered quietly and sat at the back.

'The DNA match came through an hour ago. The surviving baby's mother is Lucy Costello, living with her parents Mary and John at an address in Murrayfield. Please remember this is a vulnerable young woman who has recently given birth and who may be suffering post-natal depression. We'll have a medical crew with us including a gynaecologist. No force is to be used unless anything unforeseen happens. The home is to be secured in order to find a link to the other babies. Please behave with respect and sensitivity.'

'What did she come up on the system for, ma'am?' one of the uniforms asked.

'Supply of drugs, a year ago. It was a technical offence. She'd bought several ecstasy tablets at a rave and handed them out to her friends who'd pooled their money. There were undercover police involved. When they realised she was only fourteen years old, they opted to caution her but it was a serious enough crime that her DNA was held on the database. Let's go.'

Callanach stopped her as she was leaving.

'You got a break, then, at last. That was lucky.'

'It was,' Ava said. 'Would you tag along if you're quiet for an hour? It'd be a chance for my squad to get to know you a bit better.'

'I will. I'm going crazy sitting around here with no leads. Shall I travel with you?'

'Sure,' she said.

Murrayfield was one of the more affluent parts of the city and Callanach could see the wealth through the investment in leisure facilities. Even if you ignored the rugby stadium, there was an ice rink, tennis courts, a golf course and a well-placed private hospital for when a player got injured. An unlikely setting to house a young woman with a history of drug abuse who had recently left her child to die.

The marked police vehicles were parked a street away to avoid causing panic. Only Ava, the doctor and a Range Rover carrying four plain clothes detectives parked in the Costellos' road. As Ava knocked on their door, the sound of vacuuming could be heard through an open upstairs window. A couple of minutes later a flustered woman, presumably Mary Costello, answered.

Ava held up her badge and introduced herself.

'We're looking for Lucy Costello. Is she here?'

'No. What's this about? Is Lucy in trouble?'

'We need to talk to her urgently. Could you tell me her last known whereabouts?' Ava was firm but polite. Mrs Costello was twitchy.

'My daughter's at school. She had an exam this morning, I dropped her there myself. I think I have the right to know what it is you want.'

'We believe your daughter recently gave birth to a baby boy who she left in a park. She may also have information about other offences.'

132

'This is ridiculous,' Mrs Costello stuttered but she was tearful and obviously shaken.

'Would you accompany us to Lucy's school, please?'

'I have to phone my husband. He'll meet us there,' Mrs Costello said.

'You can use my mobile on the way. We have to get going,' Ava told her. Visibly trembling, Mrs Costello grabbed a coat and handbag on her way, and was texting on her own phone before Ava could hand her the promised mobile.

St Gabriella's High School was ten minutes from the Costellos' house and there was no choice but for the police vehicles to parade one after another through the main gates. Hordes of fascinated schoolgirls in blue pleated skirts and stiff blazers watched them stream past. Just as Ava was helping Mrs Costello out of the car, a grey Jaguar XJS streaked into a parking space next to them.

'What is the meaning of this?' the man stormed. Mrs Costello rushed to his side.

'Darling, please calm down, they just need to speak to Lucy.'

'They can speak to me first,' he said, squaring up to the detective constable next to Ava. 'Who's in charge here?'

'I am. Detective Inspector Turner. You must be John Costello. We need to speak with your daughter. You can remain with her but I have to ask you to calm down.'

'Don't tell me to calm down, miss. You've upset my wife, made all sorts of ridiculous allegations and invaded my daughter's school. How am I supposed to explain this to the head teacher?'

A group of girls was running past in tennis whites, hair flying, a teacher shouting at them to keep moving, when a voice came from below Callanach's shoulder level.

'Daddy, Mummy, what's going on?'

Lucy Costello was slim, really slim. That was Callanach's first

133

thought. More than that, she was sporty, bordering on athletic. She might have made a momentary mistake trying an ecstasy tablet but she was the picture of health – glowing skin, hair in a ponytail, clutching a tennis racket – as if she hadn't a care in the world.

'You must be Lucy,' Ava said. 'I'm a police officer. Could we have a chat, please?'

Callanach heard it in Ava's voice. A mistake had been made. There was no way this girl had recently given birth.

'What day was this baby supposed to have been born?' John Costello asked.

Ava provided the details while Mary Costello clutched her daughter.

'Lucy was on a school trip then at a residential outward bound centre. Before you start interrogating my child, I'd appreciate it if you'd check your facts.'

Ava nodded at one of her team to go inside and make the necessary enquiries.

'Do you mind allowing Lucy to accompany this doctor for a quick check-up? It will only take a couple of minutes, nothing invasive. Your wife can be present.'

The expression on John Costello's face said that he did mind very much, but his wife nodded, appeased him and Lucy was taken to the school matron's office to be examined.

'I'd better go and smooth matters over with the head teacher. I'll have your job for this, Miss Turner.' John Costello strode away.

'There must have been an error processing the DNA. Contamination at the lab or a software issue,' Callanach said.

'Have you heard the saying, if something seems too good to be true then it usually is?' Ava answered. 'I should have known it wouldn't be this simple.'

A constable confirmed that Lucy had been away from

Edinburgh the previous week. Not only that, but the girl had spent her time kayaking, rock climbing and hiking, with photos to prove it. It was no shock when the doctor verified that Lucy had not given birth days earlier. Ava went to make her apologies to the family.

'Lucy, Mr and Mrs Costello, thank you for helping with our enquiries. I apologise if it's been upsetting. Lucy's DNA came up as a match and that's what brought us here.'

'From that drug thing, I suppose.' John Costello frowned at his daughter, teeth gritted. It seemed to Callanach to be a harsh way to treat a girl who'd just been seen by a police doctor and who would face no end of gossip at school.

'It was obviously a mistake and I can only say how sorry we are. I hope this doesn't cause you any problems, Lucy.' Ava climbed back into her car and Callanach followed. She managed to keep her composure until they were on the main road.

'God, what a balls up!' she shouted, thumping her steering wheel. 'I've wasted time and resources, I'm going to be on the receiving end of a complaint and we're no further forward.'

'You were acting on the information given. What else were you supposed to do? Lucy fit the case – young girl, old enough to be sexually active but still vulnerable – local to Edinburgh. You just have to start again with the forensics.'

'And I've got to give a bloody lecture this evening. I'll be lucky if the press doesn't invade the place with questions about my incompetence. Shit!'

'Pull over,' Callanach said.

'Why?'

'Just pull over and get out.' Ava turned the car into a side road. Callanach opened her door and pointed her towards the passenger seat while he drove.

'I'm not so upset that I can't be trusted behind the wheel.'

'You have twenty minutes before we're back at the station.

135

Stop wasting your energy, get on your mobile and order every test done again. That's what they taught us at Interpol. Screw calming down when there's a problem. Work it out while you're still so angry that you'll light a fire under every other person in the chain of command. Get on with it!' She started dialling.

By the time Callanach had parked the car, there was nothing left for Ava to do but explain the situation to the Chief.

'Don't apologise, just tell Begbie what you've done about it,' Callanach advised. 'Make sure he expects a complaint from Lucy's father and warn him what type of man Costello is. No surprises. Then come and find me. I'll accompany you to the lecture so you can avoid having a uniform following you around.'

'Right, because you'll really blend in.'

'If you'd rather go with the uniformed option.' He held his hands up in surrender.

'No, sorry, I appreciate the offer. But I'm sure you've got better things to do with your evening. You know the Chief won't pay overtime,' she laughed.

Callanach found DC Tripp hunting through files in the incident room.

'What's all this?' he asked his hassled-looking constable.

'Missing persons files,' Tripp said. 'I've extended the search to cover all the other major cities and I'm matching genders, ages and similar persons. There's not much to go on, to be honest.'

'Nothing similar to our cases?'

'Not really. A couple of women of the right age who left home unexpectedly, but not high profile like Magee or Buxton, and in both cases there was evidence they were depressed. No sign of abduction, no bodies turning up. Apart from that, a known Glasgow pimp claims a girl is missing, but she doesn't fit the type,' Tripp said.

'All right. Get the details on those cases and compile them into one report for me. I'm leaving in an hour to accompany DI Turner to a lecture at the University. Is there any news about the threat the inspector received?'

'Forensics came back blank. No prints, widely used paper and ink types, no trace evidence. Whoever sent it knew how to keep the job clean. They can't find any unauthorised entry into the building. CCTV showed nothing.'

The lecture hall was packed and Ava's fears that the press would discover the day's events proved unfounded. They were met in the foyer by Professor Natasha Forge who seemed more forbidding than the night before, until she winked as she handed him a sherry.

'Is Ava all right?' Natasha whispered. 'She seems distracted.'

'Tough day,' Callanach replied. 'But she's remarkably resilient.'

Natasha stared at him, head tilted and he knew she was appraising him. 'Yes, but she's not unbreakable, so be careful.' She led Ava into the lecture theatre and they took to the stage.

Callanach got his first glimpse of his colleague's genius. Ava moved with ease from the history of Scotland's legal system, to comparative international punitive frameworks and on to the morality of punishment. The lecture hall remained silent throughout. No one fidgeted, or dropped their pen or made their way out to the toilets. When she'd finished, the students got to their feet and showed their appreciation. Next to her, Natasha looked unsurprised.

'That was impressive,' Callanach whispered to Ava as she was ushered into the foyer.

'Shut up,' she replied, reddening.

DC Tripp emerged through the crowd with a uniformed officer in tow. 'I tried to call, but you weren't picking up,' he said. Callanach sighed. He'd put his phone on silent for the lecture. 'Something's been found at Granton Harbour. You need to come to the scene. The Chief told me to leave a constable here to accompany DI Turner.'

'Is it a body?' Callanach asked.

'Not exactly. To be honest with you, nobody's sure yet.'

Callanach went to Ava, bent his head down close to her ear to speak without being overheard, explained the situation and left. Next in line to be introduced to her was a man of average height, rather overweight, with clean shoes and a well-pressed suit. Callanach didn't notice him at all.

Reginald King noticed Callanach, though. He noticed the way he was even more cocksure of himself in person than he'd been on the radio. He noticed the way women didn't flinch when Callanach went near them. He saw that Natasha's good friend seemed very intimate with Callanach indeed. King watched Natasha. If only she'd look at him the way DI Turner had looked at the Frenchman. If only King could whisper in her ear, congratulate her on her brilliance, share a private moment in the middle of such an adoring throng. He looked at Natasha for a long time and the urge to hurt her became almost overwhelming.

Chapter Nineteen

There was no body because there literally was no body. When Callanach walked into the warehouse, his eyes started watering immediately. A forensic technician handed him an anti-contamination suit, glasses and mask.

Tripp began talking as Callanach put on his gear.

'The security guard who came on shift tonight was doing his rounds and smelled something bad. By the time he'd found the source, he was worried enough to call for help and got a mate over from the harbour master's office. The two men opened the barrel and found a red–brown liquid.'

'How is it possible that the smell is so strong from just one barrel?' Callanach asked, gratefully adjusting the mask so it fit snuggly over his mouth and nose.

'They panicked. There was a tangle of human hair caught in the top of the barrel where it had been sealed. They realised there was something nasty inside, one of them tried to grab the crow bar back out, only it was stuck under the rim. Pulled the whole lot over.'

'Morons. Where are they?' Callanach wasn't in the mood to be sympathetic, however shocked the men were at their find.

'With medics. They splashed the chemicals on their clothes and both need to go to hospital. Uniforms are with them taking statements. This way, sir.' Tripp pointed to a metal walkway over a below-ground area. On the far side, the scene was what Callanach could only call carnage.

The liquid had spread across a huge area and technicians were trying to preserve what elements of the crime scene hadn't been obliterated. An empty barrel was being lifted from the middle of the puddle and a photographer was capturing the details.

'Can you identify the chemical?' Callanach asked a man scooping up samples and writing labels on test-tubes.

'Sodium hydroxide, most likely. Given how thoroughly it's broken down the bones, I'd say it's been watered down a bit. Makes the process faster and more effective. More commonly known as lye. Easy to get hold of in small quantities. You only have to provide identification if you're buying bulk.' Callanach watched him pick up an object with tweezers and hold it in the light for closer inspection.

'What is it?' Tripp asked.

The technician rotated it a few times before answering. 'There's some damage but I'm pretty sure it's a human tooth. We'll refer it to the forensic odontologist to be sure.' He bagged the tooth and took it to the police officer who was logging evidence.

Callanach didn't need to be told that finding the offender's footprints was going to be impossible. The scene was a stinking, glutinous mess. He was more interested in the security guard.

Outside, the clean-up team had arrived to neutralise the environmental threat. Callanach saw the ambulance moving off and sprinted towards it, rushing into its path and making the driver swerve.

'I don't know what you're doing, but we're on our way to the hospital . . .' the paramedic began.

'Just stay put until I've spoken to those witnesses,' Callanach shouted, holding up his badge. 'Open the back.' The door swung open to reveal two men in oxygen masks and blankets.

'Security guard?' he asked. The man on the right nodded.

'Is there any CCTV on site?' The man shook his head. 'What about daytime security? Who was on duty before you?'

He removed his oxygen to speak. 'No money for that, pal. They only bring us in at night to keep away the kids and druggies when it's dark. I kept telling the company something would happen. Didn't bloody listen.' He began to cough and replaced his mask. Callanach stepped out of the ambulance and slammed the door.

'Tripp, check every CCTV camera around the harbour area. Roads, car parks, private security systems. Find out where that barrel came from. I want a conference with the pathologist the second they've finished processing the scene.'

'Yes, sir,' Tripp said, scribbling in his notebook. 'And I thought we'd do a foot search for abandoned trolleys.' Callanach raised his eyebrows at the young constable. 'He can't have used his wheelie case this time. There must have been a trolley and I couldn't see one in the building.'

'You're assuming it's Jayne Magee's body. There's no evidence of that. This could be completely unrelated.' Callanach was testing his constable as a means of testing himself. He'd felt it too, the sense that this was what they'd been waiting for, but it was completely different to the first body.

'It just seems like he's doing it again, getting rid of the body, destroying the evidence. What are the odds?' Tripp asked.

'All right. Get a couple of men searching for trolleys. Check with workers in the neighbouring buildings, see if anyone saw someone out of place. If it is our man, I'm not sure he'll have blended in.'

The warehouse was typical of those used to store goods before shipping or inbound distribution. It had long since been stripped of the cranes that would have been situated outside but there were large doors for easy goods access, walkways on various levels and an office area with toilets and a staff room. Getting into the site wouldn't have been taxing. The surrounding wire fence was easy to lift and several smashed windows offered access from which a fire door could be opened. Getting the barrel in would have been the issue. It couldn't have been rolled for fear of spilling such dangerous cargo. But why the warehouse? The space was empty save for a few crates and long-since-retired machinery. It wasn't a chance dumping. You'd have to know where to park, how to get in and the security detail's hours. Callanach wished the crime scene hadn't been so dramatically damaged. Any evidence they did recover was certain to be successfully challenged by the defence at a trial. He couldn't shake the feeling that fate was doing everything it could to stall the investigation. The tipping of the barrel just added insult to injury. The press would be all over it. Sooner or later, a journalist would track down one of the security men and publish a tell-all, eyewitness account of the carnage on the warehouse floor. And all he could do was watch and wait. Taking a few last photos of the outside of the building, Callanach retreated to his office.

The station should have been quiet when he got back. The work that could be done overnight was being taken care of either at the crime scene or the labs. What he hadn't expected was to see Detective Sergeant Lively holding court in the incident room, surrounded by just about every member of the team and a few faces he didn't recognise. When Callanach walked in, the silence was as solid as a brick wall.

'Is it her?' Lively asked. Callanach wondered if taking the official line was better than sharing his own views. He opted for middle ground.

'The victim has not been identified yet, although there is evidence that it was a human body in the barrel. The laboratory will be processing the remains tonight and trying to salvage what DNA is feasible. Until the forensic investigations are complete, speculation is unwise,' Callanach said.

'They found hair the same colour as Jayne Magee's.' Lively's voice was high-pitched and his fists were clenched. Callanach wanted to stop the meeting and get him somewhere they could have a private conversation.

'The hair colour cannot be confirmed because of the chemical. We're not even sure that the victim is female. There's nothing more to do tonight. I need everyone on this first thing tomorrow so go home, get some rest and be back for a detailed briefing at eight a.m.'

'In the meantime it's another night wasted when we should've been finding Jayne's murderer. I'm not sitting around waiting for something to happen. There are people who can help.'

'Detective Sergeant, you need to consider that this might not be Jayne Magee before you do anything,' Callanach cautioned.

'Oh, do I?' Lively was too loud and too close to Callanach. Everyone else in the room was holding their breath. 'Maybe, sir, if you hadn't done that press conference goading the fuckin' murderer to act, Jayne Magee wouldn't be dead now. Perhaps it's you who should be considering your position here.'

Callanach knew Lively was grieving but even so he was grossly out of order. In spite of his desire to vent some frustration by giving his DS the fight he wanted, losing control in front of the squad wasn't worth the hassle it would cause. He took a step away.

'Lower your voice when you speak to me, Sergeant. Like I said, get some rest. Perhaps tomorrow you'll remember what chain of command means. If you're still struggling with that in the morning, we'll have another conversation about it.' Callanach went to his office without looking back. The last thing the investigation needed was for emotions to be running any higher. He followed his own advice and went home.

The next day brought a 7 a.m. text alert to say that the pathologist would be available to see him at half past nine. Callanach was impressed. The forensics team had obviously worked through the night, although that meant the Chief would be frowning at the overtime figures again. A second text came through as he was scrambling eggs in preparation for what he assumed would be a long day with no lunch. He ignored the beeping and buttered his toast. If it was urgent he expected a phone call rather than a text. Before eight in the morning he should be able to get a peaceful meal in his own home.

He ate, glaring intermittently at his phone, before looking at the text. The sender was DS Lively. As tempting as it was to delete before opening, the need to find out what was happening prevailed. He hit the text icon. Lively was notifying him about a meeting between DCI Begbie and what had mysteriously been called 'other interested parties re Jayne Magee's murder'. Callanach felt a surge of irritation that the victim had been named before it was official, then forced himself to consider DS Lively's perspective. It wasn't a huge leap to think that the reverend's remains were in the barrel.

'Bloody hell!' he said to the coffee cooling in front of him. 'I don't need this crap.' Callanach's first thought was that he'd begun thinking as well as speaking in English much sooner than he'd imagined. After his father's death, his mother had insisted that they should use both languages throughout his childhood, but even so it had seemed like a huge hurdle to move away from a French-speaking country. His subconscious mind had apparently made the move more easily than his stomach. The thought that followed was how the things people said aloud were rarely lies when they didn't realise they were talking. He reflected on how Jayne Magee's abductor, likely turned murderer, had been overheard on the street by a cyclist. Callanach made a mental note to pull the cyclist's statement out of the file once he got to work.

An hour later DS Salter was waiting in the corridor to accompany Callanach straight to the Chief. Ava was already there with a woman he hadn't met before.

'DI Luc Callanach, this is Dr Ailsa Lambert, Edinburgh's chief forensic pathologist. I don't think your paths have crossed yet.' DCI Begbie did the formal introductions.

It was only when Ailsa Lambert stood up that Callanach realised how tiny she was. Less than five foot tall, he guessed, and stick thin. She craned her neck up to see his face better and stuck out her hand.

'I was at the warehouse after you, I'm afraid. Caught me mid-autopsy, hence the delay. But Jonty Spurr spoke to me about you.'

Begbie coughed politely and motioned at Callanach to sit down. 'Well, Ailsa, I thought we'd review both cases together. I know how busy you are but I prefer my teams to know what's happening in each other's camps in case we have to transfer officers between cases. Where would you like to start?'

'Thank you, George.' She smiled graciously, opening a folder on the tablet in her hand. 'The baby case, I think. Awful tragedy. Both infants healthy other than the hypothermia that led to their deaths. I've spoken to the paediatrician who confirms the surviving child was also injury free. Apparently the baby is now doing well. I know you thought there'd been some mix up with the DNA, Ava, so I had the technicians double-check the results. Those came back the same again, so I asked for them to be reviewed by a professor I know. You were both wrong and right.'

'I don't understand,' Ava said. 'Was the blood a match for Lucy Costello's DNA or not?'

'It was, as far as the lab would normally cross-reference the markers. Usually they check between fifteen and twenty points of a person's DNA and this gives an incredibly high level of certainty for positive DNA evidence. On closer study, they found four mutations called Single Nucleotide Polymorphisms. In plain terms, there were four almost imperceptible differences between the DNA on file for Lucy Costello and the blood found on the baby's skin. This means that although the blood did not come from Lucy Costello, it could only have come from one other person. A monozygotic twin. She must be identical, or the DNA would have been distinguishable within the first set of tests.'

'Lucy has a twin sister?' Ava started texting as she spoke. Callanach knew he'd be doing the same – getting one of the detective constables to find a name and any accessible records. 'But neither of the parents mentioned anything . . .'

'Did you not see anything at the house?' Begbie queried. 'No family photos?'

'We didn't have a chance to go in,' Ava replied. 'Our suspect, Lucy, was at school so we went straight there. By the time the doctor confirmed she hadn't given birth and the school backed up her alibi, we had no cause to enter the property.'

'The parents didn't mention a twin sister when we were with them. They must have had their suspicions that we were talking to the wrong daughter,' Callanach said.

'Has John Costello made a complaint yet, sir?' Ava asked Begbie.

'No,' the DCI confirmed.

'Lucy's father more than suspected,' Ava said, her face reddening, 'he damned well knew. That was what all his posturing was about. I'll find out which school she's at before speaking to the parents again. Thanks, Ailsa. Do you mind if I scoot? I've got to get my team together.'

'Off you go, dear,' Dr Lambert said. 'And give my best to your mother.' The pathologist kissed her on each cheek before Ava ran for the door. Callanach wondered how small Edinburgh's community of the great and good was, that the chief pathologist should be friends with a DI's mother. No wonder Ava thought her team disliked her privileged upbringing.

'Right then, Luc,' Ailsa said, assuming the air of a matronly aunt and changing folders with a swipe across the glass. 'The remains in the barrel. Definitely human. Fragments of the pelvis confirm that the subject was an adult female. The bones, or what pieces were left, were too badly decomposed and altered by the chemicals for DNA testing but the hair caught in the rim of the barrel belonged to your missing person, Jayne Magee. Not a great surprise, if your face is anything to go by.'

'Sadly, it's not,' Callanach said. 'How long did it take for the body to decompose?'

'Our findings are less reliable than usual as most of the liquid seeped into the floor, but I'd say two days. The compound had been prepared to maximise the speed of dissolution. If whoever did this hadn't added just the right amount of water, we might still have some soft tissue.'

'All right,' he said. 'I'll notify the family and prepare a press release. Thank you, Dr Lambert. I appreciate how quickly this has been processed.'

'There was one interesting thing,' she added. Callanach stopped packing away his notebook. 'The teeth. They weren't all present, not that we could find. The ones that were in the barrel are damaged but intact enough for us to have the forensic odontologist check them against Jayne Magee's records. He's certain they're a match but we've only got teeth from the lower jaw. The upper teeth were either missing or completely dissolved.'

Callanach made notes as he considered what that meant. 'How could the upper teeth have dissolved when the lower teeth were only slightly damaged?'

'A good question,' she said. 'Not only that, but why would the teeth retrieved not have dissolved to the same extent as the bones, which was almost absolute?'

'Do bones and teeth normally dissolve at the same rate?' he asked.

'Not exactly the same, but given how thorough he was with the chemicals I'd have thought they should have suffered more damage than they did. It's a conundrum. We're doing some tests to check the breakdown rate but that's likely to take a few days. I'll get back to you.'

Callanach left the pathologist and the Chief talking crime rates and politics. He had to speak to DS Lively first and he wasn't looking forward to it. He didn't have to go far to find him. Lively was sitting in Callanach's office with a tweed-suited white-bearded gentleman Callanach didn't recognise and another man in a clerical collar. Tripp was looking distinctly nervous by the door and had obviously been waiting for him.

'I did say we should wait in a conference room. I'm so sorry . . .' the constable said.

'And I said that in the circumstances you wouldn't mind,' DS Lively interrupted. His red eyes and lank hair painted a picture of too little sleep and self-care. His voice was strained but he was keeping the volume and the language to more acceptable levels than their last encounter. Not for his benefit, Callanach thought. The men he'd brought with him commanded more respect than he.

'Don't worry about it, Tripp,' Callanach said. 'You can go.' Tripp looked more relieved than annoyed at being dismissed, and disappeared. 'I'm Detective Inspector Luc Callanach, but I'm sure you already know that.' He extended a hand to each stranger.

'This is the Reverend Canon Paul Churchill who worked with Jayne,' Lively said. 'And Professor Edwin Harris. We're here to talk about the next steps in the investigation.'

Callanach took a breath. It was normal for involved parties to want an explanation. What irritated him was Lively's rallying the troops without warning.

'Thank you, Sergeant, but the victim's family has not yet been informed about yesterday's events so this discussion is premature.'

'Let me stop you there,' Professor Harris said. 'I understand the procedures. I worked with law enforcement for a number of years. Reverend Paul spoke to Jayne's family last night so that's not going to hamper us.'

'You spoke to her family? Without police officers present who've had specific bereavement training?' Callanach turned to stare directly at Lively. 'When all you have is conjecture. It's a blatant breach of protocol. You know that's a disciplinary matter, right, Detective Sergeant?'

Harris raised a hand between Callanach and Lively to break the stand-off. Lively redirected his gaze to the professor. Callanach continued to glare at his sergeant.

'Detective Inspector, let's not get hung up on who said what and when. We're both professionals and there is a high statistical likelihood that the remains do indeed belong to the Reverend Magee. In the circumstances, I'd have hoped you might take a rather more practical approach. The main concern is that time is of the essence, and I'm here to help.'

Callanach recognised a blind-siding when he was getting one. 'And what help, exactly, are you offering?'

The Reverend Paul stepped in and the speech took on the feeling of a well-rehearsed sketch, with the professor dropping his head in what Callanach sensed was a rather false show of embarrassment.

'Professor Harris is a world renowned and respected profiler, DI Callanach. He's retired but still lectures internationally and has written books on the subject. He's also been a faithful member of our congregation for numerous years and was well acquainted with Jayne. The professor has offered his assistance and the church is happy to pay, to move forward what DS Lively has told us is a frustratingly stagnant investigation at present.'

'I'm afraid that's not appropriate,' Callanach said. 'You would need access to restricted information and profiling after only two murders isn't generally done.'

'DCI Begbie said he'll grant security clearance as Professor Harris worked with the department previously. As long as St Mary's is paying, we've got the go-ahead,' Lively said.

'We were supposed to be having a meeting about this later today,' Callanach replied.

'The Chief said I should make sure you were up to speed. I already have Elaine Buxton's mother's consent to release her files to Professor Harris.' Lively presented it as a done deal.

'I'd like access to all the information immediately,' Professor Harris assumed command, his credentials having been presented. 'And an office would be useful. It'll save a lot of time if I don't have to move around too much.' He stroked one side of his nose as he talked, his voice so soft it was almost a whisper, his smile completely self-assured. The man wasn't asking permission.

'I'd prefer to have that meeting with the Chief before I authorise the release of information,' Callanach said. 'And there are other matters that need my urgent attention. I appreciate you coming in, gentlemen.' He stood up and walked between them to open the office door.

'You know, Inspector, the sooner I assess the evidence, the sooner I can say who you should be looking for,' Harris said, smile still in place but voice firmer now.

'I'll remember that,' Callanach replied.

Lively was purple but the Reverend put a calming hand on his arm and spoke just loudly enough to make sure Callanach would hear his words.

'Don't trouble yourself, Matthew. I'll speak with the Chief Inspector personally.'

They made their way down the corridor with Harris loudly proclaiming the dangers of lost time. Callanach grabbed his phone and dialled Ava's mobile. He needed information and a sounding board before he spoke to the Chief.

'Ava, can we talk?'

'I'm getting into my car in three minutes. If you're in it too, you can have my full attention on the way to St Gabriella's High School. That's the best I can offer,' she said. He grabbed his jacket and ran.

Chapter Twenty

Callanach only just made it to the car before Ava pulled away, his foot still hanging out of the passenger door as the tyres squealed. He tried not to visibly hold on to the sides of his seat as she drove and concentrated on asking the questions he needed answering.

'What do you know about Professor Edwin Harris?' With anyone else he might have worried about diplomacy but Ava was proving to be the sort of police officer who cut to the chase.

Ava took her eyes off the road for a split second. 'The man who looks like God dressed for stag hunting?' Callanach laughed, entirely unexpectedly, and the tension broke. The speedometer needle dropped a notch and he relaxed his grip on the seat. 'He retired before I became a DI but he was involved in a couple of cases I worked as a detective constable. How come he's crossed your path?'

'I've been offered his help. Only the definition of offered means I have to take it whether I like it or not. He's heavily involved in Jayne Magee's church. The Chief has already been persuaded to agree because it's free. If I say no and there's another murder, I'll be public enemy number one.' She took a hard right that had Callanach's cheekbone against the window for a second.

'Then let me play devil's advocate. This is free advice from a man who worked with the police for a number of years. Why would you not want it and what have you got to lose?' Callanach jammed a steadying knee up against the passenger glove box.

'I'm not convinced a profile is going to take us forward and I'm worried it could lead us in the wrong direction. The worst-case scenario is that we ignore people we should regard as suspects. Also, Harris is personally involved. He's going to want to get results to appease the church and that may mean he tries too hard to find answers where there are none.'

'So let him consult, provide a profile then ignore it,' Ava said.

'I don't think I have much choice about that. What I really want to know is if I can trust his professional judgment.'

'Your gut has already told you not to. I'm sure you don't need me to tell you to follow your instincts,' she said, glancing at her watch. 'Damn it,' she hissed at a red traffic light.

'No, but I suppose I was hoping you'd reassure me that my instinct was right.'

'He's got your back up because he enjoys the process too much. He doesn't just look like a child's drawing of God, he acts like he is one. I felt the same thing the first time I heard him talk in a briefing. He was so self-congratulatory. Every good police officer I know spends their time worrying that they haven't got it right, haven't worked hard enough, that they've missed something. His whole being oozes the opposite.'

'Thank you,' Callanach said. 'That was exactly what I needed to hear.'

'Pleasure,' she said. 'Only, be smart. He's been around long enough to have the ears of a few of the top brass. It's part of what gives him his attitude. Steer clear when you can. If I were you, I'd let the Chief deal with him. You can thank me properly by having my back. It'll be reassuring to have a senior ranking witness to the complaints I'm about to attract.' She drove into St Gabriella's school for the second time. Through the rain, the place looked deserted. Callanach followed Ava to the reception area.

'Can I help you?' a woman offered with more disapproval than was necessary. It really did feel like being back at school.

'DI Turner,' Ava said flashing her badge, although there wasn't any doubt that the receptionist was well aware who she was dealing with. 'You're the last school on record as having Felicity Costello as a pupil. Is she attending currently?' Before the woman could answer, a door opened at the back of the office and a man appeared.

'Information relating to our pupils is highly confidential. Can I ask if you have the proper authority?' he asked. He was squirrelly, twitching defensively and attempting to cover it with a strained smile. Callanach longed to tell him to stay still.

'I do,' Ava replied, handing him the paperwork.

'Then I'd ask for time to contact the school's lawyers and have them scrutinise it. I shouldn't like to be accused of failing to do my duty properly.'

'Sorry, your name is?' Ava asked.

'Justin Currie,' he said. 'Head teacher.'

'This is a serious investigation, Mr Currie, and whilst you're at liberty to contact the school's legal representatives I would like access to Felicity Costello's files straight away.' Ava's voice was flat but there was no mistaking her insistence. Currie's smile began to falter.

'It can take time to locate each student's file so if you'd take a seat, I'll look it out.' Ava had no intention of taking a seat and Callanach knew it. The head teacher had exceptionally poor people-reading skills if he believed he was going to get away with anything other than following orders.

'Whilst you are at liberty to contact the school's lawyers, your receptionist should not notify any other party about our enquiries, I hope that's clear. DI Callanach and I will accompany you,' Ava said.

Currie's smile had stopped fading and was nowhere to be seen. For a second, Callanach thought he might protest but the man's emotional intelligence finally kicked in and he recognised the brick wall he'd hit.

'In here,' he said, pointing through to his office.

Currie's office was all soft leather, walnut furniture and plush carpet. On the wall above his desk, in a lavish gilt frame, was a picture of a younger version of the head teacher kneeling before some past Pope, although Callanach wasn't sufficiently good with religious miscellany to be able to recall the pontiff's name.

Two large filing cabinets stood beneath a window with a view over the girls' playing field, which today was an abandoned sea of waving greenery. There was no mistaking the benefits of working in the private education sector. Currie walked to the cabinet on the left and opened the top drawer labelled A to D.

'Remarkably easy to find, in fact, Mr Currie. I'll take it from here.' Ava's hackles were up. Whatever reason Currie had for pretending to need time to locate the file, it certainly wasn't to assist the police. Ava pulled two files from the drawer, both labelled Costello, and identified Felicity's.

'May I enquire what you're looking for?' Currie asked. Ava didn't answer. She was already flicking through the contents, concentrating on finding the information she needed.

'How many girls attend the school?' Callanach asked to distract him as Ava worked.

'Four hundred and twenty, including the sixth form,' he snapped. 'What offence are you investigating?'

Ava looked at him sharply. 'Felicity hasn't attended this school for the past five months, is that correct?' He nodded. 'And at the conclusion of her notes all I can see written is GM. What does that mean?'

There was a pause, a cough and another pause. Callanach watched Ava watching Currie and wondered how long she'd give him. Not very long, as it turned out.

'Mr Currie, is there a reason you're not saying anything?' Ava asked.

'Am I legally required to answer these questions?' Currie tried, but the defeat was plain to read on his face.

'Why would you fail to assist a criminal investigation by answering what should be a straightforward question?' Ava tucked the file under her arm.

'It's an abbreviation for another school. GM is St Gerard Majella's.' Currie wasn't happy.

'Is that in Edinburgh?' Callanach asked Ava.

'If it is, I've never heard of it.' She turned her attention back to Currie.

'It is,' he confirmed. 'Will that be all?'

Ava didn't bother with any more small talk. She had what she wanted. The school day had a couple more hours to go. They were back in the car in less than a minute. Callanach radioed in the information and the address came back fast.

'Odd to discover a school I've never heard of in the city,' Ava said. 'I know the street and I've never noticed a school building there.'

This time the blue lights went on when they hit traffic. Callanach left Ava alone with her thoughts as she drove, two marked police cars keeping pace behind them. A social worker had been called to meet them at the address with the doctor who had examined Lucy Costello previously. The school could call Mr and Mrs Costello. Ava had given them a chance to do things the easy way the first time.

St Gerard Majella's School was an ageing outer-city manor house in a road which must once have housed the area's moneyed families. It had the distinction of lacking any signage to alert visitors to the institution's name or purpose. A grand old building, slightly tatty around the edges, it initially appeared to be in need of some updating but the windows and doors were new and a state of the art security system kept them at bay outside a metal-barred gate.

They left the car on the road and were finally buzzed in on foot. Ava stationed two uniformed constables at the front gate and asked a detective to make his way to the rear of the property to ensure that no one left the premises unseen. An enormous wooden door eventually opened and a nun stood at the threshold.

'Yes?' she said. There was going to be no false friendliness. Callanach preferred it to Currie's brief, sickly attempt at charm. Once again, Ava showed her badge but this time it was taken from her and carefully inspected.

'We need to speak with Felicity Costello,' Ava said. 'You'll want to telephone her parents, but we have child-support staff with us. We'd also like her seen by a doctor.'

'Come with me,' was the reply. Callanach studied the nun's face but it gave nothing away. There was no shock, not even a hint of curiosity and she asked no questions.

'Currie phoned and warned them,' Ava whispered to him as the nun freed a heavy ring of keys from her belt. She rattled through several before extending one in the direction of an inner door. Inside, the corridor extended both left and right. Straight ahead of them was another locked door, with a glass panel through which he could see a stairway.

'Turn left,' she said and showed them to an office which contained only four straight-backed wooden chairs for visitors, a simple desk and a stool on which she sat. The only testament to the twenty-first century was the communications system on her desk. She pressed a flashing red light on its deck and spoke to someone in another office. 'Put him on the line,' she said.

Ava began to protest and was met by a hand raised palm-first in her direction.

'Mr Costello,' the nun said. 'I am in the presence of two police officers who are party to this conversation so that there are no secrets between us. I would like you to confirm that you withdrew Felicity from this school recently and that she is currently in your care.'

'That's correct,' John Costello said without a hint of his previous aggression.

'Is Felicity with you?' Ava asked, standing up to raise herself above the level of the hand.

Callanach thought he could hear muffled weeping in the background and wondered if Currie had phoned the school or Felicity's parents first. Either way, the change in John Costello's attitude was stark. 'She's here,' he said.

'We're on our way. Do not attempt to leave the house. We'll be with you shortly.' Ava was already at the door.

'Remember your duty,' the nun added. The crying at the other end was getting louder. Mrs Costello was obviously past the point of control.

John Costello added a subdued, 'Yes, Sister Ernestine,' before putting down the receiver.

'Felicity was at her home address all the time. I do hope next time you'll do your research more thoroughly before causing such a drama,' the nun said to Ava. Callanach noticed a cane on her desk and picked it up, rotating it in his hands.

'A reminder of the bad old days, Sister?' he asked.

'An educational antique, Constable.' The slight was deliberate. The nun might not have been rattled by their presence but she was annoyed by it. Ava and Callanach followed Sister Ernestine back along the corridor where she paused to unlock one door then the other.

'It's an impressive security system for a school – the cameras, the gates,' Callanach noted.

'We are a privately funded school, with the safety of many young girls in our hands. Can you imagine what would happen if the wrong sort of person entered with only myself and my fellow sisters to protect our wards? I should have thought a police officer would have been more understanding of our situation.' She closed the front door before he could answer. Ava was striding towards her car. Callanach stared up at the windows of the upper floors. Security conscious was an under-statement. The windows were sealed, no hinges in sight. Cameras from at least four different locations were trained on him, waiting for him to vacate the area. It was a fortress. What sort of parents would want their daughter educated here? That was the question he asked Ava as he climbed back into the car.

'Lucy Costello had already received a caution for dealing ecstasy. Maybe the twins are rebelling and Mr and Mrs Costello figured it was better to split them up,' Ava offered.

Callanach's mobile rang. Tripp was chasing him on the Chief's behalf. Fair enough, Callanach thought. What he'd expected to be a half hour away from the station had turned into something much more complicated. He asked for a squad car to meet him at the Costellos' house and take him back to the station. Ava was going to be some time.

They reached the Costellos' ahead of the squad car, so Callanach watched as Ava knocked on the door. The child protection social worker introduced herself first, then Ava gently explained to a pale-faced Felicity what was happening. The only words Felicity spoke were to confirm her identity and agree that she was well enough to be interviewed. There was no hint of defiance, no teenage tantrum or overacted cockiness, just a quiet, embarrassed girl whose eyes didn't once leave the ground. Felicity Costello may have abandoned her baby in a park, but she was just a child and more victim than offender. Ava put a gentle arm around her shoulders and led her to a police car.

The Chief was already ensconced with Professor Harris and DS Lively by the time Callanach got there. It was a shame. Callanach had wanted to state his case privately, in advance. No doubt, he thought, Sergeant Lively had anticipated that.

'Detective Inspector, I was beginning to think we'd lost you completely,' Harris said.

Callanach didn't grace the remark with a response, but glared at the files on Harris's lap. 'I did ask that the release of confidential information waited until after this meeting. I'm not convinced this is the appropriate way forward,' he said.

'I didn't want to waste the morning, so the Chief agreed that I could review the missing persons files your constable was compiling. I've also spoken with your team and I'm up to speed. What are your current lines of investigation, Inspector?'

'Mainly forensics. We know he's using chloroform, that he spends a long time watching his victims, planning his routes. We have a vague description from a dog walker near Jayne Magee's address but not enough for a sketch.'

'Sounds like you're reduced to waiting for him to strike again and hoping you'll get luckier next time! It's just as well I was brought in,' Harris said. Lively murmured his agreement.

Callanach took Ava's advice and conceded by ceasing to fight. At least Harris couldn't do too much damage if his only task was to review missing persons files, and it meant Tripp would be freed up.

'Review the evidence if you wish and let me have your report,' Callanach said. 'We can review the day after tomorrow at nine a.m.'

Harris shook his head and tutted. 'Tomorrow morning at eight will do nicely. I'm a speed reader, Inspector, even with this many documents I won't need two days to get myself in order. After that, I'd like to spend the rest of the day re-interviewing your witnesses.'

Callanach let Professor Harris make his remaining demands uninterrupted. If nothing else, it had the effect of speeding up the meeting. When the others had gone, the Chief called him back.

'I know you don't like it,' Begbie said, 'but work with him. It can't hurt.'

'If you want a profiler, then I'll find someone. I managed a few investigations using a very talented Swiss psychologist. I could give her a call.'

'We can't fund it,' DCI Begbie said. 'Truth is, the man gets on my nerves too, but the effort of excluding him would be a lot greater than letting him do his bit.'

'I thought you were on their side,' Callanach said.

'Give me some credit,' Begbie said. 'And just remember that if we don't catch this murderer soon, it'll be my head on the block before yours. No pressure.'

'Right,' Callanach said. 'No pressure.'

Chapter Twenty-One

Detective Constable Tripp had done well. From the photos, Callanach could see that the drum-handling trolley had been tipped off Granton Harbour Breakwater. Had it not been for the tide lodging it in the muddy sand bank at the base of the sea wall, they'd never have found it. By itself, it would have constituted no more than a vague possibility of evidence but tied to its handle was a thick plastic sack containing Jayne Magee's clothes. They'd been sent directly to the lab but it was a formality. The blood on the clothing was inevitably hers. The trolley was going to yield fewer helpful results. Dr Ailsa Lambert phoned him as he was emailing her.

'Jayne Magee's teeth,' she said. 'The test we ran with sodium hydroxide of the same concentration that dissolved the bones showed a different rate of degeneration for teeth, but even so there should have been far less of the teeth remaining than we found. As for the missing upper jaw teeth, we've no idea what happened there.'

'Can you draw any conclusions?' Callanach asked.

'The teeth from the lower jaw must have been put in separately to the jaw bone itself. Hours apart, we think.'

Callanach walked to his window and looked out over the grey road below. Why would the murderer have immersed the body parts in batches? Possibly he'd been interrupted cleaning up his carnage or maybe there was a more ritualistic element to it.

'Elaine Buxton's body was found with a baseball bat nearby which had been used on the skull and some of the teeth were smashed. Is there any sign of that with Magee?' he asked.

'I think not. The outer layer of enamel is degraded but the teeth are whole. As for the jaw itself, it's possible a baseball bat was used on it, we've only fragments left, many pieces of bone can't be anatomically positioned.'

'Thank you for the update, Dr Lambert.'

Ava walked into his office as he was putting down the phone.

'The gynaecologist confirmed that Felicity Costello gave birth recently,' she said. 'Felicity told the child support worker she's all right, volunteered that there'd been a doctor present at the birth, then shut down completely. I don't want to push her too hard, she's been through enough, but I'm going to have to get some answers.'

'Have you questioned her parents yet?' Callanach asked, pinning his recent notes on the wall next to Jayne Magee's photo.

'I've got nothing to charge them with and they've lawyered up already. We can interview them as witnesses but they're unlikely to help.'

'How about finding the doctor who delivered the baby?' Callanach suggested.

'Not as easy as you might think, assuming the health care was privately paid for,' Ava replied, plonking herself on a chair.

'Follow the money. The parents must have paid, directly or indirectly. If they're not talking then you've got cause to access Mr Costello's accounts. You can have the answers by tomorrow morning, which is a lot more than I'm going to achieve,' he said. 'Come on, I'll walk down with you. I'm going back out to Granton Harbour.'

They passed Professor Harris on the stairs, deep in conversation with DS Lively.

'You didn't get rid of him, then?' Ava asked.

'Biding my time. Did they discover anything regarding your death threat?'

'No, not that I've had time to worry about it. Even the Chief's given up having me escorted. It was strange that it got slipped under my office door though. Somehow that's more unsettling than my home, knowing they can get into this building unseen.'

'Have you considered that it might be a police officer?' Callanach asked.

'I can't bring myself to think it,' she said. 'Means I'm not safe anywhere and that way lies madness. Best to move on and assume whoever wrote the note has, too. There's Felicity with the social worker. Wait for me, would you?'

'Sure,' Callanach said, standing back while Ava spoke to the child protection team.

'Have you decided if you're going to detain her in secure accommodation tonight, only I'll need to phone the children's unit and make a room available,' the social worker asked Ava quietly. Callanach watched Felicity. The girl was listening, head down but alert.

'I don't think so,' Ava replied. 'She's vulnerable, and even though her parents aren't assisting, I'd rather she went back to her own bed. I'll go and tell the Costellos.'

'Don't,' Felicity whispered. Callanach saw it more clearly than he heard it, and he realised Ava hadn't caught it at all. Ava started to walk towards the double doors, beyond which John and Mary Costello were waiting for information about their daughter. Felicity's eyes filled with tears. She looked first at the social worker who was busy on her mobile, then to Ava who was almost out of reach and finally at Callanach. 'I don't want to go home,' she mouthed to him.

'DI Turner,' Callanach shouted. Ava looked back at him through the glass of the double doors as they swung shut. He motioned for her to return, found a chair for Felicity, then took Ava into a quiet corner to explain. Together they sat with the shaking teenager and talked her through what would happen.

'Are you sure about this? I can't guarantee where you'll go tonight and you'll be in police custody until we've decided what to do,' Ava explained.

'Are you in danger, Felicity?' Callanach asked. The girl shook her head, retreating back into silence. The social worker finished her call then joined them.

'I've changed my mind,' Ava said. 'I think it's preferable that Felicity remains in a controlled placement tonight. What's the best we can do?'

'There's a unit a couple of miles away but it tends to be used to place violent children.'

'That won't do,' Ava said. 'Is there nothing else?' Callanach watched Ava lean in closer to the social worker, almost whispering in the woman's ear. 'If it's a matter of money, I'll cover the costs personally.'

'It's not that. It's just finding a space somewhere with appropriately trained adults.' The social worker checked her watch. 'There's a foster carer, very experienced. If it's just for a couple of nights she might help me out. It's not normal procedure but . . .'

'Sounds perfect,' Ava said. 'You won't disappear, Felicity, will you?'

The girl looked her directly in the eyes for the first time. 'I won't, I promise. Thank you,' she said.

Callanach drove to Granton Harbour alone. At the warehouse, the exclusion zone formerly marked by waspish crime tape had morphed into an impossible garden, alien within the industrial landscape. Flowers, wreaths, teddy bears, cards, letters, candles extinguished prematurely by the harsh breeze, much like Jayne's too short life, surrounded the building as far as his eye-line reached. He took a moment to survey the carpet of condolences and prayers, wondering at how one person could have touched so many others. Crouching, he picked up a card bearing the simple message, 'Gone but never forgotten', and another, 'Taken from us too soon.' More of the same, variations on the themes of gratitude and loss, some personal, others obviously from admiring strangers, then in the midst of the outpouring of love, a black-edged card handwritten in ink. 'As in all the congregations of the saints, women should remain silent in the churches. They are not allowed to speak, but must be in submission, as the Law says. If they want to inquire about something, they should ask their own husbands at home; for it is disgraceful for a woman to speak in the church. 1 Corinthians 14:33-35.' He shoved the distasteful, unwelcome note roughly into his pocket and stood up, narrowly avoiding a woman placing a posy. She was crying and cooing gently to the baby bound to her chest in a sling.

'Are you all right?' Callanach asked automatically.

'I can't believe she's gone,' she said in a small voice. 'How did you know her?'

It was a question he had no idea how to answer. The truth seemed too repugnant. 'Friend of a friend,' was what he opted for. 'And you?'

She smoothed the baby's few hairs against the ruffling wind. 'This is Victoria. She'll be six months old on Saturday. She's Jayne's baby.' The woman kissed the child's plump cheek and wrapped her arms around the bundle as Callanach stared. That wasn't the answer he'd been expecting. The girl carried on before he could say anything. 'That's how my husband and I think of her anyway. We tried for years to have children but couldn't get funding for IVF treatment. There was no way we could afford

166

it ourselves. We used to attend Jayne's church before she moved to St Mary's. When I told her about it, she offered to pay. We said no at first, but with each year the pain of wanting children became less bearable. Eventually I went back and asked if she would help.'

'She could never have afforded it on her salary,' Callanach spoke his thoughts aloud.

'The money came from a trust fund. Her father was something to do with the stock market. She said she couldn't bear to spend the money on herself but that helping us have children was the best possible use for it.' She tried to smile at her baby but the expression couldn't hide her devastation. 'Who could kill someone like that? It's senseless. And you know what? She would tell us to forgive him. Well, I can't. I've prayed to put my hatred aside but it's never going to happen.' The baby began to wail, perhaps sensing her mother's distress. 'And the police seem to have done nothing,' the woman continued. 'How many more women have to die before the authorities make this a priority?'

He felt like an impostor, unable to comment, wanting to defend himself, knowing it was impossibly late to disclose his real purpose there.

'I'm sorry,' he whispered, stepping away, feeling the woman watching him even as she comforted her baby and dried her own tears, perhaps seeing more in his face than he'd wanted to give away.

Callanach took a last glance at the tide of grief and gratitude, then walked from the warehouse to where the trolley had been ditched. It was a short stroll in a quiet area. There was no discernible link between the chosen methods of disposing of the bodies, nor the locations in which they had been left. Buxton and Magee had no relationship that his team had been able to identify, yet here they were. Two individuals who had drawn the same man – both hard-working, well-respected, dedicated to their own

167

profession. Elaine Buxton had a close relationship with her mother, although the revelation that Jayne Magee came from a seriously moneyed background was news to Callanach. Each was an achiever. They were women to admire. And the Reverend Magee had left quite the legacy. Under any other circumstances Callanach might have thought the woman's language – calling her child 'Jayne's baby' – overblown rhetoric. But shocked grief brought out peaks and troughs of human emotion that tinged every memory with poignancy. Magee's good deeds might have gone unnoticed by the general public had her life followed a more normal course, but now there was scrutiny that would cast her in a near saintly light.

Callanach looked around, the breeze whipping in from the sea, bitter spray leaving its salty residue on his face. It was a starkly dull place. No one lingered longer than necessary. Only the hardiest would walk the walls for pleasure. And yet the murderer must have visited the harbour several times to have chosen the warehouse, to have decided where to park his car, where best to tip the trolley into the water. The man who had killed two women at the peak of their careers, in the prime of their lives, had stood here, gazed out over the same water, dotting his i's and crossing his t's. Callanach watched the waves. What multitude of sins had the water washed from that same spot since Edinburgh had become a thriving international city? He stared down at the mud that had captured what scant evidence of Jayne Magee's death he had to work with. Along the shore line were other tidal trophies – a deck chair, a licence plate, hub caps, the obligatory shopping trolleys, metal skeletons of umbrellas taken by the unforgiving Scottish wind, even a pram.

'He must have looked down here more than once,' Callanach said to the sea below, 'and at some point, during some visit, the tide would have been low.' The waves didn't answer, but they did deposit another object, a dented old lobster pot that might have been adrift for years. 'How could such a scrupulous murderer have missed the fact that the evidence he was trying to dump might well wash straight back up?' Callanach wondered. A gull landed next to him and squawked loudly enough to make him start. If he'd been given to flights of fancy, and he wasn't, Callanach would have thought the bird was telling him how stupid he'd been. Callanach got out his phone and called DC Salter.

He went home, remembered there was no food in his fridge, considered getting a takeaway and contemplated eating it alone in front of the television, before sending a text. An hour later Ava Turner walked into the Jamaican restaurant he'd found ten minutes' walk from his apartment. They'd agreed no work talk for the evening. She looked tired, worn down, which was how he felt. Her hair was loose, brown curls tumbling at the sides of her face. Pale with no trace of makeup, Ava Turner was the sort of woman who didn't care about impressing anyone. It was a relief to be with someone so lacking in pretence. Callanach had already ordered her a gin and tonic, handing it to her before she sat down. Half of it was gone by the time she slipped off her coat. Ava asked him to order for them both. Twenty minutes later they were tucking into jerk chicken with rice and peas.

'This may be the best food I've ever eaten,' Ava said through a full mouth. She swallowed. 'God, sorry. My manners. I hadn't realised how hungry I was. I don't think I've eaten a proper meal for a week. And where are the peas?'

'They're red beans. I don't know why they call it rice and peas. I discovered Jamaican food when I was posted there to liaise with local police about a drug lord suspected of killing numerous competitive dealers across Europe. Sometimes I dream about a shack near the beach, warm weather and this food every day.'

'You'd be fifteen stone and your skin would be leathery. Also, you'd miss the constant stress and insane bastards we work with.' Ava waved her empty glass and caught a waitress's attention.

'Are you talking about the suspects or the police officers?' Callanach asked.

'Both, but we agreed no work talk. Did you catch him then, your Jamaican drug lord?'

'I had to return to France shortly before local police arrested him. Of course, as soon as he was out of the picture, he would inevitably have been replaced by an equally evil man, commanding people happy to do whatever they're told to escape the dreadful poverty they're living in.'

'Why did you have to return to France?' Ava asked, finally throwing her fork down once her plate was clean, no trace of the piles of food that had been there.

In Callanach's mind, he saw his ranking Interpol agent getting out of the car that had brought him unexpectedly from the airport. The drawn expression on his face had been a warning that something was terribly wrong.

'Luc, forgive me. You're being transported directly back to Lyon,' his boss had said. Callanach frowned as he recalled it.

'I'm sorry, let's change the subject,' Ava said. Callanach realised he'd let his discomfort show. 'Did you want coffee?'

'Not unless you do.' Callanach drained his glass. 'But a walk would be good, yes?' He handed the waitress a credit card.

They walked in silence to the North Bridge, stopping halfway by unspoken mutual agreement to stare out across Waverley station. During the day it was an industrial eyesore. At night it became a river of light. Callanach leaned against the bridge wall and took a battered pack of Gauloises cigarettes from his pocket.

'I didn't know you smoked,' Ava said.

'I don't light them any more, but I can't stand on a bridge at night without having one in my mouth. It's the only part of the habit I can't break.'

'How very French of you,' she said lightly.

'Come on,' he said. 'I'll make coffee at mine. Even by Scotland's

standards, this wind has enough bite to do permanent damage.'
They walked back towards Albany Street with Ava pointing out
a variety of landmarks and telling tales of Edinburgh's stormy past
as well as any tour guide. The city's blackening bricks and imposing
structures lent it the feel of a gothic film set. But it wasn't the
castle or the churches, or even the grand and stately buildings
that intrigued Callanach. It was the side passages. Shadow-infested
alleyways appeared unexpectedly in his peripheral vision, trailing
off into pitch dark when he peered into them, enclosed and even
ceilinged by the surrounding structures. Late at night the walkways
might have been a time machine – the streets so little changed
over the centuries. It was both inspiring and disconcerting.
Edinburgh was a grand old onion, losing nothing of its insides,
only layering newer buildings and modern architecture around
its heart. For the first time as Ava chatted, Callanach thought that
this might be somewhere he could grow to love. Not so different,
after all, from the French towns and cities he called home.

Callanach unlocked the outer door and let Ava in. She was
in his kitchen putting on the kettle before he could remove his
coat. She handed him a coffee, slipped off her shoes and folded
her legs underneath her on the sofa. It was funny, Callanach
thought, how women were so much sexier when they weren't
trying to be. He looked at Ava's sensible boots on the floor, at
how she'd curled into a ball, wrapped around her mug, utterly
unselfconscious and at ease.

'So what about you?' he asked. 'You're not married, not
engaged. Is there no one you share your life with?'

'A couple of hundred police officers, about twelve hours a
day. I'd say that was quite a lot of sharing,' Ava joked.

'No, seriously. You go to the cinema alone, you're at work
more often that you're at home. There must be more to your
life than that.'

'Friends,' she said. 'There have been boyfriends, of course, but they didn't understand my work. Not just the hours but the fact that your mind never stops working a case, not in the shower, not watching TV, not even when you sleep. The only realistic option was to hook up with another police officer and that would be a recipe for disaster. Dating is such hard work. To start with I was too busy to try, then I got out of practice. I usually got called away or let people down. Now I think I've forgotten how. Or I can't be bothered. Not sure which. Good coffee, by the way.'

'Are you never lonely?' Callanach asked. He was on dangerous ground and he knew it. He'd kept everyone at arm's length for so long that part of him dreaded having to let down his guard. Another part of him, though, was calling time on the endless solitude.

'You sound like my aunt,' Ava laughed. 'Having the time to be lonely would be a luxury. Maybe I should call in sick for a few days and try it.' She put her mug down. 'My turn. Word is that you came highly recommended from someone several rungs up the ladder at Interpol. It isn't easy to join a police force in another country, however impressive you are. What's the story?'

Callanach sighed and shrugged. 'It's part truth and part wishful thinking. I'm sure a conversation took place. Even I was surprised to have been accepted here. But the recommendation was as much to get rid of me quietly as to assist me. What's the phrase? It was a win–win situation. Then again, it could have turned out much worse.'

Chapter Twenty-Two

King wasn't bothering to restrain Elaine any more. She didn't climb off her bed except to use the bathroom and then she dragged herself along, holding on to whatever furniture she could. He had abandoned his initial caution upon entering the room, only briefly concerned that she might suddenly find the spirit to stand behind the door and attempt an attack. He'd broken her. Entirely and comprehensively. Elaine was a puppy kicked too often, who had long since given up snapping at the foot. He hadn't intended to damage her so dramatically, and was surprised at how easily it had happened. All the trouble he'd gone to for her and she'd ended up a whingeing, shrivelled wreck.

The Reverend Jayne Magee was different. His judgment of her had been better. Was it her faith or genetic roulette that made her more resilient, he wondered. Perhaps there was an experiment he could do to test both theories. Not tonight, though. Tonight he was going to see how well they'd learned their Russian. He had lapsed terribly in attending to their ongoing education, but he couldn't be too hard on himself. He felt as if he was trying to run a puppet show with both hands tied behind his back.

Natasha had been over the moon after Detective Inspector Turner's lecture. King couldn't remember seeing her so animated. Her face had been flushed and she'd been delighted with the compliments her friend had received at the reception afterwards.

He dropped a stream of vegetables into a liquidiser and added chicken stock. It wasn't very imaginative but it would have to do for the ladies tonight. At least they wouldn't be consuming too many calories. King was trying not to think about how he'd pushed between students to introduce himself to Ava Turner. He didn't want to think about it because Natasha had upset him again. She seemed to have turned making him feel worthless into a fine art. If he thought about it, he'd end up taking it out on Elaine and Jayne and he didn't want to be reduced to that.

He put the soup in the microwave, singing loudly along with the radio, pushing the memory away, testing regularly to ensure it was no more than warm. Jayne's gums were still sore and heat would make them worse. As it was, he was having to administer huge doses of antibiotics to prevent an infection. He was pleased with himself, though. His dentistry had been much improved compared to his work on Elaine. Not that he was blameworthy for his early maladroitness. Learning the skills dental surgeons took years to perfect, from only a book and a series of clumsy online tutorials of questionable origin, was no small order. But still, it was amazing what a small amount of practice could do. He only hoped the same could be said of their Russian that evening. He needed them to begin to exercise their intellects again. Elaine was already on borrowed time. King decanted the soup into cups with straws and went to the cellar stairs. Standing still he listened carefully, hearing nothing and pleased that the sound proofing he'd installed was working so effectively. In the main body of his house he'd never heard a single sound from the concealed area. It was as if they didn't exist.

'Well, technically they don't,' he said, unlocking the door. 'Legally speaking they're both dead. I wonder what the group noun for corpses is.'

Elaine had moved, which he supposed was progress. Jayne was sitting up on her bed, one hand cuffed to a post so she could swivel her body round to a commode he'd thoughtfully purchased. Elaine had left her own bed to lie with her head on Jayne's lap, the latter stroking her hair. They grew still as he took them their supper.

King helped Elaine to the table and put the soup in front of her. She'd long since ceased resisting and began sipping the soup straight away.

'I've put clean night clothes on your bed. Leave the old ones in the basket by the door as I've shown you,' he said. 'And you must wash more thoroughly. As I'm allowing you the freedom of the room, I expect you to use the facilities effectively. Showering once a day would seem appropriate. Or if that's too much for you, at least use the sink to wash with a flannel.' Elaine didn't look up, concentrating on her supper, as mute as ever. He handed Jayne her beaker which she put down on the bedside table without touching it.

'My mouth hurts,' she said. 'I need painkillers.'

'Open,' he said. She was right, clusters of ulcers covered her lower gums. The antibiotics weren't strong enough.

'What did you do with my teeth?' she asked.

'I put them with Grace's body, to replace her own. The world needed proof that you were deceased. That tiny bit of blood you made such a fuss about my taking, I sprinkled over your clothes and left them within a locatable distance of the body.'

'They'll know it wasn't me,' she said. 'Forensics is more advanced than that.'

'I didn't leave enough for them to work with,' he said. 'Do

you think I'm that sloppy? I've researched this for months. I know precisely when they can and cannot get DNA.'

'Science progresses at unpredictable speeds. You don't know what tests they'll be able to do a month or a year from now.' Jayne was feisty tonight. He rather enjoyed her when she was argumentative. It made her so much more alive, like the first time he'd seen her, engrossed in a lively public debate.

'But there'll be no reason to test your remains again. You're dead. There's been no funeral yet but it's public knowledge.' King dropped two soluble aspirin into a glass of water and gave it to her. She wanted to throw it back in his face, he could see that, but she wouldn't. The pain was too intense for her to behave so rashly. He respected her ability to keep a cool head. 'Let go of your past life, Jayne. You've hit rock bottom. Accept it. Embrace it. There's nowhere to go but up. Life here with me could be so rewarding.'

'This is no life,' Jayne said.

Elaine began choking. He could hear the rattle deep in her throat. The liquidiser hadn't done its job thoroughly enough. Reluctantly he got up from Jayne's bed and began slapping Elaine hard on the back. With one enormous wallop she brought up a chunk of grey vegetable matter that landed on King's shoe. He grimaced and kicked it onto the carpet, pulling out a handkerchief and wiping furiously at the gleaming leather.

'You hideous creature,' he hissed at her. 'Pull yourself together or you'll leave me no choice but to get rid of you.'

Elaine began to sob, her arms clasped around her body.

'Ignore him, sweetheart,' Jayne said.

There it was again. That suggestion. That word. King's world was awash with red.

'Shut your fucking mouth, Natasha,' he shouted, leaping towards Jayne and dealing a slap to her cheek that sounded like

176

a balloon bursting. Elaine screamed and threw herself to the floor, hands over her head as if a bomb had gone off.

Jayne lifted her face and stared at him. 'Who's Natasha?' she asked.

'What?' King said. 'How do you know about her?'

Jayne blinked slowly, frowning.

'You just called me Natasha,' she said. 'When you hit me. Do you not remember?'

He didn't. He didn't remember at all. In fact he didn't remember saying anything.

'You misheard me,' he said. 'You don't know what the fuck you're talking about.'

Jayne persisted. It was an unfortunate side effect of her otherwise laudable hardiness. 'I didn't mishear it. Perhaps you weren't aware that you said her name, but it was clear. She's upset you. What did she do?'

Unbidden, the memory assaulted him.

He'd extended his hand to DI Turner, ready to greet her, about to offer to fetch her a drink.

'Ava,' he'd said. 'I'm Dr King. Your lecture wasn't bad at all.' Then Natasha's hand was on his arm, pushing his hand away before Turner took it, pulling her friend in another direction, whispering in Ava's ear but he'd heard the words.

'Sorry about that, just ignore him,' Natasha had said. 'He shouldn't have called you by your first name.'

'It's really not a problem,' Ava had responded, but she'd allowed herself to be moved away from him without a second glance. He'd been left with his hand reaching for air, looking like a fool. Ignored. Just as Natasha had intended.

'Dr King,' Jayne said, 'are you all right?'

'Quit the amateur fucking psychologist spiel!' He grabbed her by the throat, pinching hard and dragging her face towards his. 'And stop playing mummy to that pathetic parasite on the floor.'

Jayne was trying to prise his fingers from her throat and failing. King was fighting his own rising excitement and failing to the same extent. 'You should be grateful to me. I left your upper teeth intact so you didn't have to suffer the way Elaine did. I've not had to bring you into line, as I did her. All I wanted was for you to respect me, yet you're treating me like an idiot.' He thrust her backwards against the pillow, wiping her tears and saliva off the back of his hand onto the bedclothes.

King sat down and rested his feet on Elaine's curled-up, juddering back, elaborately.

'I shouldn't let myself get so upset,' he said. 'Natasha's just playing for my attention. I've been going about this the wrong way, thinking I could replace her. Not even you, Jayne, with your self-righteousness and your unshakable ideology can affect me as she does. It's time to give in to it. I see that now. It's what she wants.' He kicked Elaine under her chin, forcing her head up, making her look at him. 'And as there isn't really the space for a third bed, you'll have to earn your right to remain.' He hauled Elaine off the floor and onto her bed. 'So smarten yourselves up. We're going to have a competition. You'll like that, Jayne. You strike me as the quietly competitive type. Whoever impresses me more can stay. You're both bright enough that I don't have to spell out what that means for the other. I want to be treated with some kindness. I expect conversation, interest, debate. And I don't want you to cry!'

King was leaning into Elaine's face, spittle flying into her eyes, sweat budding on his forehead. He was overwrought. And that, he told himself, was because he finally knew that he had to address his anger with Natasha directly. He couldn't hide from it any more. With a dawning clarity, Dr Reginald King understood exactly what he had to do and how to do it.

Chapter Twenty-Three

'Felicity Costello is saying she'll talk, but only to you,' Ava said. Callanach shifted his mobile into his left hand so he could highlight some sentences in Liam Granger's statement. The cyclist who had seen Jayne Magee's abductor talking to himself was on his way to the station and Callanach wanted to be properly prepared.

'I don't understand,' Callanach said. 'Why me?'

'She said you were the first person who helped her. Can you take over the interview?'

'You don't mind?' he asked.

'If Felicity will talk, I don't care who gets the glory.' Ava sounded fired up, her tiredness from the previous evening had vanished even though she hadn't left his apartment until they'd stopped chatting well after two in the morning.

'Then of course I'll help,' he said, 'but I have Professor Harris's briefing.' Callanach didn't need to say what he was thinking. 'I can be down by nine o'clock. Could you make sure she's kept busy and distracted until then?'

'Sounds like I'm going out for breakfast,' Ava said.

Callanach made his way to the briefing room. He'd have

been happy to sit at the back but a chair had been reserved for him at the front, as DC Salter pointed out.

'Did you contact Jonty Spurr last night?' Callanach asked her.

'I did. And I've made reservations for two rooms in Braemar.'

'I'd forgotten about that hotel,' Callanach moaned.

'Don't panic,' she said. 'The pub was fully booked with a coach party. We're in a bed and breakfast up the road. We'll need to set off by four tomorrow afternoon, if that's okay.'

'It will have to be,' he said. 'What's everyone waiting for?'

'The professor likes to be introduced. DS Lively said you ought to do it.'

Callanach resisted the urge to simply remain in his seat and played along. He managed, albeit stiltedly, to thank Professor Harris for his assistance and acknowledged the funding provided by the Scottish Episcopal Church. It felt more like an awards speech than a briefing.

'Thank you, Detective Inspector,' Professor Harris said, pressing keys on his laptop to start a slide show. 'Overnight I've read and assimilated the evidence, such as it is.' DC Tripp huffed at the derogatory sub-clause. 'This first slide sets out the physical characteristics of our murderer. We know he's a Caucasian male, between thirty and sixty years of age, of average height and build. We also know that he is physically strong enough to pull the body of an adult female so we can deduce that he is not infirm.' Callanach risked a glance at his watch. He was determined not to be late for Felicity Costello but if Harris was insistent upon setting out everything they already knew, they'd be there all day.

'So in terms of your assumptions, Professor Harris, what do you have?' Callanach moved things along.

'Not assumptions, Detective Inspector, conclusions based on scientific analysis and years of experience.' Callanach bit his tongue. 'Let's deal with the inescapable first. The sexuality of the offences. This man is targeting bright, outgoing, professional women, the sort of women one can infer are out of his league. Inevitably, he will be using them to fulfil his sexual fantasies, hence the need to dispose of their bodies so absolutely. This avoids the gathering of forensic evidence of sexual assault which, for him, means that he is able to hide from what he has done. He will suffer bouts of shame, remorse, probably panic. At other times he will want to relive the experiences, may well have filmed them so he can watch them again, and is likely to access other similar pornographic footage online.'

'So should we be looking for someone with a history of sexual violence?' DS Lively asked.

'Absolutely,' said Harris. 'Sexual offenders who get to a point where they kill at the height of the assault inevitably start small and build up. Offending evolution is a clear pattern in such cases. You should be screening known offenders in the geographical area with anything from indecent exposure to rape. You'll no doubt already have checked registered sex offenders in the area where each woman lived.'

All eyes turned to Callanach. He sighed. He'd planned to avoid answering questions at the briefing. 'With no evidence of sexual assault on either woman, my feeling was that limiting ourselves to considering one type of offender might narrow the search too greatly.'

Professor Harris patted a grandfatherly palm on Callanach's shoulder, whose hands curled into tight fists at the intrusion into his personal space. Any decent profiler, he thought, would have been able to read the body language a mile away. Not so, Harris. 'Well, that's why I was brought in. In terms of the psychology of the offender, we're looking for someone chaotic. Capable of clear thought at times, but only for short bursts. He has a good scientific awareness and it's worth considering persons who work in the industrial sector.'

'He can't be that chaotic,' DC Salter chipped in. 'He's taken two women from their homes and disposed of their bodies in public places without being seen.' Callanach could have promoted her there and then.

'As I said,' Harris continued unabashed, 'capable of clear thought, but then we study the final execution. Leaving the baseball bat and Elaine's tooth, dumping the barrel trolley with the Reverend Magee's clothes. These are the actions of an offender who either panics or gets overexcited and that is what will allow us to catch him. He won't be capable of holding down long-term employment. That same inability to complete a task without making errors will carry through into his working life. He may have been in and out of relationships, capable of starting them but not sustaining them long term. Those relationships will be with women he finds non-threatening. His partners will either have had blue-collar jobs or have been on benefits.'

'What about his shoes?' Tripp interrupted. 'They were shiny, recently cleaned judging by what the witness at Jayne Magee's abduction said. How does that fit with what you're telling us?'

'Many people keep their shoes clean, Constable.' Callanach tried not to look down but he couldn't stop himself, nor could many of his team. Professor Harris's shoes were indeed spotless. 'It's a skill sadly lacking in the younger generation, apparently.'

'Exactly,' Tripp carried on. 'I'd have worn trainers to pull that wheelie case to a car. I can't understand why he didn't, unless he doesn't own any.'

'It's a fair point,' Harris conceded, 'but his footwear is really only going to tell us the size of his feet, not what's going on inside his head.'

Tripp looked disgruntled. Callanach thought that even Harris knew he'd missed a potentially important feature. The problem was that the professor couldn't admit it. No doubt he'd be revisiting the shoe issue later and hypothesising about it at length with DS Lively.

'I dedicated last night to reviewing other current missing persons files. It doesn't appear that we have any more bodies about to surface, unless he abducts again.'

That was when Callanach took out his mobile, put it to his ear and asked a nonexistent caller to wait a moment. It wasn't clever and it wasn't original but it was his only way out of the room. He poured himself an even stronger than usual coffee, would have added whisky if there'd been any to hand, and made his way down to the interview suite where Felicity Costello was waiting. Ava was positioned just outside the door.

'Ready?' she asked. He nodded and they went in.

'Hello, Felicity,' he said. 'You asked to speak with me today. Is that right?'

'Yes,' she answered, her voice timid, eyes downcast.

'You'll need to speak up,' a woman at her side reminded her. 'This interview is being video-taped. We talked about that yesterday.'

'I'm only going to talk to him,' Felicity said. 'I don't want anyone else in here.'

'I'm a social worker, not a police officer. I'm here to make sure you feel safe,' the woman said. Felicity crossed her arms and glared at the floor.

'We could watch from the filming room,' Ava suggested to the social worker. 'You can stop the interview if you have concerns and Felicity can ask for a break whenever she likes.' The social worker looked unhappy but eventually picked up her handbag in defeat.

'Felicity, my name is Detective Inspector Callanach. You understand that anything you say, any admissions you make, may result in you being charged with an offence. Did you understand that when you were cautioned before?'

'I'm not stupid,' she said.

'I know,' he replied, 'but I have to ask. It's part of the process. Also, you can have a lawyer present. Are you sure you wouldn't like us to arrange that for you?'

'No, I've seen my father's lawyer already. He told me not to say anything.'

Callanach threw a concerned look into the camera. This was dangerous ground and Ava would be worried already. He didn't want to jeopardise the admissibility of anything Felicity told him. Worse than that, he certainly wasn't about to take advantage of the girl's age and lack of understanding of the law.

'Felicity, you don't have to tell me what your lawyer said, in fact you shouldn't. You can have whatever conversations you like with your lawyer and it's none of our business.'

'He wasn't my lawyer and he wasn't trying to help me!' she shouted. 'He was telling me what my dad wanted me to do. I thought you'd understand, that you'd help.'

'All right,' Callanach said. 'I get it. I'm sorry. Do you want to tell me about the baby?'

The anger drained from her immediately.

'I didn't want him to die,' she said.

'You wrapped him up warmly enough that he didn't, so you did a good job. Was there a doctor at the birth?' Callanach asked. She nodded. 'Did you catch the doctor's name?'

'No, I didn't like him . . .' she faltered. 'I was scared. I thought he'd be nicer.'

'He wasn't?' Callanach asked. Again, the response came only from a shake of her head. 'Felicity, you had only just turned fourteen when you got pregnant, so by law that means you were raped. Can you talk about what happened?'

'Can I have a drink?' she asked. Callanach watched her biting her nails and realised she was stalling. He fetched water and waited quietly until she was ready to talk.

'I won't tell you his name,' she said. 'I don't want my parents or the police to do anything to him. I knew my father would stop me seeing him so I didn't tell them I had a boyfriend. He didn't rape me. I liked him.'

'I see. Can you tell me how old he is, Felicity?'

'Fifteen,' she said quietly.

'And he didn't force you or threaten you at all?'

'It was my idea,' she said. 'I told him I couldn't get pregnant, that I was on the pill. I just wanted to find out what it was like.' Callanach smiled at her and hoped that Ava would share his view that it was a line of investigation best dropped. Whatever the legal technicalities, this seemed to be a question of mutual teenage curiosity ending in tears, not cause for a rape investigation.

'So why leave your baby in the park? You must have been very upset to have done that.' Tears appeared in her eyes without warning. Callanach pushed a box of tissues towards her. 'We can stop if you like.'

'I made a promise,' she said.

'A promise?' Callanach asked. 'Who to, Felicity? The baby's father?'

'No,' she said. 'He never even found out I was pregnant. I promised my friends. We said we'd all do it and they did, then later I didn't want to but I felt so bad for them, like I couldn't let them down.' She hugged her knees, letting the tears run down her cheeks without bothering to wipe them away.

'Felicity,' he said. She sniffed a few times before looking up at him. 'You need to tell me their names.'

'I don't want them to get in trouble,' she said. 'It's not their fault. They didn't want those babies. We needed people to find out. It was all we could think of doing.'

'The other girls?' Callanach asked. 'The ones whose babies died in the park?'

'Yes,' she said. 'Promise me they won't go to prison.'

'I can't promise you that. It's not in my power, but if you explain what happened we'll do all we can to help them. Are they teenagers, like you?' Another nod. 'Where did you meet them?'

'At school,' she whispered.

'At St Gabriella's?'

'No, at the other place.' She was starting to withdraw again. Callanach's gut told him he didn't have much talking time left.

'Do you mean St Gerard Majella's?' he clarified.

Felicity scowled, her face pinched with anger, eyes blazing. 'Yes,' she said.

'Are the girls still there?' Callanach asked. Felicity dropped her face towards her lap.

'No,' she replied. 'They let you out once it's over.'

'Once what's over?' There was silence. 'Can you tell me anything else?' She was finished and Callanach knew it. He looked at the camera and shook his head. They wouldn't get any more from her. 'Felicity, you've done really well. You haven't hurt your friends. Is there anything else I can do for you?' He expected nothing but she slowly met his eyes.

'I want to see him,' she said. 'Would you ask if I can see my baby?'

Chapter Twenty-Four

'You're coming?' Ava asked him.

'What do you think?' Callanach replied, following her to the car.

'I traced the money. All I could see from John Costello's accounts were payments to St Gerard Majella's, none to any private hospital. The school must have organised everything.'

'Amazing, isn't it?' Callanach commented as Ava switched on the blues. 'Two cases running simultaneously, one involving a church that has been unhelpful to the point of covering up offences and the other with a church trying to be so helpful they may be making things worse. Do you believe in God?' he asked Ava.

'Ask me in a couple of hours,' she said, swerving round a cyclist. Callanach took out his mobile and left her to concentrate on the road.

'You were good with Felicity,' Ava said quietly as Callanach scrolled through a search engine.

'She's just a child,' he said.

'I know. But she trusted you, straight away. She must have felt you understood her. You were different,' Ava finished.

Callanach glanced up briefly to find her staring at him. She returned her eyes quickly to the road and he looked back down at his phone. He found what he'd been looking for just as they arrived at the school.

'What?' Ava asked as he swore loudly in French.

'St Gerard Majella,' Callanach said. 'He's the patron saint of expectant mothers.'

Ava parked the car and they walked up to the imposing gates, although this time the wrought iron barriers did not open automatically. Instead, a young nun appeared and addressed them from inside.

'Sister Ernestine is busy. She asks that you make an appointment.'

'And I require access to information relating to the deaths of two babies,' Ava said.

'We'll need to see some paperwork,' the nun said. It sounded like a line she'd been instructed to say.

Callanach stepped forward. 'I'm not entirely certain that Sister Ernestine would enjoy media attention. A delay will mean more parties having to share the information we already have.'

There was a hushed conversation through a walkie-talkie system, a buzzing noise and magically the gates opened. Sister Ernestine managed to free herself from whatever onerous duties had detained her and was waiting inside the front door.

'Come to my office,' she said, motioning towards the route they'd taken before.

'I don't think so,' Ava said. 'I have cause to believe there is evidence here and witnesses who need to be secured immediately. Unlock the inner door, please.'

'This is private property,' Sister Ernestine insisted. 'The parents of these students pay a great deal of money for their education. I won't have you rampaging in and upsetting them.'

'Let us through,' Ava said, stepping up in a manner that made her determination quite clear but which stopped short of threatening. Callanach enjoyed watching it. Detective Inspector Turner was a force to be reckoned with.

Sister Ernestine unlocked the inner door with a face that could have melted metal. Ava and Callanach made their way up the stairs as uniformed officers secured the lower floor. Along a corridor was a classroom which they entered quietly. The girls stood up automatically, showing an almost military respect to the visitors.

'My God,' Callanach said. He'd had his suspicions in the car but hadn't expected this.

'They're all pregnant,' Ava said, staring at the girls. 'Every one of them. This isn't a school, it's a maternity unit!'

'We look after these girls' spiritual, physical and educational needs. They are kept safe here, away from prying eyes and corrupting influences.'

'You mean corrupting influences like independent advice about contraception and terminations?' Ava asked. 'Do these girls leave this school at all? Who provides their prenatal care? Where do they give birth?'

'We have a fully equipped medical unit and we only use the best doctors and nurses.'

'That's why the fees are so high,' Ava noted. 'John Costello paid a fortune to have his daughter kept here. I want to see your records. I'll need the medical notes of all the girls who've given birth in the last month.'

'That's not going to be possible,' Sister Ernestine said. 'Those are confidential. You'll need to provide me with specific names.'

'Felicity Costello made a pact with two girls she met here that they would leave their babies to die in order to expose what was happening at this school. So you will give me access to those records.'

'Felicity Costello was an ungodly slut who lay with a boy then refused to confess her sins.'

'So help me, I will do everything in my power to have this place shut down. The medical staff who deliver babies here are witnesses. I want names and contact details in my hands within five minutes.' Ava was fuming. The girls in their lesson looked stunned, a few were tearful, many more were grinning at the spectacle.

'Rebecca,' one of them shouted.

'Shut up, she'll cane you,' another hissed.

Sister Ernestine tried to shut the door between the corridor and the classroom but Callanach stuck his foot out and held it open.

'Rebecca. Was she a pupil here?' he asked the group. There was a long pause before some of the girls began to nod. 'Does anyone feel able to give me her surname?' he asked, but at this there was silence, the girls glancing nervously between themselves then over to Sister Ernestine. Callanach tried a different tack. 'And has anyone here been caned by Sister Ernestine?'

'Do not answer that question,' the nun who had been giving the lesson ordered.

'You are interfering with a criminal investigation,' Callanach snapped back.

'This is an outrage,' Sister Ernestine cried. Ava stood between her and the girls, leaving the pupils no doubt about who was in control.

One pupil raised a hand. Callanach thought the girl was asking permission to speak until he saw the red welts across her palm. She was heavily pregnant, pale and obviously exhausted. Another followed suit, and finally one girl lifted her mid calf-length skirt and turned around to show the same marks across the backs of her knees.

'Sister Ernestine, you are under arrest for assault. Come down to your office with me. I'll need access to all the pupil records and I will caution you there.' Ava took the nun by the arm and led her along the corridor. Callanach looked at the expectant faces before him. As much as he wanted to get more information from them, each child was below sixteen years of age. His choices were either to obtain parental consent to interview – and what an irony that was after the parents had placed the girls there – or to get a social worker to accompany them. Anything said now would be off the record and heavily criticised later. The girls were vulnerable, and their health was the primary consideration. Proper procedure had to be followed.

'Sit down, please. I'd like you to remain calm. Uniformed police officers will come in and take your names. A doctor will be in attendance to inspect any injuries and answer questions. We will have to contact your parents but we'll be advising them that you must be seen by medical professionals independent of this school and in liaison with Social Services. You don't need to be scared any more,' he said.

Female officers entered and took over. Callanach went down to Sister Ernestine's office. He looked again at the windows and doors.

'The security wasn't to keep intruders out. It was to keep the girls in. What exactly was it you thought they were going to do? Have sex? Only that seems a little late to be effective,' Callanach said.

Sister Ernestine threw him a glare of unadulterated loathing and clutched the cross that hung on a chain around her neck.

'What they were going to do was commit a mortal sin. You think that only evil men with predatory thoughts kill people? Women do it every day, all over the world, thousands of them. Every one of the girls here had expressed the desire to do the same. We saved their souls and the lives of the babies inside them. We stopped them from becoming murderers.'

'You force these children to carry their babies to term when they want terminations, is that it?' Ava paused in the middle of opening drawers in the Sister's desk.

'I protect the sanctity and value of human life. They weren't children when they were shaming themselves, were they? Why should their unborn babies suffer for their sins?'

Two uniformed officers arrived at the door.

'Take her in for questioning,' Ava said. 'And bag this up as evidence.' She handed over the cane that Callanach had noticed during their first visit. 'We'll need to interview all the girls before we can be sure how many counts of assault she needs to be charged with.'

'You'll answer to the Lord for stopping our work here,' Sister Ernestine said.

'I answer to the courts, it's a fairer system,' Ava said, her back already turned as she continued her search.

'There'll be retribution. If not in this world, then I will pray to God you answer in the next,' the nun snarled, taking full advantage of how unwilling the uniformed officers were to use force to get her moving.

'In the place you call Hell, you mean, Sister?' Ava responded, neither turning around nor raising her face from the paperwork as she did so. 'It's an interesting debate, I grant you, the existence of a place of punishment and pain. The definition matches exactly what you've created here and in so many other aspects of your religion. For the child who's told his mother remains in Purgatory because she committed suicide. For the wives of the men in Africa who've contracted HIV because you preach that condoms are sinful even when they use prostitutes. For the women broken and exhausted from having so many children in third world countries because you tell them it's wrong to use birth control. There are many places one can describe as Hell, Sister Ernestine. One I am particularly familiar with is Edinburgh prison, and you are in the privileged position of not having to die before finding out what it's like. Be sure to exercise your right to a lawyer. You're going to need one.'

Callanach waited until they were alone. 'There's going to be a media frenzy,' he said. 'It will need to be contained until the other girls are found. You can't trust that their parents won't just send them off somewhere else.'

'It's going to take some time to go through the files,' Ava said. 'Word's going to get out faster than I can complete the investigation. That's if the good sisters haven't been on the phone to the parents already.'

'What can I do to help?' Callanach asked. 'I've got a witness coming into the station in two hours but until then I'm all yours.'

'Could you talk to Felicity again? Try to get Rebecca's surname out of her. Maybe if she knows what we've done here, she'll feel able to give us more information. I'll have you picked up. I'm going to be a while.'

'You're going to be all day,' Callanach said. 'Let me see what I can do.'

A squad car returned him to the station where the social worker met him in reception.

'Mr Costello is insisting he talks to Felicity before you interview her again,' she said. 'And he's brought the lawyer back with him.'

'That was fast,' Callanach said. 'What sort of state is Felicity in?'

'She's okay but she doesn't want to speak to her father.'

'Did she give any clear reason why not? You'd think she'd want some support from her family,' Callanach said.

'Depends what you call support. But the short answer to that is no, she wouldn't explain. If you can get anything out of her about it, I'd be grateful. Mr Costello isn't exactly my idea of a loving father, however much he was paying in school fees,' the social worker said.

'Give me ten minutes with her. You keep the parents and lawyer out of the way.'

'But I need to be with you if you're going to continue the interview,' the social worker said. 'There'll be a complaint otherwise.'

'I'm not interviewing her,' Callanach said. 'I will be having an off the record conversation to clarify a point with a witness. I'll make sure you get a copy of my notebook afterwards. Which room's she in?'

They went in different directions, Callanach with a can of Coke and a bar of chocolate in his hands, the social worker wringing hers. It wasn't exactly protocol but there was too much at stake to play it all by the book. If they didn't act fast, the school would spread its silence until they'd get nothing from any of St Gerard Majella's former pupils and that would be a dire miscarriage of justice. As Felicity was a defendant, he could interview her alone if the safety of other people was in immediate jeopardy. It was a stretch, Callanach thought, but this was one loophole he was going to have to exploit for the sake of making progress.

'Felicity,' Callanach said, handing over the food and drink as he sat down. 'There's no video recording, no one's listening. The social worker is keeping your parents busy and you don't have to see the lawyer if you say no. We've been to the school. DI Turner is still there. All the girls are getting proper medical attention. Those who need it will be transferred to public hospitals.'

'Does Sister Ernestine know it was me who told you?' she asked. Callanach saw the fear on her face and resisted the urge to express in plain terms what he thought of Sister Ernestine.

'You don't need to be afraid of her any more. She's been arrested for assault and she'll go to prison. Felicity, we still need your help. The two girls we talked about, one of them was called Rebecca, is that right? We have the school records so we'll figure it out soon enough, but if you can give me the other name we can find her faster and that would be better.'

'They'll be in trouble,' she said, 'and it's not their fault.'

'Tell me what you can. If there's a way to stop them being prosecuted, we will.'

'The nuns only keep you there until you've had the baby, then you go home. You have to register your child and your parents decide if you'll keep it or give it up for adoption. Sarah Butler was first.' Felicity paused to open the drink. 'The nuns insisted that we confess. We were supposed to talk about what we'd done to accept our sinfulness. Sarah refused to tell them anything until she was about to give birth and then it was like she broke.' Felicity was shaking, biting the skin at the edge of her nails so hard that her middle finger was bleeding.

'Go on,' Callanach said. 'Nothing worse can happen.'

'Sarah told Sister Ernestine that she'd done nothing wrong, that a man had forced himself on her. It was her priest. When Sarah told her parents what had happened they'd refused to take her to the doctor to get the morning after pill. Sister Ernestine called her a liar but you could see she was telling the truth. Everyone knew it. The nuns beat her, even though she was so big with the baby she could hardly walk. They always beat you where the baby wouldn't be hurt, on the hands, arms and legs. Sister Ernestine was still beating her when the first contraction came and still she didn't stop.'

Felicity was crying. Not the wailing sobs of a teenager but the still, unconscious weeping of a child forced into adulthood through grief, pain and fear.

'And Rebecca?' he asked before Felicity couldn't bear to talk any more.

'It's Becca Finlan. She couldn't cope with being pregnant, not from the first day I met her. She was only thirteen. I would see her clawing at her stomach, punching herself. She thought her body was being invaded. At night they used to strap her to the bed so she couldn't hurt herself. It was sick. The nuns told her God was punishing her for her dirtiness. She was convinced she would die giving birth. She never told us who the father was but sometimes, when she talked about her uncle . . . you know.'

Callanach did know. 'Was there no way of getting help, not through the nurses or by telephone?'

'All the staff obeyed Sister Ernestine. They all thought the same way as her. Your mobile phone gets taken away when you arrive. There was no internet, no landline. Parents could visit but we were never allowed out. We were cut off from everything and everyone. I didn't see my twin sister for months. I missed her so much.'

'What about your father?' Callanach asked quietly. 'Did you miss him?'

Felicity's face contorted. Her hands formed hard fists in her lap and her shoulders hunched up. She did not respond.

'Felicity, I know that what goes on inside families is often secretive and difficult to discuss. But if you need help, if there's something I should know . . .'

'He thinks I'm trash, all right? That's what he called me when I admitted I was pregnant. He sent me to that . . . prison just so he didn't have to look at me. I told him it was my life and my body, and that I would make my own decisions. He just laughed. He told me I was wicked and that I'd burn if I didn't repent,' Felicity snarled.

'And your mother? How did she react?' Callanach asked.

'My mother?' Felicity laughed, but there were tears in her eyes and her arms were clasped firmly across her stomach. 'She did what she's always done. She sat in a corner and nodded as my father spoke, and didn't say a word against him. I used to think she was scared of him. Now I just think she's pathetic. She came to visit me every Sunday afternoon. Do you know, she didn't look me in the eyes once? I showed them the marks from the beatings and my father said they should have hit me harder. He said I needed the lust thrashed out of me. So no, I don't want to see either of them. I don't care where I end up. I'm not going home.'

Callanach knew how it felt to be judged by a parent. Unconditional love was a mirage. It faded when you got too close to it. He wondered briefly what his mother was doing, and if she regretted cutting ties with him. Felicity had every right to have expected more.

'I'm sorry for what you've been through. I promise to do what I can to help and I know DI Turner will feel the same.' Callanach stood up to leave as Felicity threw herself into his arms, clinging like a toddler, her face a mess of tears against his shirt. If he pushed her away she would believe his sympathy to have been nothing more than an information gathering ploy. Against every instinct, he forced himself to let her sob against him until she had calmed down and taken what comfort she needed.

Callanach saw the social worker at the door and nodded for her to enter.

'You'll need to get a child protection order from the court,' he told the social worker as he gently extricated himself. 'Felicity, we won't let anyone else hurt you. You will still have to deal with the charges against you and Social Services will organise a solicitor. In the meantime, though, you won't have to go home. Okay?' He handed the social worker a piece of paper with the notes he'd scribbled in the meeting, slipped out of the room and dialled Ava's mobile. 'The girls you're looking for are Rebecca Finlan and Sarah Butler. Felicity says Sarah's pregnancy was the result of a priest raping her. Parents and nuns were aware but did nothing. It sounds as if Rebecca suffered a breakdown during the pregnancy and I suspect she may be self-harming or a suicide risk. There's a question mark over her uncle's involvement. You need to reach them fast.'

Chapter Twenty-Five

It was a clear afternoon, the sky coldly blue. Callanach felt the turmoil of rage bubbling inside and knew he had to find a way to empty his head. He raced home, grabbed bags untouched since his move to Edinburgh, checked the documents in his wallet and climbed into his car. It was an hour, less if he was lucky, to Auchterarder. Taking the Forth Road Bridge out of the city, oblivious to the scenery, Callanach chased the M90 north.

The day's events sat heavy in his stomach like too much fatty food. As if Sister Ernestine's grotesque delusions and Felicity's wretched disclosures had not been enough, a hand-delivered letter had been waiting on his desk. Callanach had read it three, maybe four times, and the words echoed as he drove. The thick cream paper on which much time had been taken with immaculate penmanship, was still clutched between his palm and the steering wheel, the ink staining his hand as it dampened.

My Dear Detective Inspector,
    I had only the briefest chance to meet you at my daughter's

memorial service and wanted to thank you for all the efforts you have made to find the man who stole my darling Elaine from me. She was my only living child. Her younger brother, Charlie, died when he was just days old and I never found the courage to have more. Losing him was – I had naively assumed – the worst thing I would have to survive. Life plays tricks on us though. I have a better idea now of the limitless pain with which we can be tested.

It is a shame you will never meet my girl. She was shy, surprisingly so for a lawyer, with no appetite for conflict, war or horror. To have met with such a violent death – and I pray that she left this life swiftly with little idea what was happening – is too great an injustice for me ever to come to terms with. Her friend Michael who spoke so beautifully at the church told me he was in the process of obtaining a divorce. His plan had been to move back to Scotland and find Elaine again who, in his words, had been his lifelong sweetheart, years, continents and doomed marriages notwithstanding.

So there we are. If I could change places with her I would, a million times over. I don't know if you have children, but it is a cruel fate to love another person so much that you spend your hours wishing their gruesome death had been yours instead. I know you have tried to find him. I write only to ask that you not give up. The public's consciousness of this nightmare will weaken, I know. But the monster who did this never will. For the sake of my baby, for the sake of the other mothers who will ache to hold their missing girls if he is not stopped, please do not give up.

I believe you are the right man to bring him to justice and I remain gratefully and hopefully yours,

Annabelle Buxton

He gritted his teeth. It would have been easier to bear if she had lashed out, complained or questioned his competence. He wished she'd used those neat, simple words to unload her grief. He was failing. There was no relief from the frustration of passing days and the dearth of progress.

Callanach flicked on the radio, tuning it until crashing music made clear thinking impossible, and stared at the greenness beyond the motorway. Hills rose to the west of him, and the traffic faded away as he turned off and followed increasingly windy lanes. A single-engine Cessna 206 flew overhead, its engine sounding bee-like several thousand feet above the road. It was precisely what Callanach had been waiting to see. The Strathallan skydiving drop-zone was operating.

The Centre's chief instructor met him at the reception desk.

'April Grady,' she said, holding her hand out to him. He shook it with his right hand and held his documents out to her with his left. He knew the drill. He'd be stuck going through kit and docs check before getting anywhere near an aircraft and he didn't want to waste any time.

'You've not skydived here before?' she asked, although it wasn't really a question. She was sounding him out.

'No,' he said, 'but my licence is current and I have British Parachute Association membership.'

He released the small red book to her that contained his passport photo, signature, medical certificate and licence information.

'Forgive me for asking if you have any alternative identification with you. It's just that you booked in late and I like to know who's going up in our planes. Do you mind?' He did. It was another delay and he was already irritated but reached into his wallet.

'Whatever you need,' he responded.

His passport and driving licence were at home. The only

document he had on him was his police identification. April Grady checked it without comment before moving on to his log book.

'You've got two hundred and forty jumps,' she said. 'Where did you do most of those?'

'Mostly France. My closest drop-zone was Lyon-Corbas.' He handed over the documents relating to his rig. Skydiving had been a passion of his for years although he didn't jump as often as he liked. He checked his watch, knowing it would take another half hour to inspect his kit, go through flight line procedure and get manifested onto a load. Finally he was left alone to change.

He got his jumpsuit on quietly and waited for the noise inside his head to settle as it always did when he was waiting to board the plane. Skydiving was a remedy for all troubles. Once the plane left the ground nothing else mattered except getting back down alive. In many ways it was an alien experience – the only sport in which death was the inevitable result when you left the plane until you opened the parachute and took control of your descent. It went against every instinct, was completely contrary to human nature and should never have been conceived as a sport. Yet here he was, about to throw himself from a plane for the two hundred and forty-first time, paying for the privilege, knowing he'd be back on the ground again a matter of minutes later and nothing would have changed. Except that everything he was currently feeling would have been obliterated for that time, overridden by adrenaline. That was all he wanted. To feel something other than frustration and anger for a few minutes.

At the twenty-minute call Callanach went to the flight line area. More checks, endless checks, on skydiver and kit. It was all vital and Callanach had never minded before. But today was different. He was terse with the instructor, not making any friends and he knew it. Jumping with him were two other men and a woman. The men were both in their twenties, full of testosterone and machismo, loudly comparing past jumps, outdoing one another with boyish tales. The woman was slim and eye-catching in a black and white jumpsuit. He couldn't figure out her age but she was in good shape and confident about walking over to take a seat next to him in the plane.

'I haven't seen you here before,' she said smiling, making steady eye contact, leaning close so they could talk above the noise of the engine firing up. The Cessna turned onto the runway, gaining speed and making a swift take off.

'I haven't been here before,' Callanach shouted, returning her gaze, his mood making him rash, letting his eyes wander obviously over her body.

'You're not Scottish,' she said. He grinned at her, knowing what that smile would do, how she'd react. She laughed and blushed. 'That was a stupid comment,' she said. 'Where are you from?'

'France,' he replied. 'Let me get your helmet for you.' He checked the tightness of the strap under her chin, brushing her skin with his fingertips, making her redden again. He leaned closer than was necessary, making sure their legs made contact. 'There, now you're ready.' He clicked down the visor on his helmet and double-checked his straps.

The jump-master tugged his sleeve. They'd reached the correct place and altitude. The two younger men made their way to the door and tumbled together from the plane. The woman was next, giving him a shy smile as she went, leaping into the bright sky. Standing at the door, the jump-master made sure he was fit and ready to dive, did a visual check below to make sure the others were clear and gave him the go-ahead. Callanach let himself fall.

It would take about ten seconds to reach terminal velocity.

He counted slowly, checking the altimeter on his wrist, keeping still on his belly, arms out, legs wide, watching the horizon. He tried to capture the moment, yearned for the falling sensation to spike inside his body but there was only flatness. Twenty seconds gone and the earth was closer, but not looming. He tried to clear his mind but in the fields below he saw only Elaine Buxton's face. Where there should have been nothing but the wind rushing in his ears, her mother's words whispered until he screamed to drown them out. Thirty seconds, at three thousand feet from the ground, he reached his right arm back and pulled the chute. A brief wrenching sensation and he was floating. He waited to feel what he'd come here for. The gentle flight, the calm of solitude, the utter freedom of slowly meeting the world again without fear.

But Jayne Magee screamed inside his head. Callanach closed his eyes. She couldn't be there. Whatever cases he'd investigated before, whatever stress he'd felt, was always banished in those airborne minutes. How could it not be working this time? He shook his head, tried to focus on the looming ground, pulled the toggles to steer into the wind, and bent his legs up ready to land.

He should have felt invincible. That was how he always felt when he landed. A little victory over death each time. The knowledge that he'd controlled both fear and physics. Today there was only a hard bump, a short run because his timing was off and the sensation that nothing in his life was going the way he wanted. Anxiety had got the better of him, invading every aspect of his life like a silent disease. He spent ten minutes packing up his chute before making his way back to the hangar. There was more than an hour to wait until he was due to jump again.

His head was a mess. Nothing was as it should have been – not in his mind and certainly not in his body. That was what was throwing him off-course. The lack of release. The constantly building pressure that he couldn't switch off.

'Great jump,' a voice said. It was the woman from the plane. Callanach didn't slow his pace, letting her hurry to catch up with him. 'I love skydiving at the end of the day. The light here is so beautiful. We didn't get a chance to introduce ourselves inside the plane. I'm Penny.'

Callanach stopped walking for a second. He almost told her to leave him alone, knowing that was the right thing to do. He wanted to explain that he wasn't in the mood for conversation, but didn't. Instead, ignoring every message the rational, reasonable side of his brain was sending, he held out his hand to shake hers.

'Luc,' he said. 'You've obviously jumped here before. I have some time to kill. Why don't you tell me about the place?' Her smile was answer enough. Callanach pulled off his helmet and ran a hand through his hair. They walked back making small talk and eye contact, Callanach letting the process distract him from the cacophony battering his ears from the inside.

They stripped off their jumpsuits. Beneath the skin-tight nylon, Penny was wearing shorts with a strappy t-shirt. She had a flat stomach and great legs. He didn't hide the fact that he was staring and she didn't seem to mind.

'It's a shame to be inside when it's so beautiful out there,' he said. 'Let's walk.'

They each threw on some warmer clothing and Penny led the way. The airfield was set in stunning countryside and, although chilly, the views were worth it. In every direction the landscape was a hundred different shades of green as new leaves emerged with the onset of spring, hedges lining the borders between fields, sheep dotting distant slopes. They walked for ten minutes, scaling two fences, invading land they had no right to, leaving the hangar and prying eyes behind.

Callanach took her hand as they approached a copse of trees in the middle of an uninhabited field. Her face showed no surprise. It was what she'd been waiting for, he realised, banishing the guilt at what he was about to do. Slowly, deliberately, he walked backwards until he was leaning against a tree, pulling Penny towards him. It wasn't all that unusual to end up in a compromising position with a fellow skydiver. Plenty of people did it – the result of a heady combination of danger, fear, bliss and a massive rush – although it was fair to say that doing it in a field next to the drop-zone was a little rough and ready.

'I'm not sure we should be doing this,' she mumbled. 'We've only just met.' They were familiar words that years of experience had equipped him to deal with. If a woman was having real doubts, she would say she didn't want to do it. If she wanted a little further persuasion, on the other hand, she would start with the words 'I'm not sure' or an alternative with the same meaning. It was a sexist view and he knew it, hating himself, testing himself, unable to stop. He had to feel something, anything, could only think of trying to feel alive again.

'But it feels right,' he whispered, 'out here, after what we've just done?'

She didn't answer, closing her eyes as he ran his lips down her neck to the base of her throat, sliding his other hand up under her clothing from waist to breast, making her draw a slow breath in and melt against him. It was too easy, he thought, feeling guilty, telling himself he wouldn't be there if she hadn't wanted it too.

He wound his fingers through her hair and tilted her face up towards his. Her pupils were spreading, her lips parted. When he kissed her, he knew she wouldn't bother to pretend any more that she had doubts. He felt the whole weight of her body slide against his and pushed his thigh between her legs, rubbing his thumb across her nipple, waiting for the reaction that meant he could move his hand downwards. The moan and thrust that followed were consent enough. He ran his fingers down her stomach to the button at her waist, sliding his tongue into her mouth and pulling her more firmly against him. Penny didn't protest as he undid her trousers, letting them slip down to her ankles.

Callanach tried to feel what she was feeling. He closed his eyes and pressed against her, crushing their bodies together until she moved back slightly to put her hand against his groin. That was when he froze. Penny moved her head to the side, her question more than apparent from the tiny movement. He tried to force it, fighting his own rising panic and self-loathing, easing his fingers into her knickers, touching the softness and wetness of her, telling himself he could get there too. Willing himself, cursing himself. She cried out and opened her legs more fully, letting him go where he wanted, do what he wanted. Still he felt nothing. When she fumbled for his zip he twisted his body away, wanting more time to conquer his lack of response, refusing to give in.

'Is something wrong?' Penny asked. 'Am I doing something you don't like?'

'It's fine,' Callanach muttered through clenched teeth but the moment was gone and he knew it, drawing his hand from her underwear and looking away as she pulled her trousers up.

'I'm sorry,' she said, shaking her head. 'Is there something else you want me to do?'

He should have reassured her. She was obviously mortified at her inability to arouse him. The fact that she wouldn't stop apologising was making it worse. At the very least he should have been able to tell her it wasn't her fault, but all he could hear was another woman's voice. His body wouldn't respond to a woman's touch any more. Nothing stimulated him. He hadn't been hard since his world had fallen apart twelve months earlier.

'I'm just not in the mood,' he told Penny. 'And I should

repack my chute more carefully. Let's go.' He started the walk back, keeping it brisk, staying a step ahead of her.

'We could go for a drink after your next jump,' she said. 'Maybe try again?'

'I've got work to do,' Callanach snapped. Penny took the hint. At the hangar she walked quietly away, leaving Callanach relieved to be alone.

He put his jumpsuit back on, repacked his kit, checked his phone for emails and messages, grateful when the twenty-minute call came and he could go back through the procedures that meant he would soon be back on the plane. The knowledge of his body's failure kept resurfacing in his mind like putrid gas. He couldn't keep the thoughts down. The same checks were made again before he boarded the Cessna. The two young men who had jumped with him the first time were back. Penny didn't join them, whether to avoid Callanach or because she'd finished for the day, he didn't know and didn't care.

'Callanach,' the jump-master called.

Callanach looked up sharply. 'What?' he asked.

'You all right?'

'I'm fine,' he replied.

'I had to call your name three times. Get your head together before you jump.'

Callanach stared out of the window as the plane took off and the wind began whistling through the doorway, drowning out everything but the sounds inside his head. He squeezed his eyes shut, shaking his head to banish the clamouring noise, but Elaine Buxton was screaming as she burned in a stone hut in the stone-cold Cairngorms and Jayne Magee cried out as the first drops of chemical hit her skin in a barrel in a deserted warehouse. It wasn't real. There was no evidence that either woman had suffered those fates alive, but his imagination was determined to play out the worst–case scenario.

Before he knew it, the plane was at altitude and the two younger men prepared to jump.

Callanach heard a woman screaming his name, panting, swearing at him, then finally he heard Penny's ragged, excited breathing, gasping as he touched her, sighing disappointedly as he pulled away, limp and useless.

He moved to the open doorway, held on to the frame, looked down to an Earth that seemed so distant it wasn't real. The view made the fields below appear soft and yielding, the grass a never-ending bed that would soak up his pain. Callanach jumped.

At once there was blissful silence both outside and within. The voices were stilled. The darkening blue of the sky swallowed him. He counted as he fell. One, two, three . . . the seconds were the passage of time, the movement of his body through space, a constant as he fell ever faster. Four, five, six . . . here he could control his body, make it do whatever he commanded – roll, plunge head down and back upwards again, spin left or right. Seven, eight, nine, ten . . . terminal velocity . . . rushing towards an Earth where his body would cease to be his to command, where he would be rendered impotent once more.

Three and a half thousand feet came and went, and he let the knowledge that he should have pulled his chute slide past him. His head was fuzzy, heavy. He wanted to be whole and alive again, not this half-man half-failure he'd become. Three thousand feet. He moved his right hand behind his back to grasp the cord, feeling it beneath his fingers, letting it go again, not wanting the free fall to end.

Two thousand feet before he knew it, moving too fast, the earth too close, watching as the details of the ground sharpened in his focus, understanding that he was taking a risk beyond reason, aware that his face was wet.

He didn't want to die, there was no question. But at that moment, when nothing mattered except the sensation of freedom, when he didn't have to face the shell he'd become nor answer the unanswerable questions of grieving relatives, he wasn't entirely sure that he wanted to live either. He entrusted his future to science and fate.

Fifteen hundred feet. The adrenaline was making him nauseous. His head was swimming. One thousand feet. Callanach closed his eyes.

Two seconds later, at seven hundred and fifty feet, his automatic activation device fired the reserve parachute. His head jerked up, feet swinging down towards the ground as the chute unravelled itself and caught air, no time left to steer anywhere except into the wind. If he had to survive, he didn't want to end up with both his legs, or his spine, smashed to pieces. Then he was on the ground, the jolt an awakening as if he'd only dreamed the jump.

'What happened to your main chute?' a voice called. 'Did it fail?' The chief instructor was storming towards him. Callanach turned to pick up his reserve, too dazed to answer, too indifferent to care. 'Did you lose consciousness? Are you hurt?'

'There's nothing wrong with me,' he muttered.

She put a hand on his arm and inspected his pack.

'You didn't pull, did you?' she asked. Callanach shook her hand from his arm and began to walk away. 'I was watching,' she said. 'We need to discuss this.'

'I'm not in the fucking mood,' Callanach shouted.

'You just trusted your life to an electronic gadget,' she responded, catching up and stepping in front of him. 'Did you do it for a cheap thrill or were you actually trying to kill yourself?'

Callanach stepped around her and continued walking towards the hangar.

'This isn't just about you.' The chief instructor wasn't going to be ignored. 'You put other people's lives at risk when you don't follow procedure. You're experienced enough to know that. Have you ever seen the state of a body that's hit the ground after a chute has failed?'

'I've seen that and plenty more,' Callanach said, 'and I don't need a lecture. I'm all right, no one's hurt, my AAD opened the reserve.'

'I'm banning you from this drop-zone for six months, and notifying the BPA. You can tell them your version of events if you want your insurance to remain valid. You're not fit to be skydiving with that attitude.'

Callanach stopped. In the distance he could see a small crowd gathering to witness his disciplining, the two men he'd jumped with staring openly, Penny looking at the ground as she listened, others wondering what all the drama was about.

'I'm not fit for much at all, apparently,' Callanach responded, turning his back. The conversation was over. He packed up his kit, retrieved his documentation with the chief instructor's notes about his behaviour written in red pen for every other drop-zone to see. Callanach wouldn't be skydiving again for a while. He made his way back to his car and threw himself into the driver's seat.

He was home an hour later, the miles a blur, his brief time at Strathallan drop-zone carved into his memory. Just one more thing he wanted to forget that he never would, he thought, dropping onto his sofa and covering his face with his arms, trying to block out the day. Trying to block out the whole of the last year, if he was honest about it.

He'd been suffering from post-traumatic stress disorder since Astrid had accused him of rape, but it was one of those labels he hated. There wasn't an article he hadn't read, nor a website he hadn't scoured to find a cure. He could recite the psycho-babble as well as any doctor. Everything he'd found was calmly reassuring that the impotence wouldn't be permanent, that his failure to respond to normal stimuli was a direct consequence of shock. It was an understandable reaction. His brain had assumed control of his body and was protecting him.

He flinched as he thought how badly he'd treated Penny. He tried to remember her surname and realised he'd never even asked it. Callanach drank an ice-cold pint of water and cleared his head. After a year in denial about his affliction, it was time to either accept the way he was or admit defeat.

Chapter Twenty-Six

At precisely nine the next morning Tripp brought a nervous-looking Liam Granger to Callanach's office. He was in his early twenties, with no police record.

'I just want to go over what you witnessed the night Jayne Magee went missing. You said in your statement you saw a man talking to himself,' Callanach said.

'That's right. Muttering, you know, but as if he was having a conversation with someone else. That's why I noticed it. I suppose, once I'd heard him speak, I was surprised that I didn't see anyone walking with him. At first, I thought maybe he was on his mobile or something, but his hands were by his sides,' Liam said.

'Did you see his face?'

'Sorry, only what I said already. I can't even tell you how tall he was as I was on my bike and he was in the shadows. He had a Scottish accent though, I'd have noticed otherwise, and quite a deep voice.'

'Could he have been using a hands-free kit, possibly?' Tripp asked.

'I suppose so, but it was just the way he was speaking that

struck me as odd. Mumbling to himself. I'm probably not helping,' Liam said, zipping up his jacket and shoving his hands into the pockets.

'Can you remember any of the words he used?' Callanach asked.

Liam thought about it. 'I heard two things. He said something about the lane, something like we're going to the lane. And then twelve. That I heard pretty clearly. He said the number twelve.'

That was all Callanach got from the cyclist but it was enough to get him thinking.

'Is there something called The Lane or Lanes in Edinburgh?' he asked as Tripp returned from seeing Liam out and brought a much needed caffeine reboot with him.

'A nightclub, I think, and possibly a shop. Why?'

'Get me some details. Not that I can see our suspect frequenting a nightclub.'

'Maybe that's where he went to search for victims?' Tripp suggested.

'Not these victims. Not unless both Elaine and Jayne had secret lives completely at odds with everything we know about them.'

'I'll check it out anyway. See if the club has membership records. Could it be an address? Number twelve, something Lane,' Tripp said.

'Possibly, but it would be an odd thing to say out loud, wouldn't it, your own address? I'm off to Braemar with DC Salter tonight, back tomorrow evening. Keep Professor Harris off my back and let me know what's happening.'

'Got it,' Tripp said, 'but DS Lively will ask where you are.'

'Tell him I'm working on those precious few leads he keeps pointing out that we have.'

Callanach was climbing into the car Salter had borrowed from the pool when Ava caught him.

'Luc, wait a moment would you?' she said jogging towards him.

'Sure,' he said. 'What is it?'

Ava beckoned him away from the open car door then reached behind him to close it quietly and give them some privacy. 'I just took a call that should have been for DCI Begbie. Luckily he wasn't available. It was from a woman called April Grady at Strathallan airfield. Do you know her?' Callanach glanced at DC Salter who was putting her seat belt on, then took several steps further away from the car. Ava followed him.

'This isn't a great time,' Callanach said. 'I'm just on my way to Braemar to revisit the crime scene. I need to double-check the witness views of the fire and I'd like to get there before full dark. This conversation will have to wait until I get back.'

'If you make me wait, I'll have no choice but to tell Begbie about it. I don't want to do that. Would you talk to me, please?' Ava kept her voice low.

Callanach breathed out hard and clenched his jaw. What he did outside of work was no one's business but his own. April Grady had no right discussing what had happened with anyone else.

'Is it true?' Ava asked matter-of-factly. 'Did you deliberately not deploy your main chute?'

'I got disoriented,' Callanach replied. 'It happens occasionally when you're skydiving, which is why I always set the automatic device as a backup. My rig's regularly serviced and in good working order. I'm not stupid.'

'You don't have to be stupid to be suicidal.'

'I hadn't realised you were a psychiatrist,' Callanach said.

'Are you actually going to be confrontational with me? Only in the circumstances I'd think that was rather unhelpful. What do you expect me to do – treat this like it's some sort of joke?'

'I expect you to give me the benefit of the doubt instead of being influenced by what someone else, who doesn't know me at all, thinks she saw. And I expect my private life and my work to be two different things without interference between one and the other,' he said.

Ava paused, ran her eyes over his face and his crossed arms, then put her own hands in her pockets. 'Fair enough,' she said, 'but you've been under pressure, moved countries and had a major investigation land on your shoulders. You're responsible for a team of people who need you focused. Can you promise me you've got this?' she asked.

Callanach looked her full in the eyes.

'I've got this,' he replied. Ava nodded, walked away, paused then came back.

'I'm here if you need someone to listen. You know that by now, right?'

'I don't need a counsellor,' Callanach repeated, hating the terseness of his own voice.

'Do you need friends?' Ava asked before retreating.

The hills that rolled towards Braemar were as stark as Callanach's mood. It was amazing how fast the landscape ran out of trees once the Cairngorms were in sight. There was the odd tumbledown house but farming here was plainly an exercise in futility. Signposts warned of the dangers of icy roads and steep inclines. Edinburgh wasn't that far as the crow flew but civilisation would feel a million miles away if your car broke down in the winter months. Salter tried once or twice to make conversation, carefully avoiding any mention of the scene with DI Turner. She might not have overheard anything but Callanach knew the body language must have been pretty clear. In the end, Salter gave up, put on the radio and left him to stare out of the window. The temperature was plummeting as they rose into the foothills. The paths could be treacherous in the daylight, never mind the half dark, but he had to achieve something to keep sane.

'Drive straight up to the crime scene,' Callanach said. 'Get as close as you can. Do you have a torch?'

'In the boot,' Salter said. 'We won't see much tonight though. Wouldn't it be better to go at first light?'

'We've two bodies,' Callanach replied. 'There'll be a third unless we catch him soon and the dots aren't joining up. Everything Professor Harris said made that clearer than ever.'

'But I thought you disagreed with the profile, sir.'

'I did, which is what made it so helpful. Leave the car here.'

They got out and walked. Salter was wearing hiking boots, the sensible choice. Callanach had slipped into his only pair of smart black shoes for the occasion, chosen to replicate the shiny pair Magee's abductor had been seen wearing. They had no tread at all and were a slippery nightmare.

'Look at that, Salter,' he said. 'Your hiking boots have left a deep trail.' She swung the flashlight round and it showed every detail of her footprints. He took the torch from her and tried to see his own imprints. Here and there the odd plant was downtrodden where he'd walked but the smooth, flat leather soles had left no distinguishing marks at all. The murderer might have come and gone without leaving any impression on the place.

'Do you think he foresaw that, or was it blind luck?' Salter asked.

'I think he's a man who makes his own luck,' Callanach answered, handing back the torch. At the bothy, Callanach took out a local map and set it at his feet. He opened a digital compass application on his phone and studied the surrounding geography.

'So the back of the hut is set into the rock. The view the hikers had is west of here. He can only have parked his car below and walked up. He'd never have pulled the body across the valley between us and where the hikers were,' he said.

'How did he move it, do you think?' Salter asked.

'Maybe something resembling a sledge to pull the body easily over the rough ground. I'm guessing anyone who saw him would have assumed it was sports gear or camping equipment. It's the view the hikers had that interests me. It's in the middle of a long-distance trail, right? One you'd have to set off from miles away to walk. The killer knew he wasn't going to be spotted dumping the body because no one would have set off in the dark. If they did, he couldn't have been seen anyway.'

'I agree,' Salter said, 'but I don't see how it helps.'

Callanach picked up the map, traced his finger to where a red cross was situated, checked his bearings with his phone and waved for Salter to follow him. A few minutes later, tripping where the torch light failed to show all the rocks, he stopped.

'This is where the dogs picked up the buried baseball bat. A few metres away was the tooth from which we got Elaine Buxton's DNA. This land is slightly higher than the bothy and so can't have been between the hut and his car.'

'So he ran up here to bury it, and disposing of the weapon in case he got stopped on the way down. Maybe he didn't even realise the tooth was still attached,' Salter said, kicking the dirt at her feet as she spoke.

'You don't believe that, do you? What's wrong with the theory?'

'Just doesn't feel right,' she said. 'I can't tell you exactly why.'

'For me, it's the hikers,' Callanach said. 'It's too perfect, too good. We've been looking in the wrong place for him, concentrating our efforts where he directed us, which was here. I think we should have been looking over there.' He lifted his arm to point across the valley into the darkness. 'Over here he was careful. He knew when he could come and not be seen, and he knew it because he'd walked the trail from where our two friendly hikers spotted the fire. He must have done to be sure he wouldn't be surprised any earlier.'

'What's the other side of the valley?' Salter asked.

'That's more helpful,' Callanach said. 'The hiking trail is limited. It starts at a camping ground to the north and ends up at a car park with an outdoor pursuits centre to the south. It's long and difficult and has no obvious branches off. That's why he chose this place. It's also why it makes no sense to run up here and drop the murder weapon. Imagine you've done that much research, been that careful, found the perfect place to burn the body, walked a path that starts miles away to reconnoitre, plotted daylight and average walking speeds. You've rigged up a way to get the body from the car to the bothy. You've even soaked the body in an accelerant so that it burns at an advanced speed because you know how much time you've got until the first witnesses might appear.'

'There's no way he panicked and threw the weapon into the dirt,' Salter said.

'With a tooth still attached? No,' Callanach finished. 'He knew it would be found.'

'What about the bit of scarf that escaped the fire under the rock?' Salter asked.

'I'm beyond thinking there are any mistakes, any coincidences.'

'So he's not chaotic like Professor Harris said. What else was he wrong about, then?'

Callanach hunched down and ran his hands through the dirt. 'Remorse. Harris is wrong about that. This man wanted us to find the bodies. He wanted us to know these women were dead. I'm not sure why. Maybe it's posturing, maybe it's about causing pain to the families or creating a sense of fear or panic. Perhaps he takes pleasure from the game. All I'm sure about, is that everything we've found so far is what he wanted us to find. The trolley at the base of the sea wall with the bag of clothes was the same. He knew the tide would wash it in. He left it like a gift for us.'

'Like presenting a trophy?' Salter asked.

'Token evidence,' Callanach said. 'The only way to find him is to ignore what he's leaving for us and to research his research. Come on. We've got some hiking to do tomorrow.'

Salter had done them proud with the bed and breakfast booking. Breakfast was a mountain of protein on a plate and it was the first time Callanach had ever tolerated drinking tea with milk. Their first stop of the morning was the satellite police hut in Braemar. As they crossed the bridge over the freezing and fast-flowing Clunie Water, Callanach stopped to look at the old stone well balanced precariously over the river. He wondered how long it would last, built to resemble a tiny tower, withstanding the bitter winds of the Highland winters. He ran a hand over the ageing stones and stared down into the dark waters below.

'You're in a thoughtful mood today, sir. Everything all right?'

'Detective Inspector Turner wasn't answering her phone last night,' he said quietly. He'd tried to call her three times over as many hours, wanting to make peace. 'Have you heard from anyone at the station?'

'No, I went straight to sleep. That's what happens when I stay somewhere without a television in my room. Probably good for me,' Salter said.

A car beeped as it passed them and Jonty Spurr's face could be seen momentarily.

'Let's go, Constable, we're late,' Callanach said.

The pathologist was parking his car when they reached him. He got out carrying a file and a bottle.

'DI Callanach, didn't think we'd be seeing you back here.

Shall we get started?' Spurr bellowed good-naturedly. They followed him into the police station where a few chairs had been dragged around a table. 'What was it you wanted?'

'The scarf,' Callanach said. 'What do we know about the blood on it?'

'Definitely Elaine Buxton's, no doubt about the DNA. The blood was very dry but then I'd expect that with the heat from the fire. The material only escaped because it was wedged so fast under the stone, as you know. There's a photo.' He took out an A4 sheet of photographic paper. On it was the image of a flowery scrap of material with frayed edges, a brownish stain marring one corner.

'The blood has a pretty regular shape around the edges.' Callanach ran a finger around the outside of the stain on the photo. 'What does that tell us?'

'That it didn't get there as a spatter. It's a single small pool of blood on the end of the scarf which was either dripped onto it from above or the scarf got dropped into a pool. It's not the sort of mark you'd see if it was being worn during a shooting, for example.'

Callanach nodded. 'And this, round the edge of the piece of scarf. The fibres are the same colour as the rest of the material,' Callanach noted.

'It's not burned, not at all,' Salter said. 'You were right.'

'Right about what?' Jonty asked, inspecting the photo more closely.

'That the scrap of material, just like the baseball bat and the tooth, were arranged for us to find. If it had got caught under the stone by accident and the remainder had burned, the edges would be blackened. These edges are frayed, probably cut. That means he chose a scrap of Elaine's scarf with her blood on it and planted it for us to find.'

'Clever boy,' Jonty Spurr said.

'He is,' Callanach agreed. 'Too bloody clever for us, apparently.'

'I wasn't talking about him,' Spurr said. 'Sometimes in my job I find that I look so closely at the details that the bigger picture becomes obscured. Was there anything else?'

'Only the teeth,' Callanach said.

'They're definitely Miss Buxton's. We cross-referenced her dental records. Teeth degrade slightly in high temperatures but they don't burn and the one near the baseball bat still had soft tissue firmly attached. DNA told us the same story.'

'Could you have the forensic odontologist take another look at it? Call it desperation, but anything you can find that we weren't looking for the first time, like scraps of food that might tell us what he fed her, chemicals on the tooth that suggest what environment she'd been kept in. Things that might have been overlooked when we were only trying to confirm the identity.'

'I'll get on to it,' Spurr said. 'Could you return the favour when you're back in Edinburgh?' He picked up a gleaming bottle of single malt whisky. 'Give this to Detective Inspector Turner from me.'

The label bore the name Lagavulin. It shone like dark gold honey and claimed to be sixteen years old. Callanach was tempted to open it right there.

'I didn't realise you knew Ava,' he said.

'I've not met her in person,' Spurr said, 'but I saw her speech at the televised press conference last night. All I know is she's got some guts and I admire her for expressing her point of view. Unfortunately I'd say she's headed for trouble with the brass. Thought the whisky might help.'

'What do you mean?' Callanach asked.

'You didn't see it?' Jonty raised his eyebrows. 'Your colleague has singlehandedly taken on the Roman Catholic Church. It'd be an understatement to say she didn't pull her punches.'

It took an hour of driving though unrelenting rain before they reached the camping ground. There was nothing permanent there, no toilet blocks or showers. It was unmanned, and only signposts warning campers not to leave litter or start fires in the National Park marked the area. Callanach and Salter began the hike without bemoaning the weather. It was a bad day for walking and they both knew it. There was no gain to be made from stating the obvious. It took them more than three hours to reach the valley across which the remains of the bothy were just visible in the far distance. Even then the pouring water splashed its own mist back, limiting visibility. Callanach checked the position against the witness statements, wondering at the dedication and single-mindedness of the murderer. He was driven, obsessive, almost as if it was the planning rather than the killings themselves that was his object.

'It's not about sex,' he said to the vast valley between them and the bothy.

'Beg your pardon, sir?' Salter asked, pausing between taking photos and making notes.

'Sexual crimes usually contain high levels of impulsiveness. Even when the victim is chosen for a particular reason, often the assailant gets to a point where they lose control.'

'Are you saying he doesn't rape them?' Salter asked.

'I'm not saying that, but I'd be surprised if it was his primary motivation. It's too long in the planning to be the usual type of rapist. Too clinical, too clean. Let's get back to the car. We've still got to drive across and check the other end of the trail. We won't get to Edinburgh until late as it is.'

The outdoor pursuits centre looked deserted. A mobile number on a note stuck inside the glass door looked old, but it rang when Callanach stood on a rock to get a signal.

'Yes?' a voice answered. Callanach introduced himself and

explained where he was. A couple of minutes later, the lock turned and a girl's head poked out.

Salter explained that they were investigating the fire at the bothy. The girl had the sensitivity not to say Elaine Buxton's name but it was obvious she knew.

'This is a long way away from there,' she commented. 'I'm not sure how I can help.'

'We're looking for a visitor who might have stood out, either because of his clothing or the way he was behaving. It would have been some time in the weeks leading up to the fire. He would have had binoculars, probably, and a camera.'

'Everyone who comes here has binoculars or a camera,' the girl said. 'When it's busy we have hundreds of people through each week. Sometimes there are coach parties who get dropped off then the coach picks them up at the other end of the pass.'

'This man would have been on his own, middle aged, maybe not dressed as you'd expect for hiking.' The look on the girl's face was enough for Callanach to know that she had something to tell them. 'What is it?'

'Hikers on their own,' she said, opening a cupboard and pulling out a log book. 'We keep a record, names and licence plates. It's unusual for people to walk this trail alone and if anything happens to them we may not be alerted for a long time. If a car isn't moved after forty-eight hours we check the log and give the police a name. It's a steep enough drop in places to attract suicides.'

Salter opened the log book and flicked through the previous few months.

'There aren't that many names,' she told Callanach. 'It won't take long to check them against the licence plates.'

'I hope you catch him,' the girl said. 'It usually feels so safe and peaceful here. It's ruined it a little bit.'

Salter smiled at her. For the first time since the investigation had started, Callanach saw something other than worry on his constable's face. 'We will,' DC Salter said. 'Soon.'

In the car they set the SatNav for Edinburgh. Salter drove as Callanach phoned in the names that predated Elaine Buxton's death, going back six months.

'At last, some real progress. You were right about following the research rather than the bodies. You'll be a bit more popular with DS Lively, at least, sir.'

'The murderer will have used a false name,' Callanach said. 'It's not going to be all that easy. Let's not get ahead of ourselves.'

He switched on the radio and scrolled through until it picked up a news channel. The baby death case would be headline news, especially if the details of St Gerard Majella school had got out. He'd not even had a chance to pick up a newspaper. Callanach glanced at the bottle of single malt he was ferrying back to Ava. Her failure to answer his calls last night was a bad sign. Sure enough, the media was reporting the offences in as much detail as allowed, given that the girls were minors. He turned up the volume when the reporter mentioned the Church.

'No representative from the Roman Catholic Church has been available for comment in person today,' the news announcer informed them, 'but a written statement has been released by the Vatican condemning remarks made by Detective Inspector Ava Turner at a press conference yesterday evening.' There was a momentary buzzing while a tape recording cut in, then Ava's voice came through so clearly she might have been in the car with them.

'It is beyond comprehension in this day and age, that any religion should force its doctrine upon children and deny them access to proper, balanced medical advice and care by professionals not tainted with pre-existing biases. What happened to these girls, being imprisoned at their parents' behest in a school

224

with the sole purpose of preventing them from exercising choice about their pregnancies, amounts to torture. The Roman Catholic Church should answer for this at the highest level. We're not living in the dark ages. What was happening at St Gerard Majella school was no more godly than the Inquisition burning women accused of witchcraft.'

The presenter's voice cut Ava short. 'The police have revealed that one nun has been charged with assault and that another male is being interviewed in relation to a suspected rape. Three girls are also helping police with their enquiries.' Callanach clicked the radio off and sighed.

'DI Turner is amazing,' Salter cooed. 'I'd never have had the guts to say something like that to the press.'

'She's going to pay for it,' Callanach said.

'But she was right,' Salter protested. 'How can she be in trouble for telling the truth?'

'Being right isn't always enough,' answered Callanach. 'You have to maintain the appearance of having no personal views. Take me straight to the station, Salter. I need to catch up on what's happened.'

Salter drove like a demon and they hit no traffic. Two hours later they were at Edinburgh's outskirts and they already had confirmation that half the names in the log book matched their registration numbers. DS Lively had texted to say he was personally overseeing the checks and would stay at the station all night to finish the job.

Ava was behind closed doors with DCI Begbie when Callanach arrived. Not prepared to wait for an invitation to join the party, and in no mood to be silenced, Callanach stormed straight in.

'Chief,' Callanach said before the door had even swung shut. 'You weren't there, you didn't see what we saw. Everything DI Turner said at the press conference was fair comment.'

'Welcome back, Callanach,' the Chief said, hands on hips, teeth clenched. 'I don't recall requesting your attendance at this meeting.'

'It's eleven o'clock at night,' he replied, 'so it doesn't seem to be a formal meeting, especially as Ava doesn't have a representative with her.'

'Don't quote disciplinary procedures at me, Detective Inspector. I've been round this particular block a few more times than you,' Begbie shouted.

'It's all right, Luc, I can look out for myself,' Ava said.

'I'm looking out for you, too, in case you'd forgotten. I've got half the Roman Catholics in Scotland baying for blood. They're saying you overstepped your mandate,' the Chief blustered.

'So sack me,' Ava said. 'I'll even admit it, I was expressing my personal view. I ignored my training and my position. Can I go?' She looked exhausted and fed up. Callanach held the bottle out to her.

'What's that?' she asked.

'It's a gift from Jonty Spurr, the pathologist on the Elaine Buxton case. For every person you've offended there will be a dozen more who are pleased you spoke out.' Callanach forced his voice down a pitch. 'Sir, you can't let public pressure sway you. It was a well-executed case that will save who knows how many more girls from the same torment. DI Turner deserves a promotion, not a reprimand.'

'I've got to do something,' Begbie sighed, 'or I won't be able to protect you, Ava. It'll end up going over my head. The letter in the *Herald* this morning was nothing short of a religious call to arms, raising issues about falling police standards and prejudices. I'm sorry, but I need you to accept a fourteen-day suspension during which I can conduct an official investigation and draw up a report.'

'And what good will that do?' Callanach yelled, knowing he was out of line but too enraged to stop.

The Chief got to his feet. 'It'll give everyone some breathing space, let things cool down. And it means I'll have followed procedure so that hopefully, when I find DI Turner handled the investigation in an irreproachable manner without victimising the Roman Catholic Church, the story will be about the abuse carried out at the school and not about us,' he said, punctuating his final three words by slamming the tip of his forefinger down on the desk.

'What about Ava's professional record . . .' Callanach was raising his voice.

'Leave it, Luc,' Ava said. 'The Chief has no choice.'

'The Catholic Church is kicking up to take the focus off themselves,' Callanach continued.

'So I should have seen it coming and not handed them my head on a plate. My mother always said I was my own worst enemy. Can't believe I finally proved her right.'

'And another thing,' Begbie interrupted them. 'The department received a package today addressed only to "The Detective Inspector". It was a bottle of Louis Roederer Cristal champagne which I'm sure I haven't pronounced correctly nor will I ever be able to afford. Apparently it was delivered by hand, signed in under the name Joe Smith, by someone wearing a hoodie and sunglasses. The note inside said, "What is life without pleasure?" although the sender neglected to leave their name. That little caper wasted an hour of my time having it checked out as a security risk, so whichever one of you is conducting your love life through my department, I'd be grateful if you'd tell your secret admirer where to get off.'

'Same as the roses,' Callanach muttered. 'I said you should have reported it.'

'Enough already,' Ava whispered. 'All right, Chief. Point taken. See you in a couple of weeks.'

She pulled Callanach away, shutting Begbie's door quietly and regrouping in Callanach's office.

'You should have told him,' Callanach said once they were out of earshot.

'You don't think my life just got complicated enough already?' she replied.

'One anonymous gift might have been a joke, two is harassment. And what if they're from the same person who sent the death threat?'

'Not exactly the same modus operandi, is it, or were you sick that day at Detective School? Look, I'm tired and my day is not yet over, so could you save the lecture for a more opportune moment?'

'Do you want me to drive you home?' he asked.

'Actually I need your help. I've been stuck here dealing with this, but Natasha phoned earlier really shaken up. She thinks someone's been in her house. I promised I'd call round and take a look. Given that I'm suspended I can go as a friend but if any action's required, I'm useless. Would you come?'

'Only if you bring the single malt,' he said.

Chapter Twenty-Seven

Natasha met them at her front door looking worried. Not for herself, Callanach thought. She was bright and worldly enough to know that her best friend was facing a furore.

'Come in,' Natasha said. 'Luc, good to see you again.' She caught his eyes. Was Ava all right, she was silently asking. Callanach gave a small shake of his head. 'You two didn't need to come rushing over this evening, you know. It's really nothing that dramatic. Let me get you both a drink.'

'We've come prepared,' Ava said, holding up the Lagavulin. 'Sorry I couldn't get here any earlier. What's happened?'

Natasha handed round heavy crystal tumblers. 'Nothing that can't be fixed with single malt,' she joked. 'You'll think I'm being paranoid. Nothing's broken and I can't see that anything's gone but the perfume bottles in my bathroom have been moved. A couple of my drawers weren't quite shut and I'd swear I left them closed. I had a pile of paperwork on my desk that's out of order. And one of my pillows is slightly indented. I don't want you to think I'm some sort of freak but I always make my bed and I have a way of doing it.'

'Was your alarm not on?' Callanach asked.

'I don't have one,' Natasha said. 'It kept going off and I had to leave lectures a couple of times in the middle of the day to reset it. In the end I disconnected it. There's no sign of a break-in. Either I've been burgled by a ghost or I'm going crazy.'

There was nothing to see as far as either Callanach or Ava were concerned, but Natasha's house was sufficiently well-ordered that it was easy to understand how she'd noticed things out of place. Callanach checked the doors and windows for signs of tampering but found none.

'Could I have some ice? This is a little stronger than I was expecting,' Callanach said, swirling the liquid around his glass.

'I thought you were half Scottish,' Natasha teased. 'Apparently the French part of you needs to toughen up!' She opened the ice box at the top of the fridge and stuck her hand in to retrieve an ice tray. What she pulled out was a semi frozen, red mass.

'What the hell is that?' she screamed, throwing it onto the kitchen tiles. It landed with a wet thump, fragments of red ice splattering around it. Ava knelt on the floor and poked it with a fork.

'It's a heart, way too large to be human, thankfully. Maybe from a cow or a horse,' Ava said. 'That's why nothing was taken. Whoever came here was leaving you a message.'

'A former partner with a grudge?' Callanach asked. 'Have you had any bad breakups with anyone who might still have a key?'

'I'm single,' Natasha said. 'Almost every relationship I've had has ended badly, or they wouldn't have ended. As for keys, there are probably a couple of women who still have one.' She was fighting back tears and trying not to let her shaking hands show as she cleared up the bloody mess on the floor. Ava took over from her, sitting Natasha down at the table. 'I can't believe anyone would go so far as to come into my house. It's disgusting. And why leave that in my freezer?'

'Write down the name of anyone who might have a key and I'll ask DC Tripp to follow it up. Tonight, you should stay elsewhere,' Callanach told her.

'No,' Natasha said. 'Ava got a death threat and she didn't run away.'

'You don't suppose they're linked? You've been friends a long time. Is there anyone who might be jealous of your relationship?' Callanach asked.

Ava stared thoughtfully at the heart as she scooped it into a bag to go to the lab.

'I don't see who fits that bill. Our paths don't cross socially unless we're out for a drink and Natasha rarely lets me meet any of her girlfriends.'

'It's a bizarre coincidence though,' Callanach said. 'I'll have to make this official to get forensic testing authorised and I'll need you to give a statement in the morning, Natasha.'

'You didn't say we,' Natasha noticed. 'Are you not going to be dealing with this, Ava?'

'I'm currently suspended from duty,' Ava said. 'Could be worse. Two weeks' fully paid leave is a fair trade for having my professional judgment questioned.'

'Oh honey, I'm sorry,' Natasha hugged her. 'And now I've dragged you into this. It's the last thing you need.'

'I'd rather be suspended than have someone leave that in my house. Are you sure you'll be all right tonight?' Ava asked.

'I've got chains on both doors and I'll lock all the windows. Don't worry about me. It was just a shock, that's all.'

'I'm reporting it now,' Callanach said. 'Patrol cars will go by regularly to check on you. Call me if you're worried. And I'd better get you out of here before the first officer arrives,' he said to Ava. 'Probably not a great idea to be found in the middle of a crime scene within one hour of your suspension.'

Callanach had thought he was tired, but by the time they

arrived at Ava's he knew sleep was going to be evasive and it was obvious she felt the same.

'Cup of tea?' she asked. 'Or instant coffee? Just don't come in expecting anything freshly ground.'

'I wouldn't dream of it,' he replied. 'It would ruin my bohemian, laissez-faire impression of you.'

Ava's house was somewhere between chaotic and well lived in. Most of the furniture looked antique but used and loved, rather than polished and posed. The furnishings were all about comfort and warmth. Callanach poked through collections of films and music while she washed mugs in the kitchen.

'There's no dining table,' he shouted. 'Where do you eat?'

'At my desk. Or standing up if I'm busy. Usually on the floor in front of the TV if it's late. Here you go. Decaff, I'm afraid. Can you cope?'

'Next time I'll bring my own.'

'If you're going to be like that, there won't be a next time.' She landed in an armchair and closed her eyes. 'Well, that was quite a day. Thanks for trying to stick up for me with Begbie. But he's right. A suspension is the only option to make this go away.'

'Not great for your career, though.'

'These things happen, and careers can be rebuilt. Look at you. You never did tell me what made you leave Interpol, so go on, I could do with listening to someone else's disaster story. Make me feel better about mine, if you don't mind, that is.'

Callanach considered it. It wasn't a tale he was comfortable telling. Then again, the rumours were undoubtedly already flying. Tactically it might prove helpful to have someone hear his side of it, and unburdening himself after so long might be exactly what he needed to avoid another mess like the one at Strathallan airfield. He hadn't talked to Ava about the skydiving incident yet, and she hadn't pursued the subject. It would be a while before he could deal with that one.

'It's the usual story,' he said. 'There was a woman involved.'

Astrid Borde was eye-catching. She had long auburn hair, sun-bleached at the ends, sweeping eyelashes, high cheek bones and the sort of figure men would pay good money to stare at. He'd been aware of her before a colleague had set them up, but had never spoken to her.

'My then best friend at Interpol arranged a date,' he told Ava. 'Jean-Paul would do almost anything for food and Astrid had offered to stock his freezer with enough meals to last him a month if he talked me into it. I didn't know that when I agreed to go out with her, unfortunately. It might have been enough to ring alarm bells even at that early stage. As it was, I was single, not too busy and saw no reason why I shouldn't.'

'Wasn't there a policy about dating fellow agents?' Ava asked as she sipped her tea and dragged a throw over her legs.

'She was a civilian working in the finance department. There was no conflict, it couldn't have caused problems in the field, so the rules didn't apply. Jean-Paul gave me her mobile number and I put it in my pocket, thinking I might call her in a week or two. The next day he asked why I hadn't phoned her that night, said she'd been waiting for me to call and was upset that I'd failed to do so.'

'You didn't know anything else about her? Not even by reputation?'

'Nothing at all,' he said, 'but my friend was getting hassle and all I had to do was make a call. I suppose I was a bit irritated but not so much that I pulled out. Anyway, I made the arrangements that evening, booked a restaurant. I was going to meet her there, keep it casual but she wanted me to pick her up, do everything formally.'

He recalled that phone call almost word for word, or perhaps he'd reconstructed it in his mind too many times wishing he'd seen the trouble that was coming. Astrid had a great voice, low and husky. If he was honest, that was the reason he hadn't made his excuses straight away. He knew she was going to be a bit of a princess – he'd dated enough models to know the type. There was going to be no taking it easy, no quick drink to see if they liked one another.

'She was obviously keen, a bit nervous and giggly, but I ignored it,' Callanach told Ava. 'Ironically, the idiot I used to be would never have found himself in so much trouble. Astrid Borde wouldn't have got past that first telephone conversation after requesting that I wear smart clothes.'

Ava choked. 'She didn't!'

'Absolutely, she did,' he said, smiling ruefully at Ava's astonishment.

He'd picked Astrid up as directed at seven o'clock, which was a bit early for him but she'd wanted to go for a drink before dinner. In his mind she would always be wearing the low–cut, shimmering charcoal dress that had hugged her body to within a hair's breadth of indecency. The skirt stopped mid thigh but had an off-centre split revealing enough leg that Callanach caught himself glancing at it as she walked. The dress was worn to get his attention and he had to admit that it did.

'We had champagne at a bar first and she wasn't talking much so I chatted about work, stupid things Jean-Paul and I had been up to, then I made some comment about football. I wasn't even that interested in sport but she wasn't responding to my conversation so I was just filling air space. That was when I knew for sure it was going to be a first and last date.'

'What did she do?' Ava asked.

'She said, "We won't be talking about sport. It doesn't interest me." You know those moments in your life when you look back and think, if only I'd done something different right then, it would have changed everything? For months I woke up in the night dreaming I'd walked away that minute, feigned illness, made her get a taxi home.'

'But you didn't,' Ava said.

'No, I didn't. I tried to be nice, gave her the benefit of the doubt, even thought that perhaps I'd misheard her. In my mind I just had to finish the evening, drop her home, never see her again. It seemed more effort to react than to let it go.'

He and Astrid had gone from the bar to the restaurant, the one she'd insisted they go to. It was too staid for Callanach's taste, suited and tied, with a waiter whose default facial expression was disdain, and decor designed to warn you how high the bill was going to be. Astrid had loved it.

'So what happened?' Ava asked.

'Astrid was like a child, petulant and rude one moment, tossing her hair and demanding attention the next. I honestly didn't know how to act. The waiters were looking at me as if I should have done something about her behaviour. At one point I was so embarrassed that I suggested we should talk more quietly and it made her worse. After that, I sat back and watched. She ordered fish then told me she hated it, made a point about tasting the wine, approved it, then halfway through the glass she told the waiter she'd never been served anything so revolting, and was rubbing her feet in my crotch by dessert.'

Callanach remembered listening to Astrid's whining at dinner and wishing for silence. It had seemed that she could eat without pausing once in conversation. He'd looked at his watch every few minutes during that meal, trying to do it under the table so she didn't notice, but eventually even she had taken the hint.

'Are you keen to get out of here?' Astrid had asked.

'I'm sorry. I hadn't meant to be rude, it's just that I need to review some files and I was hoping to look at them tonight. Please don't rush your clafoutis,' he'd said.

'I was going to leave it anyway.' She'd thrown down her spoon, letting it clatter in the china bowl amidst the mess of black cherries, making every other diner in the place stare. Callanach hadn't had to ask for the bill. The head waiter had brought it immediately with a look of pure relief. Callanach had left cash on the table with a generous tip, his only thought how quickly he could get out of there.

By the time they were on the street, she was asking for more champagne and complaining about being rushed. That was when he'd made the mistake that had changed everything.

'I didn't know how else to shut her up and get her home quickly, so I kissed her. It was just a few seconds, nothing intimate, just enough to take her breath away and make her do what I wanted, which was to get in my car without a fuss so I could drop her home and run.'

'You don't have to defend yourself,' Ava said. 'If I was going to judge you, I'd have done it already.'

'I'm defending myself against my own judgment as much as yours. Some part of me still thinks it was my own bloody fault, you know? That I led her on.'

'If I had a pound for every victim I'd heard say that . . .' Ava said. 'What happened when you got her home?'

'It started before then, in the car. Kissing her was the worst thing I could have done and I knew it as soon as I touched her. Astrid started acting drunk. She was all over the place, took off her seat belt while I was driving and tried to climb into my lap. By the time we reached her apartment she was saying she couldn't walk and that I would have to carry her up.'

Astrid's dress had ridden so high up her thighs in the car that he could see her underwear. If he'd been intrigued at the start of the evening, he was sickened by the end of it. Her

236

drunkenness had been an act and, with hindsight, he wondered if she'd seen through his sudden affection towards her. He'd had to half-lift, half-drag Astrid to her front door where he'd tried to make the same excuse about work until she'd literally collapsed in her doorway and started to cry. Desperate to avoid her neighbours coming out to gawp at the spectacle, he'd taken her keys, opened the door and carried her to a sofa.

'I've got to go,' he'd said, as she'd thrown her stilettos across the room.

'You don't have to go, you're lying,' she'd said, sobering up fast, the loudness gone from her voice and the low sexiness returned. 'You can't tell me you don't want me. I saw how you were looking at me earlier.' She'd twisted an arm behind her and unzipped her dress.

'This isn't going to happen,' he'd said, ignoring the clothes that were flying towards him and making his way back to the door.

'Astrid threw herself at me in the most vulgar way imaginable and I had to push her off,' Callanach told Ava. 'I was as gentle as I could be but she wouldn't let me go.'

Astrid had been completely naked by that point. Callanach remembered his disgust when she'd thrown herself against his back, rubbing her bare body against him, touching herself, trying to pull his clothes off. Eventually he'd had no choice but to use force to extricate himself. He'd heard the thud as she'd hit the wooden floor hard, looked back to make sure she wasn't hurt, then went to leave.

'Just before I got her front door open, Astrid attacked me, scratching my neck with her nails,' Callanach recalled. 'One of her neighbours came out to see what the noise was about. They saw me wiping the blood off my neck and heard me swearing.'

By the time he'd left, Astrid had been hysterical, calling him every name imaginable and sobbing. A minute later he'd been back in his car, cursing Jean-Paul for getting him in so much shit and driving home, desperate for a shower to get rid of the smell of her.

Ava leaned forward, head on hands, looking at his neck as if the wound would magically reappear.

'So what happened after that?' she asked.

'Nothing. I went to work the next day, a couple of people asked about the neck and I said I'd scratched it at the gym. I told Jean-Paul she'd been a pain but no more than that. Whatever nightmare she'd been, I wasn't going to jeopardise her job. As far as I was concerned it was over and I'm not the sort to spread rumours, so I left it at that. Two days later I was on my way to Jamaica following a lead, and the rest you know.'

'So what were you charged with?' Ava asked.

'I'm sure you've already figured that out,' Callanach said.

Ava nodded.

Chapter Twenty-Eight

Ava had apologised for prying into his past and been generously reassuring in response to his disclosures. Lyon and his lost life was a subject he tried not to think about, but the discussion with Ava had brought it all back and he gave in to the memories as he lay restless in bed. He thought about the delicatessen, hidden away in the back streets, which had sold the best meats and cheeses he'd ever tasted. He could still feel the heat of the long, hot summers and see the sun as it glinted off the imposing square glass fortress that was Interpol. After leaving France, Callanach had spent six months in Fife doing expedited training in Scottish criminal law and police procedure, before making his way to Edinburgh. By then, he'd hoped he might get a better sense of where he'd come from, but the truth was that he still felt like a cultural intruder. His father had loved Scotland with a passion. Callanach understood why, but the fact of his forced migration was still too raw for him to make a new country his home, even if he had been born there. Edinburgh was beautiful, but he longed for evenings warm enough to eat outside without the persistent rain.

DS Lively was on the phone before six in the morning, when Callanach had just fallen asleep.

'There was a name on the list, J. Locke, but the car's licence plate was last registered to a Mrs Francesca Fairbanks in Livingston. Apparently the car was written off after an accident a couple of years ago. Her husband took it to a scrap yard in Falkirk.'

'Can the husband give us more details?' Callanach asked.

'He might have done if he hadn't passed away six months ago,' Lively said. Callanach could hear the frustration in his voice.

'Get a team to visit every scrap yard in the Falkirk area. I'll be at the station within the hour.'

'And Professor Harris wants another briefing so you can bring him up to date on what you found in Braemar. Shall I tell him you're on your way?' Lively asked.

'Get straight out to Falkirk, Sergeant. I'll call Harris myself.' The last thing Callanach wanted was to lose more hours explaining himself to a man who was determined not to deviate from his own assumptions. The day was going to be busy enough that avoiding the profiler shouldn't prove too difficult.

Naturally, Professor Harris was waiting in his office when he arrived at work. Of course, Callanach thought. Why had he ever thought that Lively would follow orders? Harris had taken it upon himself to arrange for the Chief to join them.

'The team has used the profile I gave them to identify three suspects in the local area. They will each be brought in for questioning today. I should like to sit in on the interviews, if you don't mind, Detective Inspector. I'll have an accurate idea of whether or not they're telling the truth.' Harris stroked his beard as he talked. It was a habit Callanach particularly disliked.

'What makes you believe that any of the men you've iden-tified are linked to the murders?' Callanach asked.

'They all have previous convictions for violent sexual assaults. I've studied their files. In my view they all showed the potential

240

for escalating sexual violence with some psychopathic tendencies. Each lives close enough to make commission of the crimes feasible.'

'And what if you're wrong about the sexual motive for the crimes?' Callanach asked. 'You have nothing other than a history you're assuming matches the killer's psyche to connect any of these men to the offences.'

'They're also in the correct age bracket, Scottish accent, they all drive and know the city well. Statistics show that most abducted women are sexually molested, Inspector, so I'm not sure why you're so doubtful about it.' Harris was unflustered. Callanach knew he needed more than gut instinct to formulate a good argument and opted for the path of least resistance and least wasted time.

'*D'accord*,' murmured Callanach, reverting to French in his frustration. 'Fine. Bring them in. Hold them until DS Lively returns from Falkirk then you can sit in on the interviews. Check their alibis, if they have any, and contact their probation officers. Assess what current threat any of them poses. But no one talks to the press or makes any move publicly without my consent. If we arrest the wrong man, we might push the killer into proving he's still out there.'

'You're assuming I will accuse the wrong man, Detective Inspector,' Harris said, terse for the first time.

'Perhaps I am,' he said. 'Chief, there is another matter we need to discuss and I have little time.' The professor said goodbye to DCI Begbie but didn't bother with Callanach, not that he cared.

'Speaking of the press,' Begbie said, 'I'm going to need you this morning. You assisted with the baby deaths case. I have to give a statement explaining that Ava has been suspended to investigate the complaint about her comments. I'd like you to end it with a summary of the case as it stands today.'

'Which is?' Callanach asked.

'Sarah Butler's priest has been charged with rape but isn't talking. An undisclosed source is funding the best legal representation possible and those lawyers already have their hooks into the case. DNA evidence will prove if the girl's right though and she's below the age of consent. It'll take a couple of days to process everything. Rebecca Finlan is too distressed to be coherent. That will take more time. Sister Ernestine has been charged with twelve counts of assault but there are many more pending.'

'And the charges against the girls themselves?' Callanach asked.

'We had no choice but to charge the two whose babies died with manslaughter. We're anticipating that they'll both plead guilty with very substantial mitigation and receive non-custodial sentences. Hopefully, they'll have access to the support they need to rebuild their lives.'

'Poor kids,' Callanach said.

'I won't disagree with you, there are no winners here. How's Ava?' the Chief asked.

'Her best friend had a break-in yesterday. I've requested a uniformed team to investigate and I'll oversee.'

'It can't distract you from the Buxton and Magee cases,' the Chief warned, 'and keep Ava out of it. She mustn't do anything at all while we're cleaning up this public relations disaster.'

'I'll pass that on.'

'You've got to work with Professor Harris, Callanach. The Church is funding his consultancy for us to get results. I don't need conflict within your team and I can't run the risk of having to suspend another one of my detective inspectors, so play nice. Press room in half an hour.'

Callanach's phone rang from a number he didn't recognise. He almost switched it off, then thought better of it.

'Luc, sorry to bother you, only there's something new. I'm parked at the front of the station.' Natasha's voice sounded wobbly. He wondered how long she'd struggled with phoning him. She wasn't the sort of person to make a scene.

'I'll be down immediately,' he said, putting on his coat against the wind.

She flashed her headlights and pushed open the door as he got nearer. Dark circles underlined her eyes. She handed him an envelope and he put it on his lap.

'You haven't slept?' he asked.

'I look that bad? Thanks for the reassurance. I found these pushed under my back door when I went down this morning. They were loose, just scattered across the floor.'

Callanach opened the envelope and withdrew several stringy pieces of brightly coloured paper. Some were folded and crumpled. Horribly aware he was probably destroying vital trace evidence, he dropped them onto his lap before he ruined any fingerprints.

'Do you know what they're from?' Callanach asked.

'It's a photo of me at a charity fundraiser that was featured in *Scotland on Sunday*. There are six letter shapes cut from the picture, as if someone's put a stencil over the top.'

Callanach shifted the paper around with a nail. He could see an O, an N, a G and an M. 'What arc these two?' he asked of the crumpled pieces.

'C and I,' she said.

'Does that mean anything to you? Is it a personal reference?'

'At first I wasn't sure if it was an M or a W, and if the I was a 1 or an L. Then I worked it out.' Natasha reached over and took the letters from his lap. Callanach began to protest. 'Don't bother,' she said. 'I've had my fingers all over them for the last hour.' She rearranged them on top of the envelope to form a single word.

'COMING,' Callanach read. 'You need to make another statement. No arguments.'

Callanach raced to the press conference and settled himself moments before the Chief started talking. Immediately, cameras began flashing and the police media liaison officer asked the photographers to stop during filming. The Chief was sombre and to the point. Lights shone in their eyes as camera operators adjusted tripods and tussled for the optimal viewpoint. Then the focus shifted to him. Callanach ran one hand through his hair nervously. For a second, he caught a glimpse of his own face on a camera monitor and realised how tired he appeared. Natasha must have thought he had some nerve, commenting on her exhaustion. He forced his chin up, stared into the black lens transporting his image across the country and imagined Ava at home watching what should have been her moment.

He was as brief as he could be, delivering the update with clinical precision, sticking to the facts. At the end he referred back to the press liaison officer who said the Chief would take questions but limiting it to five minutes. Then the onslaught began.

'Will you be bringing in external investigators to process the complaint against DI Turner?'

'Has the Vatican been in contact regarding the criminal conduct of the school?'

'What's happening to the third girl whose baby survived?'

'Were the police investigating other possible charges against St Gerard Majella school?'

The Chief answered those he could, then stood to indicate time was up.

'Has DI Callanach still not made any progress in the Buxton and Magee cases? And if not, why has he not been replaced?'

The room went quiet. It was an ambush. The reporter who had shouted the question moved forward, microphone pointed at DCI Begbie's face. If the Chief said nothing, he was as good as hanging his detective inspector out to dry. If he made an excuse, it would look weak and defensive. Callanach stepped up to save Begbie from making the decision.

'There is progress, but you'll understand we cannot report every new piece of evidence that's uncovered. We urge you to remain calm and understand that finding Elaine Buxton and Jayne Magee's killer is our priority. A profiler is assisting the investigative team. You're right to have questions about that case, but out of respect for the victims we've been discussing today, I would ask that you direct enquiries through the press office. Thank you.'

The room exploded into bursts of nerve-frazzling light as the photographers grabbed the moment. Every journalist in the room had another question. There was too much noise, people pushing him in every direction, too much light in his eyes. Callanach tried to take a breath and found that he couldn't. He needed food and sleep. Most of all, he needed to be out of that room. Shoving his way through, he tried to cover the rising sense of panic at how ill he was feeling.

Ava was on the other end of his mobile before he could reach his office.

'Are you all right?' she asked. 'You did fine but you looked completely washed out.'

'I'm fine,' Callanach said. 'Better than Natasha, anyway.' He regretted the words as soon as they were out of his mouth. The less Ava knew, the better.

'Tell me,' she said.

'I can't. The Chief said you had to keep out of it and for once I agree. I'd feel better if she was staying away from her house though.'

'I tried to persuade her to stay at mine last night but she was adamant,' Ava said.

'No, she can't stay at yours because of the suspension. And if this is the same person who threatened you, then staying together might be the worst-case scenario. What about her family?'

'No, they cut contact when she came out. She's more stubborn than me, Luc, you won't have much luck. I'll phone her, see what I can do.'

'I can't stop you calling her, but nothing more.' Callanach finally reached a coffee machine and thrust coins into it. It didn't matter how bad it tasted. Only caffeine could save him.

'Luc, you still there?'

'Yes,' he said. 'Just getting a coffee.'

'Do you think it could be your murderer contacting Natasha? Only she fits the victim type. Single female, thirties, living alone, top of her profession. I just can't stand the thought that maybe . . .' Ava didn't finish. She didn't have to.

'Natasha's here now giving a statement,' Callanach said. 'And it's very different. The break-in, the heart in the freezer, letters under the door today. There was nothing like that in the other cases. I have to go, Ava, but I give you my word, I will protect her.'

Chapter Twenty-Nine

Professor Forge had called in sick, he'd been told when he went to the departmental reception. King had raised his eyebrows to display the right amount of surprise, asked what was wrong with her, been told predictably that they didn't know and it wasn't appropriate to ask. He'd said he hoped she would be better tomorrow and left them to their nail filing and gossip about clothes and celebrities. He retreated to his room. Natasha had been so predictable. For such an intellectually gifted woman it was almost a disappointment. To be scared by such small events showed her vulnerabilities.

As for the letters under the door, he'd been embarrassed to stoop to such amateurish soap-opera tactics but it had been easy and quick. The heart had been more dramatic, if she'd even found it yet. He'd spent an unsettled night considering how his visit to Natasha's house had altered his perception of her. In his head, her freezer was to have been empty except for a tray of ice, maybe some peas and a trout left too long at the back. There was to have been dry cleaning hanging from a doorway, recently delivered fresh to her door. A shopping order from a suitably high-class supermarket would have been imminent, with plenty of pre-prepared healthy salads, some mussels, smoked salmon, a few bottles of champagne and the harder to obtain wines. Instead he'd found a slow cooker with something resembling lamb stew bubbling away inside. The fridge was full, much of its contents home-cooked meals waiting to be reheated. Professor Forge, she of the endlessly chic clothes, tight deadlines and an unmatchable passion for hard work was a regular little homemaker, it appeared. His disappointment didn't end in the kitchen.

King thought about her bed. It had been neatly made, scatter cushions everywhere arranged just so, comfortable and clean but overwhelmingly cosy. He'd imagined the most modern of furnishings, a black and white colour scheme perhaps, minimalistic. Instead, her floral pillow had smelled of her most regularly worn perfume. King had allowed himself the luxury of pushing his face into it for a few seconds, spreading his body out across the covers as if he could soak her up. He'd watched himself in her mirror and imagined her in front of him, breathing on her neck as she put on her earrings. Enrapt, he'd spent more time there than he should have, wondering how his hands would feel around her throat, imagining her begging him to stop as he squeezed. She would have been sorry then, apologised for her lack of attention, seen the power he commanded first hand. Her breath would shorten, she would gasp, her eyes would flutter before starting to close. As if she were his lover. As if she welcomed it.

King had had to drag himself away. If he didn't remain in control of his senses he knew he'd make a mistake, leave identifiable evidence. King had made himself think of the consequences. It was not an option to be so submerged in her that he failed in his purpose. He'd entered her home to make her feel insecure. She needed to fear the unknown him. Perhaps this new her he'd found, if disappointing, was more likely to be afraid, the little lady who enjoyed her home comforts so much. Even if he preferred the old Natasha, the unreachable professional so icy he could imagine her melting beneath his touch, he knew so much more about her now and knowledge was unarguably power.

Preparing for another woman excited him. The room wasn't really suitable for three. He'd never intended to have so many there. The time was coming when he'd have to dispose of either Elaine or Jayne – a sad thought after he'd put so much time and effort into taking them – but it was thrilling, too. He hadn't wanted to admit that at first. There had been annoyance, frustration that they hadn't served their purpose as he'd wanted. Then there'd been the spark he'd tried to quell. In bed last night, he'd imagined choosing the one. It had made him feel like a god. No, not like a god, like God. He'd relived the hours spent removing Jayne's lower teeth, practising techniques learned from books and online, waiting for her to scream the way Elaine had. He'd strapped her arms and legs tightly, put down plastic sheeting so her bedding wasn't ruined and waited for the distress, knowing he'd expend as much energy calming her down as loosening the gums before chiselling and prising out each tooth. But she hadn't screamed. She'd accepted the anaesthetic injections with a grimace but without tears. There had been no hysterics. It was as if she was already dead inside.

With Elaine, he could feel her terror, see her pain, experience every emotion he wrought from her. Jayne gave him nothing. If at first he'd admired her self-control, it had become something closer to piety in his mind and he wasn't sure he liked it any more. Elaine had endowed him with unforeseen attributes. Authority. Stature. Command. But she was piteous, mewling and physically repugnant. It was an impossible decision. One which had the unfortunate side effect of making him hard when he thought about it. It wasn't just deciding who. There was the spectrum of possibilities concerning how. The last death had been clumsy and that was because it had been unplanned. Grace was always destined to die, of course, but not like that. Too much temper, not enough finesse. Perhaps he should let his next acquisition make all the choices. The thought made him shiver. She'd hate it but, then again, it would tame her.

King's to-do list was unenviable. He needed yet another vehicle and still had to find a suitable body double for his new guest. He couldn't risk returning to Glasgow's red light district. The memory of that pimp leaning into his car brought him out in a cold sweat. More research would be required, perhaps in Dundee.

An email alert popped up on his computer. Professor Forge may have been feigning sickness but it wasn't preventing her working from home. She wanted him to oversee the brochure printing for the next academic year. It was tedious work. He'd never understood why it wasn't left to the marketing department but Natasha liked input from every member of the department. She also wanted a staff meeting organised for two days' time. Not that she'd be attending, King thought. Natasha would be unavailable. The minutiae of her staff's comings and goings would be the last thing on her mind by then. Still, he had to go through the motions. There was one task left to ensure she'd be where he wanted her, in the right place at the right time. Slipping on transparent plastic gloves, he took an envelope from a plastic bag that had been tucked away in his briefcase.

He waited until lunchtime when the majority of students were clear of the building and remaining staff members were eating sandwiches at their desks, filled his arms with files and headed down the corridor towards Natasha's door. He was slow and deliberate. No one was around. He stuck the envelope to her door in one smooth move, tape positioned in advance, stripping the gloves off as he walked away. He just had to get through what remained of his working day and go home to his girls. There was much to do. Everything needed cleaning. King didn't want the guest suite to be a stinking mess before his prize possession arrived. It would create entirely the wrong impression.

Chapter Thirty

'I'm bringing in two scrap-yard owners for questioning,' Lively shouted down the phone, battling the industrial noise surrounding him. 'We'll hold them long enough that they'll think we've got something on them, give the uniforms a chance to have a good dig around at the yards and see what they can turn up. What time are you available?'

'I'm not. Another incident has taken over today and I need you with Harris to interview local sex offenders who fit his profile. I'll ask DC Tripp to question your scrap-yard owners, he's more than capable,' Callanach said as the squad car he was riding in pulled up to the pavement and parked.

'I don't see what can be more important than this. You're supposed to be leading this investigation and you're hardly around,' Lively bit back.

'Save it, Sergeant. I don't answer to you. Get on with your job and follow orders or I'll replace you.'

'When this is over,' Lively said, 'there'll be a complaint, and it'll be serious enough that not even your fuckin' bigwig pals from Interpol will be able to save you.'

The line went dead before Callanach could reply. The

constable who'd been pulled off traffic duty to drive him to the University was fiddling with her radio and doing her damnedest to pretend she hadn't overheard, but the expression on her face said it all. She was waiting for Callanach to explode. Instead, he sat back in his seat and drew long, slow breaths. He had to get through this, go back to the station, check what everyone was doing then make it home without punching anyone. That was all. Right then, it was enough.

One of the Philosophy Department's administrative staff had phoned Natasha to say that an envelope had been found stuck to her office door. The girl had removed it and dropped the contents on her desk, then called her colleagues over who'd helped unscramble the mysterious letters, moving them around until they'd made a word. The envelope and its contents were covered in fibres, fingerprints and assorted DNA. You couldn't blame them, Callanach thought. It was the natural thing to do and they'd had no reason to exercise caution. Natasha had decided she wanted to keep what was happening secret from her staff, so that it neither upset them nor caused unnecessary fuss. Unfortunately, that meant they hadn't been alerted to the possibility of contact from Natasha's stalker. Callanach sighed. He just couldn't seem to get it right at the moment.

In the office, the girl giving her statement was none the wiser as to the relevance of the letters scattered across her desk. An officer photographed them, then went off to take pictures of the door where they'd been stuck. Callanach retrieved the envelope from a bin, placing it and each letter carefully in an evidence bag and labelling it.

DS Salter was out locating two of Natasha's ex-girlfriends who might still have keys. Natasha, watched over by a uniformed officer, was at home compiling a list of anyone who might hold a grudge against her. A forensic team was working its way around her house checking for fingerprints, but it was a reach.

Callanach approached the officer coordinating the University crime scene. 'Speak to each staff member individually, see if anyone saw anything suspicious, anyone they didn't recognise in the building, and establish a time frame. I'd like to know when the envelope appeared on Professor Forge's door.'

The incident room was buzzing when he got back to the station.

'What's going on, Salter?' he shouted through a mass of bodies.

'One of the three Buxton/Magee suspects has been released. He was on a probation assessment during the relevant period and his alibi checked out immediately. Of the other two, one isn't talking and has lawyered up, the third has apparently made some admissions. Professor Harris is observing while DS Lively conducts the interview.'

'Get Harris out of there, this second,' Callanach said.

'But the Chief said . . .'

'I don't want to know. Just do it. And get me the file on the suspect who's with them now.'

Callanach made his way down to the interview suite, flicking through paperwork as he went, reading up on Rory Hand. At fifty-two years of age with previous convictions for rape and using threats to procure sexual activity with a person suffering a mental disorder, he wasn't someone you'd want to share a lifeboat with. Hand had served eight years for the rape and then, after five years trouble free, or at least without getting caught, he'd served another four.

In both cases he'd been working as a carer, the first time in someone's house, the second time under an assumed name in a care home. Callanach glanced through the glass in the interview room door. DS Lively and Harris were packing up their notes. There was only one other body in the room. Hand was red faced, an oily sheen of sweat across his skin, breathing faster than normal but he was a big man.

Harris was first out of the room. 'Well, Detective Inspector, we've a lot more work to do but I'd say this was a major breakthrough. And the sexual motivation was as I'd suspected.'

'How much did you give him?' Callanach asked.

'I'm not sure what you mean,' Harris said. 'DS Lively conducted an entirely professional interview. In my experience, offenders like these often want to be caught. The interview is their big moment. They fantasise about it. Their confession and the horror they cause by revealing the details of their crimes is the ultimate high.'

'He had no lawyer with him,' Callanach said.

'Hand was cautioned and urged to get representation,' Lively said. 'I know what I'm doing.'

'I want to see the tapes.' Callanach walked into the media control room. A technician rewound the video record of the interview and pointed at a monitor.

The usual introductions and legal necessities completed, Callanach saw Hand twitching slightly in his chair, fingers scratching at the surface of the desk, frowning as he was asked repeatedly if he wanted legal representation. He certainly couldn't argue that Lively hadn't done his job properly on that score. That was when Professor Harris had dramatically pulled a bundle of A4 photos from his lap and dropped them one by one in front of Hand.

'Elaine Buxton,' Lively had said. 'This is what was left of her.' The photos showed the charred bones in the dust of the bothy. Pictured in another were the baseball bat and tooth. Callanach studied Hand. His body had relaxed and Callanach could have sworn that Hand's pupils had dilated. 'And this is Jayne Magee,' Lively continued. More photos were placed before the suspect. 'Did you ever meet either of them?'

Hand rocked in his chair. His shoulders had relaxed out of their hunched position, the nerves were gone. Instead, there sat a man struggling to restrain the physical urge to reach out and touch the photographs.

'See how excited he becomes at the sight of his victims. I imagine it would have been too great a risk for him to photograph them himself, so when he's finally faced with the imagery he's tried so hard to reconstruct in his mind, he can't control his physical reaction.' Harris was triumphant, bordering on smug.

Callanach turned to the technician. 'Rewind it a minute please,' he said.

The video went back to the point when the photos were first put before Hand. Callanach stared at Hand's face as the images hit the desk. There was a slight frown as the suspect worked out what he was seeing, then Lively said the victim's name. Hand's eyes widened suddenly and sharply but only for a fraction of a second. His mouth formed a tiny 'o' and Callanach saw the intake of breath.

'He was surprised,' Callanach said. 'Genuinely surprised.'

'Well, he didn't think he was going to get caught. I've never yet met a suspect who says, "I've been waiting for you, I figured you'd be arresting me today." The whole point is to take them by surprise, or is that not how you did it in France, sir?' The title on the end of Lively's question was pure acid. The sergeant was so defensive that Callanach guessed Lively was equally worried about how easily the interview had produced results.

'These deaths have been all over the news. The papers have released every detail they could uncover. This suspect will be familiar with times and dates and places. If he gets gratification from this kind of thing, and it's fairly obvious from his state that he does, he'll have read every tabloid and watched every second of television coverage,' Callanach said to Lively. Harris stepped forward to insert himself into the conversation.

'I understand that it's hard to accept, but sometimes profiling gets these sorts of results. You'll not be the first investigating officer to have their nose put out of joint, but I assure you the whole team will get the credit for this arrest.'

'This is not about fucking credit. This is about you making assumptions then turning them into self-fulfilling prophecies. The man in there had no idea what he was about to be shown!' Callanach shouted.

'You're not qualified to decide that,' Harris came back at him.

'Maybe I'm not, but this is still my investigation. Lively, get back into interview. Ask him where he held and killed the women. I want locations. Get a team there and find me some tangible, evidential link. Then we'll talk.'

'I'm about to charge him. He's made a full confession,' Lively said but the bullishness was dissipating.

'You charge him and the investigation into other suspects is dead in the water. Is that what you want?' Callanach asked.

Lively was, for once, silent.

'Sergeant, the Reverend Jayne Magee's killer is sitting in that room. You and I have brought this case to a successful conclusion. Surely you're not going to allow yourself to be swayed at this point,' Harris said, his voice little more than a whisper.

Lively's hand crept towards his neck, stopping just below his collar. Underneath his shirt, Callanach suspected, was an item the sergeant shouldn't have been wearing on duty for safety reasons. Silver, he thought, small and plain. A crucifix Lively was so attached to that he couldn't bear to take it off, even at the risk of having it twisted around his neck in a brawl. Callanach knew then that he was fighting a losing battle.

'I'm going to get the Chief's authority to charge him. I've done everything by the book. The team will start gathering evidence.' Lively's voice was unusually quiet.

'Rory Hand just confessed to two murders without being presented with any evidence against him. That means he cannot continue killing. Serial killers crave their next kill, don't they, Professor Harris? It's why they work so hard not to get caught. This makes no sense,' Callanach said.

'You're neither a psychiatrist nor a psychologist, Inspector. The complexities of these men's brains are never singular in terms of motivation or behaviour.' Harris had one arm around the back of Lively's shoulders as if to shield the sergeant from any more persuasion. Lively looked as uncomfortable as Callanach had ever seen him.

'And they rarely evolve from rape in a care home, with victims who are specifically targeted for their reduced mental capacity, to kidnapping, torturing and killing high-profile women in one move,' Callanach replied.

'You can't be sure what he's been up to in the intervening period. It may be that he's been progressing slowly over a number of years.' Lively backed Harris up, but didn't seem to be taking any pleasure from it.

Callanach turned his back on them. Hand's identification and arrest had been neat, quick, simple and completely contrary to everything his years of experience had taught him to expect. The Chief would be under pressure to release a statement to the press, and if he didn't it would have leaked before the end of the day anyway. Rory Hand was undoubtedly scum. He was clearly getting off on the carnage in the photos. Callanach had not one ounce of pity for him. It beggared belief that anyone would admit to offences carrying a life sentence just for the notoriety that would come with the conviction. In addition, Hand would have to be given access to all the evidence – photographs, videos, autopsy reports, forensics, details of the women's lives. He was sick and the world would certainly be a better place with him behind bars. What worried Callanach was the possibility that the real murderer had just been gifted more time to kill again with the hunt called off. If, as he believed, arresting Hand was a mistake then it was going to be a costly one. Callanach left a message on the Chief's phone telling him exactly that.

Tripp was waiting in the incident room.

'What's happening with the scrap-yard owners?' Callanach barked.

'Not getting much. Does it matter? Word's out that a suspect has confessed.'

'And I've just won the lottery. One of those online competitions where I didn't buy a ticket but a nice man from Nigeria emailed to say I'm owed three million pounds.' Callanach stood with his hands on his hips. Tripp handed him a coffee and opened a file.

'The first scrap-yard owner wasn't bothered at all, so laid back he barely answered anything but it seemed genuine. Nothing to hide but not a particular fan of the police, if you know what I mean. The second has served time in three different prisons, all petty offences, handling stolen goods, burglary of commercial premises twenty years ago and benefits fraud. He was more interesting, slightly on edge, thinking before he answered every question. I got nothing from him but I'd say there's something he's not telling us.'

'Get some ammunition, anything he's doing wrong even if it's health and safety. Find an excuse to shut down his yard while we investigate. Every offence he's committed was motivated by money so that's how you'll get him talking. Move fast and under the radar. There'll be an announcement later today that will shift all our resources elsewhere.'

Callanach was at Natasha's house half an hour later. He was avoiding the Chief and letting every call go to voicemail. He should have expected Ava's car to be outside. She was never going to be told what to do. He rang the bell and waited.

Natasha opened with an altogether brighter face than he'd seen earlier at the station.

'Come in,' she said. 'I was just making coffee. You want some?'

'Am I French?' he asked in response.

'Actually, you're half-Scottish, so by rights I should be putting a dram in the top. I'm guessing you're still on duty though.'

'I am,' he said, 'and you're not supposed to be here,' he directed at Ava who was sitting at Natasha's kitchen table eating a biscuit.

'I'm suspended,' Ava said through a mouthful of crumbs. 'What better opportunity to spend time with my oldest and best friend?'

'I need to go through a list with you, Natasha, to get more information. We have forensics working on the new letters and envelope but it'll take time to process. Are there any students we should be aware of as suspects, anyone you've failed or a kid with a crush on the teacher?'

'All right, but I think it's ridiculous. I hope you won't say I gave any names out.'

'We'll say we're talking to everyone, don't worry,' Callanach said.

'Giles Parry, second-year student, went through a stage of bringing me gifts. I had to formally write and ask him to stop. He hasn't spoken to me since. Marcus Turnbull, I caught taking photos of me during lectures. When he followed me into the toilet I warned him about his conduct. He said he just wanted to discuss a paper, but it was creepy. And there's a first-year student, permanently wrapped around one male or another, big opinion of herself but she stares at me, waits in corridors, looks at my legs so that I'll notice. There's something just not right about it. Her name's Jaclyn Best. I'd love it if you gave me a reason to get rid of her.'

'Great,' Callanach said. 'Now, staff and faculty. We'll need to check each one, but any information will help. Stop me if anything strikes you. Anthony Allardice, Simon Cordwell, Clare Edgerton,' Natasha held up a hand.

'Clare was given a verbal warning last year for calling in sick then being seen at a music festival. No biggie but she was disgruntled.'

'Naomi Fuller,' Callanach continued. 'Edgar Groves.'

'He wanted my job,' Natasha said, 'and spread a few nasty rumours about me when I was appointed instead. He was also suspected of having an affair with a student last year and got quite antsy when I asked him about it. He hates me,' she finished simply.

'Delia Inman, Reginald King,' Callanach went on.

'Hopeless,' Natasha said. 'Thinks he's God's gift to academia but couldn't get beyond an admin position. He's snooty and irritating, but that's as bad as it gets.'

'Vera Lesley, Dean Oppenheim,' Callanach went down the list.

'This is being taken very seriously,' Ava said, as he came to an end. 'Don't get me wrong, I'm all in favour, but what exactly did that last note say to pull you away from your murder investigation?'

'I'm not being pulled away from anything. There's a suspect at the station being charged with the Buxton and Magee murders as we speak,' Callanach said.

'Why didn't you tell me you'd got him?' Ava asked, standing up.

'Because I'm not convinced we have,' Callanach answered. 'And as for the note, I'm here because it's become more specific. It said TOMORROW.'

Chapter Thirty-One

Callanach chased up the three less than exemplary students the next day. He hadn't turned on the television or radio, had refused to take part in the media madness following the announcement that Hand had been charged, and had spoken to the Chief only briefly. Rory Hand had finally requested a lawyer and the Chief wanted all available resources dedicated to documenting the previous few months of Hand's life. Callanach had made it clear he wasn't convinced and that was how it had been left. There was no argument, no orders were given that would prevent him pursuing his own leads, only the fact that charging Hand had been unavoidable. What followed was that pursuing other suspects would give Hand's defence team a stick to beat the police with if Hand changed his plea. Callanach hated it when the lawyers got involved. It made decisions tactical, evidence double-edged and the most innocent of actions and words became fodder for cross-examination. He was, to all intents and purposes, acting alone.

Natasha's troublesome students Marcus Turnbull and Giles Parry were unlikeable but pathetic. Jaclyn Best was a piece of work with a huge opinion of herself and an impressive ability to lie but Callanach's gut told him she wasn't involved. The letters were the work of someone careful and committed. The students were all about quick gratification and reactionary behaviour.

By then it was eleven in the morning. If the threat against Natasha was real, then the sand was already falling through the hour glass. Tripp's name appeared on his ringing mobile.

'What's the progress?' Callanach asked.

'We got the scrap yard closed down by the Health and Safety Executive. The owner's buying time saying he needs to go through his records, but he can't stall much longer. He's losing money by the hour.'

'And what's happening with . . .'

'That's not why I called, sir,' Tripp interrupted. 'DCI Begbie wants you back here straight away. Rory Hand's lawyers are making demands. There are uniformed officers with Professor Forge and the Chief says that's all the personnel we can afford at the moment.'

'I made it clear last night that I'm not prepared to have anything to do with Rory Hand. It wasn't me who arrested him.'

'The Chief said you'd say that.' Tripp's voice was quiet on the end of the phone.

'And?' Callanach asked.

'The Chief said he didn't give, well, I don't need to repeat it. He just said you're on the clock so get back to the station.'

Callanach climbed into his car. In the rear view mirror he saw his bloodshot eyes and wondered why he was so shocked at the sight. He hadn't slept for . . . he gave up calculating the hours. He'd lost count of the days. There was no choice but to return to the station. That was what jobs with hierarchies were all about. You could complain or question but ultimately you did what you were told or the whole system fell apart. If you couldn't stomach it, you were in the wrong profession – and Callanach wasn't. He was right where he was supposed to be, doing a job he loved. He needed to remind himself of that occasionally.

At the station, Hand's lawyer was waiting for him.

'My client has confessed to the murders,' the lawyer said as if it was the most boring case in the world. Callanach wanted to arrest him just for being so disrespectful to the two dead women. 'He will give a full statement with details only when his conditions have been met.' Callanach was obviously supposed to chip in at that point and ask what the conditions were. Instead, he folded his arms across his chest and waited. The lawyer tutted at the pause and carried on. 'He wants to visit the site where each woman was abducted and the warehouse where Magee's remains were found. He wishes to be taken there today to refresh his memory or he will be unable to make a full statement.'

'I wonder why that might be,' Callanach said.

The lawyer raised his eyebrows. 'What are you suggesting, Detective Inspector?'

Callanach very much wanted to answer but self-preservation kicked in.

'Just that it seems to be a common feature among murderers that they have recollection problems only when it suits them. I'm sure your client's memory will improve when he has what he wants.'

'Detective Chief Inspector Begbie said you'd be leading the visit. I shall be with my client and require your officers to keep a sufficient distance from us that we won't be overheard.'

The day was wasted. Not so for Rory Hand. He had a gratuitous tour of crime scenes that Callanach knew would feed his sickened mind for years to come. Hand was given all he needed to add colour and texture to his confession. There would be nothing more to link him to the crimes. Forensics were already drawing a blank. It was six o'clock before the most recent addition to the list of Scotland's infamous murderers had had his fill, sucking out what little life remained in the atmospheres of the dead women's homes. By the time they were done, Callanach was almost hoping Hand would be convicted of the crimes. He deserved a minimum of twenty-five years in payment for the thrill of the afternoon.

DS Lively didn't show his face during the crime scenes visit. Callanach wondered where he was but decided against asking. It was better that he and his sergeant remained separated. Once Hand was back in his cell, it was close to seven and dark. He was eager to get to Natasha's house. Although he'd had uniformed officers stationed there and reporting to him every hour, Callanach had the unremitting impression that these weren't hollow threats. They were too plain for that. Natasha had insisted upon remaining in her own home in spite of multiple warnings. Perhaps it was better to keep her there and see what happened. The best-case scenario was that they caught the stalker trying to get in. At least it would ensure her future safety.

He grabbed his overnight bag from the boot of his car. Natasha had asked him to stay before he'd suggested it, not that he'd have given her any choice in the matter. As backup, there would be a uniformed officer to the rear of the house and the fire service had been alerted, too. Nothing would be visible from the front of the property.

Callanach breathed in roasted garlic and beef, and for a second he forgot why he was there.

'Hello, darling, good day at the office?' Natasha joked, taking the coat from his hand and replacing it with a glass of merlot. She was more collected than he'd expected, wearing a crisply ironed white shirt and black jeans, an apron over the top.

'I can't drink, Natasha, I'm on duty,' he said ruefully.

'You can have one, make it last all evening if you like. Dinner's in half an hour. Why don't you put your bag in the guest room?'

He did so. On his way back downstairs he checked the windows were locked, closed the curtains, looked in each cupboard and under every bed, then rang Ava.

'Where are you?' he asked.

'At home, like a good girl,' she said. 'Is Natasha all right?'

'She's cooking. Nothing to report here. I wanted to make sure you were being sensible, only if you get involved the Chief will have to do more than just suspend you for a fortnight.'

'I know that and I also trust you've got it in hand,' Ava responded breezily.

'You don't have to worry,' Callanach replied, wondering why she wasn't pushing harder for the security details and demanding hourly reports by phone. Somehow he'd expected Ava to find it harder to separate herself from the action.

'I don't intend to. I'm watching *The Magnificent Seven*, eating a takeaway chow mein and drinking ice-cold beer. As tempting as it is to race over and watch the clock with you all night, I'd rather have some alone time with Yul Brynner, Charles Bronson and Steve McQueen, who in my humble opinion may be the best-looking man who ever lived. Have a pleasant evening,' she said.

'Maybe the Chief should extend that suspension anyway,' was all Callanach could come back with as she ended the call. The truth was that he wished she was there with them. He dismissed the thought. Ava Turner was a colleague and unimpressed by him at the best of times.

In the lounge, he picked up the remote control and flicked through channels until Yul Brynner could be seen biting the end off a cigar with McQueen brandishing a shotgun next to him on top of a funeral coach.

'He's not that good-looking,' Callanach said.

'Who are you talking to?' Natasha asked as she entered the room.

'Just having a long-distance disagreement with Ava. Dinner ready?' he asked.

'Yes, sir,' she gave a mock curtsy. 'Hope you're hungry.'

The food was good. It reminded him of France. If they hadn't been waiting for a dangerous criminal to break down the door, it would have been almost perfect.

'Talk to me,' Natasha said as she rinsed plates before loading up the dishwasher.

'About what?' he asked.

'Ava told me about the girl who accused you of raping her.' Callanach took a breath, trying to get a handle on how he felt about having his private life discussed. He was surprised to discover that rather than annoyance, he felt a sense of belonging and acceptance. Whatever Ava's motivation for sharing had been, it certainly wasn't malicious. 'I know you didn't do it,' Natasha continued. 'I just don't see how that can happen. Surely there has to be evidence for the police to charge a man with sexual assault?' She flicked the kettle on and got out a cafetière. Callanach waited for her to ask if he minded talking about it, but she didn't. It was her way, that straightforwardness. From anyone else it might have seemed intrusive. From her it was genuine curiosity. Callanach could see why Ava liked her so much. Natasha Forge obeyed no one's rules but her own. No doubt that had helped draw her stalker's attention. 'Milk and sugar?' she asked.

'Neither, thank you. Ava explained about my evening with Astrid?' he asked.

'Yes,' she said. 'But not what happened after you were arrested.' She passed Callanach a mug and sat down opposite him at the kitchen table.

'There was evidence, enough to charge me, anyway. She'd apparently seen a doctor the day after our evening out, although she didn't report it to the police for some days after that. I think she was waiting to see if I would call her. When I didn't, she had already laid the groundwork for the allegation. I'd pushed her to get away at her front door. She'd landed hard and the medical report noted bruising to her buttocks. Astrid had told the doctor that the bruising was caused when I'd forced her to the floor and climbed on top of her.'

Callanach frowned. It wasn't an easy thing to recall. The memory of how sick he'd felt when presented with the evidence was even worse than the moment he'd been arrested. At the start, he'd been so sure he'd simply explain the course of events and walk away. The reality was very different. The local prosecutor was investigating without any input from Interpol, so there could be no suggestion the complaint had been handled with anything other than absolute independence and fairness. They had a medical report, forensic analysis, photographs and statements ready on his return from Jamaica and took him through it piece by piece. His vision had blurred, he'd wanted to vomit, it had been hard to talk. He knew he must have looked guilty but he couldn't speak up to defend himself. That moment, when he'd realised he hadn't simply been accused of a crime, he'd been set up with a skill and determination that left him entirely at the court's mercy, was the single worst feeling he'd experienced in his life.

When his father died, Callanach had been devastated but wrapped up in the love of his family. When he'd been arrested for drunk driving, he'd thought his life was ruined, but knew in his heart that he had it within himself to turn things around. But a rape charge? No one could protect him from it. No one could bail him out. He'd been powerless, and flat denial was his only option. The defence that he'd been the subject of a woman's obsession sounded like so much bullshit he was afraid to make the case. He'd answered no questions at all during that first interview. Later he realised he'd been in shock, trying to process the wreckage of his life. By the time he was interviewed again, it could only have looked like he'd had time to rustle up a story that would explain away the evidence. He'd been paralysed and it had done nothing but seal his fate.

'Surely the bruising to her buttocks wasn't enough. That could have happened any number of ways,' Natasha interrupted his thoughts.

'That wasn't all. She'd snapped a nail scratching my neck, had asked the doctor to photograph and keep it. My blood was underneath it. Astrid claimed she inflicted the wound on me when acting in self-defence. Her neighbour had seen me wiping the blood away and swearing at her as I left, and had caught a glimpse of her naked and crying.'

'Oh, shit,' Natasha whispered.

'Yes, oh shit,' Callanach echoed. 'And I'd lied to my friend, Jean-Paul, said the scratch had happened during an accident at the gym. I'd tried to be a gentleman and keep quiet. It turns out that was a bad idea.'

'What about more intimate evidence?' Natasha asked quietly. 'What you've listed is enough for assault but . . .'

'That part I can only guess,' he said. 'The doctor, and I had no reason to think he falsified his report, said Astrid had bruising and scratching both outside and inside her vagina. She claimed I had used a condom and taken it with me which was why there was no semen. The injuries were more than enough for them to charge me. The only logical conclusion was that she'd been raped.'

'She did it herself,' Natasha breathed out hard. 'Holy fuck. You must have wanted to kill her.'

'I believe Astrid used her own nails or an implement and created those injuries after I'd left. And yes, I wanted to kill her and myself, a few times.'

The photographs of the external scratches were as clear in his mind as when he'd first seen them. The skin between Astrid's legs was a mesh of angry red lacerations as if someone had torn at her. If she'd done it herself, she must have been crazed. The image was like a sickness in his mind. The police had left that detail until last and he'd known then that he was hung. Claiming that a woman who held down a responsible job at Interpol was unbalanced enough to self-harm for revenge was not going to help.

'She'd ripped her underwear and her dress, phoned a friend sobbing and incoherent. Even now it sounds like I'm guilty, doesn't it? The detail was incredible. A few times, even I wondered if I had done what she'd said and simply blocked it out.'

There was silence. Natasha had tears in her eyes and he was grateful for them. They made him feel less of a monster.

'No one who knew you could possibly have believed her,' Natasha said.

'That's the thing about rapists,' Callanach said. 'They can be charming, sociable, well integrated, boring, quiet or shy. There's no type. Astrid said I made a pass at her but as it was our first date she'd refused me. She claimed that I'd become enraged and, I quote, "He told me that no woman had ever refused him, that he always got what he wanted, that I should have been flattered he wanted me," and I guess there were people around who were happy to believe it. Jean-Paul and my other friends abandoned me and I don't blame them. Guilt by association is real. Only my boss at Interpol stood by me. Even my mother . . .' Callanach still couldn't talk about that final, devastating blow. He opted for the most impersonal, understated summary he could give. 'It was a lonely time. When Astrid finally changed her mind about giving evidence against me, it was too late to undo the damage. She pursued me for a while. Eventually I took out an injunction to prevent her from contacting me. She didn't even turn up to court for that. I think she thought it was all just part of the game. My superiors at Interpol never prejudged the outcome of the trial, and I think they were genuinely pleased when I was acquitted, but there's only so far you can go to repair a career following such a serious allegation. So they helped pave the way for my move to Police Scotland. It avoided the struggle of trying to reintegrate me into my former Interpol department. Leaving France felt like my only option. You never really walk away, though. It's as if you're left stained. And everyone can see it.'

'Ava said when you told her about it she knew perfectly well you weren't capable of such an atrocity.'

'Ava is kinder than most people,' Callanach said.

'She's more perceptive than anyone I've ever met,' Natasha said. 'And enough of that's rubbed off on me to see you care about her.'

'I have a huge amount of respect for her. She's unafraid, principled and not interested in promotion politics. There aren't many police officers like that around.'

'It's more than that, but you can play the work card if you like. Just don't let what happened to you ruin your chance of a relationship.'

'Natasha, my relationship with Ava is entirely professional. And you know she'd be incensed if she heard you talking like that.'

'Tell me I'm wrong,' she said.

'There must be a thousand men who would happily lose a body part to go out with Ava. She deserves better than me,' Callanach said.

'She certainly deserves better than someone lugging that boulder of self-pity around with them. You may have been through a hard time, but you're going to have to get over it sooner or later.' Natasha stared at him, unabashed by his outraged expression.

'You have no idea what you're talking about. Just because I'm no longer facing a trial doesn't mean I'm not still . . .' His voice trailed off.

'You're not still what?' Natasha asked gently. Callanach breathed heavily, the edge of his temper only half a step away. 'Luc? There's very little in life that can't be fixed.'

270

'I can't, all right?' he shouted. 'No matter how many weeks and months pass, whatever else I concentrate on, I can't be bloody well fixed.'

There were three loud blows to the kitchen door. Natasha jumped and screamed as the glass cafetière fell from her hands and smashed on the tiles. Callanach leapt to his feet and the uniformed officer ran into the kitchen.

'It's all right, sir, that's just my replacement. I'm off shift. We agreed he'd come to the back door.' He radioed through and the man outside confirmed his rank, name and that it was he who had knocked on the door. Callanach let him in as Natasha cleared up the shards of glass.

'You should probably get some rest,' Callanach told Natasha once the replacement officer had settled in.

'We were talking,' Natasha said.

'We'd finished talking and I'd started shouting, which is not how I want to end the evening. My head needs to be clear for the night. I'm going to stay down here a while,' Callanach decided. 'Call if you need me.'

'Luc, I didn't mean to upset you.' Natasha put her arms up for a conciliatory hug. Callanach stepped away.

'You didn't,' he said, busying himself with checking the settings on his phone. 'It was my own fault. Forget it, okay? Sleep well.'

They said subdued goodnights and Callanach settled on the sofa. He mulled over what Natasha had said about Ava, tried to dismiss it then considered it some more. Even if he'd been capable of having a relationship, Ava was off limits. He shrugged the thought away and performed an unnecessary additional round of checks on the windows and doors. It was quiet. Eventually the sofa's comfort was too powerful to resist and sleep took him.

Chapter Thirty-Two

King was slumped low in the four-wheel drive he'd paid to use for the night. The weasel had charged him double for the late request but the vehicle was worth the money. The rear windows were darkened, the back seats would lie completely flat and the number plates related to a similar make and model of car long since written off.

A ritual had evolved in preparation for this acquisition that he'd been unaware of with Elaine and Jayne. He'd cooked a meal during the day, preparing it exactingly. Pasta with paprika-baked salmon and bok choy. The pasta had been selected to give him the slow release energy he'd need to get through the evening and night. The kitchen clock had ticked steadily as he'd seasoned the fish and laid the table. The clock reassured him that time was absolute, that the floating sensation he felt with the passing minutes was an illusion. The routine stabilised the world around him. King's car, the one he drove to work and to the supermarket, was parked in front of his house on the road. His replacement vehicle, the one in which he would make only four journeys and never touch again, was in his garage. He'd caught a bus to the weasel's yard. Public transport was anonymous. He disliked the inescapable proximity to people who stared, coughed, sneezed and played tinny music through headphones – the scratchy sound set his teeth on edge – but it was a necessary discomfort. He always left the bus two stops away from the weasel's. So careful was he that he called into a nearby bakery on each occasion and bought fresh croissants, providing an excuse for the journey. Planning, detail. It was all in the detail.

Once he'd consumed his meal, followed by green tea in a china cup, he'd showered. He had the water hotter than he usually liked, soaping and scrubbing his skin, to minimise the transfer of physical evidence at the crime scene. What few hairs he still had, he combed obsessively for ten minutes before leaving the house, ensuring as far as he could that there were no loose hairs left to fall. The male-pattern baldness was a hand-me-down from his father, a sick joke really. His parents had regularly expressed their disappointment that he had inherited so few of his father's traits. At least they had this one thing in common. King always wore a hat when he was out collecting a woman, but he brushed his hair anyway, better safe than sorry. On this occasion he'd been anticipating the pounding of the scorching water on his skin. He knew it would bring his blood to the surface, invigorate him, infuse him with a cocktail of relaxation and readiness. He conjured Natasha's face in his imagination. She was crying. As he looked up into the shower stream, he saw her tears falling on his face and body. He ran one hand over his full belly and felt the softness of her skin. He longed to hear Natasha sobbing. She would sob once the night was over. She would sob and scream and curse and plead.

He dressed in clothes that had been inspected, cleaned with a sticky roller to remove stray fibres and hung in his closet. Finally he polished his shoes. It was his finishing touch. It signified that he was ready, that everything was perfect. If his shoes were shining then his preparation was complete. He'd left food for the other women and prepared a makeshift bed until he could reduce his staying guests to only two. That might take a week but he was clear in his own mind that it was necessary. Elaine had learned nothing, contributed nothing, wouldn't speak any more, and as for Jayne . . . she spent every moment he was there praying. Last night he'd washed her mouth out with soap. She'd gagged and spluttered then carried on. When he'd hit her, the lower denture he'd fitted the previous week went flying. He'd waited for her reaction. When she'd begun to pray again he'd had to leave. He'd wanted to throttle her, to squeeze the piety from her with his bare hands, but he wasn't ready for that yet. If he chose to sacrifice her from their number, the task had to be discharged with fitting ceremony.

Tonight was a risk. He had to believe he'd laid the groundwork with sufficient skill that it would proceed according to plan. He knew where Natasha would be, that precautions were being taken to protect her. He had an escape route if needed. Her road was free of CCTV cameras and would be quiet as a graveyard after midnight.

'You can expect a new colleague to be joining you,' he'd told Elaine and Jayne. At least that had silenced the chanting reverend. 'Make her feel welcome and don't scare her with unpleasant tales. You'll find her most impressive. Help her settle in so we can begin the next phase of growth together.' There was electricity in the air. He could feel it. This was what he'd been steering towards all along. It was as if he'd been holding a part of himself back, honing his technique on the first two. Strange how the human brain chose its moment to reveal its true purpose, he thought. His phone vibrated in his pocket. It was time.

Dr King drove to the corner of Natasha Forge's road, pulled up at the far end and checked his watch. It was one in the morning, dark but not raining, and the two street lamps cast an orange glow without shedding light into the shadows. Her car was where he'd expected it to be. He began to congratulate himself on his good fortune, then stopped. There was no luck, no chance. He'd formulated and schemed. This providence was entirely of his own making. It was proof of his prowess.

Through the dark, he watched. She was her usual poised self in spite of the drama of the night, in spite of the threat. His heart was hammering in his chest. The intoxication rose like a surfacing whale, engulfing him, astounding him. His initial reaction was to quell it, but why should he? Wasn't this all part of the experience, a reward in and of itself? He waited, settled himself, let his equilibrium rebalance at its own pace. At last, he prepared to take his prize.

He drew the bottle of chloroform from his bag, using a dropper to withdraw the precise amount required into a clean, white handkerchief. He looked up and down the length of the road. King knew the exact distance from where he'd parked to the outside of Natasha's home, had walked it so many times he could cite the number of footsteps. He released the catches to flatten the back seats, knowing his hands would be too full to do so later, made sure the picnic blanket, gag and cable ties were handy, and slipped noiselessly from his vehicle.

A few steps up the road, he knocked on the window of an occupied car. 'Detective Inspector Turner,' King panted. 'Thank goodness you're here.'

Ava Turner had parked in the darkest section of the road under a tree, in a spot neither visible from Natasha's house nor obvious to any passing police officer. King put on his most benign smile. There would be no perceivable threat. He looked to the world like a man winding down to retirement, who had only cardigans and easily digestible food to look forward to. She jumped. If he hadn't been watching for it, he might not have noticed how well she covered it. He stepped back to allow her to open her window without anxiety. DI Turner, so sure of her ability to look after herself and therefore so easily duped by the man in his well-ironed shirt and unfashionable tie, dropped the glass a fraction.

'I was on my way to Natasha's,' King said. 'She called my mobile. I recognised you from the lecture you gave . . .' She was opening her door already. Her expression was mixed, partially unreadable in the shadows, but he saw flickering uncertainty replaced by concern for her friend and that made her careless. As she unlatched the door he yanked it fully open, shooting his right arm in, covering her mouth with the handkerchief. He pressed his left arm against her throat so her instinct was to gasp for air. She was obliging, gulping in a cloud of chloroform as she thrashed. She fought longer than the others, better aware of how to deal with the attack, her hands grabbing his face rather than her own throat, turning her head left and right to shake off the drug, losing the battle. More than anything else, she kicked her legs. He could hear them thumping the underside of her seat, as if they were trapped. It took longer than he liked but there it was, that instant of softness when she swooned in his arms, not so fully unconscious as the others. King needed her to be able to walk, but not talk coherently. She was as compliant as a teenager drunk on snakebite for the first time. He hauled Ava's body out, hoisted one of her arms around his shoulders and manoeuvred her the short distance to his car. He'd rehearsed his speech to imaginary passersby.

'Too much to drink, the temptations of Edinburgh on a Friday night,' with an expression of long-tested tolerance, was what he would say. It was unnecessary, in the event. His car would be as untraceable as ever. He'd even dyed his hair a silvery grey for the evening and worn glasses from a charity shop. The gloves were a necessity but then, it was Scotland.

When did the wind not blow? King tipped Ava's body across his back seat, smiling and shaking his head like an irritated but loving uncle dealing with a wayward niece, covered her in the blanket then climbed into the front. From there he fastened the cable ties around her wrists and ankles, slid the gag over her mouth and flipped the blanket over her face. Ava Turner was his.

Natasha was losing someone she loved and didn't that feel good? So good he was dizzy with it. So extraordinarily fulfilling to know how much pain she would experience. And she didn't even know it yet.

He reversed, performed a quiet three-point turn and went back the way he'd come. There was no point driving past Natasha's house. DI Callanach or, more likely, one of his underlings might still be awake and watching. King had bet everything on Ava being unable to stay away, the disciplinary investigation that the press had announced with such grim satisfaction notwithstanding. How could she keep her distance from her best friend's house when the threat was so imminent and so credible? He'd even dug the knife in to accelerate her suspension with that letter to the *Herald*, complaining about her outspoken criticism of the Roman Catholic Church, under a false name, naturally. It wouldn't have worked if he'd been unable to get inside and leave his ridiculous trail. Natasha was slapdash with her keys at work, often leaving them in her pigeonhole. It had been child's play to have a copy of her house key made. There was a key cutter within a two-minute walk of the department.

King drove carefully, ensuring there were no traffic infringements for which he could be pulled over, hat low, shielding his eyes from prying CCTV cameras. He could hear snoring in the back, as if they were taking a Sunday afternoon ride. It allowed him to imagine an alternative scenario with her. Perhaps, if Natasha hadn't whisked her away when he was about to introduce himself, things could have ended differently. Ava would have held out her hand to shake his and smiled sweetly. A dimple formed at one side of her mouth when she smiled. He'd seen it as she'd settled the audience at the start of her lecture. Her face might have lit up when he'd spoken to her.

'Dr King,' he would have said. 'Call me Reginald. I'm on the departmental staff in the Philosophy Department. Let me fetch you a drink, save you from the great unwashed.' He'd have nodded his head at the milling students and Ava would have shared a knowing smile.

'I'd appreciate that,' she would have said. 'It's been quite a day.' He might have guided her out of the crowd and towards the bar with the lightest of hands in the small of her back. She would have noticed but not objected. There would have been eye contact, fleeting, hers shy, his confident.

'So you're an old friend of Natasha's?' he would have asked silkily, handing her cold champagne, heads bent towards one another so they could talk without being overheard.

'More an acquaintance to be honest. You know what it's like, you grow apart over time,' Ava says inside his head, raising one eyebrow so he couldn't mistake her meaning.

'I see,' he would reply knowingly. 'Yes, she can be a bit . . .' He would leave the end of the sentence hanging subtly.

'Absolutely,' she would agree, giggling at their private joke.

That was when the banging started.

He jerked his head round. They were paused at traffic lights next to a mass of bodies exiting a nightclub, bouncers herding the rabble. Ava was shrieking through the gag, kicking at the inside of the rear passenger door with both feet, thrashing under the blanket.

'Shut up, you stupid bitch,' King swore through clenched teeth. He revved his engine to drown her out until the lights went green and saved him. It was taking too long. Furiously he fiddled with the radio, a nightmare of buttons and dials in an unfamiliar dash. At last, music filled the car, not a bad match for the rhythm of her feet bashing the door. The youths going past peered in to see what was going on but looked away, full of contempt. He was too old, unfashionable, out of place. Loud music and revved-up engines belonged to the young in their arrogance and disbelief that the passage of time would never affect them. The traffic lights finally released him from their derision.

'Too close, why couldn't she stay still?' he hissed. 'Got the chloroform dose wrong, maybe she didn't breathe as deeply as I thought. Maybe the bitch was pretending. Were you pretending?' he shouted. 'Are you that deceitful?'

A screech from the back was indication enough that she was conscious and understood him.

'You have to be a good girl for me, Ava,' he cooed, self-control only a matter of breathing deeply and remembering the greater plan. 'If you're good, there'll be rewards. You're doing this for Natasha, so she can learn humility. She needs some loss to humanise her. I'm taking you somewhere safe. You won't be alone. I have friends for you. Dr King has thought of everything.'

Chapter Thirty-Three

Natasha woke Callanach to say that the uniformed officers were changing shift again.

'Seven o'clock and all is well,' she boomed with a smile. 'You were sleeping like a baby.'

'Are you all right?' Callanach asked, but she looked rested and refreshed.

'All my limbs are still attached and none of the windows are smashed, so I'd call that a successful operation, Detective Inspector. Why don't you use the bathroom while I make French toast. House specialty.' He was going to insist that she not bother but his stomach said yes. Twenty minutes later he'd changed his clothes and retaken his seat from the night before.

'I've texted Ava to let her know I'm fine. No response yet. She's probably sulking because you insisted she couldn't be here last night.'

'In her best interests,' Callanach said through a full mouth. 'The sooner the Chief can put this complaint to bed, the better. What are your plans? We're still following up the list of departmental staff so you probably shouldn't go in to the University yet.'

'As fond as I am of sitting at home, I have work to do. I'm bored of being scared. I'll be sensible, nothing risky, but I have to go in to my office. There's work building up. You can phone me every ten minutes if that helps.'

'Certainly, I will,' Callanach said. 'If anything happened to you, Ava would never forget it. I can't lose her as a friend. She's the only one I've made since I got off the plane.'

'Oh, I think Ava would forgive you almost anything,' Natasha said. 'All right, maybe not that, but anything else. Can we talk about how our conversation ended last night?'

'I have to go,' Callanach said, shoving his arms into a jacket. 'Do what the police officer tells you and don't speak to any strangers.' Callanach put his plate and mug in the dishwasher then picked up his mobile. 'I'm glad last night turned out okay.'

'Luc!' Natasha shouted as he dashed out of the back door. He looked back. 'Ava's not the only friend you've made since you arrived. You have at least two.'

Outside was a blue sky and the absence of rain. Even the wind was taking a day off. It was far from sunny but Callanach decided he'd happily settle for not freezing. His car was parked opposite Natasha's and he started the radio before putting on his seat belt, adjusting it to make room for the enormous amount he'd eaten in the previous twelve hours. Pulling away, he gave the house one last external inspection, checking up and down the road. That was when he spotted the silver Mercedes parked under a tree at the far end of the street.

'Just couldn't stay away, could you?' he said through his open window, slowing down, expecting to see Ava waving at him. He'd have no choice but to tell her to go straight home. Daylight wouldn't make her presence at Natasha's any more acceptable to DCI Begbie. Callanach was parallel to her car when he saw there was no one inside. He parked and got out.

The Mercedes was unlocked, the driver's door not quite fully closed. Convinced he must have missed her on foot as he'd been getting into his own vehicle, he called her mobile. There was silence, then ringing. With a growing wariness he realised it was coming from the passenger seat of Ava's car. He reached in to pick it up, instinct stopped him and he withdrew, phoning Natasha as he stepped away.

'Natasha, I know this will sound strange but is Ava with you?' he asked as lightly as he could manage.

'No, you know that, you just left,' Natasha said. A pause. 'Why?' Callanach couldn't reply. Lines were forming to make a shape inside his head and he didn't like what he was seeing. 'Luc? Say something.' She slammed her phone down hard. He heard it hit what he guessed was the kitchen table. Seconds later Natasha was running down her pathway into the road, looking left and right for him along the street. When she saw him she froze, then she spotted Ava's car and began to sprint. It wasn't far and running would achieve nothing but she raced towards him as if to stop a child from falling off a cliff.

'Where is she?' she screamed. 'What's happened? Tell me what's happened!'

'I don't know,' Callanach said, catching her before she could tear through the vehicle. 'You mustn't touch it, Natasha, please.' The uniformed officer was behind her, puzzled, out of breath.

'Call the station,' Callanach ordered. 'Get a location for Detective Inspector Turner. Tell them her car and mobile are here. I want officers at her home immediately. Contact her family and ask if they've heard from her in the last twelve hours.'

Natasha collapsed to her knees. 'She's gone,' she cried. 'Oh God, we were in there eating and drinking while she was being taken.'

'We don't know that,' he said. 'Ava could be anywhere. She could be up a tree in your back garden for all we know.'

'No,' Natasha sobbed. 'No, she's not. Her keys are in the ignition, Luc, and her handbag's on the back seat.'

Callanach stared through the window. Natasha was right.

He wanted to believe there was a better, more rational explanation. He wanted to explain where she might have gone. In the end he knew the simplest explanation was the most likely. The woman he had claimed just minutes ago as his only friend in Scotland, had been abducted.

The sirens could be heard coming from every direction. The forensics team arrived in tandem with the Chief Inspector. Out of nowhere, a press van followed before the road could be closed and constables hastily formed a line around the car to block the camera's view. Not that there was anything dramatic to see. It was what was missing that was so damning.

Callanach wanted Natasha to go back inside but she refused, stubborn, furious with grief and panic. Instinctively and without hesitation he put his arms around her shoulders and held her tight as she fought back tears.

'What was DI Turner doing here last night?' the Chief demanded.

'I don't know,' Callanach replied quietly. 'As far as I was aware she was at home. She must have been keeping her movements quiet because of the suspension.'

The implied criticism was below the belt and Callanach knew it, but he couldn't stop himself. It wasn't lost on DCI Begbie.

'Don't make this about her suspension, Inspector. Turner knows better than to put herself in harm's way.'

'It's my fault,' Natasha said. 'She was here to protect me.'

'It's not your fault,' Callanach told her. 'There's nothing anyone could have done to stop it. Whoever is responsible played us.'

'Where's your team?' DCI Begbie barked.

'At the University checking out the other departmental staff,' Callanach said.

'Get them out of there and into the incident room. If this was a set up with DI Turner as the intended victim, then the University was just a means to an end. Pull every uniformed officer and detective from any other investigation that can spare them. Check who might want retribution from the baby case and revisit the death threat. And get the bloody press out of here. If I see Ava's face splashed over the news, heads will roll.' Callanach saw that the Chief was reeling. Ava had been under his command for years. He'd been responsible for promoting her. She was a difficult person not to love.

'Come on, Natasha, I need to get you home,' he said, walking her back up the road towards her house. As he did so, there was a shout from behind.

At the Mercedes a forensic technician was waving and shouting for an evidence bag. Callanach left Natasha and went back.

'What is it?' he demanded.

'A trainer, lodged way back under her seat. Just one. Could have been there some time, fallen out of a gym bag, maybe.'

'At the end of a gym session she'd have undone the laces to remove the trainer, and even then it wouldn't have fallen out of a bag and ended up lodged under the driver's seat. If she was conducting surveillance last night, this is the sort of shoe she'd have been wearing. It seems more likely to me that this came off her foot at some point during . . .' He looked up the road towards Natasha, the will to finish the sentence draining from him. Ava had known exactly what she was doing even in the stress and panic of the abduction. She'd shed the shoe to prove beyond doubt, as soon as the car was found, that she'd been taken by force. It was typical of her to be planning even in chaos. 'Don't tell Professor Forge,' he said to the officers around him. 'Enough hope's been lost this morning.'

He returned to Natasha, whispering urgent but distracting nothings about procedure and priorities as they went.

'She'll fight. I've never seen anybody get the better of her,' Natasha said.

'We don't know what's happened yet,' Callanach replied. 'Ava might have had a blow to the head and wandered off, or followed a lead on foot with no time to pick up her bag. Anything's possible. Panicking won't help.'

'Don't patronise me,' she said quietly. 'I get it. We talk facts not hypotheses.'

'Exactly,' he replied. 'Ava would tell you the same.'

'Ava can't tell me anything right now.' Callanach didn't respond. Natasha was right. 'She's all I've got, Luc. My parents cared more about maintaining their social status than they did their own daughter. That's why they ditched me when I came out. I didn't fit their ideal of a wholesome, socially correct child. The day I told them, my mother asked if I'd done any research into where I could be treated for my "perversion". My father just never spoke to me. He was the centre of my world until that day and he never spoke to me again. Ava looked after me, rebuilt my confidence and loved me enough that she very nearly made up for the whole rotten lot of them. I was depressed for the best part of a year, wavering between hanging around bars picking up any woman I could and phoning bizarre churches in America who claimed they could cure me. Ava didn't once tell me to stop feeling sorry for myself. She didn't make helpful suggestions. She just let me get on. The life I have now was all built through her and if I have to live it without her . . .' She dropped her head as she fought not to cry, tensing her shoulders, gritting her teeth. 'I refuse, Luc. I refuse to go on without her. So just fucking well bring her back. If you're one ounce of the detective and the man she seems to believe you are, then prove it now.'

Callanach didn't make any promises. There was no comfort to be given. He simply let himself out of Natasha's house and did as she wanted. He got on with the job.

The incident room was a parody of a child's game of sardines, body crushed against body, no one seated because chairs would take up too much space. The Chief took charge and Callanach was glad. He was too full of self-loathing to be trusted to lead the team dispassionately.

'You all know what's happened by now,' DCI Begbie began. 'DI Turner's home was securely locked and undisturbed, as was her garage. In addition her handbag, found in her car, contained her house keys. The conclusion is that she was abducted between the hours of nine last night and six this morning. Door-to-doors have been conducted in Professor Forge's road and there's no information. It's a quiet area, no local pub, people tend to be indoors at a reasonable hour. Low footfall. The majority of people living in the vicinity drive to and from work.'

Salter shouted across a sea of heads.

'Is it the same man who took Buxton and Magee?'

Professor Harris stood up before the Chief could answer. Callanach hadn't even realised he was in the room, not that it was possible to see further than the people immediately in front of him.

'The man who took Miss Buxton and the Reverend Magee is in custody and this abduction does not shake my faith that we have the right man. Whilst there are similarities, there are also wild variations. The break-in at the professor's house, the two rather crass notes, the fact that the assailant wasn't waiting at DI Turner's home but lured her to a public location. It's a well-executed offence, I grant you, but the modus operandi is completely different. I suspect that what we have on our hands is a copycat.'

Callanach raised his voice to be heard above the sighs and moans rippling through the crowd.

'DI Turner was an extremely difficult subject to choose to abduct if this was a copycat,' Callanach said. 'Why risk kidnapping a police officer?'

'Kudos,' Harris replied immediately, as if he'd foreseen the question. 'The glory of going one better than the man whose work he is emulating. He wants the same recognition, probably hopes Rory Hand himself will admire his daring. These are crimes of ego, DI Callanach. They are bold and unafraid. The copycat wants to show that he is even more outrageous than his idol.'

'So why the clumsy notes and the heart in the freezer?' Callanach wasn't going to be silenced so easily. 'That was just trickery, not a device Buxton and Magee's killer has resorted to.'

'I believe our new player is trying to put his own stamp on his work, to be unique. The outcome is a tribute to Hand's work, not the minute detail.'

'Could you not call the person who abducted DI Turner a player, if you don't mind, Professor Harris,' DCI Begbie said. The room was silent. It was a reprimand. 'This is no game.' Harris opened his mouth to apologise, knowing he'd been too clever for his own good, knowing he'd lost the respect of the men and women in the room, but Begbie wasn't going to let him get another word in. It was the only moment of satisfaction Callanach got from the briefing. There was no other good news at all.

'I'll be revisiting the baby deaths case and chasing leads on anyone who might have felt retribution was necessary. DI Callanach will be following up the death threat DI Turner received. Anyone not allocated to those teams will be conducting further checks in the crime scene area, CCTV, studying recent personal and professional communications to see if there were any other threats she didn't report. DS Lively will be continuing to process the case against Hand. I want updates by noon. Now get moving.'

Tripp caught up with Callanach in the corridor. 'I just thought you should know, sir, the scrap-yard owner finally found his records. He passed the car to a dealer in Edinburgh. Name's Louis Jones. Shall I bring him in?'

'Not at the moment. That car could have gone on to another four or five dealers after Jones. Get me the file on the death threat, then find Sergeant Lively. Tell him to ask Rory Hand for the dates and times when he killed Buxton and Magee. I want to know how long each was alive. And tell Lively he's to indicate to Hand that the police already know the answers to those questions, as if there's a right or wrong. Professor Harris is not to be involved or I will personally see to it that DS Lively is the subject of a rapid transfer to traffic.'

'Using those exact words?' Tripp looked concerned.

'Those exact words.'

'You don't really think it's the same murderer who's got DI Turner, do you sir? Only if it is . . .'

'I have no idea, Tripp. It's a mess. There are more differences than similarities and we're all chasing our tails. But I want some answers and I want them right now, if only to rule a few possibilities out.'

Callanach arrived home at two in the morning, and then he'd only abandoned his desk because Begbie had seen his light on and issued a direct command for him to leave the office. Outside Callanach's flat was a tall stick leaned carelessly in the corner, wrapped in brown parcel paper. He recognised the handwriting on the attached card as Ava's.

He opened his door, grabbed the parcel and rushed inside. He tackled the wrapping paper first, desperate to believe that inside was a clue as to her whereabouts, that it had all been a terrible mistake and that Ava was alive and well, having run away after her suspension. What he found was a gleaming wooden fishing rod, reel already attached, with a small box of flies and a rolled-up woollen hat. Callanach opened the note. It was scribbled, the penmanship not a concern, with what looked like tea spilled on one corner of paper that had clearly been ripped roughly from a notebook. It was typically her.

'Luc – I've decided you need to learn to relax. Enclosed is a fishing rod in case such things had passed you by in France. Next time you've a weekend off, we're going to Loch Leven near Kinross. There I will teach you to catch the finest trout in the world, which I will also cook for you. We'll hire a cottage (you'll be paying as I'll be sharing my fishing expertise with you). It's a beautiful place – only sky, water and more sky. Just so we're clear – this is not a date. The fish are much more interesting to me than you!' The final phrase was followed by a huge smiley face, below which was a PS. 'You'll need the hat. We have to fish from a boat and it gets cold. Sorry if it messes up your hair!!!'

He picked up the fishing rod. It wasn't cheap. The wood was velvety smooth and the reel made the softest of clicks as he wound it, balanced faultlessly against the weight of the rod. The present and note had been left before she was taken, he knew that. Presumably while he was settling in at Natasha's, so she could be sure he wasn't home.

The thought of what Ava was suffering was unspeakable. Callanach held a pillow to his face and yelled.

Chapter Thirty-Four

Ava's face was swollen and disfigured. It was a shame. He'd admired her handsomeness at the lecture.

'If only you hadn't made me strike you, this would have been altogether less difficult and you wouldn't be in so much pain,' King had told her as he'd dragged her into his house from the garage. Ava had been unconscious, so he supposed talking to her was a little odd but at least she couldn't answer back. He'd had to hit her to silence her. The second he'd stopped the car she'd begun the kicking and screaming again and, without the engine noise to drown it out, there was a possibility that a passerby might hear.

He'd used the back of his fist, lashing one of her temples hard enough that it had put him in mind of a cat o' nine tails on a Napoleonic ship. He'd enjoyed the comparison. It made him feel like a captain. At sea, strict discipline was necessary to maintain order. The ranks had to be kept in line or rebellion would occur. Wasn't that the most apt analogy to their situation? Regretfully, after the cracking sound his fist had elicited from her face, he feared he might have broken her cheek bone. The bruise was already blooming.

In the lounge he'd drawn the curtains, checked the cable ties and fastened her to the legs of a massive, old oak table. As a thoughtful final gesture he'd slid a cushion under her head.

'You don't want to wake up with a crick in your neck, do you?' he'd asked as he picked up the car keys one last time. He still had to drop off the borrowed vehicle before he could relax. 'Not that you're going anywhere,' he'd whispered in Ava's ear. 'And when I get back, we'll make plans for your stand-in's death. You can help, if you like. You know the tricks of the trade even better than I.'

Dr King spent the intervening period returning the hired vehicle, and considering whether or not it had been too rash a move, taking a police officer. Not that there was any real danger she might prove to be a match for him – his ability to foresee and prepare for all eventualities was his ultimate weapon. But he was aware that she wouldn't be intimidated as easily as Elaine or Jayne. The battle to break her would be more prolonged, require a greater level of dedication. There was a risk, in fact, that she might never bend to his will. It was possible that her stubbornness might be greater than her desire to better herself. If that was true then he had no qualms about dispatching her. He didn't want to lose Ava, aware that he was tiring of Elaine and Jayne. Some fresh blood was definitely needed. But if she proved too dangerous, Ava might leave him no option. He considered the possibilities. Without an element of natural justice to her death, it would be plain old murder. And he was no common-or-garden murderer.

She was stubborn, he focused on that. Stubborn like a mule. And what did mules do? They kicked, which would leave him no choice but to kick back. He imagined the sound of his foot contacting her abdomen, like deflating a football. Her ribs would break too easily. He would have to remove his shoes, he thought. He would hurt his feet but it was a proper and necessary sacrifice.

It wasn't fair to kick with shoes on. That would be wrongful. Yes, kicking it would have to be. Thinking about it, it seemed more than likely that she might prove implacably stubborn. And the more he thought about the consequences of that, the more colour and texture the sight of her bruised and fractured body took on in his mind. He wondered briefly if he weren't creating a self-fulfilling prophecy. But that was absurd. After all, he was nothing if not open minded.

It was three long hours before King made it home again. He'd had to walk miles back from the weasel's. No buses at that time. And by then, very much awake, Detective Inspector Ava Turner was waiting.

Chapter Thirty-Five

Falling asleep had proved an insurmountable task, so Callanach had risen again, dressed, taken his car via the station to pick up keys from the evidence store and made his way to Ava's. He was aware that it was four in the morning, that it looked odd going there alone at that time, and that he was doing more wallowing than police work, but it was the only place he wanted to be. He'd been there just once previously, but the familiarity from that sole visit lent a small measure of comfort. It wasn't simply that it was the place Ava inhabited away from work, more that everything in it was the embodiment of her. Mugs were bright, colourful, larger than life. Every wall was covered in a painting, a print, postcards, maps or shelving that housed endless DVD cases and music. It was both functional yet brimming with life as only Ava lived it. In front of her washing machine was a pile of clothes, t-shirts, jeans with socks poking from the feet, half upright, that she had clearly stepped out of in the utility area, saving the walk from the basket to the laundry. He fought the desire to shove it all in the washer for her. To do one tiny, stupid thing to make her life easier when he brought her back. If he brought her back.

His mind rewound time to the day she was sent the roses. What had he said when she'd refused to report it? 'It's your funeral.' That was it. Only time would tell how prophetic that might prove to be. With a roar he hadn't even known was coming, he rammed his fist full force into the wall, pulling it back, connecting again and again until he felt the snap of his little finger and an exploding firework of pain shot up his arm. There was a dent and a bloody mark in the plasterboard. He took a cloth and did what he could to clean it with bleach from beneath the sink before raiding her first aid kit and binding two fingers together. He knew he should leave. It wasn't healthy to be there, immersing himself in memories of her. Yet the temptation of her bedroom proved too strong, of finding out who she was in her most private moments.

Ava's bedroom was calmer and more ordered than the rest of the house. A plain white duvet cover was laid across a neat bed. A few ornaments decorated surfaces, but it seemed that this was where she came to clear her head and shed the chaos of the day. Callanach sat on the edge of the bed, feeling like an intruder, but knowing he was as close to her as he could get for now. Slowly, he slid open the top drawer of her bedside cabinet. There was jewellery, a notepad, a diary, and below that pushed to the back, was a tiny slate painted with a child's prayer. 'And now I lay me down to sleep, I pray the Lord my soul to keep, If I should die before I wake, I pray the Lord my soul to take.' He ran his fingers over the thin, smooth slab of grey stone, the irony of the words a twisting vine of ice in his guts. If she should die . . . No amount of prayer could protect her now. Ava's alarm clock buzzed. It was time to go to work.

Callanach stared at the useless facts and figures on the page before him. His brain was frustratingly slow. Instead of trying to read it a fourth time, he picked up the phone to speak to the forensics assistant who'd compiled the report.

'So the death threat letter gave us no leads. There's not one unusual aspect about it that might help?' he asked.

'Nothing, I'm afraid,' the girl said.

'Is there anything you could have missed, something you might test again?'

'Nothing. You've got the grammage of the paper, the ink type. They're all commonly used. Most businesses buy these in bulk just because they're so cost effective. We use both.'

Callanach stopped flicking through the report. 'We, meaning, the people in your lab?'

'We, as in the Edinburgh stations within Police Scotland,' she said.

Callanach hung up. The flowers and champagne had been delivered to the station but that didn't mean they hadn't been ordered by someone on the inside. Someone who had access to exactly the same paper and ink as had been used to write the death threat. Someone who had developed an impossibly deranged obsession with Ava, who had manipulated Natasha to get Ava where he wanted her. It was time to go back to basics. No amount of forensic investigation would solve this.

Callanach took the stairs to the ground floor. Every police officer had been called in for the day. All leave was cancelled. Only those holidaying abroad or off sick were not on duty. He didn't even know what he was looking for. He simply had to believe that when he found the person who was doing this, their reaction would give them away. He started on the ground floor and slowly worked his way up.

Office by office, corridor by corridor, floor by floor he went. He spoke to everyone, asked if they'd had any contact with DI Turner in the last twenty-four hours. Every person took his questions seriously, no one was evasive, they all understood what was at stake. Callanach wasn't listening to their answers, not the words they used, anyway. He was watching faces, looking in their eyes for avoidance, excitement or fear. He kept his manner stern, businesslike. Two hours later, as he reached the top floor, he was starting to doubt the sanity of what he was doing thinking he could find the needle in the haystack. Once he reached the administrative offices, he was lost. He'd never been up there in the most distant corridors, had always sent Tripp with paperwork queries.

He kept on going through human resources, past the press office and up to support staff. A woman crossed the corridor into an office carrying a bundle of folders. He followed her.

'DI Callanach,' he introduced himself. 'Do you mind if I ask you a couple of questions? Have you had any contact with Detective Inspector Turner in the past twenty-four hours?'

The woman shook her head. 'I haven't. I only do the finances for the uniformed divisions. My colleague handles yours and DI Turner's accounts. She's in the other office. I wish I could've helped.' She seemed genuinely upset. Callanach thanked her and went to the office opposite.

A woman was at her desk in the corner with her back to him, eyes fixed on a screen, tapping fast on the keyboard. Callanach waited a second before knocking on the open door to announce his presence.

'Excuse me,' he said. 'I appreciate you're busy but I need to ask you a couple of questions.'

The woman turned around. Her hair was streaked different shades of blonde and cut into a short bob. She was skinnier than he remembered and wearing black-rimmed glasses. He'd never have recognised her from the back or the side, and even front on he might not have noticed her if he hadn't been looking directly. But the smile was exactly the same.

The woman he'd spoken to across the corridor walked in and stood at his side.

'There you are. You probably haven't been introduced yet. Detective Inspector Callanach, this is my colleague, Astrid Borde.'

Chapter Thirty-Six

King was tired, and when he was tired his manners suffered. It was a flaw he disliked in himself but then he always had been his own harshest critic. What he didn't enjoy was having his faults pointed out by others.

On his return home, legs and arms punishing him for the physical exertions of his night, skittish with the after effects of too much adrenaline, he had tried to be welcoming to his newest guest. She'd been unreceptive. Tempted as he was to resort to an extra dose of chloroform, he couldn't imperil her with too great a build up. More importantly, he'd decided that he was beyond dragging bodies up and down the staircases. Tilting the heavy table, he allowed Ava to slip her cable-tied hands free of the table leg, and sit up.

'There,' he said. 'You'll be groggy for a while and your hands and feet will be numb from the restraints, but that'll go. I'm Dr King.'

'Moffboars,' she said through a swollen face, puffy lips, eye badly disfigured. He'd have to get some ice on that.

'I can't understand what you're saying, I'm afraid. Perhaps better to stay quiet and listen at this stage. I need to get you to a place where you can rest properly. You're going to have to walk. It's not far. Every door and window is locked so there's no point running. Your hands will remain as they are and I will cut the tie around your ankles, but you and I need to understand one another. I have this knife,' he picked it up from the sofa. 'It's a carving knife. I sharpen it myself and take quite a pride in doing so. Given that the world will be mourning your passing anyway in a couple of days, it would be advisable not to give them better proof of your demise than I had planned.'

Her face could put lemons to shame, he thought. Quite the vixen. She hadn't even glanced at the knife. He'd expected toughness from a police officer but this hostility was unfortunate. King pointed the blade at her for effect, letting the lamp light glint off its edges and reflect in her eyes.

'This knife will be at your throat as you walk. Do not kick or trip or launch yourself at or away from me. If you do, I will not hesitate to dirty the steel.' He put the knife to the cable tie around her feet and demonstrated the truth of his claim. It sliced the toughened plastic as if through butter. Ava watched him do it, but he saw calculation in her eyes rather than distress. He'd have to be careful with this one. No wonder Natasha had been drawn to her. They were well twinned in cunning and guile.

'Stand up,' he said. Ava didn't hesitate. She was bright enough to know which battles to fight and which were beyond her. They walked across the lounge, through the hallway and into the cupboard under the stairs. From there, the door to the cellar was discreet but far from hidden. The cellar was a feature of all the houses in the road. Pretending it didn't exist would look suspicious if anyone ever got close enough to enquire. It was down those very steps, tragically enough, that his sister had slipped and broken her neck aged just fourteen, wasting so much extraordinary genius and potential. Thirteen-year-old King had thought they might move from the house then, that it would be too full of memories to tolerate, but it had only served to become a shrine to their darling Eleanor, and both his father and mother had spent the rest of their days there.

DI Turner was walking as he'd instructed her, but her eyes were darting left and right. Well, left anyway, he thought, allowing himself a grin. She couldn't look to the right with the damage to her face.

'I know what you're doing,' he said. 'So study away, get a feel for the terrain, know your entrances and exits. It won't help. The staircase from the cellar to the guest suite has been there for years. My father used to escape to his private rooms when my mother was in one of her less sociable moods. It was only when they both passed that I put in the false wall, converted the space so I could use it in my own way. It took me the best part of a year just to fit the wood panelling.'

At the bottom of the first staircase he unlocked the door and flicked a light switch to illuminate the stairs hidden behind the wall. Ava turned to look him in the eyes. She was brave. He could see it. Not bravado, not an act. Perhaps she genuinely had no fear. Perhaps some part of her, that sixth sense that everyone had like a parasitic worm in their guts, had always suspected this might be her fate.

'I know who you are.' She spat out each word through the swelling so he could be left in no doubt. 'You smell of mothballs. You murdered Elaine Buxton and Jayne Magee.'

'Is that what Detective Inspector Callanach told you when he was so unsuccessfully investigating the case?' King asked, bristling at the mention of how he smelled but more determined than ever to get her up the stairs. 'You police are all so self-assured, aren't you? So keen to label and box and solve. Perhaps you'd like to join Miss Buxton and the Reverend Magee?' he asked, pushing the knife into her throat until he could see the veins starting to bulge.

Finally she looked afraid. She took a step backwards, then another and another, following the orbit of the knife as he circled it from left to right in an infinite loop before her face, forcing her upwards, closer to the top of the hidden staircase, further away from her old life with every step.

'You don't have to kill me,' she said, finding her voice as the upper door loomed closer.

'If only that were true,' he said. 'But if you don't die, then you'll never be mine, not properly. There will always be people with hope in their hearts, people who won't stop searching, police officers for whom the case will grow cold but never lie still in their memories. With death, Detective Inspector, comes grief and with grief there can be an ending.'

Ava stood on the top step, her back to the door. She put her hands in the air and the gesture said more than words ever could. She had surrendered, accepted her fate, made herself his. He wished he could stop time, could study the expression on her face as she transcended into his world, could fill himself forever with the delight of knowing he had won.

'Ava, don't be scared. It's time to meet your new dead friends.'

King pushed open the door. He held Ava's hand as she went in, like a bride walking to the altar, watching her eyes widen as she recognised the women on the beds.

'What the fuck?' she whispered.

Chapter Thirty-Seven

'DI Callanach,' she said, adopting a superficially demure air before her coworker. Only Callanach could hear the mockery in her voice. 'How nice to meet you.' Astrid held out her right hand to shake his. He stared at it as if she were offering him a slab of maggot-infested meat. He hadn't been able to tolerate anyone touching him, however fleetingly or well meant, since she'd accused him of rape. Now the thought of Astrid's flesh making contact with his made him feel physically ill.

'I'll need to talk with you privately,' he said, his voice hoarse, fighting his disbelief.

'Certainly,' she replied sweetly, 'anywhere you like.' Astrid beamed at the woman she shared an office with as if she'd been given the rest of the week off. Callanach stepped back to let her through the doorway without giving her an excuse to touch him.

'Down the stairs, ground floor, far end of the corridor to the right,' Callanach said, keeping his eyes in front, counting his breaths to combat the light-headedness that was blurring his vision. Astrid took her time on the stairs, greeting every person who passed them with a cheery hello. Callanach could feel the muscles in his shoulders and back seizing up with every passing step. It was all he could do not to scream at her to hurry.

'Are we not going to your office?' she asked, sugary and compliant. Her voice grated inside his head like vuvuzela at a football match.

'No,' he said, walking ahead down the final corridor, and opening the interview room door. 'And we're talking in English only. No French. I'm not prepared to lose time with allegations that we've had any improper conversations.' He pulled a chair out from under the table and motioned for her to sit. Callanach punched buttons on the monitoring system, setting both video and audio recording in motion. Astrid slid her hands across the table to within a centimetre of his, flashing a bright smile.

'Luc, this is an interview suite. I don't understand what the problem is. And why the machines? Just ask me whatever it is you want to know.'

'I want to know what you're doing here,' he said, endeavouring to keep his voice unthreatening. It shook with the effort.

'I work here,' she said. 'I have not been hiding. I even sent down some time sheets you hadn't filled in properly. My initials were on the note. Unfortunately, you sent one of your boys to sort it out. Sloppy not to get your paperwork right. Your standards must be slipping.' Astrid played with a lock of hair that had fallen across her face. Another man might have thought it alluring. What Callanach saw was a viper planning her next strike.

'I meant, what are you doing in Scotland? There's an injunction, Astrid, a court order to prevent you from coming near me. You're not allowed to have any contact at all.'

'Only in France, silly. That injunction ceased to have any effect once you left the country. And you didn't get another one here, so I'm not restrained any more. That's how you wanted it, no? You came here so we could have a new start?' She touched his hand. Callanach reacted as if a scorpion had crawled on his skin. He kicked his chair away and backed off to lean against the far wall.

'I didn't come to Scotland for you to follow me. I came because you ruined my life in France. You took everything – my career, friendships, reputation. How the hell did you get this job?'

'Interpol was not entitled to write anything about it on my reference. It was not relevant to my professional conduct. I was a victim who had felt unable to go ahead with a trial. If that had prevented me getting this job, I'd have been entitled to sue them. And my immediate superior at Interpol had no idea you were here. I actually think the bitch was pleased I was leaving, so I'm sure she wrote me a glowing reference.'

'That doesn't explain why no one here realised who you were. They did a full background check. I disclosed everything.'

'You were never convicted – in fact you were legally declared not guilty of any wrong-doing. The administrative system does not cross-reference the names of employees in such circum-stances, especially given that I only applied here after your posting had been finalised. And your boss who worked so hard to get you this job presumably arranged to keep all the paper-work nice and clean on your behalf.'

'You had no right to follow me here and you know it.'

'Luc, darling . . .' She stood up and began to step around the table.

'Sit down,' he ordered.

'Am I under arrest?' she asked.

'You're being questioned.'

'Then caution me,' she teased, undoing her top button and flicking her hair, but she sat. 'I don't understand why you're so angry. I decided against giving evidence.'

'Not until the day before the trial. I lost months of my life! My own mother can't bear to talk to me any more. And the worst thing is that I don't believe you ever intended to go through with the fucking trial. You just wanted to destroy everything I had!' Callanach's hands were fists in his pockets.

'I saved you. You really shouldn't be telling me off.' Her eyes were huge and teary.

'It was a lie, Astrid. Every bit of it was a lie. I didn't rape you, we didn't have sex. How can you possibly think you saved me?' Callanach was at shouting point. A curious officer put his face to the glass in the door to check what was happening. Callanach nodded at him and he walked away.

'You'd have been in prison now if it weren't for me. Is that what you'd have preferred? Ten years of shitty food and dirty, stinking men for company. How long do you think you'd have lasted?' Astrid was angry. At least that one emotion was real, Callanach thought. 'I made sure you were released so we could move past the unpleasantness and start again. That's why your choice to move elsewhere in Europe was so perfect. We both speak English, we both have transferrable skills.'

'Please, stop!' Callanach's hands were over his eyes. 'Astrid, listen, you need help. I know this is hard for you but we don't have a relationship, we never have. You can't keep doing this.'

'You're so kind, Luc. You've always been kind. No one else sees it but me. We are destined to be together. When I'm with you, the pain inside me goes away. That's why I came after you. I feel how much you love me and I know it's scary, but I can be strong enough for us both.'

'How did you think this was going to turn out?' he asked. 'Were you planning on just walking into my office one day and throwing yourself at me?'

'I had already let you know I was here. I sent you champagne. Nothing but the best. And roses like the ones that grew at the

Parc de la Tête d'Or in Lyon where you used to run every lunchtime.'

'That was you? We assumed . . . never mind. At least it makes sense now. But I want to know everything. No more games.' He changed tack.

Astrid considered it. 'What do you want me to say?'

'Just the truth,' he said. 'There has to be honesty between us if you want me back. Only you could have thought so carefully about the things I like. The roses were stunning and they did remind me of home.'

Her face darkened. It was like watching a storm roll in.

'Only me, Luc, or has there been someone else?'

'No one else,' he said, sitting down again.

'Liar!' she shrieked. 'I saw you with her. I watched you flirting. And I saw the way she looked at you. Did you share my champagne with her? Did you give her the flowers I sent you?'

'I don't know who you're talking about, Astrid.'

'Yes, you do,' she spat.

Callanach was making headway. 'No, honestly, I don't. There's been no one since you.'

She grinned at him and it was like teetering on the edge of an abyss.

'You're playing me,' she said. 'I know what you want me to say, Luc, and I'm not going to. No one since us? I thought there had never been an "us". I thought you'd scuttled here like some big, fat, nasty spider hiding under a rug to get away from me. You want me to say her name. I'm not going to.'

Callanach checked his watch. He'd tried his best with her, but having a personality disorder wasn't the same as having a low IQ. He would need a lot more time to get her to admit what she'd done and the clock was stealing minutes Ava didn't have.

'Did you send DI Turner the death threat?' he asked plainly. The emotion dropped out of her face.

'I want a lawyer,' she said.

'Did you abduct her?'

'I'm not answering any more questions.' Astrid buttoned her shirt back up dramatically, crossed her arms and stared at the desk.

Callanach considered the lengths she'd gone to. It took a peculiar state of mind to pursue someone so far and with so much passion. She would keep the game going as long as he was here to play it. The only way to win was to deprive her completely of her goal.

'All right,' he said, 'but I'm busy. We have sufficient grounds to question you further. I have more important matters to attend to, though. Wait here. I'll get a constable to conduct the interview. You won't have any further dealings with me.' He walked to the door.

'Stop,' she said. 'You stop right there. You're just going to walk out, after everything?'

'Yes,' he said. 'I have priorities.'

'You bastard,' Astrid hissed. 'Priorities? You think you can find Ava Turner without me? Within two hours you'll be begging for my help.' Her face was snarled, twisted. As much as Callanach longed to race back in, grab her by the neck and wring the information out of her, he knew it wouldn't work like that.

'Like I said, I'm very busy. I'll have an officer with you soon. In the meantime, I'll send the custody sergeant to process and caution you.' He let the door swing shut.

A few seconds later he heard the latch go. He was halfway up the corridor when Astrid began yelling.

'Fuck you. I saw him take your precious Detective Inspector Turner. He'll kill her. You get back here right now or her blood will be on your hands.'

Callanach turned, moving back down the corridor towards Astrid, stopping opposite the interview room door, leaning against the wall and staring in. 'Where?' he asked her through the open doorway. 'Where did you see this?'

'I'm saying nothing until you come back into this room,' Astrid screeched.

'Give me some facts so I know I can believe you, or I'll make sure you never see me again.'

'I followed you after work,' she said. 'You went to that professor's house, the one your girlfriend is so keen on. I waited all night for you to come out but you didn't. You stayed pandering to that stupid woman, making a fuss about those little notes. And yes, I know all about the case. Don't make the mistake of thinking I don't have friends inside this police station.'

'I don't give a damn who you're friendly with. I want to know why you stood by and did nothing while a police officer was being abducted!' Callanach growled.

'I had no idea it was Turner until he pulled her out of the car.'

Callanach moved through the doorway so fast that Astrid had no time to brace. He pulled her against him, gripping her upper arm with one hand, raising the other to point in her face.

'If you're lying . . .' he said. He didn't have to finish the threat — his face said it all.

'I'm not,' Astrid replied, 'but I'm saying nothing more until you guarantee in writing that I won't be prosecuted, not for the letter I sent her, not for anything I tell you about last night.'

'Astrid, there's no time,' Callanach said, torn between violence and begging.

'And you'll stay with me until it's sorted out. We'll talk about France, about our old friends, how it used to be. That's how this is going to work.'

Tripp entered the interview room, followed by Lively. They both froze when they saw Callanach with Astrid in his grasp.

'Constable, get me someone from the Procurator Fiscal's office who has the authority to grant immunity,' Callanach said. Tripp was gone without a second's pause. Callanach looked at Lively. 'What do you want, Sergeant?'

'Rory Hand. He couldn't answer the questions about when he killed Buxton and Magee. He went no comment then lawyered up. I came to say I'm sorry. I think maybe you were right.'

'It's a bit bloody late for that,' Callanach said, pushing Astrid back down into her seat.

Chapter Thirty-Eight

King relished the confusion in Ava's eyes when she saw the women on their beds. Neither of them said a word. He gave his latest guest the opportunity to use the toilet before securing her to the bed. The intimacy with their personal habits was an aspect of being a guardian he disliked, but it gave him an additional element of power.

'Could I have more painkillers, please, Dr King?' Elaine whispered.

He thought about it. She was consuming an awful lot lately. Still, there were worse things than an addiction to prescription drugs and it certainly made her easier to bear.

'I'll get you some paracetamol but you have to help me with your new friend. Secure that cable tie around her wrist and the bed post. Not too tightly! We don't want to cut off the circulation.'

'Don't do it,' Ava said to her. 'Elaine, I'm a police officer, you don't have to help him.'

'She does have to,' King whispered, 'don't you, my dear?'

Elaine nodded feebly.

'Or what will I do?' King kept the knife pointed at Ava while Elaine tied her up.

'You'll get the ruler out again,' she said.

Ava looked to Jayne. It didn't take a genius to realise he'd broken Elaine, snapped her inner fortitude into so many useless fragments, but he hadn't expected the gutsy detective inspector to give up on her quite that fast. Jayne was praying. Same old same old.

'Now, Ava, I don't want you inciting these girls to riot.' He giggled at the notion of it. 'Let me explain why. If one of you behaves in a way that is detrimental to the well-being of our community here, I will have to punish another among your number. Hence, if you are difficult with me, I shall have to do things to Jayne that she really will not enjoy.'

'Jayne,' Ava said. 'Can you talk to me? Jayne Magee, help will come.'

'That's exactly what I was talking about,' King said. 'Normally I would be more lenient on your first day. I expect a bit of kerfuffle while you get settled, but I'm shattered and I think you need to fully comprehend the position you're in.' He unlocked a drawer, took out two tablets and gave them to Elaine with a plastic tumbler of water. 'See how kind and considerate I can be?' He withdrew another item from the drawer that he kept folded in his hand. Ava strained her neck to watch what he was doing.

King stood at Jayne's bedside. The chant of her prayer had risen in volume and she wasn't making eye contact with him. Elaine had swallowed her medicine and was in the process of sliding under her bed clutching a pillow and blanket. There was a vague humming coming from where she was hiding, something childish and repetitive.

'She's regressing,' King said sagely to Ava. 'Lesson number one, DI Turner. Do not think you can ignore the warnings I give you.'

He grabbed Jayne's nose with his left hand, pinching it

viciously. She squealed, heaving her body up and down, on and off the mattress, fighting to get away but his grip was vice-like. It was odd, he thought, as he positioned the bulldog clip in his hands, how he had been so weak as a child. No good at sports, never strong enough to help his father with lifting or woodwork. But recently, in his late middle age, when he'd needed it most, he had the strength of a bear. It wasn't so much mind over matter as freedom from worrying about it. His brawn in the heat of the moment was effortless.

He squeezed then released the metal clip onto Jayne's tongue, allowing the spring to close with a twang. Her eyes rolled as the pain dug in, then she was awake again, crying, screaming, gagging.

'You have Miss Turner to thank for that,' King said. 'Perhaps later today when I return you'd like to think of some way to repay her. It being a Saturday, and as I've not slept for eighteen hours, I'm off to rest. I'm sure you could use some as well.'

'Take it off her,' Ava shouted.

King could hear Elaine's mantra of 'no, no, no' from beneath her bed. She was shaping up to be the most sensible of them all. Even Jayne was fighting through the agony to shake her head wildly at Ava.

'I don't think the good reverend wants you to intervene any further,' he said. 'I think she'd like you to behave in a way that does not result in me taking more drastic action.' Jayne was nodding fiercely, almost growling at Ava.

'I'm sorry,' Ava said quietly.

'I don't think we could hear you over the other ladies' noise,' King said. 'Say again, please.'

'I said I'm sorry,' Ava yelled at him. 'All right? I'm sorry.'

'Good,' King said. 'Now, Jayne, don't you move that clip! You'll find that the pain will die down naturally in a couple of hours. And Elaine, don't you be tempted to help your friend by relieving her of it. You may be unrestrained now, but that doesn't mean you're free to do as you wish. Not if you don't want to experience first hand just how excruciating this is. Very interesting history, though. It's a form of punishment that was used popularly in Colonial America to encourage nagging wives to talk less. Seems appropriate. I shall leave some music on for you. Might help take your mind off it, Jayne.'

As he left, one of Rachmaninoff's piano concertos filled the air. King listened at the door for a moment after he locked it, but heard no voices. They would talk later, when he was asleep. It didn't matter. They would say what a monster he was and how they hated him, make plans and imagine rescuers winging their way to them. Let them have their fantasies, he thought. If that was all they had left of their former lives, who was he to deprive them of such paltry comfort? They would adapt very soon and, if any of them failed to do so, he'd have one less decision to make.

Chapter Thirty-Nine

Callanach was back in the interview room. Astrid's deal had been done. Lively was in the monitoring room, watching the remainder of the interview unfold. Callanach wished he could change places with him. He had no desire to be in such close proximity to Astrid for a single second longer.

'You have everything you wanted,' Callanach said, 'and I'm losing my patience.'

'Not everything,' Astrid replied. 'I want a signed letter guaranteeing you will not apply for another injunction.'

'Ava Turner is in the hands of a madman. Stop playing fucking games, Astrid.'

'Write it out and I'll start talking.'

'God damn it,' he shouted as he grabbed a sheet of paper and scribbled. 'There, tell me what you saw and make it fast.'

'You admit you have feelings for her, then,' Astrid said. 'I thought so when I saw the two of you going to her car.'

'DI Turner is a colleague and I'm doing my job. If you don't start talking, though, I can be replaced by someone less tolerant.'

'All right, calm down, Detective Inspector,' she said acidly. 'It was about one thirty in the morning. I didn't know who it was at first, you understand. Turner's car was parked a long way from mine and under trees. I noticed the car door opening because the interior light came on. There was a minute when I couldn't see what was happening, then a man hauled her out of the car and walked her up the road, towards me, into another vehicle. I only recognised her face as he dumped her in his car.'

Callanach interrupted. 'Can you describe him?'

'Not really, it was too dark. He wasn't that tall, Caucasian, rather heavily built, out of shape, you know, wearing a hat and glasses. I can't do any better than that.'

'What then?'

'He put her in his car, must have been the back seat because he opened and closed two doors before driving off.'

'She was in the rear passenger seat?' Callanach asked.

'I assume so,' Astrid said, leaning her head on one hand as if bored. Callanach fought his temper. 'When the car pulled out, I still didn't realise what was happening but I watched more closely.'

'Why?' Callanach asked.

'Because he failed to put his headlights on straight away, not until he was nearly out of the road. And he did a three-point turn to leave in the opposite direction, not past me.'

'I don't understand how this helps,' Callanach said.

'It helps because I had binoculars and I took down the registration number. He was driving a black four-by-four, a Nissan.' She took out her mobile and opened a notebook app. 'Here's the plate.'

Callanach took her mobile and read out the licence number so the officers watching from the monitoring room could start checking it. That was when the interview room door burst open and Lively flew in.

'You had the licence plate all along?' Lively yelled, grabbing Astrid. 'You might have cost her her life!'

'DS Lively,' Callanach said. 'Take your hands off her and get out.'

'Your bloody fan club doesn't get special privileges here,' Lively shouted at him.

'We have a lead, which is more than you managed by arresting the wrong man. Now leave.'

Lively cursed a few more times but did as he was told.

'Thank you, Luc,' Astrid said softly. 'That was very gallant of you.'

'Not out of choice,' Callanach said. 'I agree with my sergeant. But I'm not finished yet. How did they get from Ava's car to his? Did he carry her?'

'No,' Astrid said. 'She walked, sort of, as if she was staggering and he was supporting her.'

'Chloroform,' Callanach said. He stood up.

'Wait!' she said. 'Is that it? When will I see you?'

'You're unwell, Astrid. I pity you, but there is no us and I never want to set eyes on you again. Try to understand.'

She smirked. 'I hope he kills her. He'll break your heart like you broke mine. Then you'll come back to me. You'll want me like you did before.' Callanach left.

The licence plate came back within five minutes as having been scrapped. It only took one phone call to the Falkirk scrap yard and the threat of another red tape visit from the Health and Safety Executive to persuade the owner to reveal that the wrecked Nissan, presumed by the owners to have been crushed, had also ended up at Louis Jones's.

'Tripp!' Callanach shouted as he stormed along the corridor towards his office. 'Get Louis Jones here. I want every sheet of paperwork, his computer, mobile, absolutely everything, in the incident room straight away. Identify where those cars ended up. And I want to know Jones's whereabouts each minute for the last month.'

'Yes, sir,' Tripp replied, poking his head out of the incident room and into the corridor. 'And Dr Spurr's waiting in your office. Said he knew you were busy and he'd wait.'

Callanach picked up Detective Constable Salter on his way back to his office. The pathologist greeted them with a heavy smile.

'Detective Inspector,' he said. 'I wanted to come in person. I'm sorry about Ava. She sent the loveliest note to thank me for the Lagavulin. It's hard to remain objective when one of our own is taken.'

'I appreciate the visit,' Callanach said, 'but it's bad timing. We're waiting for a witness to be brought in and I need to read his file.'

'It isn't a social call,' Spurr said, taking a file from his case. 'I'd like you to take a look at these.' He held up several large – scale photos.

'What am I seeing?' Callanach asked.

'Teeth,' Spurr said. 'This was the one found near the baseball bat and not fire damaged, so it's in the best condition to see the marks.' He pointed out small shaded areas, linear, about two-thirds of the way down the tooth. 'They look like deep ridges, don't they? The forensic odontologist didn't pick them up at first because we were only using the teeth for identification purposes.'

'So what are they?' Salter asked. 'And how did they get there?'

'We suspect, and I put it no higher than that, that they are damage to the enamel from a tool.'

'So the marks could have been made by her dentist previously?' Callanach said.

'I don't believe so,' Spurr said. 'The marks go below where the gum line would have been. The fact that this tooth still had healthy root attached means there was no reason for a dentist to have done this. The tool most likely to have caused this damage is dental extraction forceps.'

'What about the other teeth?' Callanach asked. 'Are there marks on them?'

'We think so,' Spurr said, turning to other photos. 'Look, here and here. It's harder to see because of the fire damage but on this one,' he held an extreme close up of a molar, 'you can see the scrapes. They're deep and they go right to the base of the tooth.'

'So you're saying the baseball bat wasn't the cause of the teeth dislodging?' Salter asked.

'I'm saying that someone used forceps on her teeth and it seems logical that the damage occurred while the teeth were still in Elaine's jaw, not afterwards. I checked with her dentist. He can't guarantee she didn't ever visit another practitioner but he certainly didn't do this. He also said the marks were clumsy, misplaced. If we're right, then . . .'

'Then Elaine Buxton was tortured before she was killed. You believe her teeth were pulled out with forceps while she was still alive,' Callanach said. Salter was a shade of green.

'That I can't be sure about,' Spurr said. 'But it seems more likely than after he killed her. There'd have been no point.'

'Amateur dentistry?' Salter said, her voice strangulated with the effort of not gagging. 'How do you get the tools for that? And how could he have learned to do it?'

'The implements can be ordered online from numerous websites and as for the training, there are emergency medicine manuals online. Not recommended reading, but they'll do the trick.'

'What about Jayne Magee?' Callanach asked. He thought about each woman's family and the fresh torment this news would add.

'I checked with Ailsa Lambert. She's terribly upset. I gather she's a friend of DI Turner's mother.' Callanach nodded. 'Magee's teeth were so badly damaged by the chemicals that the odontologist couldn't discern any specific marks. But if the teeth were extracted before death, it would explain the differing degrees of deterioration between the teeth and jaw bone.'

'Oh, shit,' Salter said.

'I quite agree, Detective Constable,' Spurr said. 'If Ava Turner's still alive then you need to find her quickly. A man capable of this . . .' He didn't finish and Callanach was grateful. He was all too aware of what the man holding Ava was capable of without anyone lending his brain images.

'Thank you,' Callanach said. 'Forgive me for not being able to give you more time.'

'Don't apologise,' the pathologist said, 'just find the monster who did this.' Jonty Spurr left and Callanach closed the door behind him.

'Sir . . .' Salter began.

'No,' Callanach said. 'We're not telling anyone, not yet. Everyone is working to full capacity. We won't get them to achieve more or better. At the moment, this is supposition. There's not even any hard evidence that the man who has DI Turner is the same man who killed Buxton and Magee. At best, it's an allegation we'll prove when we find where he kept them. All right?'

'Yes,' Salter whispered. 'It's just so awful to think of them being tortured like that.'

'Don't think about it,' Callanach said. 'You learn that after a while. You mustn't put yourself inside their bodies. Keep busy, Salter. Get me a list of websites where you can buy dental tools.'

'We will find her, won't we, sir?' Salter asked quietly.

Callanach wanted to lie but years of police work counselled against it. 'Keep busy,' he said again. 'We can only try our hardest.'

Chapter Forty

Louis Jones was proving elusive. Tripp was emailing photos of Jones's office, if you could call it that, back to Callanach in real time. There wasn't a calendar or diary to be found, no paperwork on the desk. The drawers were full of paperclips and ancient DVDs but nothing relating to his car business. Mounds of vehicle parts cluttered the lot, numerous cars with dubious histories were randomly parked, but there wasn't a computer in sight. Likewise, Jones's file was taking its time being brought to him. After an hour of waiting, Callanach finally lost it.

He was about to hammer on DCI Begbie's door when the Chief opened up.

'Come in, Inspector,' he said. 'I was on my way to find you.'

'I've requested a file and it's . . .' Callanach said.

'I know,' Begbie said. 'It's on my desk. Before you start, there's a reason. It's marked not to be opened without the authority of my rank or above.'

'I don't understand.'

'Louis Jones is on his way here, voluntarily. We'll speak to him together,' Begbie said.

'I can't run this case if you're keeping information from me.

I want to know exactly what's going on.' Callanach's hand slammed down on the Chief's desk. Begbie glanced at it then picked up a thin, tatty file and handed it over.

'The file is confidential because Jones, previously known to some of Edinburgh's less law-abiding citizens as Louis the Wrench, was an informant. Fifteen years ago, a three-year investigation was about to collapse with no prosecutions, not even an arrest. It was organised crime. The gang had men on their pay roll inside the police, government, everywhere. Each time we made a move they knew about it in advance. Louis was their go-to guy for vehicles and drivers. He didn't speak publicly, he wouldn't have survived long if he had, but the information he fed us was what we needed to close them down. We had a gentleman's agreement and he's been left alone ever since.'

'This is too serious to worry about past deals. We can't even be sure he's not the man responsible.'

'I can,' Begbie said. 'The man you're looking for is Caucasian. Louis is black. He's also not the type. I got to know him well enough to be able to tell. He was my source. He'll talk to me.'

True to his word, Louis Jones appeared twenty minutes later. Callanach watched Begbie greet him with a handshake and the sort of look that suggested they'd genuinely missed one another. The interview room was forsaken for the privacy of Begbie's office.

'This is Callanach,' DCI Begbie told Jones. 'He's got hands-on control of the investigation.'

'I thought it'd just be you and me, George,' Louis said, his voice soft and easy, belying a well-practised watchfulness.

'Not enough time for that. Callanach needs to speak with you. He can be trusted.'

Callanach wasn't sure that was true, not if it turned out that Jones had known what was going on.

'Two cars,' Callanach said, handing over the details. 'They came to you from a scrap yard in Falkirk. I need the records for each vehicle.'

'I don't keep records,' Jones said. 'It's all in my head. When you've seen the things I've seen, you don't write anything down. What's this about anyway?'

'Elaine Buxton,' Begbie said. 'You know about her?'

'Everyone knows,' Jones said. 'What've my cars got to do with that?'

'These cars were used by the man we think killed her. So who's got them?' Callanach asked.

'That prissy fuckin' snob? You're fuckin' messing with me!'

'Who?' Callanach shouted. 'I want a name!'

'I don't deal with names. What planet is he off?' Jones asked Begbie who held up a subduing palm.

'What can you tell us, Louis?' Begbie asked quietly.

'He paid cash. Only uses the cars for twenty-four hours then drops them back. That's what I do, hire out vehicles, no questions asked. He's been back six or so times, seemed like such an uptight ass that it never crossed my mind he could be doing anything bad. He joked once about needing a bit of private time away from the wife. I assumed he wanted to be able to cruise for a bit of tail without his other half getting a call from the polis.'

'Description?' Callanach said.

'Fifties, fat round the middle, bit of a comb-over on top, grey overcoat I remember, jowly face. I don't want my name dragged into this, George. This is bad news.'

'We need more than that, Louis,' Begbie said. 'I owe you and I know it, but I can't keep you out of this one. You loaned him cars with no checks or records. If this guy turns out to be the killer, even I won't be able to protect you.'

'I saved your fuckin' life, George, remember that?' Jones stood up.

'Yes, you did,' Begbie replied, 'but one of my officers is going to lose hers if we don't find this man, so let's cut the bullshit, shall we? You've never done business without certain precautions in place and I don't believe either of us has changed very much over the years. What were you going to do if he didn't bring a car back? No name, no address? That's bollocks.'

Jones landed back in his chair, swearing at the ceiling. 'I'm ruined if this gets out, so usual rules apply, right?'

'Usual rules,' Begbie said.

'I had one of my boys follow him. Standard when people won't give me details. I take a deposit so it doesn't really matter if they don't bring the car back but I need protection in case they use it in a robbery or . . .'

'Or a murder,' Callanach finished for him. 'So you lend the cars but bank the information to bargain with the police.' He ended the sentence with lengthy swearing in French.

Begbie ignored it. 'So what do you know?'

'He took the cars back to a lock-up on Causewayside, dodgy area, not much to see. I can give you the address. It was enough that I'd be able to find him if I needed to.' Louis scribbled on a notepad on Begbie's desk. Callanach ripped the paper off and went to the door.

'My name never comes out, you don't tap my fuckin' phone, and you don't quote me in any prosecution papers. Me and my business get left completely alone. We've got an agreement, and as far as I'm concerned it still stands,' Jones shouted after him.

'We understand,' Callanach heard DCI Begbie say, more for his benefit than Louis the Wrench's, he was sure. Interpol and its procedures, triple checks and no-compromise policy seemed further away than ever. Callanach wasn't sure if he should feel disgusted or grateful. At that moment, it didn't matter. He began to sprint.

The garage was one of a block in a back street off Causewayside. There were at least thirty with front-lifting doors so faded and chipped that the colours they had once been were now a distant memory. Disintegrating concrete made rubble of the ground outside and the street lighting was nonexistent. Most of the numbers had been knocked off or graffitied over. Tripp was waiting at the end of the street to wave in the forensic team whose sirens could be heard as they fought traffic. Callanach counted his way down the even side until he reached eighteen. He put on gloves and tried the handle. It was locked. Fetching a crow bar from the car boot, he shoved it into the gap between door and ground. A shearing sound ripped through the air as the wires at the top of the door fought the lock and then it was up, the metal too weakened by age and lack of maintenance to resist for long against Callanach's determination to get in.

From the entrance he shone the torch into the darkness at the back, flicking it left and right.

'What's in there?' Tripp yelled from the end of the street.

Callanach, hands on hips, head down, kicked the crow bar into the distance, ignoring the pain it sent through his toes and into his ankle.

'*Merde!*' he shouted. 'There's nothing here, not a single damned thing.'

Tripp abandoned his post and came running, staring into the empty hole that was the garage.

'Maybe forensics will find something,' he tried, but Callanach saw from Tripp's face that he didn't believe it.

'Even if we find his DNA, and there's a chance we might, this bastard's not in our system. He's obsessive, has probably been planning this for years. He's the opposite of a sex offender. Professor Harris had it all wrong. This man is not the least bit compulsive. It's a matter of pride for him that he's not that type of person.'

The forensics van pulled up and a team took over, leaving Callanach and Tripp staring on uselessly.

'I need a cigarette. Come and sit with me.' They walked around the corner as the crime scene was taped off. No houses overlooked the garages, no pubs exited onto the side road, nobody would hang around there at night, at least not innocently. It was a place designed for the business end of nasty criminal enterprises, the low-rent jobs, burglaries of people who couldn't afford insurance or alarm systems, organised muggings of the elderly or infirm. It was somewhere the murderer could be anonymous in the company of the nameless and faceless. Perfect for him.

'So he just swapped his vehicle over here then drove his own car home, right?' Tripp asked.

'Must be,' Callanach confirmed.

'Damn, he's good,' Tripp said. 'Control room says the garage is owned by a woman who advertised it in the local paper. Man renting it paid for the whole year in cash, which he put through her door in an envelope. That was six months ago. She never met him, just left it unlocked with the key inside. One phone call was all she remembers. Envelope and cash all long since gone.'

Callanach took a cigarette from the pack in his jacket pocket and stuck it, unlit, in his mouth, dragging air and tasting stale tobacco. His imagination did the rest, spiking nicotine into his blood and blowing out smoke in blue-grey puffs. He felt guilty for wanting it and pathetic for doing it. How could he give up smoking and not be able to give up pretending to smoke?

'What did I miss?' he asked, leaning back on his elbows and turning his face into the weak sun. 'There was something, somewhere. What do we know that he doesn't want us to know?'

'We've figured out how he gets his cars, where he does the

changeover, the extent of his planning. We even know what he looks like,' Tripp said.

All of which should have been vital information, Callanach thought, had real value, moved them closer to him. Only the murderer was still a step ahead, knew exactly which battles he could afford to lose.

'I think he plays it all out in his head. Almost as if he imagines it backwards. He knew we might find the lockup so he paid cash, never met the owner. Same with the cars. It's all information he knew we might uncover and he's allowed for it. What could he not have planned?'

'How he chose them. That bit's personal because the women had to be to his taste, fulfil whatever need he has for them.'

'But we don't know how or where he saw them. Every lead we've had he practically dropped in our laps, except for being seen by Astrid and that's brought us to yet another dead end. The only thing he couldn't control was being overheard by the cyclist when he was taking Jayne Magee.' Callanach walked to a drain where he let the crumpled, unsmoked cigarette fall into the watery depths as Tripp flicked through his notebook.

'I meant to bring you up to date on that,' Tripp mumbled as he read. 'The nightclub, The Lane, had no membership for Magee or Buxton. There's also a shop in the city called "Goodies in The Lane" but no relevance that I can see.' Tripp flipped over a couple of pages.

'What was it the cyclist heard exactly? Remind me,' Callanach said, kicking a can against a wall like a teenager, taking his rage out on metal and brick.

'Something about going back to the lane . . .' Tripp's voice rumbled beneath the sound of the can bashing against mortar.

Callanach stopped kicking and glared at the wall. 'Say it again,' he said. 'Whatever you just said, say exactly the same words again.'

'Liam Granger heard him say something about going back to the lane.' Callanach stared at Tripp who stared back. 'Are you sure you're all right, sir? Only you've gone an odd colour.'

Callanach bent over, head down almost to his knees, panting like a freight train, seeing stars. He'd skipped several meals and missed even more sleep than food. But the phantom nicotine, dredged from the depths of his memory, had worked its magic.

'They're not dead,' Callanach whispered. 'Tripp, they're not dead.'

Tripp put a gentle hand on his inspector's shoulder.

'Can I get you some water, sir? Perhaps you should sit down.'

'Listen to me. The cyclist heard the words "the lane" but what he actually said was "I'm taking you back to Elaine". It's what I thought you said when I wasn't listening properly.'

'But Elaine Buxton's body had been found by then. He can't have been taking Jayne Magee to her.'

'No, I don't think so. And Jonty Spurr won't either. Get in the car.'

Spurr abandoned whatever he was doing and got straight on the line to Callanach.

'DI Callanach,' Spurr said. 'Is there news?'

'No,' Callanach answered, 'but there's hope. The teeth, extracted before the body was burned, we think, and if I recall none still in position in the jaw.'

'That's right,' Spurr confirmed. 'Several smashed though, consistent with use of the baseball bat.'

'Could the teeth and jaw bone have been smashed with the bat after the extractions?' Callanach asked. There were a few seconds of silence on the line.

'Yes,' Spurr said.

'So he gave us a body too badly burned to retrieve DNA, left in a place where it wouldn't be discovered too soon, but sufficiently intact to indicate that the deceased was female and get an estimate of the age. We have blood, but not enough for blood loss to have led to her death in situ . . .'

'That's right . . .' Spurr said.

'A baseball bat positioned to look hidden but close enough to ensure we'd find it and one tooth with soft tissue attached for DNA. Also, luckily for us, part of her scarf that didn't burn around the edges. Tell me, Jonty, what of that evidence means the body was Elaine Buxton's?'

'All of it,' Spurr replied hesitantly, 'if this was a normal killer.' There was a long pause while Spurr took on board the conclusion Callanach had led him to. 'Or none of it, if he was determined – as well as clinical, precise and obsessive – absolutely determined to make us believe that it was Elaine Buxton and willing to kill a different woman to use as some sort of corpse proxy. You think they're still alive, don't you?'

'I do,' Callanach said. 'Because that's the one conclusion he absolutely did not want us to draw.'

'Tell me how I can help,' was Spurr's response.

'Compare notes with Ailsa Lambert about the body presumed to be Jayne Magee's. This scenario might explain why the bones and teeth in the barrel degraded at different rates, and why there were no upper teeth found at all. It was your identification of the tool marks in the enamel that did it, Jonty. I can't thank you enough.'

'Just find DI Turner alive.'

'It's not Ava I'm worried about,' Callanach said. 'It's the identities of the two dead women and the fact that he's going to need a third to put in Ava's place.'

Chapter Forty-One

It was a Sunday, and a day and a half since Ava Turner had first set foot in his house. King had lost track of the time, waking in a panic and believing he was late for work. In his exhaustion, he'd fallen asleep a second time until well into the afternoon. He'd been too stressed to eat and the fracturing of his usual routine was irksome. Worse than that, he'd tried to call the weasel at the car lot several times and been met with either a busy tone or the answer phone. It wasn't as if he'd been able to call from his mobile, either. Each time, he'd had to go to a different pay phone. In the end, he'd had to settle for changing the licence plates on his own car and adding loathsome transfer stripes along the sides. It was the best he could do as a disguise and he'd had the necessary parts ready. He'd always known he wouldn't be able to rely on the weasel for long. In an hour, when daylight turned to dusk, he'd be on his way to Dundee. He needed a favour from a girl there.

King went to feed his ladies before leaving. The room was unnaturally quiet, as if he'd disturbed witches in their coven, he thought. They were all eyes watching him enter the suite, suspicious, tense.

'Boo!' he shouted suddenly, eliciting a scream of terror from Elaine who was under her bed, surrounded by pillows and blankets, shivering on the floor. He let out a belly laugh that felt so good, he wondered why he hadn't come up earlier in the day.

'Jayne, your poor tongue, I'd completely forgotten,' he said, pulling the clip away with a smacking noise. She shrank back from him, crushing the pillow behind her, mouth firmly closed. King could well imagine she would never open it again in his presence.

'I take it that Detective Inspector Turner has learned not to make so free and easy with her temper,' he said, 'and I hope Elaine has been out from her cave often enough to bring you both the bedpan as required.'

He sat down next to Ava and stroked her hair, expecting her to flinch from his hand. She didn't. 'You have remarkable skin,' he said. 'And the swelling has reduced already. Later tonight, when the unpleasantness is over, I'll bathe you. I've bought fresh clothes, quality ones, not tat.'

'Thank you,' Ava said. 'What's happening tonight?'

'He's going to pull out your teeth,' Jayne lisped, her swollen tongue making it hard to understand her. King made a disapproving circle with his mouth and tutted at her.

'Now, we don't want to scare our new guest, not when she's settling in so well.'

'That's how you convinced the pathologists of their identities,' Ava whispered. 'Clever.'

'Do you really think so, Ava? What's that quote . . . "True praise comes often even to the lowly; false praise only to the strong." I have longed to be strong. It seems I've finally achieved a goal.'

'Seneca, advisor to Emperor Nero. You don't need to prove how strong you are to us. Why are you doing this?' Ava asked, bending and stretching her fingers in their bindings.

'You've read Seneca?' he asked.

'Some,' she replied. 'You didn't answer my question.'

'There's no answer. I did it because at some point I couldn't resist.'

'But why Elaine?' she pushed. He tucked the bedclothes in like a kindly matron then took a brush from a shelf and began to smooth her hair.

'She was brilliant, single-minded, focused. I especially liked that about her. She could command an audience like no one you've seen. I attended more than one public speaking engagement of hers. Skills acquired from all those years in court, I suppose. She would have become a judge eventually.'

'You wanted someone you could be proud of,' Ava commented.

'Exactly. Proud. It's a compliment. The other two haven't grasped that. When I saw you lecture at the Philosophy Department, I knew we would understand one another.'

'So why not approach me, ask me to dinner, talk to me? Would that have been so hard?'

'Would you have said yes?' he asked, narrowing his eyes, waiting for the lie.

'No,' she said, 'but I'd have respected you for asking. It's difficult to respect you when I'm tied to a bed.'

'It won't be for long,' he said. 'You're a woman who values mind above body, who can analyse and comprehend. You'll be able to see the world from a new perspective.'

'You mean from your perspective,' Ava said. 'What if I disagree with it?'

'All views are equally valid here,' he replied. 'We'll listen to each other, share our learning.'

'Through fear? No one learns that way. It's called conditioning.'

'There will only be fear if punishment is necessary, and that only results from bad behaviour. Without one there will be no need for the other.'

'Your rules, then,' Ava said.

'My rules.' He kissed her hand and put the brush back on the shelf.

'So we're not all equal. If we can't contribute to the rules, it doesn't work.'

'I have to go,' King said, 'but I've enjoyed this.'

'Let us go,' Ava said calmly. 'Elaine is close to breaking. She hasn't been out from under her bed in hours. She even slept there. Jayne has bed sores and her wrists have been in the metal cuffs too long.'

'She brought that on herself,' he snapped. 'Don't expect sympathy.'

'I thought you were our protector,' Ava said. 'To whom else should we turn?'

'Cunning pythoness, aren't you? It won't work,' he smiled.

'Carl Sandburg wrote, "The greatest cunning is to have none at all." What will you hide behind when we're telling you nothing but the truth?' Ava asked. King left without answering.

Chapter Forty-Two

Detective Constables Salter and Tripp were in Callanach's office surrounded by paperwork.

'So you're saying these women are still alive, but they've had their teeth pulled out,' Salter said. 'Is Hand still in custody?'

'Yes,' Tripp told her, 'but only for giving false information and the indecent images found on his computer. Sergeant Lively is handling it. The Chief's about to announce the reduction of Hand's charges at a press conference. Professor Harris is in with DCI Begbie now. I told them you were still out at Causewayside.'

'Good,' Callanach said. 'That should buy us some time. I want those missing persons files back from Harris without him figuring out what's going on or he'll interfere. Salter, can you get them for me?' A purposeful exit from the room was her answer. 'Keep a unit watching that garage, Tripp. He may yet return there. Ask Salter to take those files down to my car. I'll read them at home. Figuring out the identities of the dead women is the only way to catch him, and I need some peace and quiet. Stay here and keep everyone else away from me. All right?'

Tripp nodded. 'Sir,' he said. 'Good job.'

'Not yet,' Callanach answered, 'but let's keep hoping.'

He drove home. Daylight was dying. The news would be full of Hand's release on bail, his charges reduced from murder to attempting to pervert the course of justice. The headlines, though, would be about police incompetence and the spectre of a killer going undetected. Not unfairly, he thought.

Callanach felt bruised from his day, having repeatedly taken one step forward and several more back. Progress, failure, revelation, frustration. And in the midst of it all had been Astrid. Seeing her had been the last thing he'd expected, but somehow he hadn't thought about her all afternoon.

Now, alone in the dark as he drove, Callanach could still see the inside of the police cell in Lyon. He could hear his lawyer telling him it might be best to plead guilty, to get credit from the judge by not putting Astrid through the trauma of giving evidence. A guilty plea meant a substantial reduction in the time he would serve. The fact that he was an Interpol agent would be an aggravating enough factor when it came to sentencing. He'd considered it too, falsely admitting guilt to minimise the prison time, hoping he'd be sent to a secure wing. He knew what treatment he could expect inside. Then twenty-four hours before the case was due to open, with no warning, Astrid had announced that she wouldn't give evidence. It was like a sick joke. All he'd been able to think about was getting as far away, as fast as he could. For him, every colleague's face was permanently masked with the first reaction they'd had to his arrest. Pity, smugness, disbelief, horror. After months of bail conditions – a 6 p.m. to 9 a.m. curfew, surrendering his passport, not leaving the Lyon area, not visiting the Interpol building – he felt as if he'd already served a sentence.

His mother had done her best to stand by him at first, but as she'd heard more and more of the case details she had slowly distanced herself. It was the one relationship he'd assumed could never be weakened. She'd remained unshakeable through his early years as he'd come to terms with the fury he'd felt at losing his father. Even his behaviour at university and his journey into adulthood hadn't diminished her belief that he would turn out well. But after proving everyone wrong, after taking control of his life and pursuing a career in which he sought to do nothing but good, she had fallen away when he'd needed her most. That had been the most painful loss imaginable. The closest thing to an explanation from his mother had been a clipped voicemail message, saying she couldn't bear to watch him destroy himself any more, that every time she thought he'd changed there was one more blow to come. It was as if she had finally run out of the strength to love him.

The fact was that Callanach had been declared not guilty on a technicality. Astrid hadn't admitted lying. The truth never came out. And here he was again, facing the same demons he'd tried to leave behind. Astrid Borde had threatened Ava's life and wasted an opportunity to catch a killer because of her obsession with him. Callanach had come full circle.

He glanced down at the passenger seat. There sat the same pile of files he'd been preparing to read when the Chief had handed them to Professor Harris instead. At the time, Callanach had been grateful to have the professor distracted by what had seemed a low priority task. Look where that had got them. They were back checking cold cases, clueless, chasing their tails. He was no further forward and his friend and colleague was in the hands of a psychopath. Women were dead, and more were sure to die unless the murderer was caught.

He was certain that Ava was in the city somewhere. He had no idea if Elaine Buxton and Jayne Magee were with her or what they'd suffered. All he knew was that another victim was waiting to be saved. A woman who had no idea what was coming and who'd done nothing to deserve her fate.

Back in his apartment, Callanach showered, getting his head in order before he started reading. In the cupboard next to the sink was a pile of towels, at the bottom of which sat a paper-weight, a globe key ring and a child's prayer slate. If anyone found them, he would be accused of taking trophies and his guilt of their theft was undeniable. But holding those items, sensing the ghosts of their former owners' hands, had kept each woman alive for him. Now he knew that they were, in all probability, still alive, he wondered what he would do with his stash of intimate treasures.

Back at his desk, he spread the missing persons files out in a line. The lives of more than one hundred women, each no longer where their loved ones wished they were, had been reduced to tiny summaries. Some had run away. The majority, he suspected. There were suggestions of drug abuse, alcohol addiction, abusive partners and mental illness. Many had taken a credit card, or clothes, or a treasured photo. Not much, but enough to deduce that wherever they'd gone, they had made the decision to leave. Only the ringing of his doorbell snapped Callanach out of the daze of reading too similar, too depressing stories.

Natasha was at his door. If he'd passed her on the street in such a state he might not have recognised her.

'Sorry, Luc. I couldn't sit at home and wait for news any longer,' she sobbed.

'Come in,' he said. 'I'll get you a drink then I should call a constable to take you home. You're a witness and I'm still in the middle of the investigation.'

'You're working,' she said, staring at the mess of scattered papers. 'Can I help?'

'No,' he smiled, 'unless you feel like cooking. I apologise for the sexist undertones of that comment.'

'I'd love to cook. Don't send me home. I never want to set foot in that road again.'

336

'I don't blame you,' he said. 'There are eggs and salmon, probably some asparagus, brie.'

'Just carry on,' she said. 'I need to be busy. I promise not to disturb you.' She bustled into the kitchen and Callanach picked up the files where he'd left off.

Two teenagers from the Highlands, best friends, had apparently packed their bags and disappeared. The father of one of them had given a statement talking about his daughter in the past tense, like some contrived eulogy, full of self-glorification about his extraordinary relationship with her. Callanach had the chilling sense the girls were long since dead, not partying with secret boyfriends in a distant city, but they didn't fit the age range as a match for either Elaine or Jayne. He put the papers aside to request follow-up action.

The next file related to Grace Smith from Glasgow. The missing person report had been registered by a man with an eastern European name who claimed he was her business partner. It was an interesting euphemism, Callanach thought. Her lengthy previous convictions for soliciting, combined with the street from which she'd disappeared, were enough to tell Callanach that the statement had been given by her pimp. He must either have been sleeping with her or short of cash to go to the police for help. Natasha emerged from the kitchen clutching two plates, an omelette and salad on each.

'Here you go. When did you last eat?' she asked.

'Can't remember,' Callanach said.

He skimmed the statement as he ate, reading the pimp's account of the last time he'd seen his prostitute. It might be a ruse. Sometimes when a pimp didn't get the full amount of cash they were expecting after a night's work, they got violent. He wouldn't be the first, or the last, to kill with a misjudged punch then try to cover it by reporting the girl missing. There was detail in the statement, though. A broken interior car light, the girl was jittery, the pimp had demanded cash up front. That was odd, Callanach thought. Admitting that he'd been pimping. Not the actions of a man creating a false history. Other than describing a musty, lemony odour coming from inside the vehicle, the pimp had given little detail about the client. Male and white was as far as the statement went. There was no make or model for the car either, and Grace hadn't had a phone with her.

'Maybe she just saw her chance and ran away to a better life,' Callanach said.

'Pardon?' Natasha asked.

'Talking to myself,' he said, still scanning the pages. 'It must be catching.'

'First sign of insanity, apparently. Who was it who said that?' Natasha mused.

'Lemony,' he said.

'Lemony?' Natasha echoed, refilling her wine glass.

Callanach was up and dashing to another pile of files heaped on an armchair. He threw one then another to the floor, but opened the next, running his finger down the index.

'Here it is, Isabel Yale,' he said.

Natasha had forsaken her omelette to look over his shoulder. 'Who's that?' she asked.

'The witness who saw a man with a wheelie case leaving Jayne Magee's road.' He speed read the statement, flipped the page then ran his finger under a line of text. 'Natasha, what do mothballs smell like?'

'Acidic, I suppose. A bit unpleasant, cloying. Citrusy would be the kindest description.'

'Grace Smith,' Callanach muttered to himself. 'Right age range, easy target. He broke the light deliberately.'

Natasha had begun picking up the discarded files and putting them back on the chair to create a stationery-free pathway back to the kitchen.

'I hate the smell myself,' she said. 'Reminds me of my departmental administrator. Did you meet him at Ava's lecture?'

Chapter Forty-Three

It had been a disastrous trip and Reginald King was spitting nails. Dundee had seemed the easy choice, close enough and he'd not visited before, so he couldn't be recognised by some eagle-eyed pimp seeking new regulars for his girls.

He'd found the slut, lit by her own cigarette as she fouled up a pavement with her advertorial presence, wearing a fake fur jacket with its hood pulled over her face, stockings and no visible skirt. She'd been too far away to get a decent look at her face but he'd guessed from the bend in her back and the sag of her shoulders that she'd been around the proverbial block more than a few times. The height was right, at least.

He'd wound down the window and she'd shouted over to him.

'What d'ya want?'

He hated that part of it: the filthy talk, the negotiating.

'Straight sex,' he'd said. 'It'll be quick.'

'Fuckin' right it will,' she'd said. 'Show me the cash.'

He'd waved the money out of the window. It would be the last she'd see of it, he'd thought. The girl had weaved a drunken line to his car, yanked open the door and all but fallen through.

'Mind the seat,' he'd hissed. 'Don't dirty it.'

He was peeved that he'd had to use his own vehicle. The girl had reeked of cheap liquor and urine. Her hands were scabbed. Cigarette burns, no doubt. Probably doing her a favour. At least whoever was abusing her would be deprived of their sport. She'd sent tiny hands skittering like sick spiders into his lap, fumbling for the zipper, as she'd swayed and mumbled.

'Get off me,' King had ordered, unable to maintain the charade when the stench of her was so overwhelming. That was when he'd seen her face.

The eyes were old, hollowed out, the life inside them extinguished as effectively as if he'd already completed his task. The rest belonged to a child. Painted like a sex-shop doll, crudely, grotesquely, with false eyelashes that were sliding down one cheek and stuck too high on the other side, the skin beneath was unlined. No more than fourteen, he'd thought. Then she'd vomited.

'No!' he'd screamed, shoving his fist out without thinking, pushing her head as far away from him as he could. When her face had smashed into the window, he'd known the chloroform wouldn't be necessary. The passenger seat looked as if an animal had exploded on it, covered in the slick dripping contents of her stomach and laced with blood from her nose. It was gushing down her body and still she wasn't regaining consciousness. Wrong age or not, there was no way he could let her go. She'd seen too much. And she needed to pay for the damage to his car.

King reprimanded himself. He didn't kill for petty reasons, not in anger, not for vengeance. He killed only to free the women in his life, to give them the ultimate and final alibi. The girl had to die. He'd make it part of his plan, use it to further his work. Ava Turner still needed to witness his authority first hand.

First, he had to transport what was left of the girl whose life he was certain no one would miss. King pulled her more upright in the seat, lifted her hood as if she were sleeping, and did his best to wipe the mess off the window. If he could just make it home and into his garage, he could get properly cleaned up in private. For the first time, he was pleased that he'd been unable to hire a car. Whilst picking up the prostitutes or disposing of their bodies, he would usually have left his own vehicle at the Causewayside lockup and changed cars there, but with all the bodily fluids swimming around there was no way that would have been practical this time. It would take him two days to valet the car to acceptable standards. Two days he couldn't spend with his women. At that moment, it seemed reason enough for the girl to die. An hour later he was home. It was eleven o'clock.

Chapter Forty-Four

Callanach was on his mobile to the control room, as Natasha was on hers to University security getting out of hours numbers for other staff members. They finished their respective calls and regrouped with notes in hand.

'Reginald Andrew King,' Callanach said, 'Scottish national, fifty-three years old, no previous convictions, not so much as a speeding ticket. Is he married?'

'No,' Natasha said, 'no partner or children to my knowledge. But I have found something. Jayne Magee gave a lecture at the School of Divinity eight months ago. I just checked with the department head. I remember King raving about it the next day. At the time I hadn't paid any attention to who the speaker was.'

'What about Elaine?' Callanach asked, grabbing trainers and frantically tying the laces.

'She addressed Edinburgh Law School students a little under a year ago. It was an open lecture so he could have attended,' Natasha said.

'That's one hell of a coincidence. All three of them.' Callanach swiped his car keys off the table. 'Do you have his address?' he asked.

'I'm coming with you,' she said.

'You're staying here, Natasha. This might be nothing.'

'Call it in,' she said.

'Not yet. I've reached this conclusion by leaping from hunch to hunch. Maybe it's just what I want to believe. DCI Begbie is in the middle of a shit storm from the media. We've just released a man who confessed to the murders. There is no forensic or witness evidence linking King to the crime. Legally speaking, I can't even justify searching his property. If I get other units involved and they handle it wrong, we'll scare him off and we might never find those women. We might never find Ava.'

'He's five foot seven, pale skinned, heavy around the waist and he calls himself Dr King as if he's the most important man in the world. He had access to my office and tried to introduce himself to Ava the night she gave a lecture. What else do you need?' she asked. 'If he's going to answer the door voluntarily, it'll be to me.'

'I'm not taking that risk,' he said.

'You think he's going to invite you in?' Natasha asked, incredulous.

Callanach held the front door open for Natasha, locking it behind her. They ran down the stairs and along the corridor, out into the night.

'Here's my car,' Callanach motioned, starting the engine before he'd even closed his door. 'Listen, we're just going to take a look at the place before I make this official, all right? No heroics,' Callanach said, pulling out into the traffic.

Natasha punched the address into the SatNav.

'How far away is that from Ravelston Park?' Callanach asked her.

'Ten minutes or so, if you don't get caught in traffic.'

'Or maybe twelve,' Callanach mused. 'Maybe exactly twelve

minutes' drive if you're careful about the speed limit and allow for stopping at every traffic light.'

'How could you know that?' Natasha asked as she switched her phone to silent.

'It's what Jayne Magee's abductor told her as he wheeled her along the pavement, I think. "I'm taking you back to Elaine, we'll be there in twelve minutes." He's an obsessive planner and timer. Have you ever overheard your Dr King talking to himself?'

Natasha stared at him. 'Drive faster, Luc,' she said. 'Much faster.'

Chapter Forty-Five

As he approached home and turned into his driveway, King opened the garage door with a remote clicker. It rose noiselessly – he was particular about keeping it well oiled – and he drove the few metres into darkness, closing the electric door behind him as soon as the car was clear. The lights inside the garage wouldn't turn on unless he got out of his car to switch them on manually. He'd had an automatic system previously which he'd disabled when his life had become more complicated. There was no point attracting the attention of nosy neighbours.

He was out of the car in the dark, hand searching for the switch on the wall when the girl bolted for the only door out of the garage. The one that led directly into his meticulously locked and sealed house. He'd assumed she was still unconscious. Apparently, her survival instinct had kicked in. He hadn't bound her, unwilling to pull over with the car in such a state, certain she wouldn't wake up for hours, if at all, given the ferocity with which he'd had to deal with her.

King turned the light on and plucked a hammer off the tool rack on the wall. It was fortuitous really, he thought. At least he didn't have to carry her inside. It wasn't as if she'd be able to escape. He followed her, slipping off his shoes and padding inside.

'I won't hurt you,' he called softly, turning on lights as he went, checking each corner and cupboard. 'It's just business. I'm sorry I hit you, it was a mistake. Come out, let me clean up your face.' There was no response. He hadn't expected one. She, on the other hand, would be expecting him to say all these things and it was always an advantage to behave the way people supposed you would. It gave you more scope for surprising them. A door creaked in the hallway, a sound that could only have come from one place. She'd gone into the cupboard below the stairs. It was the one door he never oiled. He wanted to know if anyone went in there or, God forbid, came out unexpectedly. Hammer held aloft, King went to find her.

'Are you scared?' he asked as he walked. The toady little man who had pandered to Natasha Forge for so long was gone. He barely recognised his own voice, so full of confidence, with a lack of care he could embrace without analysis. The hand that had written so many notes, ripped them up, rewritten them countless times for fear they wouldn't meet Natasha's exacting standards, did not shake when it held a weapon. For the first time his feet were happy unclad, free of their polished shoes, feeling the wood beneath his feet, toes gripping, using the silence. And there was silence. He wasn't talking to himself. He knew he never would again. The nerves, the desperation to impress, to be liked and accepted, had slipped away like excrement slithering down a drain. This was who he was. This was what Reginald King was always meant to be. No titles, no certificates, no pretence. Just this.

Placing one unwavering hand on the door handle, he raised the hammer higher in the other. Filling himself with several deep breaths, drunk on the influx of oxygen, he yanked it open. She wasn't there. He began to swing round to exit as a knife

347

sliced the back of his arm, running across the rear of his rib cage. King clasped the hammer and smashed as he spun, bashing the knife away from his spine and sending it flying across the hallway. He kept on punching as he went, moving towards her, striking another hammer blow and watching blood fly, ruining wallpaper, carpet, ceilings. It was beautiful.

'Come here, you little cunt,' he raged. The hammer had knocked her off balance but she was coming back, going for the knife again, howling with a pain and fury that matched his own. 'You want to draw blood?' he growled. 'You want to paint my house red with it? Come on then.' He advanced on her, raining blows left and right as she ducked then fell and scrabbled sideways on hands and feet like a demented crab. Finally she stopped, her back against his front door, panting like the dog she was. Like a rabid, mangy cur. 'Get up,' he shouted, hammer held in front of her face as his free hand explored the horizontal gash across his back. It should have been sore, would be in the morning, but it wasn't dangerously deep and the truth was that he was finding the pain enlivening. It felt good to experience something other than shame and rejection, the sure knowledge that you were only ever second best.

'You should have stabbed, not sliced,' he told her. 'If you'd put that knife in my lung I'd be dead. Stupid girl.' He walked backwards, picked up the knife she'd stolen from his kitchen and tucked it in the back of his trousers. 'Get up,' he said. She didn't move, tears streaking the blood that had spattered her face. 'I'll help you, then,' he said, marching forwards and grabbing a handful of hair, wrenching it upwards, dragging her whole body weight through it. She screamed. 'Do you not like that? It's okay. You don't have to like it. You just have to move.'

King kept the hammer before her eyes so she was in no doubt what would happen if she attacked him again. He dragged her into the under-stair cupboard. It was tight for them both but it

348

didn't matter that she was dirtying the walls. Some redecoration was due anyway. Unable to release the girl or the hammer, he kicked at the door in the back to reveal the steps to the cellar.

'Please don't hurt me, I'm only fourteen. My mum makes me go out on the streets, she'll pay if you take me back. I was scared, I didn't mean to hurt you with the knife. Please don't, please don't, please.' She went on and on. King felt the slice in his flesh burning as he dragged her down the cellar steps. It felt like immortality.

At the bottom he threw her against the wall, took the key from his pocket and unlocked the door in the panelling.

'No,' she said. 'I won't go up there. What is it? What are you going to do to me?'

All bark and no bite, King thought. It was sad given how impressive she'd been earlier on. It had taken some guts to go for him rather than just hide.

'You must have had a terrible life,' he said. 'Your own mother pimping you out on the streets. Does she give you drugs to make it easier?' She nodded. 'And you don't go to school?' The girl shook her head. 'So what good are you?' he asked. Her face showed confusion, then upset and fear again. 'What good are you to me? To anyone, except your lowlife mother?'

'I don't want to die,' she sobbed.

'Of course you don't,' King raised his eyebrows. 'Nobody does.' He took her by the hair again, let the weighted door swing shut behind him and jerked her, one thud at a time, up the last steps.

Unlocking the final door, careful there were no unwelcome surprises waiting beyond, he thrust her into the room.

'What have you done to that girl?' Jayne asked breathlessly.

'Don't start,' King said, throwing the hammer onto Ava's bed, careful to avoid the area where her feet would be able to grasp it. 'Where's Elaine?'

'Under my bed,' Jayne responded. King could see a shivering ball of bedclothes at the very back wall, below the headboard.

'Don't hurt the girl any more,' Ava said quietly. 'She's just a kid. I don't mind if she shares a bed with me, we'll look after her.'

'Do you know what she is?' King asked, turning up the classical music he'd switched on.

'Young, vulnerable, innocent, terrified. That's what she is. Leave her alone.' Ava was straining against the ties around her wrist.

'She's detritus. This girl is living, breathing proof of what happens when poor genes meet poverty and an unwillingness to educate or work oneself out of the gutter. Can you see what she did to me?' He lifted his arm and leaned to one side to give Ava a good view. She didn't flinch.

'She was protecting herself,' Ava said. 'It's human nature. What did you do to her?'

'Broke her nose, probably burst an ear drum, concussion for certain and a sore scalp. I brought her for you, but she's not suitable. And I've ended up with a gash that needs stitches, a car to clean and a hallway to redecorate. Not to mention one too many house guests. Or maybe two too many. I seem to have created something of a harem.' He laughed. The girl began to clamber towards the door. King kicked her in the ribs without breaking eye contact with Ava.

'Do you like me, Detective Inspector Turner? No, you couldn't possibly, stupid question. How about this then: do you think I'm fun?'

'I'm not doing this,' Ava said, concentrating on the winded, struggling girl.

'Yes, you are. I'm not going to plead or cajole. You don't have any choice. How does that feel?' He ran a hand down Ava's face leaving red streaks on her pale skin. He was unsure if the blood was the girl's or his. He liked the way it made Ava look wild, like an injured animal.

King picked up a rope and began to bind it around the girl's feet.

'What's your name?' he asked. 'The last girl I had in here was called Grace. Please tell me your mother came up with something more appropriate.'

'Billie,' she said. 'Why are you doing that? I don't want you to. Can I go to that lady? I'll be good. I'll let you do anything you want. I won't fight no more.'

King threw the rope over a high beam, stood back and began to yank it. She was light. Presumably that's what consuming drugs instead of food did for you. Either that or he was stronger than he'd realised. The pain from the gash had disappeared. He savoured the dull ache in his muscles and wondered why he'd spent so many years dreading exercise. It really was about finding the right activity for you, after all.

Billie began to grab hold of things, desperate to remain on the floor, but King was unstoppable. He hauled, dragged and lugged, and finally she was where he wanted her, feet two metres off the floor, head down, swinging as she struggled, tears hitting the wooden planks below her in a shameful puddle of hopelessness.

'I have a problem, DI Turner, and it's taken a while, but it's just dawned on me how to solve it. I've been wondering whether to get rid of Piety Magee or Insane Elaine. The inccssant praying is sickening but at least the reverend is lucid. Elaine on the other hand is useful for carrying out simple commands with minimal syllables but she'll never recover her faculties. No natural resilience. I've been struggling to choose who should go and suddenly I don't have to.' He took the kitchen knife in hand and walked to Ava, cutting the cable ties from her wrists and stepping quickly backwards.

'Pick up the hammer,' he said, 'and, should the thought of hurting me go through that well-educated mind, know the girl will die if you do.' He retreated to Billie, holding the knife to her exposed throat, pushing the tip of the blade in just far enough to produce a bead of blood. 'Ava's choice,' he said. 'Who's destined to leave us? One blow should be all it'll take. Aim well and you'll minimise the pain. If you have the guts, you can save the girl's life. I'm giving you five minutes, starting now. If you don't kill either of them I'll bleed little Billie like a hog. She's fourteen, by the way. Too young to die, I'm sure you'll agree. What you need to remember is that I don't fucking care who you choose. Someone needs to die.'

Chapter Forty-Six

Callanach parked a couple of houses away from King's address. He and Natasha opened and shut their doors quietly, watching the house from the edge of his driveway, shielded by bushes.

'That's a substantial property for a university administrator,' Callanach said.

'He inherited it from his parents. Believe me, I've heard all about it. He invited me over for coffee once. I made an excuse.'

'I'm calling one of my constables to get him to organise backup. I just need a mobile signal. Wait here.' Callanach began to walk a few metres up the road staring at his phone.

'You haven't got grounds for an order to break down his door, you said so yourself. The only way is for me to make up an excuse for an impromptu visit,' Natasha said, following him.

'Too risky,' Callanach told her as his call was answered. 'Tripp, it's Callanach. I'm going to give you an address. Grab a pen and paper . . .' By the time he'd finished Natasha was gone. Callanach raced back to the gateway. She was already knocking on King's door.

'Natasha,' he hissed. 'Don't you dare go in there!' She raised her hands to the stained glass in the door, standing on her toes, trying to peer in. No one answered. Checking around, she waved to Callanach, pointing to the front windows and beginning to move. Balancing on a plant pot, she peered through a crack between the curtains, tilting her head to the side as if studying one aspect of the scene more closely. Then she froze. Natasha began to shake her head, small movements at first, then more violently. Callanach didn't need to be close enough to hear what she was saying. Her body was doing it for her. No. No, no, no. He was sprinting before she could face him, too late for caution. He joined her at the window. A trail of congealing blood snaked through the lounge, glistening along the wooden floor. Natasha directed his gaze to a doorway with a view into the hall. The tasteful blue and white striped wallpaper was streaked with bloody droplets.

Callanach ran to his car, returning seconds later with the same crow bar he'd used on the lockup. He ran to the garage that was attached to the side of the house, and jammed the bar underneath the door, levering it upwards. This time he knew he wouldn't be leaving empty handed. Natasha was behind him as the door came up. The garage lights were on, and the car's front passenger door had been left open. Natasha pressed a hand to her nose.

'God, that smell,' she said. Callanach checked the car. The passenger footwell was awash with vomit and a sticky blackening fluid.

'Go out to the street and wait for Tripp,' he said.

'Ava's in there,' she replied. 'You're not going to stop me.'

Callanach tried the door into the house. It was unlocked. King must have been in the throes of an unexpectedly dramatic event if he'd forgotten to lock up after himself, Callanach thought. Crow bar still in hand he crept inside, finding the trail of blood. He dipped a finger in it.

'Not congealed yet,' he whispered. 'Whoever bled here did so very recently.'

It was quiet and bare. No television or radio played in the background, no forgotten mug sat on the coffee table, no coat was slung casually over the banisters. But a smell lingered beneath the recent and explosive fouling of King's home, one that Callanach thought must have hung there, unnoticed by its owner, pervading every fibre and fabric for years. It was like cleaning fluid only more sickly, a sweet, tangy odour. He took hold of a curtain as he passed a window, breathed in hard and there it was, mothballs, harsh in the lungs, making him wince. Reginald King would have stopped smelling it years ago, like a perfume too frequently worn.

The blood spatters led to a door beneath the staircase, left ajar. Callanach braced himself.

'Unlock the front door,' he told Natasha. As she did so, he pulled the under-stair cupboard fully open, expecting the worst, finding nothing but hanging jackets and shoes in rows. 'There's nothing here,' he said. 'Fuck!'

Natasha pushed past him, ripping the coats from their hooks, while Callanach went to the kitchen. The back door was locked from the inside, so King hadn't made his way out of that exit.

'I'm going to check upstairs,' he said, poking his head into the under-stair cupboard. There was no response. He took one step further in, then another. A hand shot out from beyond the coats and grabbed him. It took a second to realise it was Natasha.

'Don't do that, I nearly punched you.'

'Shush,' she said. 'It leads down to a cellar. Come on.'

It was dark, and a damp chill hung in the air although it wasn't exactly cold. Callanach reached out to his side and felt a wall of wood panelling.

'It's a dead end,' Natasha said from the bottom of the steps. 'There's not even a grate for air up to the garden.'

'Check the floor,' Callanach said. 'There may be a trap door leading further down.'

They got on their hands and knees, feeling around the floor for unseen cracks or levers, finding nothing.

'Wait,' Callanach said. 'Just listen.'

They stayed completely still, heads cocked, breath held.

'I can't hear anything,' Natasha said.

'One moment. There was something, faint. I think it's voices.' Callanach walked back to the staircase, climbed a few steps and stood motionless once more.

The sound was as vague as if they were underwater, a vibration of air, nothing more. This time, though, Natasha heard it too. Callanach saw her straining her neck to catch it better.

'There's a torch,' she said, grabbing a black handle from a shelf and swinging the beam of light to and fro.

'This way,' Callanach said. 'The noise is coming from behind the wall.'

Natasha shone the torch along the panelling looking for a way through.

'On the floor, here,' Callanach was on his knees pointing at a dark blotch. The light made it a rusty brown colour. He rubbed a finger in it and held it to his face.

'Blood,' he said. 'Give me the torch.'

Callanach knocked gently on the wood. It was solid adjacent to the steps but at the base there was an echo when he banged. He found what he'd been looking for.

'Finger marks,' he said. 'Look at the prints on this panel, clusters of them. And there's a nick in the wood here.' He slid the square of wood across to reveal an inset keyhole. 'Shit,' he said. 'Needs a key.'

Natasha yelled with fury, shoving hard on the panel, and went flying through to hit a wall the other side. Callanach pulled her up.

'He must have had his hands full. God knows what we're going to find up there,' he whispered. 'Please, Natasha, go back out. Someone needs to show them where to find us.'

From above them, as clear as if they were in the midst of it, the screaming began.

Callanach took the steps two at a time with Natasha racing behind. The staircase was narrow, enclosed. At the top was another door, thick, solid wood with a huge lock.

They gritted their teeth and pushed, hoping he'd been too sloppy to remember to lock this one too but, finally, their luck had run out.

Chapter Forty-Seven

'I won't do it,' Ava said. 'You're not going to make me respon-sible for taking a life, either the girl's or theirs,' she pointed at Jayne. Elaine was nowhere to be seen.

'You think I'm bluffing?' King asked, digging the knife further into Billie's neck. 'You think I won't, because she's so young, maybe? Let me tell you what young women think of me, Ava. They walk behind me in the corridors at the University and giggle. They turn their snotty noses up at the way I dress, whisper unkind words about my hair. Then they flash their bare legs and their under-developed tits at the childish boys who strut around campus as if they were gods. Well, who's the god here?'

'Put the knife down,' Ava said. 'That's enough.'

'Pick up the hammer or I'll cut,' he answered. 'You're running out of time.'

'I won't,' Ava shouted. 'When you've cut her throat, what'll you do then? You don't want to kill Jayne or Elaine yourself. That's why you're trying to make me do it.'

'You think I'm that gutless?' King screamed at her. 'I've slaughtered two women in this room. You doubt I can kill two, three, twenty more?' He removed the knife from Billie's throat and took a step towards Ava, pointing the blade at her instead. 'You think I won't kill you?' He lunged towards her, making Ava gasp and shrink backwards in a way he found unexpectedly enticing. 'You want to know why I'm doing it? Because I want to see Natasha Forge's best friend butcher another woman in cold blood. I want to hear you scream with more than pain. I want to witness the humanity ripping out of you.'

'Is that what it was all for?' Ava asked quietly. 'To get Natasha's attention? She must despise you.'

'Pick up the hammer,' he said. His voice was ice. 'Twenty seconds. Choose one or I'll catch the girl's blood in a bucket and make you drink it.'

'No,' Ava screamed. King stepped back to Billie's upside down body. Her face was purple and swollen. Ava stared at the girl. 'Please, please don't kill her.'

'It's all right, Ava. Choose me,' Jayne said. 'Cover my face first and make it a good blow. I'm not scared of dying. Truth is, I'm more scared of watching him kill again.'

'Jayne, no. We're not doing this,' Ava said, putting a gentle hand on the other woman's forehead.

'This isn't heroics. Believe me, the thought of the pain is terrifying. But you can't let him take her life. She's a child and she's been through enough already. Save her. Do it for me.'

'Ten seconds,' King said.

'Fetch the hammer,' Jayne told Ava. 'I'm closing my eyes.'

'No,' Ava whispered although suddenly she was a step closer to her bed, reaching out her hand. Tears were spilling down her cheeks. King tried to stop the grin spreading over his face, realised he couldn't, and allowed himself to simply enjoy the moment.

'Know that you're doing what I want,' Jayne said. 'And that no one will ever think you did anything but what was right.

Tell my mother I love her. Ask my congregation to forgive this man. It's true that you can't conquer hate with hate.'

Ava was in front of her, the hammer's old wooden handle rough against her palm, its metal head stained from years of use. She looked at King, her eyes pleading, beyond words. He responded only by positioning himself behind Billie's inverted body, one arm gripping her around the waist, his other hand sliding the knife blade through the air in front of her windpipe. His message could not have been clearer.

'May God forgive me,' Ava said, covering Jayne's face with a blanket and lifting the hammer up high, gripping it with both hands, sobbing as she spread her feet for balance, to get her aim clean and the blow hard. She could only bear to do it once, and she knew that when the blow had been struck she might as well have died, right there, with Jayne.

The hammering on the door came from nowhere, hard, insistent.

There was a moment when King's eyes met Ava's, each assessing the other, planning their next move. King wavered, at first taking the knife from Billie's throat to run towards the door, then returning to cling to her hanging body, knowing he would need the leverage.

'Don't touch that fucking door,' he shouted but the hammer was falling from Ava's hands to the floor, her post as executioner abandoned, and she ran for it.

The key was in the back of the lock. King cursed himself. It was Billie's fault. She'd been too difficult, made him too angry. He wondered how they could have found him.

'Open that door and she'll only survive for seconds. Do you want that?' King screamed. 'Do you want to see her bleeding out every time you close your eyes?'

'Open the door,' a male voice demanded, heavy with an accent King recognised.

'Luc, I can't,' Ava shouted, 'he's got a girl strung up. If I open the door, he'll kill her.'

'He'll kill her anyway,' Callanach shouted back. 'He killed two women before. I'll take responsibility, Ava. Unlock the door.'

'Ava?' another voice called, this one female. 'Ava, you've got to do as Luc says. You have to let us in so we can help.'

'Natasha?' King said, before the word could come out of Ava's mouth. 'Is that you?'

'Yes,' came the reply. Silence. Waiting. Even Billie was mute, her struggling ceased.

'Open the door,' King instructed Ava. 'I won't hurt the girl. I'd like to see Professor Forge.'

Ava reached out with shaking fingers and turned the key. The door swung open and Callanach and Natasha stared in.

Chapter Forty-Eight

As the door opened Callanach took a step in front of Natasha. There had been an eerie quality to King's voice as he'd spoken her name, part childlike, part menacing – the bully who offers sweets to lure a smaller child behind a tree to hurt them unseen.

Ava's face was battered. One cheek was badly swollen but she was still standing. That was good. Across the far side of the room, a woman was tied by the wrists to a metal, hospital-style headboard. Her face and body were covered with a blanket. Only her arms were visible. She was moaning and chanting.

King was only partially visible, his body shielded by another female, this one upside down, hanging from a beam by ropes tied around her ankles. The state of the floor below showed she'd already lost some blood. She'd lose consciousness if they didn't get her down soon. King was holding a long, serrated kitchen knife to her jugular. One wrong move and she'd be beyond help.

'Reginald,' Callanach said. 'My name's Luc. Can we talk without the knife, do you think?'

'Don't even start with the Psychology for Dummies speech, DI Callanach. I'm beyond it. It's Natasha I want to talk to. Can

I call you by your first name, here?' he asked her sarcastically. 'As I'm in my own home, where you're no longer my superior. I guess I'm not welcome back at the University anyway. Human Resources probably doesn't have a standard warning letter on file for this scenario.' He laughed and Natasha brushed Callanach's restraining hand off her arm to step into the room.

'You're not going to hurt that girl are you, Dr King?' Natasha said.

'Why do you care?' King asked. 'You never cared about me, never asked my opinion, never once in all the time we worked together did you enquire how I was. But this girl, this faeces on the shoe of humanity, her you care about.'

'We had a working relationship, the same as I do with every other member of the department. I'm sorry you thought I didn't pay you enough attention.' She took another step towards Billie, showing King she was unafraid. Callanach tried to edge into the room.

'That's as close as I want you, Detective Inspector. Remember what's at stake,' King said.

'Let me get her down,' Natasha said. 'You've proved what you're capable of. You've shown me that I underestimated you. Nothing more is needed.'

'No, I won't let her down, not yet,' he said. 'But you can comfort her if it'll make you feel better, if you want to show your friends how kind and compassionate you are. Be my guest.'

Natasha took one of the girl's hands in her own. There was a flicker of life from the teenager. Callanach heard Billie sigh as their hands made contact, saw her look into Natasha's eyes with shining gratitude.

'You see,' King said. 'You are capable of it. I don't know why you always had to be such a fucking bitch to me.'

Dr King sliced, severing long and swift, cutting deep. Billie's face had no time to register the pain. With the tension from her throat gone, the front of her head slipped downwards to face the floor. Natasha tried to make sense of it, held her hands out to catch the blood, to push the girl's face back towards her throat, both of them swimming in red.

'No!' Natasha screamed at him. 'Oh God. Please no. Why did you do that?' Ava ran towards Billie and Natasha. Callanach rushed for King, but too late. He was at Jayne's bedside before Callanach could intercept.

Billie's body emptied itself of the remainder of its life-giving fluid. Natasha was on her knees, howling with grief and fury as Ava wrapped herself around her.

Callanach watched as King whipped the blanket off Jayne's face. His face was flushed and sweaty. He was enjoying it, had a taste for death. He wouldn't stop.

'No,' Ava said. 'You're not going to hurt Jayne. You won't get out of here alive if you do.'

'Would you like to come and comfort this one as well, Natasha?' he asked. 'Hold her hand while I gut her?'

Natasha pressed her face into Ava's shoulder.

'Your valiance was remarkably short lived. What a shame. Jayne doesn't mind dying, do you? Presumably you think Heaven awaits. But what if the afterlife is only you, me and this room, the two of us trapped together forever, as I slaughter you over and over again?' Jayne didn't respond.

Callanach heard a noise behind him, cast his eyes around and put one hand backwards to the doorframe.

King was stroking Jayne's cheek with the knife. She was shaking, her eyes bulging with fear. Callanach walked forward to Ava and Natasha, pushing them behind him.

'Are you going to have a go, Inspector?' King asked him, grinning. 'Only it seems to me that I can slice faster even than Interpol's brightest and best can run. Surprised? Well, you're not the only one who's done your research. Left France under quite the cloud, didn't you? Although I dare say your colleagues weren't upset to lose you. How was it being the golden boy and having it all ripped away? Let me recall . . . you've got a good degree, you spent time modelling, magazines and newspapers back then had you linked to more than a few celebrity names. After that, a brief but impressive period with the police in Paris, transfer to Interpol. And then your great downfall. Of course, I had to read it all in French, but then I'm self-taught and fluent. We have more in common than you realise, actually. I had my future cruelly stolen from me too, didn't I, Natasha?'

King glanced briefly in her direction. She opened her mouth to reply, but no more than a whisper and a sob came from her lips. Callanach did his best to remain impassive at the details King had been able to provide about his life. The fanatical ability to research was exactly the trademark of the killer they'd been hunting. His obsessive nature was what had made it so hard to catch him out. He must have planned the abductions for months, known everything there was to know about Jayne and Elaine.

'Shall we try it, then, Callanach?' King continued, waving the knife at the space between the two of them. 'Ava didn't want to play my game. Perhaps you'll be a better sport.'

'All right,' Callanach said. 'What's the distance between us, do you think? You know this room better than me.'

'I do,' King said. 'It's approximately eighteen feet. Enough time for me to kill her and turn the knife on you. Fancy your chances?' he asked.

Callanach nodded.

'Luc, don't!' Ava shouted. 'You'll never make it. For God's sake, stop!'

'Any last prayers, Reverend? Only the inspector here is taking a substantial gamble with your life and you might want to be prepared for the worst.' Jayne began furiously straining against the cuffs around her wrists and thrashing her legs.

King put the knife to her throat with studious care, adjusting the angle, adding pressure as if he were about to carve a roast.

He looked at Callanach and opened his mouth to give the go-ahead.

Callanach jerked his hand from behind his back and fired. The taser wires hit King full in the chest, sending twelve hundred volts through his body. He dropped like a rock, and the knife went with him.

Tripp's face appeared from the stairwell. 'Did you get him?' Callanach nodded. 'Medics and back up will be here in one minute.'

Callanach started walking towards King's body when a woman he hadn't seen before, at least not in the flesh, stood up and held one hand out to stop him.

'No,' she whispered. 'Don't come any closer. He's got to die.' In her hand was the hammer Ava had thrown to the floor.

'Elaine,' Ava said. 'It's over. We're going to arrest him. King's going to prison and he won't be let out in his lifetime, I promise you.'

'It's not enough,' she said. 'I don't care if he's locked up and tortured every day for a hundred years. It can never be enough.'

She pulled out false teeth from red raw gums and threw them across the room. They landed at Callanach's feet.

'Elaine,' Jayne whispered. 'Honey, you can't kill him. That's not you.'

'How can you say that after what he did to us? After what he did to the others?' she asked, lisping and spitting saliva.

'I want him to face trial,' Jayne said. 'I need justice to be done. It's not up to us to take a life. Please, untie me and let me look after you.'

Elaine held up the hammer and looked Callanach straight in the eyes.

'Don't I deserve something for this?' she asked, pointing at the sores in her mouth. 'Isn't it right that he pays, instead of hiding behind lawyers and psychiatric assessments? I know how this works. I've been on the other side of it. I remember him when I gave a talk at the University Law School, coming up at the end, fawning over me. He scared me. It was in his eyes even then. He has to pay.'

'Elaine,' Callanach said. 'I cannot give you permission to hurt him. And I need to secure him while he's still incapacitated.'

Callanach saw on her face the vivid scar of terror that would never leave her, not at work, not in her car, not even while she was sleeping. There were things from which a person could never recover. In his right hand was Max Tripp's taser, handed to him from the stairwell. He kept it ready in case King moved. With his eyes, Callanach motioned down towards his left hand, seeing Elaine follow his line of sight. Slowly, deliberately, saying nothing, he held up his forefinger. Just one. For the first time, an emotion other than dread passed over her face. She nodded her understanding back at him.

Elaine didn't raise the hammer too high nor hit too hard. She didn't risk death or even brain damage. She aimed carefully and the blow was accurate. When she brought down the metal head of the tool it smashed into King's lips, through the flesh and into the centre of both rows of teeth.

Ava went to her, put an arm around her shoulders, took the hammer from her hand and led her out. Tripp took Natasha down the stairs where medics were waiting. Callanach cut the ties from Jayne's wrists, rolled King over and handcuffed him. There was nothing he could do for the poor lost child hanging from the beam, except stand with her and wait until she could be taken down and treated with dignity. It was over.

Chapter Forty-Nine

Callanach had refused to take part in the press conference. He'd had enough media attention to last him a while. DCI Begbie handled it with fitting brevity and lack of self-congratulation. Three women were dead. There was no cause for celebration.

Elaine Buxton and Jayne Magee's families and friends were overwhelmed, having held memorial services, mourned and grieved. A psychological support team had been called in to help the abducted women come to terms with their experiences. Callanach thought privately that nothing except a decade of passing time would begin to dull the agony of such recollections. Elaine Buxton's corpse double turned out to have been another missing prostitute from Glasgow. A memorial service for all three victims was to be held the following week.

Tripp entered Callanach's office holding a long box that could only contain a bottle. Callanach felt sick. He'd forgotten about Astrid in the days since King had been arrested. The thought of more anonymous gifts arriving was too much to deal with. He wanted to be left in peace.

'For you, sir. Just arrived,' Tripp said.

Callanach opened the box and pulled out a bottle of Lagavulin with a handwritten card.

'Your turn,' the note said. 'Pleasure working with you. Share it with the team. Jonty Spurr.'

DCI Begbie walked in as Tripp was leaving.

'Are you staying in Scotland a while longer, Luc?' he asked.

'Did I hand in my resignation without realising?' Callanach replied.

'No,' Begbie said, picking up the Lagavulin and eyeing it appreciatively, 'but you came here because you were running away from what happened in Lyon. In my experience, people who start running often can't stop. You should know that I don't want to lose you from my team.'

'I'm not going anywhere, Chief. It's taken me this long to get used to the rain, the coffee and the accent. Might as well stick with it.'

The Chief nodded at him. 'Professor Harris meant well, you know. There are times when we all try too hard.'

'Next time, I choose who I work with though, no?' Callanach asked.

'No. Tight budgets, restricted overtime. This is no frills policing, Inspector. Get used to it.' He put the bottle down and gave Callanach back his room. DS Lively knocked two minutes later.

'I'm popular today,' Callanach said. 'I should get some sort of sign made for my door.' Lively didn't respond to the joke, handing him an envelope and stepping back. 'What's that?' Callanach asked.

'My resignation,' Lively said. 'I was out of line with you on more than one occasion. Much more than just out of line. It didn't help the investigation. My fault, not yours.'

'It's funny,' Callanach said, 'but this is the second conversation about resignation I've had in as many minutes. The Chief didn't

369

want mine and I don't want yours. You were rude, really rude and you needed to apologise but I don't want to lead a pack of yes men. Next time my instincts will be wrong and yours will be right. I should have taken you off the case the moment I knew how involved you were and I take responsibility for that. Don't tread on my toes, Sergeant, and I'll try not to tread on yours. Take this bottle down to the briefing room and tell everyone well done from me.' He threw Lively's envelope in the bin. 'And tell DC Salter to start preparing for her sergeant's exams. You can make things right by mentoring her.'

'Will you not join us for a drink, sir?' Lively asked.

'I've got somewhere to be,' Callanach said. 'Make my excuses, would you?'

By the time he reached Ava's house, he felt ready to collapse. The hospital had phoned to say she was discharging herself, ignoring their wish to observe her for another day. Callanach didn't know why he had expected any different.

Natasha opened Ava's front door, throwing herself into Callanach's arms, hugging him until he felt able to prise her off. He allowed himself to be touched for longer than normal though, without feeling threatened or claustrophobic. It was progress.

'Is she okay?' he asked.

'Pretending to be. You know how she is,' Natasha said. 'She's in the lounge. I'm staying for a few days, for my own benefit as much as hers. I'm cooking, if you're hungry.'

Natasha wandered back into the kitchen and Callanach put his head around the lounge door.

'Fit for a visitor?' he asked.

'Only if you brought flowers, chocolates and single malt,' Ava said.

'I forgot the flowers, decided you wouldn't eat the chocolate and gave the single malt away,' Callanach said. 'So you'll just have to appreciate my company.'

'Bugger,' she said, turning off the television. 'I'll make do.'

'I'm sorry,' he said, sitting next to her on the sofa and trying not to stare at the yellowing bruises on her face. 'If I'd done my job properly you wouldn't have gone through any of that.'

'Your ego really is astounding,' she said. 'I got too emotionally involved in a case, ended up suspended, didn't stay at home as I should have done and opened my car door to a stranger at night. And yet you're still claiming responsibility? Get over yourself, Luc.'

'Well, that sorted that out,' he said. There was a moment of silence. 'Do you want to talk about it?' he asked.

'No,' she said. 'Some time, maybe. Definitely not yet. What about you? No problems after Elaine's swipe at King?'

'I couldn't do anything to stop her,' he said. 'I'm sure she thought King was about to get up, which explains why she needed to strike that blow. But if I had indicated to her that she could have a single stab at vengeance, my conscience would be flying high. He's evil. And she was right. He's pleading insanity.'

'Of course he is,' Ava said.

'It's not just the three women we know about. Forty years ago his sister allegedly slipped down the cellar stairs breaking her neck. King, thirteen years old and only one year younger than his sister, was alone in the house with her at the time. The notes from the investigating officer show that he never believed King's version of events. It took the sister some time to die and yet the call to the ambulance wasn't made until it was too late. He claimed he was in shock. There was no evidence though, you know, the usual story. His father died twelve years ago, apparently of a stroke. Two years after that, his elderly widowed mother slipped getting out of the bath and drowned, leaving King the sole beneficiary. No clear evidence of foul play. No charges were brought, but the officers' statements show that they

371

felt King's behaviour seemed rather . . . smug, I think that was the word. But no way to disprove his story, just as before. We have no concept of what his motivation to murder the sister might have been, but it's a lot of deaths for one property.'

'I knew I shouldn't have asked.'

'How about some good news, then? Felicity Costello has been moved to a mother and baby unit with her son. Social Services are going to assess how she gets on.'

'That is good news,' Ava said. 'And the lovely Sister Ernestine?'

'Will be serving a term of several years. She's facing multiple counts of assault with complaints going back a decade. You uncovered a monstrosity. The girls are getting proper care now. You should be proud.'

'Pep talk over, thank you, Inspector. What happened to the finger, by the way?'

Callanach looked her straight in the eyes. 'I punched a wall. Your wall, actually. It may be slightly dented. I'll make good any damage.'

'No need. I prefer my home to have plenty of character. That was very honest of you. Almost as if you've realised we actually are friends. Been skydiving recently?'

Callanach rubbed a hand over his eyes. 'No,' he said. 'I don't think I'll be welcome at Strathallan for a few months. And about that . . .'

'Are you going to tell me the whole truth?' she asked. 'I mean everything, no more righteous indignation and angry avoidance?'

Callanach couldn't answer. Lying to Ava wasn't acceptable – not when he'd come so close to losing her. His physical issues were no closer to resolution, but at least he hadn't thought about them for a while. He opted for shaking his head.

'I find a fishing lake's a good place to bare one's soul. Spring is finally here, which means the lochs are about as beautiful as you'll see them. Nothing except a small boat between you and the forces of nature. No one to judge you except a few trout and they don't make good listeners. I, on the other hand, do.'

'I love the rod,' he said. 'Does it rain a lot at Kinross?'

'It's Scotland,' she said. 'If it's not raining, you're not fishing properly. I heard on the grapevine that you had a surprise visitor from France.'

'She was responsible for sending the champagne and roses gifts, meant for me rather than you, by the way. Except for the death threat. I have no idea why Astrid targeted you with that.' It was a small lie. Callanach did know. Astrid had seen something between Ava and him, something in the way they communicated with one another. Natasha had picked up on it too. 'She's mentally unstable. I'm afraid I had to agree immunity from prosecution.'

'Thank goodness for that. You think I want a court case where everyone finds out that I only attracted a second-hand stalker? I'd prefer my own, instead of your wacko hand-me-downs. How is life as a French–Scottish former Interpol agent in the wilds of Scotland, by the way?'

'No one appreciates how sensitive I am,' he laughed. 'And I'm considering asking the Chief for a pay rise just because the accent's so difficult to understand.' Ava laughed and it made him smile. For a while, although he hadn't admitted it to himself, he'd been certain he would never hear her laugh again. 'So, as an act of charity, would you like to catch a movie this week?' he asked. 'Only I find your choice in films helps my insomnia.'

'Philistine,' she replied. '*High Noon* is the midnight showing this week. Even you couldn't fail to appreciate its brilliance.'

'Is Steve McQueen in it?' Callanach asked, his hand finding the miniature slab of slate in his pocket that he'd been determined to give back. He let it fall deep into the pocket once more, and crossed his arms instead.

'No,' Ava said. 'Sadly not. He's probably the only actor who could have improved it. I'm hungry. Make yourself useful and find out what's happened to dinner.'

Callanach got to his feet. 'You don't seriously think he's better looking than me?'

'Blonde hair, blue eyes,' she said. 'My kind of guy.'

Callanach checked himself in the hallway mirror on his way to the kitchen.

'Steve McQueen,' he muttered, running one hand through his hair. 'I don't think so.'

Loved *Perfect Remains*?
Then turn the page for an exclusive sneak peek of
Helen Fields' second book, *Perfect Prey* . . .

PERFECT PREY

by Helen Fields

PART ONE

Chapter One

There were worse places to die. Few more terrifying ways of dying, though. It was an idyllic summer backdrop - the cityscape on one side, the ancient volcano Arthur's Seat silhouetted in the distance. The music could be felt before it was heard, the bass throbbing through bones and jiggling flesh. Sundown came late in Edinburgh in early July and the sky was awash with shades of rose, gold and burnt orange. Perhaps that was why no one noticed when it happened. Either that, or the cocktail of drink, drugs and natural highs. The festival was well underway. Three days of revellers lounging, partying, loving, eating and drinking their way through band after band, bodies increasingly comfortable with fewer clothes and minimal hygiene. If you could take a snapshot to illustrate a sense of ecstasy, this would have been the definitive scene. A sense of communal joy washing through the crowd, jumping as one, as if the multitudes had merged to create a single rapturous beast with a thousand grinning heads.

Through the centre of it all, the killer had drifted like smoke, sinuous and light-footed, bringing a blade to its receptacle like a ribbon through air. The slash was clean. Straight and deep.

The extent of the blood loss was apparent on the ground, the wound too gaping for hands to stem the flow. Not that there had been time to get the victim to a hospital. Not that anyone had even noticed his injury before he had almost completely bled out.

Detective Inspector Luc Callanach stood at the spot where the young man had taken his last breath. His identity had not yet been established. The police had pieced together remarkably little in the hour since the victim's death. It was amazing, Callanach thought, how in a crowd of thousands they had found not a single useful witness.

The young man had simply ceased his rhythmic jumping, crumpling slowly, falling left and right, forwards and backwards, against his fellow festival goers, finally collapsing, clutching his stomach. It had annoyed some of them, disrupted their viewing pleasure. He'd been assumed drunk at first, drug-addled second. Only when a barefooted teenage girl had slipped in the pool of blood did the alarm ring out, and amidst the decibels it had taken an age for the message to get through. Eventually the screams had drowned out the music when the poor boy had been rolled over, his spilled entrails slinking closely in his wake like some alien pet, sparkling with reflected sunshine in the gloss of so much brilliant blood.

The uniforms hadn't been far away. It was a massive public event with every precaution taken. But making their way through the throng, police officers first, then paramedics, and clearing an area then managing the scene, had been a logistical disaster. Callanach looked skywards and sighed. The crime scene was more heavily trodden than nightclub toilets on New Year's Eve. There was enough DNA floating around to populate a new planet. It was a forensic free-for-all.

The body itself was already on its way to the mortuary, having been photographed in situ for all the good it would do.

The corpse had been moved so many times by do-gooders, panicked bystanders, the police, medics, and finally left to rest on a bed of trampled grass and kicked-up dirt. The chief pathologist, Ailsa Lambert, had been unusually quiet, issuing instructions only to treat the body with care and respect, and to move him swiftly to a place where there would be no more prying cameras or hysterical caterwauling. Callanach was there to secure the scene - a concept beyond irony - before following Ailsa to her offices.

In the brief look Callanach had got, the victim's face had said it all. Eyes screwed tight as if willing himself to wake from a nightmare, mouth caught open between gasp and scream. Had he been shouting a name? Callanach wondered. Did he know his assailant? He'd been carrying no identification, merely some loose change in his shorts, not even so much as a watch on his wrist. Only a key on a piece of string around his neck. However swiftly death had come, the terror of knowing you were fading, of sensing that hope was a missed bus, while all around you leapt and sang, must have seemed the cruelest joke. And at the very end, hearing only screams, seeing panic and horror in the sea of eyes above and around him. What must it have been like, Callanach wondered, to have died alone on the hard ground in such bright sunlight? The last thing the victim had known of the world could only have been unalleviated dread.

Callanach studied the domed stage, rigged with sound and lighting gear, and prayed that one of the cameras mounted there might have caught a useful fragment. Someone rushing, leaving, moving differently to the rest of the crowd. The Meadows, an expanse of park and playing fields to the south of the city centre, were beautiful and peaceful on a normal day. Mothers brought their toddlers, dog walkers roamed and joggers timed the circuit. Strains of 'Summer is A-Coming In' sounded in the back of Callanach's mind from a screening of the original version that DI Ava Turner had dragged him to a few months ago. He'd found Edward Woodward's acting mesmerising, and the images of men and women in animal masks preparing to make their human sacrifice had stayed with him long after the projector had been switched off. It wasn't a million miles away from the circus in the centre of which this young man had perished.

'Sir, the people standing behind the victim have been identified. They're available to speak now,' a constable said. Callanach followed him to the edge of the field, leaving forensics constructing a temporary shelter to protect the scene overnight. Leaning against a tree was a couple, wrapped together in a single blanket, their faces tear-stained, the woman shaking visibly as the man comforted her.

'Merel and Niek De Vries,' the constable read from his notebook. 'A Dutch couple holidaying here. Been in Scotland ten days.'

Callanach nodded and stepped forward for quiet privacy.

'I'm Detective Inspector Callanach with Police Scotland,' he said. 'I know this is shocking and I'm sorry for what you witnessed. I'm sure you've explained what you saw a few times now, and you'll be asked about it many more. Could you just run over it for me though, if you don't mind?'

The man said something to his wife that Callanach couldn't follow, but she looked up and took a deep breath.

'My wife does not speak good English,' Niek De Vries began, 'but she saw more than me. I can translate.' Merel rattled off a few sentences, punctuated with sobs, before Niek spoke again.

'She only noticed him when the girl screamed. Then Merel bent down to shake him, to tell him to get up. He was on his knees, bent forward. We thought he was drunk, sick maybe. When Merel stood up again her hand was covered with blood. Even then, she says, she thought maybe he had vomited, ruptured something. Only when everyone stepped back and we laid him out, did we see the wound. It was as if he had been cut in two.' Niek put one hand across his eyes.

'Did you see anyone before he fell, near him, touch him, push past him? Did anyone seem to rush away from the area? Or can you describe any of the people standing near you in detail?' Callanach asked.

'Everyone was moving constantly,' Niek answered, 'and we were watching the stage, the band, you know? We don't have any friends here so we were not really looking. People were jumping up and down, screaming, going this way and that to get to the bar or the toilets. We were just trying not to get separated. I hadn't even noticed the man in front of us until he fell.'

'Did he speak at all?' Callanach asked. Niek checked that question with Merel.

'She thinks he was already unconscious or dead when she first spoke to him. And anyway, the noise was too much. She would not have heard.'

'I understand,' Callanach said. 'Officers will take you to the police station to make full written statements and then transfer you to your accommodation.'

'Not British?' Merel stuttered, addressing Callanach directly for the first time.

'I'm French,' Callanach replied, 'well, half French, half Scottish. I apologise if my accent's hard to understand.'

'Le garçon était trop jeune pour mourir.' The boy was too young to die, she said, continuing in French although Callanach found he was hearing it in English, so fast had his translation become.

Merel De Vries recalled one other thing. Above the music, a woman laughing in the crowd, so loud she could hear it even as she'd bent down to help the victim. What struck Callanach as odd was Merel's description of it. That it wasn't a happy laugh. In her words, it had sounded malicious.

Chapter Two

'The cut came from a single weapon, but the implement would have been customised by skilled hands,' Ailsa Lambert said. 'Two perfectly paired scalpel blades must have been bound together with a spacer between them creating a gap of four millimetres. The combination would have rendered the wound impossible to close or suture, even had he been on a hospital ward when he'd been attacked. The twin incisions are . . .' she paused as she picked up a flexible measure, 'twenty-eight centimetres in length. They have pulled apart substantially causing a gaping wound resulting in massive trauma. His organs then moved, sliding down and forward, so that much of what should have been in his abdominal cavity exited his body as he fell and rolled. Some of it even has identifiable shoe marks from those around him. Blood loss caused his heart to stop.'

'I get it,' Callanach said wearily. 'Not much doubt over cause of death. Anything else I need to know?'

'Tox screen will be a while. He has no other visible injuries, seems superficially healthy, his lungs tell me he wasn't a smoker, good boy.' She patted the corpse's hand with her gloved one and smiled. 'But this weapon, Luc, this weapon wasn't designed for self-defence. And you can't pick it up at the hardware store either. Someone crafted it, adored it. The cut was deep, even, and yet very little force seems to have been required to puncture far into the abdominal cavity. Whoever did this took pride in it, thought about efficiency, understood the mechanics of it. This was no impromptu stabbing or weapon grabbed in the heat of an argument.'

'An assassination then?' Callanach asked, bending over the body and taking stock.

'More like a ritual, if you ask me,' she said. 'This was dreamed up, practised and perfected.'

'How old is he?'

'Between eighteen and twenty-two, I think. Five feet, eleven inches. Active, no spare fat, good muscle mass but not one of those types who live at the gym. Size ten shoe. Brown hair, hazel eyes. No defence wounds. Never saw it coming.'

'So he didn't recognise his attacker as a threat when they came for him?'

'Most unlikely. You don't look well yourself, Luc. Are you sleeping?' Ailsa asked as she peeled off her gloves and made notes.

'I'm sleeping just fine,' he lied.

'Eating properly? You're pale and you have broken blood vessels in your eyes.'

'I'll phone you tomorrow for the tox results,' he evaded. 'Anything before that and you have my mobile number.'

'Give my love to Ava. I haven't seen her for an age,' Ailsa said, stretching her back. In her mid sixties, tiny and birdlike, she was a force to be reckoned with. Today, Callanach didn't have the energy.

'I'll pass that on,' he said, stripping off his own gown and dropping it into the bin outside the door.

On his return to the station, a grim welcome party sat around in the incident room. Callanach looked directly to Detective Constable Tripp.

'Just following up a lead from a phone call, sir,' Tripp said. 'Young woman called in to say she and her boyfriend got separated at the festival. He hasn't turned up yet. I've sent a car to pick her up.'

'Did she give his name?' Callanach asked, grabbing coffee as he sat at a computer.

'Sim Thorburn,' Tripp replied, pressing a couple of keys and waiting for a photo to load, one step ahead as ever. Some new social networking site popped up in seconds with a multitude of larger-than-life photos. In each one, the lad was smiling, laughing, his expression care-free and guileless. In the last, he was hand in hand with his girlfriend. Without a doubt, it was the same hand that Ailsa Lambert had been patting a short while ago.

'That's him,' Callanach said. 'So what do we know?'

'At the moment, everything that's on his home page. He didn't bother with privacy filters, so it's there for the world to see. He's twenty-one, Scottish, lives in Edinburgh.'

'Police record?'

'Not that we can find.' A phone rang behind Tripp and someone passed him a note. 'The girlfriend's here, sir. And DCI Begbie wants to see you as soon as you're done.'

'Of course he does,' Callanach said, standing up. 'Do you have any idea where DI Turner is, Tripp? Only Ailsa Lambert was asking after her.'

'Off duty,' DC Salter shouted from the corridor. 'Said something about maybe being in late tomorrow too. Did you want me to get a message to her, sir?'

'No thanks, Salter,' Callanach shouted after her. 'It's nothing that can't wait.' Unlike Sim Thorburn's girlfriend, no doubt already suspecting the worst but who'd be downstairs holding out for a miracle. She would be imagining some mistake, hoping perhaps that in spite of the evidence, her boyfriend had met some friends and wandered off without telling her. Any number of excuses for his disappearance would be going through her mind. Until she saw Callanach's face, he thought. People always knew, the second they looked at you. He couldn't recall delivering the news of a death at any time in his career in the French police or Interpol, nor in his brief time in Scotland, where it had actually been necessary to say the awful words.

'I'm sorry,' he said, as soon as he saw her. Introductions were pointless. She wouldn't remember Callanach's name in a few seconds' time, anyway.

'You can't know that yet,' she whispered. 'You haven't even asked me about him.'

'We found several photos on an internet site of the two of you together.' He held out an example that Tripp had printed off in anticipation. 'Is this Sim?'

She sobbed and took a step away from the photo as if the paper itself was a weapon.

'Have you seen him?' she asked. Callanach pulled a chair out for her and she sat.

'I have. I'm sure it's him.'

'What . . . what . . .' she couldn't say the words.

'He received a knife wound. It proved fatal. It would have been very fast. The ambulance didn't have time to get to him.'

'A knife wound? I heard that someone had collapsed. I thought maybe a ruptured appendix or a blood clot or . . . a knife wound? It's not him. No one would do that to Sim.'

'He wasn't in any trouble that you knew of? It might be something as simple as a family feud, money problems, someone settling an old score?'

'Don't be so stupid!' The girl snapped. It was an understandable reaction given what she was going through. What she didn't understand was how cold the trail would get with every passing minute. 'He was a charity worker. He earned minimum wage and still spent every spare moment doing extra unpaid voluntary service.'

'Can you tell me more about that?' Callanach asked.

'He worked in the homeless shelters, ran the soup kitchens in the city, organised fund raising. Sim was the gentlest, kindest person you could ever meet. He gave away every last penny. It was the only thing we ever argued about. Enemies? No.'

'And you didn't see anything strange yesterday. No one following him?'

The girl shook her head, shock taking hold. Callanach knew he'd got all he was going to get from her by then. He handed over to Tripp to organise the formal identification of the body and obtain family details. Callanach had to get a break, and fast. Somewhere the man or woman who had slaughtered Sim Thorburn had undoubtedly already hidden the weapon and neutralised any incriminating forensic evidence.

'Salter,' Callanach shouted on his way towards the incident room. 'Find out who's controlling the footage from the concert. I want it available tonight. And try to keep the Chief off my back for a while, would you? I've got work to do.'

'So have I, Detective Inspector,' DCI Begbie said, appearing in the doorway. Lately he seemed larger every time Callanach saw him. It wasn't healthy, putting on weight that fast. The Chief hadn't been exactly slim when Callanach had joined Police Scotland, but now he was working his way towards an early grave for no apparent reason. 'Is something wrong, DI Callanach?' Begbie asked. He realised he'd been staring at Begbie's straining shirt buttons.

'No, sir, just distracted.'

'Frankly, that's not very reassuring. What leads have we got?' Callanach tried to find a way to express the completely negative nature of the case so far, and struggled to answer. 'That good, huh? Well, somebody must have seen something. Thousands of potential witnesses and we're stuck. Bloody typical. Have media relations organise a press conference. Might as well do it immediately. We can't have people scared on the streets. There'll be a rational explanation for this. No one walks up to a complete stranger and slashes them. Get answers, Callanach. I want someone in custody in the next forty-eight hours.'

'Chief . . .'

'Got it. You don't like doing press conferences. Duly noted.' Begbie walked off, puffing as he went. Callanach considered following to ask if his boss was all right, then recognised that for the career-ending move it would be, and made his way back towards the incident room. He was starving, but the fish and chip supper being consumed straight from newspaper was making him queasy. There was no prospect of getting home for twelve hours and the healthiest food at the station was probably an out-of-date packet of crackers abandoned at the back of a cupboard. Callanach was getting his thoughts together to lead a briefing when someone thrust a carrier bag into his hand.

'Stop looking at everyone else's food as if they're eating poison. It's off-putting. You're not doing anything to help your reputation for French snobbery,' DI Ava Turner said, pushing a fork into his free hand. 'Prawn salad. Not home-made, so you're safe from my pathetic efforts.'

'I thought you were off duty and not coming in until late tomorrow. Have you been demoted to the catering division?'

'You can always hand it back,' she said, checking her phone and frowning.

'Too late,' Callanach ripped open the packaging and tucked in. 'Ailsa Lambert was asking after you. Said she hasn't seen you for a while. Do I take it that Edinburgh's elite social circle is not functioning properly?'

'How do you tell someone to shut up in French?' Ava asked without looking up from her phone.

DC Salter interrupted, handing over two pages of A4 and checking her watch. 'DCI Begbie said he knew you were busy so he's organised the press conference for you,' Salter was trying not to smile. Turner ruined the effort by laughing out loud. 'I've written out some notes for you, sir. Media will be gathered in about an hour.'

'Wow. Reduced to using the media circus already? This time tomorrow morning women will be swooning over your face on the front cover of all the papers. So Police Scotland's pin-up detective is getting back out there, is he?'

'It wasn't my idea,' Callanach muttered. 'Merde!'

'Language,' Turner admonished.

'I thought you couldn't speak French.'

'Calm down. I was only teasing. It's that bad then? You've really got nothing to go on?'

'Less than nothing,' Callanach said.

'DI Turner!' Begbie shouted from the corridor.

'I'm off duty, sir,' Turner shouted back. 'In fact, I'm not even in the building. You're imagining me.'

'Too bad for you I have such an active imagination. Saves me a phone call though. Get a squad over to Gilmerton Road. A woman's been murdered.'

Chapter Three

The house in Gilmerton was an unpretentious semi-detached, with a plain but carefully tended garden and a Mini in the driveway. A high wooden gate allowed access to the rear garden. The upper windows of the property were small, but at one corner, presumably where the internal staircase ran, an unusual slit of window spanned both floors to look out over next door's driveway. Two uniformed officers had been posted at the gates and the circus of forensics, pathology, and photography had yet to properly begin. The area was peaceful, the streets asleep.

'What happened?' Ava Turner asked the officer guarding the front door.

'A neighbour heard a disturbance, phoned it in. There was no answer when we knocked so we went round the back to find the kitchen door open. Body's in the bedroom, ma'am. Do you want me to come in with you?'

'No, stay put. And keep people off the garden. Who's the victim?' Ava asked.

'Mrs Helen Lott, mid forties, lived alone as her husband passed away a while back, apparently. Neighbour was quite friendly with the deceased. We haven't told her what we found yet . . .'

'Good. Where the hell are the rest of the team?'

'All still over at The Meadows dealing with the murder at the festival. No one was expecting a second murder on the same night,' the officer said, rubbing his hands together. Even in July, Scotland was no place to stand outside in the small hours.

'Damn right. That's Edinburgh's murder quota for the whole year. God almighty, the press will have a field day.'

Ava pulled gloves and shoe covers from her bag and made her way in through the kitchen door, careful not to disturb anything as she went. The lock had been broken, although there hadn't been any chain or secondary security. She cursed how cheaply people valued their lives.

The house was dark, as it would have been when the intruder crept through. Ava kept the lights off, imagining how the killer had moved and navigated the property. There was enough light from a street lamp to make it easy. None of the stair floorboards were squeaky. There was every chance the killer had got all the way to Helen Lott's bedroom without disturbing her at all.

The smell of vomit was noticeable from halfway between floors, beginning as a sharp twang, growing riper and more meaty as she got closer. Something else, too, when Ava pushed open the door to the main bedroom. A rotten smell. Human faeces.

In the bedroom, she turned on the light, taking an involuntary step back from the carnage on the floor. The body was difficult to see at first, hidden as it was by a wooden chest of drawers. Clothes had tumbled out everywhere, hiding all but the woman's right foot and right arm. Ava tiptoed across and peeled the corner of a jumper away from the face. Blood had erupted from her mouth, nose and ears. The vomit was already crusting on the carpet and in the wrinkles and folds of her skin. The victim's eyes, a vivid and unusual shade of blue, bulged in their sockets, and stared somewhere over Ava's shoulder as if watching, terrified, for her attacker to return. There was very little white remaining in her eyes, the haemorrhaging like crazing on an antique vase. Her neck and face were swollen solid, a deep shade of purple. It was as if she had been painted from the neck up by an angry toddler in all the colours of fury.

The chest, a broad, weighty piece, lay across her body. Its position there was no accident. Ava looked carefully at the damage. The chest's back panel which now faced the ceiling had been smashed in, the sides caving inwards. Faint boot prints marred the floral pastel bed linen. The attacker had jumped from the mattress onto the chest, adding to the murderous crushing pressure that had squeezed the breath from the victim's lungs as she'd lain terrified beneath it. Helen Lott's visible leg was twisted to an unnatural angle, and the nails of her free hand were bloodied and hanging. Ava folded the arm upwards to where they would have made contact with the chest of drawers. Sure enough, corresponding scratch marks ran down the polished surface. The poor woman would have been conscious then, enough to have done all she could in those last desperate minutes to fight her way out. Death would have been the only kindness, Ava thought. Mrs Lott would have been grateful when the darkness finally swallowed her.

'Oh, my dear,' a small voice came from the doorway, 'what on earth is this, now? I was just saying to Luc earlier how I was missing you. I certainly didn't mean to see you under these circumstances.'

'I need as much as you can tell me about the killer. Single assailant or a gang, was there a weapon? Just give me enough to get started, Ailsa,' Ava said.

The pathologist, covered head to foot in a white suit, making her appear smaller than ever, opened her bag and withdrew a thermometer and a variety of swabs.

'It's a difficult scene, not much room. Keep your squad out until I'm done. Get me some decent lighting and I'll need the photographer immediately.'

'That's fine,' Ava said, as Ailsa knelt next to the body.

'She's still quite warm, so the attacker, singular or plural I can't say, hasn't gone terribly far yet,' Ailsa said, photographing with her own tiny camera as she went, shining a light in Helen Lott's eyes, ears and mouth. 'Death was within the last forty-five minutes, that's the best I can do for now. I'd put money on the perpetrator, if it was one person acting alone, being male and very large. This took an absolutely extraordinary amount of strength and overwhelming rage. No weapon other than this furniture was required to cause these injuries. Whoever it is must be covered in blood though. They'll be keeping out of sight until they've cleaned up. This blow to the face, you see the swelling and discolouration here,' Ailsa pointed to the side of Helen Lott's head, 'probably fractured the cheekbone, maybe the jaw too, and would have put her on the floor so that the furniture could be pushed on top of her. It's unusual. Very personal. I've never seen a crushing death outside of a car or industrial accident before. And these blood spatters here and here,' Ava followed Ailsa's eye-line outwards from the chest along the carpets to the walls and wardrobe, 'suggest to me that the crushing wasn't a single continuous force.'

'Meaning what?' Ava asked.

'Meaning, I'm afraid, that whoever did this jumped again and again, causing individual injuries and almost explosive bleeds each time they landed. When we've moved the furniture and the body, we'll see a star shape coming out around her.'

'Bastards,' Ava said, hands on hips, hanging her head.

'I bet you don't let your mother hear you speak like that,' Ailsa said, smiling gently. 'Now let me take care of her.'

Ava went back down the stairs turning each light on as she

went, issuing orders through her radio. Technicians were carrying lights and sheets in before she'd even reached the kitchen door. She saw that the lock had been sliced through. If it was a burglar, then it was a highly professional job as opposed to the usual smash and grab whatever was nearest to the window. The perpetrator had paid a lot of money for decent tools, must have known what he'd need for the lock.

Ava walked out onto the street and looked around. It was a quiet residential area, devoid of CCTV and not wealthy enough for any of the residents to have invested in their own surveillance systems. It would have been obvious that the house was occupied, so late at night with a car on the driveway. The burglar - if it was a burglary gone wrong - would have been cautious about the residents.

'Officer,' Ava called to the uniform she'd spoken to on the way in. 'Is there anything obvious missing or any sign of ransacking?'

'Handbag with purse in it still on the kitchen table, ma'am. Other than that we didn't want to disturb too much.'

She went back to her car and dialled Begbie's number.

'Turner here. It's a bad one, Chief. Female victim, living alone. Crushed to death with a piece of her own furniture.'

'You've got to be bloody kidding me,' Begbie sighed. Ava could almost see him scratching his head as he tapped his pen on the desk. He sounded exhausted. 'Sexual assault?'

'No idea yet. And we won't have confirmation until Mrs Lott has been taken in for a full autopsy. The torso and two limbs have been pretty comprehensively flattened.'

'Suspects?'

'Nothing yet. Pathologist's still with her. Everyone was over at The Meadows so it's taken a bit longer than usual to get going. Almost certainly a male attacker. Not sure yet if there's more than one. It's brutal, a lot of force. We have a boot print.

Officers are with the neighbour taking a statement. After the incident at The Meadows, the press will . . .'

'I know, I know,' Begbie said. 'But they'll have to be told. They'll find out soon enough anyway. Better from us.' Ava could hear the Chief's heavy breathing down the phone. His chest sounded as if it was chugging between words.

'Sir, nothing else will happen tonight. Maybe you should just go home. Callanach and I are both available to take calls.'

'Don't you start too, Turner. If I wanted another woman nagging me, I'd have committed bigamy long ago. Just seal off the scene and bring back some useful bloody info. The very least I expect is one hundred per cent more than Callanach's turned up from The Meadows. Not that that's setting the bar very high, mind you.'

Chapter Four

Callanach sat with an expressionless video editor, and tried to avoid the pile of newspapers that some helpful person had left on his desk. What he needed to do was sift through the footage from four different cameras and see if anything recorded might resemble a lead. Thankfully the timelines were such that the job, initially at least, was a limited one.

The first two tapes were from static cameras, no operators. They both covered the front areas of the crowd, and the place where Sim Thorburn had been standing was a distant blur. The remaining footage was more difficult to navigate. One camera operator had been moving around on the stage, intermittently filming the band and looking out at the crowd. The second camera operator had been on a cherry picker crane to give more dynamic angles. It was painfully slow to sit through, but finally the first glimpse of the thankfully tall Niek De Vries emerged amidst the masses.

'Stop it there,' Callanach said, leaning forward and peering hard at the screen. 'That area, can you make the section larger?'

The editor pressed a few keys and leaned back, hands behind his head.

'Is that it?' Callanach asked. 'It's too blurry.'

'Yeah, you know that stuff in films where they can suddenly zoom in and it all goes super-sharp and you can see inside people's pockets and read what's written on a note? That's all bollocks,' the editor said. 'There's one picture, it consists of a certain number of dots. You can see closer but then it gets less sharp. If I had a pound for every time I've had to explain that.'

'Zoom back out then, left a bit,' Callanach said. 'That's Sim,' he said. 'Play it from there.'

As the screen came to life, Callanach could see Sim's head bouncing up and down, in and out of the line of sight. It was sketchy, but unmistakably the victim. Behind him and slightly to the right stood Merel De Vries. Sim was singing along with the rest of the crowd, one arm in the air pumping in time to the music. He looked relaxed and happy.

'He has absolutely no idea what's coming,' Callanach said to himself. The camera began to shift to the right, and Sim's face edged towards the far side of the screen. 'No,' Callanach shouted. 'It's just about to happen. Freeze the frame or something.' The editor tapped the space bar. Callanach searched the picture but found nothing new. 'Damn it. Let it play,' he said. Another tap and away slid Sim's face, about to shift fully out of frame as he seemed to bump into the body of someone passing by in front of him. 'Stop! Right there. That's it.'

Callanach's mind filled in the blanks. The subtle shift of a body through the crowd, slipping the knife out of a pocket, pulling off the sheath, sliding the razor-sharp blade along Sim's naked stomach as they passed, ready with a cloth to clean up and avoid bloodying anyone else. Slipping quietly away before the victim had hit the floor. They would have moved in a zigzag through the crowd. Taking a straight course through the masses, directly out of the area, would have been too obvious.

'Play it back again,' Callanach ordered. On a second view, it was clearer that Sim's head hadn't even turned. There had been no distraction, no conversation, no recognition. Had there not been the movement of a few blurred pixels, dark in colour, vague in shape, passing just in front of the lower half of Sim's face before he'd fallen, it might have been murder by ghost. 'You're going to tell me we can't improve that section of the picture, aren't you?' The editor simply raised one eyebrow. 'I need the best quality print off you can get of all the frames when his face and that blur are in sight.'

Tripp entered holding a document that he was reading as he walked.

'Forensics, sir. Just came through by email. Nothing on it.'

'What do you mean nothing?' Callanach asked.

'Only what you already found out at the autopsy. Victim had no drugs in his system, trace amounts of alcohol. Healthy, no previous injuries except what looks like a childhood broken leg. He was clean. Cause of death as you'd expect,' Tripp said.

'Any response from the press conference?' Callanach asked.

Tripp looked edgy. 'You've not heard, sir?' Callanach's face was a blank. 'Someone started a media site, people have been uploading every bit of footage from their phones. There are thousands of hours to view. Other than that, no useful leads. Then there's the uproar. I think DCI Begbie may have barricaded himself into his office. You turned your mobile off again, then, did you sir?' Callanach's hand went to his pocket and came out again clutching a black screen. 'Media relations have been trying to get hold of you. Some journalist wants an interview.'

'Do you think it will help?'

'Not my call, sir. But I think one of the papers dubbed you Police Scotland's answer to Brad Pitt, so maybe you won't want to . . .' Tripp's voice faded out.

'That'll be all, thank you Tripp. Is the DCI available?'

'He said only for people with good news,' was Tripp's parting reply.

'Seems like we're all going to have a disappointing day then,' Callanach muttered.

He knocked on Begbie's door and walked in to find the Chief handing a bundle of files to a plain-clothes officer he hadn't seen before.

Begbie pointed to a seat which Callanach decided not to bother taking.

'No idea how long we'll be here, I'm afraid,' the plain-clothes officer continued, ignoring Callanach's presence. 'Obviously we'll be working with your regional squad. We may also need a few of your men for on-the-ground inquiries.'

'I'm afraid that as of yesterday all my lot are taken,' Begbie growled, eyes closed. 'Unless Callanach here has some unexpected news for me.' Callanach stared out of the window. 'Well then, you can have what office space you need, all the facilities, local knowledge to your heart's content. Manpower is your problem.'

The officer made a non-committal noise which Begbie ignored as he flicked the switch on the small kettle he kept in his room, presumably to minimise the need to walk the few yards along the corridor to make tea. Callanach took the opportunity to study the newcomer. The accent he recognised as upper-class English. In his time at Interpol he'd worked with enough of Scotland Yard's favoured few to see money, education and a corresponding attitude when it walked through the door.

'Right, I'll be getting along then. We'll review our requirements and revisit the manpower issue at a later date, DCI Begbie.' He left without a thank-you, not quite bothering to ensure the door was shut. Callanach followed him and finished the job.

'Anything I should know about, sir?' Callanach asked.

'Not today,' Begbie muttered. 'Got a suspect yet?'

'Dark hair, either natural or dyed. Maybe even wearing a dark hat. Could be male or female. Short, probably below five foot five. Slight build, but that's a guess as the crowd wasn't disturbed by them passing through. My best description would be something along the lines of Professional Grade Murderer.'

'Thank you Detective Inspector, be sure never to repeat those words in front of another living being. DI Turner is currently in her office trying to organise an investigation into a man she has, much like yourself, already named inappropriately. You may have a professional grade murderer on your hands. Turner has The Crusher. Almost certainly male, heavy, strong, brutal and a raving psychopath if the autopsy details are anything to go by.'

'Two in one night? Isn't that unusual for this area?'

'Unusual? It's a disaster of monumental proportions, is what it is! Do you know what the headlines said this morning?' Callanach still hadn't braved the papers. 'No? Well, let me halve my burden by sharing it with you. "Not safe on the streets, not safe in our homes. Edinburgh's Night of Monstrosities". Not catchy but pretty bloody appropriate, don't you think?' Begbie threw himself into the chair behind his desk so hard that it skidded backwards half a metre. 'And I don't have the money in the budget to pay for any overtime for the remainder of the year! Do something about it Callanach. I've got two bodies in the morgue and I daren't so much as pick up the phone.'

Callanach exited. It wasn't as if he could offer any consolation. Ava sounded like she was having an even worse day than him. He wandered in the direction of her office for some mutual bemoaning of fates.

He didn't bother knocking. As he opened the door there was a sudden pulling away of bodies, Ava stepping quickly backwards and banging her hip on the corner of her desk, the man she was with looking more annoyed than embarrassed to have been interrupted. He recovered faster than she.

'Begbie didn't introduce us. Seems he's having rather a busy day. I'm DCI Edgar.'

'Callanach,' he said holding out his hand and shaking the detective chief inspector's. 'I interrupted. Apologies.'

'No, you didn't. What was it, Luc?' Ava asked, brushing hair away from her face.

'Thought I'd just see how you're doing. The Chief said you've picked up a rough one.'

'That's the best kind, isn't it?' Edgar chipped in. Ava made her way to the other side of her desk and sat down.

'Joseph's here from the National Cyber Crime Unit in London. An attack is imminent and there's intelligence that it's being organised from Edinburgh.'

'Probably best to limit the spread of the information, Ava. I gather Callanach has matters of his own to worry about.'

'I do,' Callanach said, 'so I'll catch you later. Good to meet you.' He closed Ava's door, grimacing, and wiping the palm of his right hand on his trousers as he went.

Chapter Five

'Some bastard leaked the autopsy summary!' Ava yelled, slamming Callanach's door and throwing herself into a chair. 'Which means either someone in Ailsa's office or a police officer here is responsible, as if this wasn't bad enough already.'

'Have you slept?' Callanach asked.

'Listen to this,' Ava tore open the newspaper she was clutching and began reading. ' "Helen Lott, a forty-six year old palliative care nurse, was deliberately crushed to death in her own bedroom." Of all the monsters I've ever dealt with, who would want to kill a nurse who looks after terminally ill patients? "Injuries included multiple fractured ribs and sternum, a collapsed windpipe and severe damage to internal organs, resulting in internal bleeding and asphyxiation. A neighbour alerted police after loud noises were heard coming from the property late at night. The autopsy report suggests that the murder was torturous and orchestrated to cause as much pain to the victim as possible. Mrs Lott will be sadly missed by work colleagues and patients alike, who have described her as nothing short of an angel who had dedicated her life to nursing." Did you know there's graffiti about the murders on the city walls and concerned citizens are planning a Take-Back-The-Night style protest march. Like we don't have enough to do. What the fuck is going on?'

'You want coffee?' he asked.

'Sorry about yesterday. With Joe. It was . . .' Ava's voice dwindled.

'None of my business,' Callanach said.

'Joe and I were friends at university. He phoned me a few months ago to say he was likely to be posted here. You know how sometimes you just pick things up where you left them as if no time had passed at all . . .'

'Forget it. You want to get something to eat on the way home? If I don't get a shower soon my clothes are going to sue me for hygiene abuse.'

Ava looked down at her hands.

'It's fine,' Callanach said, Ava's unspoken plans hanging in the air between them. 'I'll catch you tomorrow. And don't worry about the papers. New story every day, remember?'

That turned out to be good advice. In spite of the endless coverage afforded by two murders in one night, the media headlines the next day focussed on an altogether different target.

The largest incident room was taken up with an array of well-dressed plain-clothes officers, freshly washed and scrubbed, who obviously had not been up all night watching endless mobile phone footage and scanning photos with no results.

'Something happen overnight?' Callanach asked Sergeant Lively as he passed by.

'Fuckin' snobby idiots strutting around, acting like they own the place. Hunting a bunch of nerds no one in their right mind gives a damn about. Makes you look almost like a frigging native.'

'Look almost like a frigging native, *sir*,' Callanach reminded him. Lively sniggered.

'Aye, whatever.' Lively wandered off stuffing a sandwich into his mouth. Callanach and he hadn't hit it off properly since day one. At least the influx of Scotland Yard's finest had provided a favourable comparison.

Callanach's phone was ringing as he reached his office. He took the call as he threw his jacket onto the desk. It was too hot for any sane person to be wearing more than shorts and a tee-shirt. Shirts and ties were one of the drawbacks of promotion.

'Callanach,' he said.

'DI Callanach, I've left several messages for you,' was the opening line. 'This is Lance Proudfoot. I'm the editor of an online news and current affairs blog. I was hoping to get a statement about the festival murder.'

'How did you get this number?' Callanach asked.

'Switchboard put me through.'

'That'll be a career-shortening decision then,' Callanach said, imagining the conversation he'd be having later with the idiot who had answered the phone. 'No statements. You had every-thing we're giving out at the press conference.'

'To be fair to the young lady on your switchboard, I may have given the impression that I was a family member,' Lance said. Callanach sighed. 'And your media office rarely bothers inviting the online only press to your conferences, hence the need for a certain level of . . . inventiveness about sourcing information.'

'While you're on the phone, what was the big story over-night? I haven't had a chance to pick up the papers yet.'

'You mean the hackers? Brilliant bit of anti–establishmentar-ianism,' Lance laughed.

'I have no idea what you just said,' Callanach replied.

'Some group calling themselves The Unsung hacked into the accounts of a load of banker types who'd just been awarded some mega-buck bonuses and transferred the funds.'

'That's it?' Callanach asked. 'Theft? Hardly seems worth all the fuss here.'

'They've called in the cavalry, have they? Doesn't surprise me at all,' Lance said. Callanach mentally kicked himself for his indiscretion. 'Take benefits away from single mums and the disabled and there's not one politician available for comment. Nick some cash from a load of rich boys and the government mobilises. And anyway, it was a bit cleverer than theft. They transferred the funds into the accounts of a variety of good causes, anything from children's hospices to animal shelters. Only took twenty-five per cent of each bonus, too.'

'I don't see how only taking twenty-five per cent makes a difference,' Callanach said, knowing he should end the call but too intrigued to put the phone down.

'Well, they've not lost all their money, have they? Not even half of it. Some of those bonuses ran into multi-millions. So now the losers have to report each unauthorised money transfer as a crime, which is how the press gets to know about each offence, and they have to ask for their money back. What would you do, DI Callanach? Say you got a four million pound bonus on top of already obscene wages, three million is still in your bank account. You going to make a spectacle of yourself and insist that the local chemotherapy treatment centre gives you your million back? Named and shamed doesn't even start to describe how little love the public have for these guys. Quite some stunt, isn't it?'

Callanach didn't answer. Quite some stunt indeed. It certainly explained the peacocking going on in the incident room.

'And now perhaps you can help me, too. I just need one comment on the record.'

'No,' Callanach said. 'This is a murder investigation. Have some respect.'

'Listen, I do this because I care about getting news stories out. I don't want to work for a paper that'll twist my words to meet the owner's political agenda, or to maximise advertising revenue potential. Do me a favour. Just one line. We're not all bad, you know.'

'Fine,' Callanach said, feeling resigned and having no idea why his natural defences weren't shutting him up. 'But unnamed. An anonymous source inside the police. The festival attack appears motiveless. Whilst the majority of murders are committed by persons known to the victim, this does not appear to be the case. We ask the public to remain vigilant and for anyone with any information to come forward as soon as possible.'

'That's all?' Lance asked.

'Don't push your luck,' Callanach said. 'Use my name and we never talk again.'

'Does that mean I can call you if I have any more questions?'

'No, it doesn't. And the next time you lie to switchboard to get put through, I'll have you arrested.' Finally common sense kicked in and Callanach hung up, but he was smiling as he did so.

Ava's friend DCI Edgar was going to have his work cut out wading through the mire of public relations mud about to rain down. The Unsung may have committed grand scale fraud and theft, but it was hard to imagine many people condemning them. And it was a big enough story, just about, to deflect the media's attention and provide some breathing space while they made headway on the murders. Couldn't have happened to a nicer guy, Callanach thought, wondering how long Joe Edgar would be using Edinburgh as an investigative base. He reached for his coffee and for an unlit Gauloises cigarette to suck.